Praise for *The Housemaid's Daughter*

"The dignity and defiance that defined the towering life of Nelson Mandela can also be found—in a smaller, quieter way—in Ada, the title character of Barbara Mutch's fine new novel about two women caught between South Africa's racial divide."
—*USA Today* (4 ½ of 5 stars)

"I was struck with the grace of *The Housemaid's Daughter,* not only in the characters but in the style of Mutch's writing as well. While she does not gloss over the struggles and hardships prominent during this segregated time in South African history, she writes with clarity and hope. *The Housemaid's Daughter* is a great book-club option, and a shining example of strong female characters who rise above their unfortunate circumstances to care for themselves and for those they care about."
—*Spencer Daily Reporter*

"Few of us . . . really know or understand the personal history of South Africans who lived under [Apartheid's] horrifically damaging set of policies. Barbara Mutch's *The Housemaid's Daughter* changes all that. . . . [and] is a brisk reminder of just how far South Africa has come—and how fast things deteriorated there in the years before Mandela came to prominence."
—Bookreporter.com

"With memorable characters and vividly exploring the landscape and the cruelty of the apartheid years, this is a powerful, moving, and beautifully written novel of hope, love, and caring across South Africa's racial divide." —*Choice* magazine (UK)

"Exquisitely written, I felt transported in time and place, and was so engrossed in Ada's life that ~~there was no convincing me to~~ put the book down. Mutch seen~~...~~ g of what the South African people must have gone through during the Apartheid. She sensitively conveys their hopes and fears very well indeed, and in her very down-to-earth manner, doesn't shy away from the truth of what South Africa experienced. A true modern classic." —*Bookworm Ink* (UK)

"A rich novel set in an era of political unrest . . . has echoes of the bestselling *The Help* with its portrayal of friendship across divides." —*Sainsbury's Magazine* (UK)

"This debut novel has echoes of Kathryn Stockett's *The Help* and is equally compelling. . . . Ada's story is both an enjoyable and a very moving one, told with sensitivity and feeling." —*We Love This Book* (UK)

The Housemaid's Daughter

BARBARA MUTCH

St. Martin's Griffin ⚑ New York

THE HOUSEMAID'S DAUGHTER. Copyright © 2012 by Barbara Mutch Limited. All rights reserved. Printed in the United States of America. For information, address St. Martin's Press, 175 Fifth Avenue, New York, N.Y. 10010.

www.stmartins.com

The Library of Congress has cataloged the hardcover edition as follows:

Mutch, Barbara.
  [Karoo plainsong]
  The housemaid's daughter / Barbara Mutch.—1st U.S. edition.
      p. cm.
  ISBN 978-1-250-01630-0 (hardcover)
  ISBN 978-1-250-03196-9 (e-book)
  1. Women pioneers—Fiction.   2. Irish—South Africa—Fiction.   3. Apartheid—Fiction.   4. South Africa—History—1909–1961—Fiction.   5. South Africa—Social conditions—Fiction.   I. Title.
  PR9369.4.M88K37 2013
  823'.92—dc23

                                                            2013026243

ISBN 978-1-250-05446-3 (trade paperback)

St. Martin's Griffin books may be purchased for educational, business, or promotional use. For information on bulk purchases, please contact the Macmillan Corporate and Premium Sales Department at 1-800-221-7945, extension 5442, or write to specialmarkets@macmillan.com.

An extended version of The Housemaid's Daughter was first published by Troubadour Publishing Ltd. under the title Karoo Plainsong

First published in Great Britain by Headline Review, an imprint of Headline Publishing Group

First St. Martin's Griffin Edition: January 2015

10   9   8   7   6   5   4   3   2   1

For

L, W, H & C

Author's Note

This is a work of fiction. Apart from recognised historical figures, the names and characters in the novel are the product of the author's imagination. Any resemblance to actual persons living or dead is entirely coincidental. The places they inhabit, however, are real, even if they have strayed a little from their original sites. The Karoo itself is eternal.

Prologue

Ireland, 1919

Today I left for Africa.

Out of the front door I went, and down the flagstone path. The gulls were shrieking over Bannock cliffs and my dearest sister Ada was crying. Mother – in the brown dress she wore for weddings and christenings – looked the other way. Remember this, I kept telling myself as I climbed into the pony trap.

Remember this: the wheeling gulls, the click of the waves on the pebbles in the cove, Father's hands red and chapped, Eamon shifting from foot to foot, a waft of peaty earth and chimney smoke and lilac . . .

Remember this, hold it tight.

Chapter 1

I wasn't supposed to be born in Cradock House. Not me.

But my mother Miriam stayed by the *kaia* round the back, under the bony shade of the thorn tree, moaning quietly in the midday heat until Madam returned from school with the children and came down the garden to look for her.

By then it was too late to go to the hospital.

Master Edward was at home, seeing to his papers in the study. Madam sent him out to fetch the family doctor from his surgery on Church Street. It was lunchtime and Dr Wilmott had to be interrupted at his meal. My mother told me that Madam shooed the children – Miss Rosemary and Master Phil – away from the one-room *kaia* and helped Miriam up to the house. There, she held her hand and wiped her forehead with her very own hanky, the one Miriam had ironed the day before.

The doctor came. Master went back to his study.

I was born. It was 1930.

Mama named me Ada after Madam's younger sister across the sea in a place called Ireland.

I think that being born in Cradock House has made me grateful all my life. It makes me feel I am part of it in a way that my mother Miriam never was. The narrow stairs and the brass doorknobs know my hands and feet, the bony thorn tree and the apricot bush hold me inside them, carrying me in their sap from year to year. And I own a tiny bit of them in return. So when Cradock House was taken away from me I could not understand my life after that.

Cradock lies in the Karoo, the great semi-desert of South Africa that you find whenever you go far enough inland from the green mountains that edge the coast in a steep frill. The Karoo is the hard place you have to cross before you reach Johannesburg, where you can dig gold out of the ground and become rich. None of this I knew, of course. My whole world was just a square, two-storey house of cream stone with a red tin roof in a small town surrounded by rocky *koppies*, brown dust and a lack of rain. The only water I knew about lay in the Groot Vis – the Great Fish River – and sometimes stirred itself to flow along a furrow outside the house, from where it could be led into the garden for the plants to drink. On the edge of town where the sky met the earth, tough Karoo bush hardly ever taller than the height of a child clung to the dry soil. Above the bush poked the withered trunks of aloes, topped by orange flower spikes that stood out like flames against the scrub. There were some trees, like bluegums or frothy mimosas, but only in front gardens or down on the banks of the Groot Vis where their roots could burrow for water.

On those few times when it did rain, the hammering on the tin roof was so loud it sent Miss Rosemary and young Master Phil into fits of screaming. My mother and I – in the *kaia* at the bottom of the garden – also had a tin roof but ours was grey and overhung by the thorn tree. It damped the hammering into a hiss. I didn't scream at the rain, I stood at the *kaia* door listening to it and looking out over the veld beyond the fence. When my mother wasn't watching, I would put one bare foot out into the tiny rivers that crept over the hard ground and watch the water pool and sink reluctantly into the ground around my toes.

Cradock House sat on Dundas Street, just up from the Groot Vis and just below Market Square. Dundas became Bree Street about halfway along its length. I don't know why one street needed two names – Mama said perhaps it was a matter of honouring ancestors equally – but that was the way it was. Once the street with two names crossed over Regent Street, it ran out of steam, fell into a township and disappeared.

Cradock House had a wooden *stoep* with shell chairs to sit on that went almost the whole way round the house, like a circle. It stopped at the kitchen and then picked up again after the laundry, which was just as well, said my mother, otherwise we'd want to sit there all day when we should be washing or cooking or ironing.

But although I longed to sit in one of those chairs, I was forbidden by my mother to do so. They were for the family, she said. 'But I am also part of the family,' I would say hopefully in return, stroking the grainy wood. 'Shoo, child!' Mama would mutter and tell me to get on with the polishing. Mama and I mostly talked in English, unless she was really angry with me, or singing to me in the night: *Thula thu' thula bhabha . . .*

Hush, hush, hush, little baby . . .

I didn't mind too much about the chairs. There was a secret lookout upstairs that was far better than the *stoep*. In the mornings when the children were at school, and while I was busy dusting on the top floor of the house, I would creep into Master Phil's room, climb on to his toy box and peer out of the window.

There it was: the whole of Cradock – perhaps, I thought, the whole of the Karoo – unfolding in the yellow morning sun like a map Master once unfolded for young Master Phil under the yellow lamplight in the study. If I narrowed my eyes and ignored the window frames, I could imagine flying right over the broad streets of the town, past the spire of the Dutch Reformed Church – far higher than St Peter's, the Master and Madam's church – then out over the brown shallows of the Groot Vis with its mimosas digging for water, then through dust devils that twisted into the sky above the stunted veld, then over rocky *koppies* piled high with polished stones in the early sun, and finally, as the desert heaved upwards, over mountains thick with forest. I could hardly see the mountains, but everyone talked about them as if they were there, especially when it was cold and frost coated the ground like sugar.

As I stood there every day, craning out, it seemed to me that for one special moment the whole town, the whole Karoo, was mine. From this spot, from this window, it belonged to no one else.

Like Cradock House belonged to me.

Maybe Madam felt the same way about the place called Ireland across the sea, where she had come from. She, too, seemed to stare out of windows, looking for something beyond the bluegums and the Groot Vis and the brown dust that hung over Market Square when there were too many horse carts and no rain.

Mother and Father don't mind me going to Africa – in fact they rather need it. But they won't say so openly. And I don't mention it. They can rent out my room for more than I can pay from my salary. Eamon needs boots, Ada's coat – my old green – is worn out. There isn't enough money for me to stay.

I am looking forward to going, yet dreading it as well. For I know that once there, I will not be able to return. This is a commitment that will last a lifetime. And while I will keep up with friends and family through the letters we will exchange, I will never see their dear faces or hear their Irish laughter again. This is what it means to emigrate.

Mrs Pumile, from the *kaia* next door, was jealous of my mother Miriam and me. She said that our Madam treated us well, unlike her own Madam who watched the level of the sugar in the kitchen and made Mrs Pumile turn out her pockets if she thought they were bulging with stolen goods.

'Eeeh.' Mrs Pumile would suck in her breath and waddle back to her *kaia*, *doek* askew, apron pockets flapping, the biscuits or whatever she had borrowed now lying in the bottom of Mrs Pumile's Madam's rubbish bin. Biscuits handled by Mrs Pumile were no good to her Madam. I never found out Mrs Pumile's Madam's name. She was just Madam, like most Madams were Madam.

Our Madam's name – apart from Madam – was Cathleen. Mrs Cathleen Harrington née Moore, as she once wrote for me in her swooping hand, though she didn't explain why she had so many names. Madam was tall and gentle and had green eyes and brown hair that she twisted into a round ball at the back of her head during the day. I saw her once with her hair out of the ball and it floated about her head like smoke. She was in her pale blue nightgown at the dressing table, writing in her special book, and I was only there because my mother Miriam told me to fetch Madam as young Master Philip was getting sick in the children's bathroom.

'Ada!' Madam said, getting up straight away, her nightgown with its embroidered flowers on the hem brushing the floor. 'Is something wrong?'

'Just Master Phil oops-ing,' I said from the doorway. 'Mama says to come.'

Madam was a good mother, and not just to Miss Rosemary and Master Phil – although Miss Rose spent a lot of time arguing with her. But then Miss Rose didn't often agree with anyone.

'So perverse,' Madam would sigh to Master, using a word I did not know but could guess what it meant. 'Whatever shall we do?'

Madam's goodness to me meant letting me sit in the chair next to her on the *stoep* – despite my mother's frowns – or by her side when she played the piano. Madam made me feel like it was my chair after all. She made me feel like I was hers, too.

Master Edward didn't make me feel like I was his, which was a pity because I didn't have any other father. For a long time I didn't think you needed a father to have a baby. In any case, I thought only white children had fathers.

My mother Miriam had left KwaZakhele township outside Port Elizabeth when she was eighteen years old to go to work for Master Edward in Cradock. He had just bought Cradock House and was waiting for Madam to arrive from across the sea. Master had been saving for years, Madam said, before he could buy Cradock House for Madam who was to be his bride. Yet Master never came into Madam's dressing room, and only sometimes into Madam's bedroom. I could tell: the bed, when I made it each morning, carried the imprint from Madam's body on its own. I was surprised about that. I thought that married people always wanted to be together, especially after saving for so long for Cradock House. But I didn't ask my mother why not. It would be unfair to ask such a question when she didn't have a husband of her own. But having no husband was not unusual. There were many like Mama. Mrs Pumile next door, for instance, although she had many callers to her *kaia*. But callers were not husbands and could never be relied upon to keep calling.

When I asked my mother Miriam about her early life, before the possibility of husbands, she used to say that she came with the house. I don't know if that's true, I don't think you could buy people along with houses, even then. But perhaps you could – perhaps that was why next door's Madam kept Mrs Pumile even when she ate too much sugar and entertained too many callers?

But it is true that Mama worked all her life in Cradock House and died there one day while she was polishing the silver at the kitchen table.

I wanted to stay in Cradock House all my life as well. I didn't want to live in that place where Bree Street ran out of steam, fell into a township and disappeared. I wanted to live and die in Cradock House, where I'd been born. Where I surely belonged because of that?

But I wanted to die while I was polishing silver under the kaffirboom tree in the garden, where the emerald sunbirds darted among the red flowers and the sky poked bright blue between shivering leaves.

Chapter 2

The distance we are from Bannock village, Ireland, is further than a hemisphere.

And yet I do feel a curious sympathy with the townspeople I've met, though I know nothing of their past and they nothing of mine. And I remind myself that wherever one finds oneself, home and love is lent to each of us only for a while. We must care for it while it's ours, and cherish its memory once it's gone.

So I embrace this new life, and these new people.

Soon, I hope, we will no longer be strangers to one another.

My mother Miriam never went to school and neither did I. Mrs Pumile never went to school either. There was a small school in the Lococamp township that served the railway workers across the Groot Vis, but the children there were always dirty and played wild games, my mother said. A bigger school lay in the township on our side of the river beyond Bree Street. It was called St James and it was run by the Rev. Calata. It had sports fields and a choir and it looked away from the town and towards the open veld. It was much more strict, Mama said, and that was a good thing for a school to be, but it was too far for me to walk to such a strict school on my own.

We didn't go across the Groot Vis often, only on Mama's Thursday afternoon off, when we went to visit her older sister, my aunt. 'So many people,' Mama would gasp, perhaps reminded of her old KwaZekhele days, as we pushed across the bridge. 'Stay close to me, child.'

Auntie lived in a mud hut with no door and she had to wash her clothes in the river. Bad people came and stole the drying clothes off the bushes along the riverbank when Auntie went home for the next bundle of washing. Auntie washed for a living. In the matter of schools, Auntie agreed with Mama that the Lococamp school was not to be trusted. Auntie said it was as rough as life on the riverbank.

It fell to Madam and Master to talk about a school for me.

'Edward,' I overheard Madam say one day as I was coming out of the kitchen carrying the ironing for my mother, 'we can't ignore it, we have a duty. The township school is too unsettled, perhaps Lovedale Mission?'

'It'll only lead to trouble later on, expectations and whatnot,' said Master Edward, flapping a page of the newspaper over. 'But look into it if you must. Will you play the Beethoven for me this evening?'

I don't know what 'trouble later on' Master was afraid of. And going to the mission school might have meant leaving Cradock House and leaving my mother, who needed me to help her as she got older and smaller, like a bird, while I got bigger. It seemed to me that life was strange in the matter of size, but maybe it was meant to be that way; you grew from a tiny baby into a tall grown-up and then you shrank until you died and were small enough for God the Father to deliver you to the ancestors.

'I'm grateful, Ma'am,' Miriam said to Madam when the subject of school came up again. 'But Lovedale Mission is far away and Ada would be alone.'

Leaving to go to school, and leaving to go to Africa must be about the same, I calculated, hiding behind the door while Madam and Master talked one evening in the lounge. Both meant losing your family and never seeing them again. I didn't want to lose mine, like Madam had lost hers. I watched through the crack above the door hinge. Master was reading the paper and Madam was shaking her head. The round green stone she wore at her neck caught the lamplight. She had changed from the loose, low-waisted dress she wore during the day – Madam's day dresses were made to withstand the heat, and were the colour of cream on the top of milk – into a fitted one in pale green to match her brooch.

'I'd like to get her into the children's school here in town but the head won't hear of it,' she said. The stone flashed at me again. I didn't know what it meant when people wouldn't hear of things. I didn't think it had anything to do with being deaf. 'Why is everyone so difficult about this, Edward?'

'For the simple reason, my dear,' Master said, frowning at her over the top of his newspaper, 'that if you let one in, they'll all want places.'

'Is that so wrong?'

He didn't answer but instead turned another page, his dark head with its side parting disappearing behind the paper. I don't know what he meant, or what Madam meant. But I don't think Madam agreed with him. Perhaps she didn't understand the trouble he said he was afraid of later on if I went to school. The trouble that I didn't understand either. I would never want to cause Madam and Master any trouble. If going to school meant trouble, then I should not go.

I watched as she stood up, looked out of the window for a moment, then walked over to the piano. When there was silence between Madam and Master, she would often go to the piano.

Sometimes she played straight away, and sometimes she sat stiffly, staring at the keys.

'Ada!' hissed my mother, pulling me away. 'The *tokoloshe* comes for bad girls that listen at doors!' I ran back to our room and lay down, covering my eyes so I couldn't see the evil *tokoloshe* when he crept on to the bed and took me away to hell. But he didn't come. And Madam played Beethoven. The *Moonlight Sonata*. But she was distracted, I could tell. I could hear it in her fingers.

'The child can learn all she needs here, Madam,' Mama said firmly the next day as she looked for elastic for young Master Phil's garters in Madam's sewing basket. My mother had given me a talking-to when she later came to bed. She said that I didn't deserve Madam's kindness if I listened at doors. And that she wouldn't have my schooling bothering Madam and Master.

Madam pushed her needle into young Master Phil's sock that she was darning. There was always a lot of sewing to do with young Master Phil. He seemed to be able to walk out of the house and tear his shorts or lose a button straight away. But all boys tore their clothes, Mama told me. It's what boys do. But it didn't seem to matter, for we all loved Master Phil, who was as sunny as Miss Rose was forever peeved.

'We'll see. I won't give up just yet. You didn't have the chance for school, Miriam dear, but Ada should.'

But I never went to school.

Instead Madam started to teach me my letters at home at the dining-room table when Master was at work and the children were busy. I don't know why she wouldn't teach me when Master was at home, but that was the way it was. We always had to pack up very quickly when Master's footsteps were heard coming down the path. And my mother Miriam and Mrs Pumile from next door clapped their hands and said I was very lucky to be getting something they called an 'education'.

I began to read from the book Madam left in her dressing room as well, on the table next to her silver brush and her powder box where I dusted every day. No one else saw that book, not Master or Miss Rose or young Master Phil. I knew this because I could tell from the outline it would make in powder or dust if it had been moved by anyone apart from Madam and myself. I watched for this every morning when the sun came through the window and fell upon Madam's dressing table in a revealing, yellow beam. And I made sure to put the book back to the page she'd been writing so she would never know.

There were often sentences that I didn't understand but I could think about them all day as I went about my dusting and polishing, and sometimes the meaning that had been hiding within them would jump out at me long after I had read the words. Musical notes, I later discovered, were also like words: they meant one thing when played on their own, and quite another when strung together.

I don't think that Madam knew I was reading her book, but maybe she did. Was that why, many years later, she left the book behind when she went away to Johannesburg? Left it for me? After all, without Madam and the children, Cradock House would be empty and silent. There would be only my footsteps and Master's footsteps on the narrow stairs.

Once I started to understand letters, I began to make out words on the front of shops in town when I went to post Madam's letters to Ireland at the post office on Adderley Street. I started to search out new ones every time I went to town, peering into windows for so long that often the shopkeeper would come out and shoo me away.

I learnt to walk slowly one way up Adderley, cross over the

broad dirt road with its donkey carts and snapping dogs and fine gentlemen on horses and then slowly the other way so I never missed anything. Madam didn't seem to notice if it took a while to post letters, so I could return via the Karoo Gardens on Market Square where there were wooden benches that I was allowed to sit on. I could stare up at the palm trees over my head, or at the flaming aloes in their square flower beds, and repeat the words I'd read while the sun warmed my bare feet. Then it was along Church Street – like Adderley, also broad on account of wagons and oxen needing to turn about in years gone by – and the last signs before the shops ran out at the edge of the Groot Vis.

The first words I learned on my own like this were 'Austen's the Chemist', 'White and Boughton for paper and ink', 'Cuthbert's Shoe Store for personal fitting', and 'Ladies find Quality at Anstey's Fashions'. Outside Badger & Co., there was often a table with rolls of cloth, saying '. . . for a bolt". I never could work out what those missing words were – I saw them in lots of places – but they weren't made of letters I recognised, so they must have come from another sort of language that I didn't yet understand. I never found any of those unknown words in Madam's writing. I longed to ask her what they meant but I didn't want to seem ungrateful for all that Madam was teaching me anyway at the dining-room table, and secretly from the book on her dressing table.

So I asked Miss Rose and young Master Phil instead.

'I don't have time to explain,' said Miss Rose over her shoulder, as she brushed her yellow hair in front of the mirror. 'You haven't any money so you probably don't need to learn to count.'

'Why, they're numbers, Ada!' said Master Phil, grabbing a pencil with a chewed end and drawing some of the strange shapes on a piece of paper. 'They tell you about quantity, how many of something you've got. I'll show you some more after cricket practice – here, take this, you can try.' He stood over me for a moment, and corrected the way I held the pencil. 'That's right, just like that!' then ran off, his cricket bag banging against the banisters as he raced downstairs.

'Less noise, Philip!' came Master's voice from below.

But before the possibility of numbers, there was Madam's book in her dressing room. It had a cover of dark red velvet, with a red satin ribbon that tied round its centre in a bow. I would stroke the velvet and the satin, and bend down and rest my cheek against them. Very often Madam didn't bother with the bow and simply wound the ribbon around the book. I never meant to read it, I only started when Madam left it open one day and I had to move it during dusting. And it wasn't as if I was stealing anything from Madam, like Mrs Pumile stole from her Madam. This wasn't sugar or biscuits or jewels.

At first I read each letter, beautifully formed in black ink, a slanting pattern of unrelated thick and thin strokes.

'*TomorrowIsailforAfrica* . . .'

Then, after many times of struggling, I began to separate the words. '*Tomorrow I sail* . . .'

What was this thing, 'sail'?

And then the words joined together to become sentences. And then the sentences began to tell me what Madam was saying to the book. And sometimes what she wasn't saying. '*Five years of betrothal, Edward in Cradock, self in Ireland. Marriage is a step in faith, Father o'Connell says. But of course I still love him. And everyone says we're made for each other.*'

The book became a secret conversation between Madam and myself.

Chapter 3

A whole summer of heat and flies passed. In the garden of Cradock House the orange and blue strelitzia – crane flowers – swelled into huge clumps and the pampas grass waved feather heads that made you cough when you passed by. Invisible beetles rasped all day in the plumbago hedge, and yellow bokmakieries with black collars called to each other from opposite ends of the garden. In town, the new bank was finished on Adderley Street and everyone came to look at it; ladies in dresses with tucked bodices that needed lots of ironing, gentlemen in suits with watches on chains like the Master's, little girls in smocked dresses, and boys in shorts and long socks and caps on their heads. People like Mama and I watched from the back of the crowd, although at first young Master Phil pulled me along to stand at the front. Master Phil often pulled me along with him.

'Look, Ada – there's Father!' he cried, jumping up and down and pointing out the Master on a platform with a lot of other men beneath a sign that said 'Bank' and another word that I didn't recognise. 'Doesn't he look important?' And he did, in his best suit and with the shirt that Mama had starched so carefully the day before.

'What does a bank do?' I asked, pulling on young Master Phil's sleeve to get his attention. Several of the white children nearby giggled.

'What?' He was craning forward to get a better look.

'A bank.' I cupped my hand towards his ear, so the others wouldn't hear. 'What is it for?'

'It's where you put your money,' he said, then shouted, 'Father, Father!' waving his arms and jumping up and down again to get the Master's attention. The nearby children stared, the girls among them covering their mouths against the dust from his jumping boots. Master turned impatiently in our direction, then turned back to a man who was cutting a red ribbon across the front door of the bank with a pair of scissors. I suppose young Master Phil shouldn't have tried to inter-rupt the Master, but he never thought too much before he did anything – like eating too many apricots without worrying about the consequences for his stomach. Unlike Miss Rose, who could be silent for ages when she really wanted some-thing, storing it up with sighs and shrugged shoulders until the moment when she knew Madam and Master could never refuse her.

Rosemary has not been an easy child. Perhaps I was spoiled with Phil, whose good cheer was evident even in the crib. In contrast, Rosemary finds fault with the world in general, and her mother in particular.

Such ill temper has been thrown into sharper relief by the demeanour of Ada, who has Miriam's stoicism but also a lightness about her that is immensely appealing. Perhaps the fault lies with me. In my inability to be the right sort of mother. Yet every effort I have made has been rebuffed. There seems to be no pleasing Rosemary.

Note to self:
Try to find some simple readers for young Ada. I am determined her

reading should progress, whatever Edward's reservations. Perhaps the school library could oblige. I could say they are for a private pupil.

I wasn't allowed to go into the new bank, but you could see big ceiling fans and brown desks through the windows and signs that I could read saying, 'Enquiries' and 'Manager', although I didn't understand what they meant. Mrs Pumile's cousin was allowed to go into the bank because she polished the floor with red Cobra floor polish every morning. She brought Mrs Pumile sugar that was left over on the tea trolley. People went into the bank to give them money to look after. That's what young Master Phil meant. But my mother Miriam said her money was safer in a shoebox under the bed, where she could watch it.

There were many days that summer when I was too busy with the necessary sweeping and tidying, and with the washing of the family's clothes that got dirty trailing in the dust, to spare much time to read. I would stare at Madam's book on the dressing table in longing while I ran the *lappie* in slow circles around it and then Mama would call and tell me there was washing to take off the line.

A whole winter of cold winds passed too; winds that blew in from the mountains I couldn't quite make out from the top of Master Phil's toy box. Sometimes I thought I saw in the distance a light dusting of white, like icing on top of fairy cakes, but I could never be sure that it wasn't just me wanting to see such a sight. I have always wanted to see further than my eyes can manage.

'The roof would be better for sightseeing!' laughed Master Phil coming upon me one day as I craned out of the window when I should have been dusting.

'Sorry, sir.' I scrambled down and grabbed my *lappie*. 'Just going.'

'Wait! Wait, Ada!' He grabbed my arm. 'What're you looking for?'

'The mountains,' I pointed over the brown veld, 'where there is snow. Have you ever seen snow?' I could never ask such a question of Miss Rose. And I would never want to trouble Madam.

'Once.' He grinned, slinging down his school blazer. I noticed one of the buttons was missing. 'It was like wet cotton wool. You could roll it into balls and throw it. Snowballs!' He mimed a bowling action, hair flopping forwards on to his forehead as he swung his arm. Master Phil always answered my questions. He never made fun of me, like Miss Rose did. Then he climbed up on the toy box himself, and showed me how he could brush the ceiling with his fingers as he pretended to bowl once more, and said he often did it to check how tall he was and that one day maybe even his head would reach the ceiling.

That winter, the cold winds from the snow that Master Phil knew about cut through my uniform and numbed my face when I went down Adderley Street to post Madam's letters to Ireland across the sea. Did those letters hold the same thoughts as the book on Madam's dressing table? Or did Madam leave some things out of her letters, like she left some things out of her book?

I hurried on my journey, wrapped in Mama's old funeral coat, too cold to search for new shop signs or to read the words outside the newspaper office. Back at Cradock House, Mama and I made pumpkin soup and roast chicken stuffed with last summer's dried apricots, and hot sponge puddings that young Master Phil loved. 'More, please, Miriam,' he would say after eating a mountainous bowl. 'Best sponge ever.'

Only after the winter was past did I realise that, in one

important way, Madam was the same as me: we both carried sentences inside ourselves that we never spoke out loud. The difference was that she could tell her sentences to the book, or to her letters, whereas I had to keep mine forever inside my head. Because, you see, even although I could read, I wasn't yet able to write.

Chapter 4

Miss Rose took piano lessons.

Not at Rocklands School that I couldn't go to because of trouble later on, or from Madam who was a music teacher herself, but from another lady teacher in narrow glasses who came once a week.

'Arch the fingers, Rosemary,' she instructed. 'Up, up, up!'

I used to dust the piano every day, so I could see what Miss Rose was learning. I could see the book with its pictures of white and black keys, and how they were named like the letters Madam had taught me – only the piano letters didn't go all the way to the end of the alphabet. I wondered why not.

So I could tell where Miss Rose needed to put her fingers to make a tune.

Sometimes if I was dusting in the room and she made a mistake, I could show her where she should have put her fingers.

'Smarty-pants!' Miss Rose stuck her tongue out at me and tossed her long yellow hair back from her face. Miss Rose knew she was very beautiful but still spent hours looking at herself in the mirror in her bedroom to make sure, widening her eyes and turning from one side to the other. Unlike Madam's soft green eyes, Miss Rose's were dark blue, like slate on a roof or the Karoo sky just before night. Mrs Pumile had no time for Miss Rose because Miss Rose would never say good morning to her when she passed her on the street. My mother Miriam said that Miss Rose would 'grow out of it'. Certainly Miss Rose seemed to grow out of her clothes very quickly because she always needed new ones, but how you grew out of rudeness I didn't know.

One thing was certain: Miss Rose did not love music.

'I hate the piano!' she would hiss at the back of the teacher in glasses as she and Madam talked in low voices at the front door after each lesson. 'Arch, arch – I hate it!'

This pained Madam, who had played the piano since she was a child over the sea. Indeed, one of the first things that Master Edward bought when he moved into Cradock House, and was waiting for Madam to arrive, was a piano.

'It was made in Leipzig, Ada, in a country called Germany,' Madam told me the first time it was my job to do the dusting. 'Look,' she pointed at gold lettering, 'here's the make – Zimmerman. We don't often find words with a z, do we?'

'Only "zebra", Ma'am. How did it come here?'

'Across the sea by boat, dear, just like I did. How kind of Master Edward to buy it for me.'

I watched Madam as she looked up from the piano and out of the window towards the Groot Vis.

Will I still love Edward?

Will I be able to play for him as passionately as I play for myself? Will he want me to?

All I knew was Cradock and the Karoo with its dust and rocky *koppies* and its lazy river, so a sea with endless water and places beyond such a sea were a mystery. Even the ragged place where Auntie lived across the river, and the crowded township at the far end of Bree Street where Mama sometimes took me to visit friends, and where the strict St James School lay, were better known to me.

I could not imagine what a boat looked like. Clearly the people who lived in those faraway places were very clever and could make things like pianos and boats that we weren't able to on our side of the sea.

'Will you ever go across the sea?' I asked Master Phil one day as he did his homework upstairs with the door shut, while Miss Rose fought with the piano downstairs.

'Maybe,' said Master Phil, considering. 'You'd like to, wouldn't you? I know you like new places, that's why you climb up on my toy box to look out—'

'But will you?'

'I guess so,' said Master Phil, his eyes wandering from the exercise book in front of him to the cricket bat and ball propped near the door for a quick getaway.

He brightened. 'Tell you what, we'll go together one day. To Ireland, to see my Aunt Ada that you're named for!' He leant back dangerously in his chair.

I giggled. Silly Master Phil. Such things weren't meant for girls like me.

'Even so,' the chair wobbled as he flung an arm wide to take in the bedroom and the vast Karoo beyond the window, 'what could be better than here?'

Madam practised every day for an hour first thing in the morning before school. The whole house woke to her music except for the weekends when she and the Master rose late. And she played in the evenings as well, when Master asked her or when there were visitors who asked her. I grew to know what she would play at different times and for different people.

The mornings were full of scales and arpeggios. Scales made smooth sweeping sounds that ran up and down the piano like wind, while arpeggios leapt off the keys like hail on the tin roof. Mrs Pumile used to say she could hear Madam's scales rush all the way down the garden every morning and into her *kaia* next door.

In the afternoons, when the children had finished their homework and Master Phil was restless, Madam would play marches for him to stamp about to as if he was a real soldier. Or, for Miss Rose, pieces with a swinging beat that made your feet want to tap in time – to encourage her to practise.

But at night, after Miss Rose and Master Phil were in bed, Madam would play quieter tunes, tunes that slid about in your head and came back to you the next day while you were busy with washing or dusting. I used to creep out of Mama's room – for by then we were living in the main house – and listen in the corridor leading to the lounge. It was dark there and I was afraid the *tokoloshe* would come.

When Madam and Master had guests, Madam wore dark green satin and played bright music like waltzes. Sometimes the guests would sing along. Madam loved the songs from across the sea where her family lived and would sing them on her own or accompany a guest who had a fine voice; songs like *Galway Bay* and *Take me home, Cathleen*, which was the Master's favourite. Except he liked to hear her play it when there were no guests. Master wanted Madam to himself. He did not want to share her. But Madam was happy to share herself, and her music.

'*This is the future*,' I read one day hurriedly during my chores. '*Edward, a man whose face and touch I haven't known for five years, and*

Cradock, a small town at the foot of Africa. This is where I will make my
home, start a family, find new music . . .'

And what was this 'future'? People talked about it and always
sounded worried. Was it something you had to pay for? Like
Master paid for the piano? Or was it something Madam brought
with her from Ireland?

I asked Master Phil one day, and he said it was something
that you got when you grew up, so I shouldn't worry about it
just yet. Miss Rose said the future was something I wouldn't get
at all unless I went to school, so there.

While Madam was playing, Master would stand straight by
the piano and smile for the guests and pull out his watch from
his waistcoat when he thought she'd played enough. When I was
young Cradock House was never quiet.

One day, Madam caught me correcting Miss Rose's piano-
playing.

'Rosemary, dear, that sounds so much better!' she had called
cheerfully, coming into the lounge with floury hands from
making scones, then stopped, seeing my fingers on the keys.
Miss Rose tossed her yellow hair and paged noisily through her
music book.

'Sorry, Ma'am, I'm just going,' I said and ran out of the room
and into the laundry where Mama was starching Master
Edward's collars. Miss Rose would not be pleased to be shown
up in front of Madam.

'Why do you rush so, child?' my mother asked me, thinking
I had done something wrong.

'Ada,' Madam said, hurrying in and finding me behind my
mother's skirt. Maybe Miss Rose had already complained to
Madam? She knelt down and looked me in the eye, like she did
when she was first making me repeat my letters. 'Would you like
to learn to play?'

Chapter 5

I discovered Ada correcting Rosemary at the piano today. This has happened before. Rosemary was annoyed but I pretended not to notice. I remember the first time I encouraged Ada to sit by my side and watch me play. The child was nervous, but then put out a finger to touch a note and turned to me with such wonder that the breath caught in my throat.

I learned to play the piano while something called the War grew.

I also learned, through the words of songs, about English things like woods and maypoles and grass that was always green and never brown like ours was. *Come to the Green Wood* became my favourite piece. And *Dance of the Gnomes*.

I learned history from Madam's stories of the great composers and I learned geography from the routes they travelled in search of new tunes. I hadn't realised that the piano did more than train your fingers. I hadn't realised it could show me a world beyond Cradock House. The first time my fingers touched the ivory keys I knew music would lift my heart, but I didn't expect it to stretch my head as well.

The piano taught me more about numbers. I learned to count the beats in a bar up to eight. There was now a connection between the counts and the figures I saw on shop signs in town.

For a while I could not work out quite how they were related. How could 'four' beats in a bar of music mean the same as 'four' on a bolt of cloth in town when there was only one bolt? Numbers, I decided, were unreliable things.

There was no war while Madam and I made music.

As I sat beside her on the piano stool, her soft cream dress against my blue overall, her hands on either side of mine as she helped me, I began to picture the world like she did, although most times I had never seen the things she talked about.

'A stream, the cry of seagulls, the curl and suck of the sea make a pattern over and over, one inside the other. Like the counterpoint we see in Bach . . .' She floated a series of repeating melodies that wove around each other, her hands rippling over the keys.

'What did the stream across the sea sound like on its own?'

'Ah, if you could only hear it, Ada.' She smiled fondly, as if the sound was echoing in her ear at that very moment. 'Over Bannock cliffs and into the cove, it was Grieg . . .' Her fingers danced across the opening chords of the piano concerto.

I nodded. Her hands stilled and she glanced away out of the window in the direction of the Groot Vis, brown and sluggish in the heat.

'A minor,' she turned back to the piano, 'falling into E – remember?'

And I would feel the tune rise in my hands and join her in the tumbling cascade down the piano.

A strange thing happened just after the start of the war. The sun disappeared one day. The *koppies* changed from brown to purple, and the birds in the garden stopped singing – even our bokmaki-eries. A man called General Smuts that I had heard people talking about, a man who had warned about Jerry controlling the sea route, visited Cradock to look at this daytime darkness. Crowds gathered outside the town hall on Market Square to hear him speak. Red and blue streamers flew across the front of the buildings to welcome him, and he was cheered all the way down Church Street as the skies darkened.

'It's an eclipse, Ada,' Madam said, on her way out to listen to him, 'nothing to be afraid of.'

She said it was the moon that was hiding the sun from us, and that it happened from time to time. Miss Rose said everyone knew what eclipses were. Master Phil was away marching so I couldn't ask him what he thought. Mama went to lie down in our *kaia*, so I crept upstairs and tried to see Market Square from the toy box as the light faded across the distant Karoo. Clapping reached me through the open windows. Perhaps General Smuts would call upon his powers to bring back the sun. I was sure it was the war that was to blame, just like it was to blame for the shortages we had in the kitchen. What else would cause the moon to cover the sun after all the time that I had known it to stay in the sky without trouble?

So there was Cradock House in the middle of the dry, sometimes dark, Karoo, and there was Mama and Madam and Master and Miss Rose here, and young Master Phil going away to war. There were the sinister hadeda birds that flapped and honked overhead every evening against a sky streaked with orange and pink. There was Mrs Pumile next door complaining at the extra work because of the war.

And now, instead of the occasional rain song on the *kaia* roof under the bony thorn tree, there was Mozart and Chopin and Beethoven every day – more tunes waiting inside the piano than I would ever be able to play. And more world beyond Cradock House than I had ever imagined. There was war, certainly, but there was also enough music to make you forget it.

⟨※⟩

Miriam and Ada are becoming my family, too.

No one warned me of this. They rather talked of heat, biting insects, restless natives. The possibility of finding companionship with my black housekeeper and her child was not even a remote consideration.

I suspect Edward finds my attitude disturbing. But he can have no complaints about my devotion to my own two. Phil and Rosemary have my total attention, and where Rosemary is concerned, I take particular care to encourage her in her various pursuits. I am sure we shall find something that will capture her interest.

Chapter 6

Young men like Master Phil appeared on the streets of Cradock in smart uniforms and caps with badges. When they marched, their boots beat time against the brown earth like the staccato notes I learnt to play. Older men like Master did not march, they went to meetings in the town hall opposite the Karoo Gardens where I used to sit under the palms, and talked for many hours about somewhere called 'Up North'.

One day Madam gave me a message for Master and I stood at the back waiting to give it to him. All the important men in Cradock – or perhaps the whole Karoo – sat around a table, and talked in loud voices and sometimes banged the table with their hands like you do when you are making bread. There was a man in a gold chain, and many with long beards. They did not look at me, so I listened to what they were saying. I often listened to what people were saying when they didn't expect me to hear them.

'Why should our boys have to fight and they don't?' I heard one man say loudly.

'Throw them in jail,' said another. 'It's treason!'

I didn't know what treason was. But it must have been bad because jail was where you were sent when you had killed or hurt someone so badly that you had to be locked away forever. There was a jail at the far end of Bree Street, and I think that was one of the reasons Mama would not let me walk to the strict St James School that lay beyond it. And jail, Mama once said, was not just for bad people. Jail could reach out and snatch you if you weren't careful.

'What is it, Ada?' Master had come over to where I was standing. He was in his shirtsleeves, and I noticed that his collar was drooping. It was hard to find starch because of the war. I held out the note. He read it, passed a hand over his thinning hair and then crumpled the note up in his fist. There were small drops of sweat on his forehead.

'Tell the Madam I will be back as soon as I can,' he said, not looking at me and turning quickly to go back to the table of shouting men. That was the time when we found out that young Master Phil was to go to the war.

At first, Master Phil just had to wear a uniform and practise the sort of marching he used to do while Madam played the piano when he was a boy. He would come home each night after a day of marching in the veld, and have dinner and then go again in the morning while Madam's scales swept through house. I was very proud of him and took extra care with the ironing of his khaki shirts. He even had time for the odd game of cricket with the other boys who were learning to be soldiers, although the dusty marching square where they played dirtied his cricket whites and gave me extra scrubbing that he was always sorry about.

'What do you do in the war?' I asked him one day when he came home early and was lying on his back in the grass watching the sky through the kaffirboom leaves. I was pegging washing on the line. 'Is it very hard?'

He sat up on an elbow and looked at me. Master Phil and I

had always talked easily, from the time he first showed me numbers and even when he seemed to be growing beyond me. Master Phil was my friend, the first friend I ever had. 'It's not hard yet,' he said after a pause, 'but it will be when I'm sent off to fight.'

I thought about this as I pegged up a pillowcase. 'Will you be afraid?'

He looked across at the house. Madam was at tea with friends, my mother was in the laundry, and faint sounds of dance music filtered from Miss Rose's open window.

'I hope not, I . . .' he reached for a leaf and began to tear it into neat pieces along the line of the veins. His fair hair flopped on to his forehead. 'I don't want to be afraid – but what if I am?'

A silence fell between us. His sleeves were rolled up and I could see where the marching had made the muscles of his arms rise in strong cords under his skin. Dear Master Phil, always so keen, always at the front of every game, always wanting to play his part. I was sure he would make a great soldier, too.

'I don't want to be afraid of the *tokoloshe*,' I said, leaving the washing, and kneeling down at his side, 'but it is God the Father's way of teaching me to be brave.'

His hands stilled from their shredding and he stared at me.

'But war's about killing, Ada. Killing,' he repeated, his voice not much more than a whisper. 'Not ghosts or evil spirits! Does God want us to be brave for that?'

Master Phil's eyes were very light, much lighter than the sky, much lighter than Miss Rose's steely blue, you could look almost all the way through them as if they were water. They were searching me now, and I had no answer for them.

He picked up another leaf and began to break it into pieces once more.

I got up and fetched the next shirt from the washing basket. Silence stretched between us. What could I say to reassure him? I ought to help, as he had helped me in the past. But I knew nothing of war and what it demanded. Then another thought came to me and I tried to turn it away but it kept coming back. Was it possible that Master Phil, despite his energy and his good heart, was not meant to be a soldier?

And what would Madam have said to his question if he'd asked her? Was there a lesson on God and war to be taken from Madam's book in her dressing room?

'I will pray for you, sir,' I said, holding the damp shirt against my chest and feeling the cold on my body, and hoped my praying would be enough. 'And Madam and Master will, too.'

He smiled up at me with his mouth. Then flung off the torn leaves, jumped to his feet and strode back inside.

While young Master Phil marched, my mother Miriam and I saved food in the kitchen and Madam collected spare cake tins and knitted socks for some of the young men who might get cold in boats – strange machines that I had never seen but seemed to be necessary for war and for taking pianos across seas. In the town square there were rallies with important people coming to tell us to 'support our lads and smash the enemy'.

During the war, some of the men in uniform were coloured people, a lighter colour than Mama and I. They lived in a part of the township that I had never been to, above a drift in the Groot Vis where it was possible to get over the river when the water was low. The coloured soldiers were very proud of their khaki kit and marched around the edge of Market Square, kicking up puffs of dust to dirty their new boots. This I could see when they stopped in front of the town hall for some saluting. Then they started off again down Church Street and across the bridge to the railway station to go away to war. One handsome boy winked at me as he stamped by and my mother pulled me away from the front of the crowd. 'Cheeky,' she muttered. 'Just because they got uniforms like whites.'

The whole town came out and cheered them and waved little flags.

There were no black soldiers the same colour as Mama and I; they stayed in the crowded township beyond Bree Street or worked on the farms. I don't know why they didn't go to the war. I asked my mother but she said it was because they hadn't been asked to go, and that it had something to do with not being trusted with guns.

A few white men didn't want to fight and were put in jail – I heard this from the corridor one night when Master leant over the piano as Madam finished playing. They'd be left to rot there, he said, sounding satisfied.

I remembered the meeting in the town hall and the shouting of the word treason and Mama's fear of jails and what they could do to you even if you had never hurt anyone badly enough to be put there.

But I couldn't understand about the men being rotten as well. Only fruit like apricots went rotten when they fell from the tree on to the ground. Not people. Maybe the white men didn't want to fight because they were already frightened, like young Master Phil had said he might be?

'They see no reason to fight for England,' Madam said sadly. Master patted her shoulder. He touched Madam a lot more since the war started. And Madam walked away to the piano a lot less than she did before the war. Maybe war makes you value things and people more than you did when there was Peace and you knew there would never be a shortage?

I wondered about the black men who hadn't been asked to go to war. If ways could be found to trust them with guns, then they could take the place of the white men who didn't want to go. And no one would have to go to jail. I wanted to say this to Madam, but my mother Miriam said it was not my place to question Madam and Master about such things.

I didn't understand about the sides in this war either. Especially as I remembered Madam saying that our piano came from Germany. This must mean that the clever people who had made our piano were now our enemies. It seemed to me that this might be the worst thing about war: that friends could be enemies-in-waiting.

Chapter 7

'Ada!'

I looked about. No one ever shouted to me on Church Street. The town streets were mainly for white people to shout on, black people did their shouting in the township alleys where Auntie lived. As if, Auntie used to say with a sniff, they lived on opposite hills instead of just across a dirt road from one another.

'Ada!' Young Master Phil in his khaki uniform marched across the gravel, avoiding a horse and cart coming along at a trot. 'What are you doing here?'

'Posting Madam's letter, sir.' I showed him the envelope with Madam's beautiful thick and thin pen strokes. I had been hiding it in my pocket so it wouldn't get dirty from the dust of the street, or smudged from the heat of my hand. It was a letter for Madam's sister, Ada, who I had been named for. I wished I could write to this Ada and ask her about her life in Ireland, if it was less dusty there, and if the stream still played Grieg as it fell over the cliffs into the sea.

'I'm leaving soon,' said young Master Phil, standing like a soldier, feet apart, shoulders square.

I looked up at him. His pale eyes were staring down the road, where the horse and cart were heading in a brown cloud. Only his hands moved, flexing themselves against his drill trousers. 'Where will you go, sir? To protect Madam's country? To Ireland?'

He laughed then, but it wasn't a happy laugh. 'Oh no, Ada, there's no war in Ireland. I'll be sent up north, probably, to north Africa. Come with me.'

He began to walk up the road. I didn't know whether to follow. He turned and looked at me. I could walk and talk with Master Phil at Cradock House, but here, on the street, in front of white people, it was different. I'm not sure why it was different, skin difference was not a matter of law at that time and there were no signs saying benches and entrances were for white people only, but already I knew it was so. Even when I was on my own, the shopkeepers shooed me away if I hung around too long reading their signs. Church Street with its line of pepper trees and its soaring Dutch Reformed Church was not meant for people like me. Walking along Church Street by the side of a young Master in the uniform of a soldier was certainly not meant for people like me.

Already someone had noticed.

A lady in a pink frilled blouse and a darker coloured skirt was coming out of N.C. Rogers General Dealers, fanning herself. I saw her look from Master Phil to me, and back to Master Phil once more.

'Why,' she said, turning her back to me, 'it's Philip Harrington, Cathleen and Edward's boy. How smart you look!'

Young Master Phil took his gaze away from me and walked across to shake her hand politely.

'I believe,' she lowered her voice, 'you lads are to leave soon.'

'I don't know yet, Ma'am.' Young Master Phil's words were steady, but I knew the fear that lived just beneath them. I had heard it in his voice in the garden at Cradock House, just as I'd seen the sun shine on the muscles he'd grown for war. I hated the lady from the General Dealers. I hated her for reminding young Master Phil that not only he, but others as well, would soon find out if he was too afraid for war.

I waited, just behind them. Master Phil's eyes as light as water met mine over the lady's frilled shoulder. Some men clattered out of the store and went over to check on a horse tied up nearby, its nose deep in a bag of oats.

'Sir,' I called, over their talk of the horse, 'here is Madam's letter for posting.'

The lady turned, her lips tight from the interruption.

'Thank you, Ada,' said Master Phil, and touched his cap to the lady. 'Please excuse me. It was very nice to meet you. Ada,' he turned to me, 'we must also check if Father's parcels have arrived.'

With a bob of the head, he began to march up the road towards Market Square. I kept my eyes away from the frilled lady and hurried after him, keeping a distance behind. Once he was alongside the Karoo Gardens, he stopped beneath the striped shade of a pepper tree and waited for me to catch up. Across the square, carts drawn up in front of the town hall wavered in the heat as if readying themselves to drive off on their own. Master Phil wiped his forehead.

'You'll be a good soldier, sir,' I said, looking around to check no one was watching. I reached a hand across the space between us to touch his arm. 'I know you will.'

Some nights during those first seasons of war, while young Master Phil trained in the veld nearby, Madam and Master would cluster about the radiogram and listen to a man with a deep voice called Mr Churchill. Mr Churchill, it seemed, was more important than General Smuts. Sometimes Madam wept at his words, and Master paced up and down, squeezing his hands, his jacket thrown aside on the chair, his normally flat hair in tufts. The radio talked about things called bombs making fires in a town called London, which must be near to Madam's home in Ireland for her to be so worried. They talked about aeroplanes that dived to deliver the same fire from their guns and caused great ships – still I could not imagine these, nor could I imagine the endless seas on which they floated – to sink beneath the oceans forever. And Miss Rose would run upstairs and shut herself in her bedroom and cry that she was tired of the whole war and why couldn't everything be just like it was before.

'When will it end?' Madam would whisper. 'So many boys lost. Ada,' raising her voice, looking about for me in the corridor, 'come and play for us.'

And I would play quiet nocturnes, or a prelude like Chopin's *Raindrop*, its single notes falling into the anxious, pressing silence. Master would return to his newspaper, smoothing down his grey hair. Madam would sit pale in the lamplight, hands clasped in her lap, for once not keeping time with the music.

Phil has received his orders.

We try to be cheerful.

Miriam makes his favourite jam sponge, Ada plays marches, even Rosemary rouses herself to be agreeable. But Edward and I remember too much about the Great War to be swept up in any sort of euphoria.

Ada has ironed his khakis obsessively. She wants everything to be perfect when he leaves.

Mr Churchill sent young Master Phil 'up north'. There was no ocean or great ships there, but a desert more vast and more dry even than our Karoo.

I asked to go to the station to see young Master Phil off. The station was across the Groot Vis, on high ground some distance from Auntie's small township. My mother Miriam said later that it was not my place to ask such a thing, but seeing as I asked Madam when Mama was busy in the kitchen, it was done before she could forbid me.

'Why, Ada,' said Madam, with a quick glance at Master behind his newspaper in his chair opposite her, 'of course you can come.'

It was the busiest I had ever seen the station. Young men stood about with kitbags over their shoulders and talked in high voices and punched each other with their free arms. A train waited for them, its dark red carriages dusty even before the journey had begun. With an explosion that shook the air, the train's engine began to work up steam into white clouds, forcing smart ladies on the platform to turn their faces away from the blasts of grit. A conductor in a blue uniform and cap paced up and down the platform and then, at some signal that I did not see, began to blow hard on his whistle to get all of the excited soldiers on to the train in time.

'Darling,' Madam hugged Master Phil who towered over her from all the growing he had done, 'come back soon!' She stepped away from him and clasped her fingers together.

'Philip.' Master offered his hand, although some of the other fathers were hugging their boys. 'Keep your head down, son. Rosemary,' he turned quickly to gather Miss Rose who was making eyes at a young man nearby, 'come now, say your goodbyes.'

Miss Rose flung herself at young Master Phil and then raced off to be with her school friends. I waited a little way behind Master. I was the only black person standing with a white family.

The station entrance was behind me, I could slip out, no one would know. I could say that I went back to help my mother Miriam with tea. Yet it felt good to be part of such a crowd, even though I was an outsider. There was laughter and crying all about, and children waving little flags. I wondered what it was about war that made people laugh and cry at the same time. Perhaps crying always lies behind laughter but only shows its face when we say goodbye.

Three soldiers with bugles lined up in front of a carriage and began to play a short tune – Madam told me later it was called a fanfare – that made the crowd cheer. 'Ada?' Young Master Phil was looking for me, and I went and stood in front of him.

'I will miss you, sir,' I said, raising my voice over the noise, and offering him my hand. 'Good luck to you, sir.'

And then young Master Phil did a strange thing. He opened his arms and he leant down and hugged me. For a moment I felt his cheek against mine and the prickle of his beard where he had forgotten to shave, and then he was gone, shouldering his bag and leaping up the steps to the carriage.

I felt Madam's hand on my shoulder. I stole a look at Master. He was staring at Master Phil on the train, and frowning.

'All aboard,' shouted the conductor and blew a further blast.

The buglers tucked their bugles under their arms, grabbed their bags and rushed on board as the train began to edge forward under a balloon of smoke. All around us, people on the platform called out to their boys who leant out of the windows and sang and banged the sides of the carriages in time to a song I had heard on the radiogram at Cradock House. 'We'll meet again, don't know where, don't know when . . .'

Ladies who had turned their faces away from the smoke now looked back, and wiped their eyes with lace handkerchiefs and waved gloved hands. The train blew its own whistle in a high screech, higher pitched than the conductor's whistle. A group of children nearby squealed and clapped their hands over their ears. Dark blue pigeons took off from the beams under the station roof.

I turned to look at Master again, to see if he was sad he had not hugged his son like the other fathers had, and found that instead of watching the packed train carry Master Phil to where Mr Churchill was sending him, Master was staring at me.

I have no father.

Well, perhaps that is not right. I have no father that I have ever seen. He must be somewhere, living at his home or with the ancestors, but I have never known him. Mama does not talk about him, and he has no face for me. Madam and Master don't talk about him and young Master Phil and Miss Rose have their own father and do not seem to think it strange that I can't show them a father of my own.

The day that young Master Phil left made me think of my father again. Madam was a second mother to me, but Master was too busy to notice me enough to be a father. I didn't expect his attention, and I didn't receive it. I never felt that he didn't like me; it was just that he didn't notice me.

Except for today.

His look across the heaving platform carried as much attention as I'd ever seen him give Miss Rose or Master Phil. Yet it was not kindly attention. Master looked at me with no particular sympathy. Instead his look was one of dismay.

Chapter 8

'Who is my father?' I used to ask Mama after I had realised that it was in fact necessary to have a father in order to have a baby.

'Just a man I knew once,' Mama would reply, turning away so I could not see her face.

'Did you marry him? Like Master married Madam?'

'He was gone before you were born.'

I would pull up the blanket and stare at her. I always started these talks when I was in bed at night, after Madam had finished her evening playing and the house was quiet except for the creaking of the tin roof as it cooled down after the heat of the day. Mama used to crochet in the chair by the window, her feet in slippers, her hair freed from its usual *doek*. She would wrap a blue shawl she'd made around her shoulders and I would fall asleep to the sound of the roof, and the owl in the kaffirboom, and the rhythmic movement of Mama's crochet hook through her wool.

'Master never went away when young Master Phil and Miss Rose were born,' I persisted, the last time that we talked about the father I never knew. 'Why did my father go away?'

My mother didn't often get really cross with me, especially at the end of the day when she was tired, but now was one of those times. She pushed aside her crocheting and came to stand over me, as if what she had to say must be for my ears only and never escape from the room. *'Tula!'* she hissed. 'I will not speak of these things. You have the best of growing up here, you have no need for a father that does not return! Be grateful to the Lord and go to sleep!'

But I couldn't sleep. I watched her as she picked up the shawl where it had fallen to the floor, and bent back over her work. Mama was not one to give her heart away easily. She was devoted to Madam and Master and the children, so what sort of man could have won her love? Surely only someone fine and kind, who promised to marry her. I knew Mama disapproved of Mrs Pumile with her many, unreliable callers, so she would never have taken up with a man who was not prepared to stay. But a man she looked up to, a man prepared to stay could have won her heart and been a fine father for me. I wish I had known such a father.

And yet all around Cradock – all around the Karoo? All around the world? – it seemed to me that very few black families lived together. It could be, I reasoned, because men and women worked in different places. Men wanting to dig gold out of the ground needed to be in faraway places like Johannesburg while their women remained at home working for white families like Mama and I did. Or was it because black men liked to have many wives and many children to keep them wealthy in their old age? And so staying with one particular wife would be seen as a cruelty to the others?

In Mama's case, the other possibility was that my father was not a man to be looked up to, or a man who worked far away, or a man with other families that claimed his time, but a man who had deceived my mother, who had tricked her into believing that he was a good man when he was not. A man who had talked of marriage but run away before it could happen. A man who probably never knew he had a daughter.

I never spoke about my father after that. Or fathers in general. Even when I wanted to, on the day that young Master Phil left.

I wanted to know what made fathers angry. I wanted to know why Master looked at me the way he did. But I never asked Mama, so she never knew what began that day.

Chapter 9

When I was fifteen I learnt that the war was over and that peace had arrived. We had last had peace before the war – I remember it written on some of the posters outside the newspaper office when I went to post Madam's letters to Ireland. But it hadn't lasted long. Before there was any time to get used to it, war had arrived.

'Is there always peace when there is no war?' I asked Miss Rose one day while I was folding away her clean blouses.

She looked up from the bed where she was arranging a collection of scarves – bright, thin, slippery pieces of material, softer than anything Mama and I washed in the laundry downstairs.

'Don't be stupid, Ada,' she snapped. 'Of course there is. What else would there be?' She began to move the scarves about, holding them up against a knitted jumper or a skirt, or winding them round her neck while she watched herself in the mirror.

'But there is still killing,' I said. 'I've heard the Master say so.'

'There's always killing somewhere or other, it doesn't bother me, so I don't see why it should bother you.' She held up a light blue cardigan. 'I think I prefer the blue-and-white spot rather than the plain next to this.'

'But I want to understand the difference between peace and war,' I said. This seemed very important. War had changed Cradock House; it had left us short of sugar and cake tins and laughter and young Master Phil. I wanted to be prepared for the next time, for the enemy-in-waiting. But Miss Rose was too far away in her own world, and she did not hear me.

Before Master Phil arrived home, my mother and the Madam talked in the kitchen with the door closed. I polished the dining-room table and strained to hear what they were saying but the door was too thick. Miss Rose returned from buying a new dress in town at Anstey's Fashions.

'Look, Ada!' She spun around in it, yellow hair flying about her face. The dress was blue like the sky through the kaffirboom leaves and had a white collar with blue embroidery. It was the most beautiful dress I had ever seen.

I won't need the fur muff or my one good silk hat, not in Cradock. Edward says the ladies wear practical clothes. And Mother, who knows about foreign parts from her brother Timothy in India, says the most important thing is to protect my complexion. Although what Uncle Tim actually wrote to say was: never dispute with the natives, it shows weakness!

So – sadly, for I love the silk even though it's ancient – I shall leave it and the muff behind and take three plain bonnets and a spare parasol. After all, Mother says – a little harshly, I thought – South Africa isn't India.

I didn't know what silk was or where India was. But Miss Rose's dress was surely as beautiful as any sort of hat.

'Madam and Mama have been talking in the kitchen,' I said to Miss Rose while she twirled about, blue skirt flying, 'and they're not cooking.'

'Silly Ada! Why can't they talk? This is one of the dresses I've got for Jo'burg. They said at the store all the girls will be wearing them now the war's over!'

'I think it's about Master Phil.'

'Have you ironed my petticoats yet? Please, Ada.' She leant forward and put on her widest smile. 'I'll buy you peppermint creams!'

'Now then, Rosemary.' Master appeared suddenly from the study. 'Ada can't run after you all day. It's high time you did some of your own ironing.'

'Mean Daddy,' Miss Rose said, linking her arm in his. 'Do you like my new frock?'

Master gave a grudging smile and fiddled with the watch on a chain in his waistcoat. He couldn't resist Miss Rose. Not many people could, especially men.

'When is Master Phil coming back, sir?' I ventured.

I didn't often speak directly to the Master. And the only time he looked directly at me was at the station when young Master Phil left. There was always something fierce about Master's face – the greying eyebrows above pale eyes, the silence in him, the stern lips that only ever softened for the Madam and Miss Rose, or when I played the piano and he didn't know I could see him out of the corner of my eye.

He turned away from Miss Rose, now admiring herself in the hall mirror I'd cleaned that morning, and looked down at me. There was still fierceness, but also something else, something strange that I hadn't seen before in Master's face. It was, I realised suddenly, the look of my young Master in the garden before the war, when he'd wondered if he would be brave enough to fight. Yet what nervousness could Master possibly feel on the return of his beloved son?

'Soon, Ada,' he said quietly and touched my shoulder. Master had never touched me before. Perhaps he was distracted by Miss Rose. 'Soon.'

Master Phil arrived the next day. They carried him up to his room on the top floor. All I saw of him was his face above a blanket and the face was different from the face he'd taken to the war with him. Madam told me that Master Phil was very tired and needed to sleep a lot. I could understand that. After all, Mr Churchill had required very great actions and bravery from all of his soldiers. There had been a church service at St Peter's for the families of Cradock boys who never came back. Madam and Master went along and said prayers to God to thank Him for sparing Master Phil and bringing him home. The other boys had mostly died and been buried in the desert 'up north' or in another country called Italy, where Mendelssohn went to find a new symphony in a land that was said to be almost as hot as our Karoo.

'But why,' I asked my mother in our room after a week had gone by and Master Phil still slept, 'why are some of the other living soldiers walking around town? Didn't they fight as hard as Master Phil?'

My mother looked up from her crocheting. She crocheted tea cosies and bed socks for the church. They always were short of tea cosies and bed socks.

'Master Phil is wounded, Ada,' she said and laid the work aside.

'Then why can't I help you nurse him, Mama?'

My mother Miriam smiled but it wasn't a happy smile. 'Some of Master Phil's wounds are inside, Ada.'

'Under the bandages?'

'Further inside than that. These are wounds that don't have blood.'

I stared at her. She picked up her crocheting. The owl hooted outside in the kaffirboom. I wondered if Master Phil could still hear owls, or if the inside wounds had taken sound away from him as well.

Miss Rosemary left for Johannesburg soon after Master Phil returned. I don't know why she went, although she seemed very happy to be going. She said that the future would be better in Jo'burg. I remember reading about the future in Madam's book at about the time she was to leave Ireland for Cradock. It was clearly something that rich people needed in their lives. I wished I could find people who had already found the future, and then I could ask them what was so special about it.

'Wish me luck!' Miss Rose called from the window of the car taking her to the station. There were more cars and fewer horse carts these days since the war. Miss Rose looked very happy, waving her lace handkerchief from the car. She was wearing the new blue dress from Anstey's and red lipstick from Austen's the chemist. She hadn't wanted Madam and Master to go to the station to see her off – 'Too much fuss,' she laughed gaily. Perhaps she wanted to spare Madam and Master the reminder of her brother leaving for war? But I don't think so. Miss Rose was not that thoughtful. I think she just wanted to be away with as little delay as possible.

Master stared down at his shoes that I'd polished that morning, then up at Miss Rose in the car and lifted a hand to shade his eyes from the sun. The breeze fluttered Madam's cream skirt against her legs. Upstairs in his room, Master Phil slept.

'Take care, darling! Write every week!' Madam blew kisses and felt for the brooch at her throat.

'*Cathleen Moore for Union Castle Steamship* Walmer Castle, *Southampton*' – *it says on the label on my trunk. Train from here, boat to England, train again to Southampton and then the* Walmer Castle. *I've never been further than Bannock village.*

'Well, Ada,' Madam said, blowing her nose as we closed the garden gate behind us and went back up the path to the house, 'you're the daughter of the house now.'

'Then let me help you with Master Phil,' I said, watching the Master's straight back climb the step up to the *stoep* and go inside, 'like a daughter should.' Madam stopped on the path. She bent down and nipped the dead head off a rose. Afterwards, when I told Mama what I'd said, she was angry with me. But she knew and I knew – and Madam herself knew – that Miss Rose had never been helpful, never been the sort of daughter Madam needed.

'Perhaps you can, Ada,' Madam said, straightening up. Her eyes looked sore, like when you've been standing with your face into the wind and there's snow on the mountains. I had still not seen that snow – it lived high up, about two hours away across the Karoo. It sent hard white frosts that fell in the night, and crunched under my bare feet at sunrise when I fetched the milk.

And so I began to take care of Master Phil.

'Remember that night I got sick, Ada?' Master Phil turned his thin face towards me.

'Yes,' I said. 'You'd eaten too many apricots from the garden.'

He smiled a little and shifted in the bed. His arms weren't brown and strong like I remembered, and long bones pressed against the skin like the washing line under a wet sheet. When he walked to the bathroom, his steps were the steps of an old man. When he bent to get back into bed, the knobs of his spine showed through his pyjama top.

'Do you want to sit up, Master Phil? Shall I open the curtains? It's a lovely day, you could watch the clouds.'

'No, no.' He subsided on the pillow. 'The light hurts my eyes.'

'That old apricot still makes fruit,' I said, after a while. 'Did you see apricot trees in the war?'

Master Phil stared at me, his eyes pale as the lightest sky, like that time in the garden when he said he might be afraid. Then he began to cry, his shoulders hunching under the flannel pyjamas that Mama and I had to wash every day on account of his sweating in the night.

'Sorry, sir,' I said, trying not to cry myself. 'Sorry for disturbing you.'

He didn't turn away when he cried, like he used to do as a boy when he'd fallen and hurt himself. Now he just lay there in bed facing me, the tears going down his cheeks, his shoulders shaking. He didn't make much noise either. Maybe soldiers learn to cry quietly in a war.

I didn't know what to do so I took his hand. He placed his other hand on top of it.

'Play for me, Ada,' he muttered. 'Play something gay.'

And so I did. I left the door open and went downstairs and played something cheerful and gay to cover his crying. Maybe a waltz, like Madam used to play when there was a dinner party before the war. Or a polonaise with its lively march up and down the keyboard. And Madam would come in and say thank you with her eyes. And Master would open the door to the study and listen as well.

I learnt about 'Up North'. This was where Mr Churchill

had sent Master Phil in the war. I wanted to learn about it, I wanted to understand what sort of place could have wounded Master Phil so deeply. Perhaps then I would understand about war.

But I also wanted to know about it because it was a new place for me. Was this wrong? Was it wrong to have such thirst for new places even though they had caused such pain?

All I knew was Cradock. All I could see from Master Phil's toy box was the Karoo. What, I would ask myself as I peered over the veld, what lay beyond the brown *koppies* and the distant mountains with their imagined snow? Books and music could only take you so far. Words, drawn from real life, took you further. Madam's words had taken me to Ireland and a blue stream that tumbled over cliffs to the sound of Grieg . . .

At first I asked him nothing. I cared for him quietly, and cut his once-bright hair, and shaved his thin face when he was too weary to do so, and held his hand while he fell asleep, and waited in the chair across from him so he wouldn't be alone when he woke.

Then he began to talk about it. And so I discovered the desert from Master Phil, a desert that made our Karoo with its struggling bush seem rich by comparison. The Sahara he spoke of was a place where life had given up trying. Not even a bony thorn tree found the will to grow. Brown sand dunes, bare of plants or animals, smothered the land and rose higher than our *koppies*. Yet what the dunes lacked in inhabitants they made up for in movement of their own. They moved, Master Phil told me, his face for once keen. Whole dunes moved!

'But how?' I gasped, peering at him through the gloom of the dark bedroom, dark on account of the sun hurting his eyes.

'Why, it's the wind, Ada,' he said patiently, like his patience had once explained words with strange meanings, or numbers I'd not yet understood. 'Wind shears the top of them, you see, or shifts them sideways. Into a new place, a new shape.'

He grimaced a little, and I wondered whether the inside wounds became sore if he spoke too much. It would be a pity if the first time he'd shown some spirit was to be the cause of more pain. After the tears over the apricot trees, I'd been careful not to ask too many questions. I waited for him to tell me things while we sat together in the fading afternoons, or over the mid-morning cup of tea I brought him during my daily chores. Sometimes he talked, like today, sometimes he stayed quiet for days at a time. In this respect, Master Phil was very changed for me. Gone was the laughter, the keenness, the energy he'd had as a young man, even the fear he'd been able to confess before he went away. What was left was as empty and as dry as the place he described.

'There's a strange beauty,' he once said of the desert, when I risked a further question. 'But it's cruel, Ada.' He stared down at his fingers in surprise as they fidgeted on the bedspread, almost as if their movement was happening outside his control, like the sands of the desert had no control over where the wind sent them.

'What's beautiful about it?'

Were the dunes purple at sunset, was the sky coloured more vividly than I saw above Cradock House each evening? Or did the beauty come from the hardness of the place, from the power of the wind to lash sand into new shapes?

'There's no shade,' I heard Master Phil say, drawn back to the cruelty. 'Flies on your face, in your hair, sand stinging your eyes, scratching your throat till it bled.' He lifted one of the restless hands and put it against his neck as if the dryness still held him in its grasp. 'Half a cup of water to shave in, no way to get clean. Heat dried you to a crisp, cold froze you as soon as the sun went down.'

'Where did the water come from, sir, that you were given?' For there could have been no rain in such a place, no Groot Vis winding between sand mountains to bring relief.

'They carried it in trucks,' he said, smiling for once all the way to his light blue eyes. 'From miles away, where there was a river, or an oasis.'

'An oasis?'

'A spring in the middle of the desert,' he lifted himself up a little against his pillows, 'a place where water from deep down bubbles to the surface.'

'Did you see such a place?'

'Yes,' he said, before putting his head back and lifting a thin arm across his face. His hair was no longer wavy, and lay pale and flat against his head. He spoke again with his eyes covered. 'When I was injured. It had palm trees, and there was shade.'

'Like our palms? In the Karoo Gardens in Market Square?' I broke in, excited at the possibility that I knew of something that was also found far away, that I'd sat in the shade of trees that grew at the other end of the world, that I could touch something that was part of war.

'Yes.' He took his arm away from his face. 'Just like them.'

I stared at him. I had read music that came from across the world, I had felt it quicken beneath my fingers. And down in Market Square there was shade that I had shared with Master Phil without knowing.

'But it's the sand you remember the most.' He brushed his fingers, as if they would never be free of it. 'Funny, isn't it,' he murmured, 'how in a desert it's the sand that flows . . .'

The house was quiet. Madam was teaching at school, Mama was resting downstairs, Master was at the town hall. I had already peeled the vegetables, and made the pastry to go on top of the steak and kidney pie. The ironing was done. I waited for a moment.

'How were you injured, sir?'

He glanced at me, the light blue eyes suddenly focused, as they were when I shaved him and felt his gaze on my face.

'I want to understand about war.'

He hesitated, his eyes probing mine. 'It's not something to admire, Ada.'

'I still want to understand.'

From the station came the irregular sound of shunting. Low pitched, a drawn-out semibreve, then a rush of crotchets. It carried me back to the laughing and crying crowds on the platform, the buglers playing, and the quick warmth of Master Phil's hug. Perhaps he remembered it too, for he gave a sad smile and then nodded. Maybe he knew my plan. Maybe he knew it was less about me than about him. Maybe in remembering out loud, he might learn to forget.

'We were ambushed,' he began after a pause. 'That means to be caught, to be surprised by your enemy.'

'What happened, sir?'

'Don't call me sir.' He shifted in the bed irritably and looked down at his narrow, veined wrists. I waited in the shadows, pushing down my questions. I knew that men fought each other in war, but surely not like this? Only animals ambushed one another. Lions of the veld lay in wait to attack buck, for buck were their prey. Did war force men to lie in wait for one another, to stalk one another as prey?

'They had tanks, with mounted machine guns,' he went on, his voice clipped with remembered detail. 'We had rifles. They could move about, we were in slit trenches – holes in the ground, Ada, just a foot deep. They pinned us down, we couldn't dig deeper because the sand became rock.' He covered his ears with his hands.

I realised, then, that it wasn't only the sights of war that returned to soldiers, but the sound and feel of war as well. Perhaps the closed curtains that I'd thought were Master Phil's way of blocking out the world were also necessary to deflect the remembered rip of bullets over his head as he cowered in the shallow hiding place, and to expel the grit under his finger-nails as he scratched desperately to deepen the trench . . .

'There were shells, too, that whistled before they hit,' he muttered, hands still over his ears, as the battle pounded against his skull. I had to lean forward to catch what he was saying. 'You could hear them coming – high pitched, like a screaming violin – coming faster than you could get away – they explode, they splash sand – and blood.'

He stopped suddenly, and wrapped his arms round his thin torso and began to clutch at himself, as if wondering again how it was possible that he could still be whole despite the terrible rain of death all about. I put out a hand and touched his shoulder. The bones felt jagged under the cotton of his pyjamas.

'I still see them, Ada.' He grabbed hold of my hand and stared wildly at me, his eyes aflame. 'Ben, Frank, my sergeant . . .'

'I will pray for them, sir,' I said, trying to stop my hand shaking within his frenzied grip. 'God the Father will make them well, I know He will.'

He stared at me, but I'm not sure he saw me at all.

'Did this battle have a name, sir?' I didn't want him to stop talking. It was too soon. He needed to talk more, he needed to let the poisonous memories escape. I knew battles were given names. I had learnt of Waterloo, and other places in France with difficult names where many men had died in a previous war. But in that war death had come in mud, not sand.

'Sidi Rezegh,' he said wearily, his hands falling to rest limply on the covers. 'It was called Sidi Rezegh.'

I wanted to ask him something else but I never did. I wanted to ask him if his fear of war had gone away during the actual fighting. Or whether it was to blame for what had happened. Whether fear – and not just the enemy – had pinned him down and drawn the bullet to his chest, and left him with a wound that no longer bled but still gave him no peace.

I wanted to ask him, but I never did.

A season went by. Master Phil stayed in his room. The inside wound and the memory of the cruel Sahara never left him alone. His hands fidgeted. The heat of the desert came on him in the night to make him sweat and cry out. Then, as if to remind him even when he needed no reminding, a drought fell on the Karoo and brought winds that scoured the veld and dried the skin on the tips of his fingers until they cracked, and attacked his throat with familiar grit.

'Why won't it leave me?' he would mutter with quiet despair as I brought wet flannels to lay on his forehead, and my mother Miriam's cold lemonade to soothe his throat.

The ground between the *koppies* broke into steep gullies. The water in the town dam went up into the air and left a line where it had been – like a ring on a bath that hasn't been cleaned. The Groot Vis was reduced to a trickle and Auntie's washing business struggled. In the town's gardens, dogs panted in the shade of the bluegums. Our apricot tree dropped hard, wrinkled fruit. Water was rationed, and Mama and I washed from buckets. As I read to Master Phil each day in the close darkness of his bedroom, Church Street rumbled with the sound of farmers driving animals to slaughter because even the Karoo bush dried out. Dust devils blew into Cradock House and stained the curtains where they hung limp behind the fanlights we kept open to catch a breeze. I had to take the curtains down one by one and wash them in the smallest amount of water and then haul them over the line outside to dry while I prayed that the dust would stay away. The furrow in front of the house that used to carry brown river water to the garden no longer ran. The only wetness in the world seemed to be the thin stream of water from the tap in the laundry where, after morning cleaning, I would hold my neck and feel the coolness trickle over my cheeks and into my hair.

The drought lived with us until one day I heard the chirp of the *langasem* – the rain grasshopper – that only spoke when rain was on its way. The same day Mama pointed out to Madam how the songololo worms knew what was coming, for they began to creep inside and curl up into neat circles on the wall.

'How do they know, Miriam?' Madam wondered, carefully moving one out into the garden.

'They know, Ma'am. They knew long before we did.'

And so it came. Mama and I watched from the *stoep* as the sky turned black and cracked open, spitting silver hail on to the roof in a fearful racket, stripping Madam's few wilted shrubs and covering the hard ground between them in a stony carpet. I put out a foot and felt the iciness beneath my toes. After the hail finished its noisy business, the rain hissed sweet music and filled up the water tanks and the town dam and the Groot Vis, and I knew we were saved. Even Master Phil roused himself to look outside and marvel at the kaffirboom leaves bending in the downpour against an overflowing sky. I think it washed away some of the desert from his heart.

The nights were difficult in Cradock House. During the day, it was the memory of sand and thirst and whistling death that tormented Master Phil. At night, his fellow soldiers came to him and called for help.

'Sarge! Sarge!' he would scream, and twist his sheets into knots. 'This way!'

I would listen for the first cry and run upstairs and stroke the sweat from his forehead with a damp cloth.

'Covering fire, the flank, the flank!'

'Hush, sir,' this from me. 'The war is over.'

Thin hands scratching the covers, head tossing from side to side, the racket of the battlefield making his eyelids flicker.

'Ben, hold on! I'll come for you!'

'Shhh, Master, shhh.'

'No ammo, no ammo, Father – Father?'

Sometimes the only way to calm him was to take him in my arms and sing to him like Mama had once sung to me, *Thula thu'* . . . and feel the rigid cords of his arms slacken and the terrible, wracking battle fade from his face.

Sometimes Madam would reach him before me, and together we would hold him and soothe him, Madam's eyes bright with tears, her hair falling about her face in a cloud, her hands trembling as they never did at the piano.

'When will it end, Ada?' she would whisper, as she'd whispered to Master during the time of war when bombs fell and ships sank. 'Will there be no end?'

Master never came to comfort Phil, even when he called out his name. Perhaps he felt it was woman's work. But he did come to stand at the door. I looked up once, and saw him there. It was hard to see because of the darkness, but he stood there in his dressing gown and slippers and watched me with my arms round Master Phil, and with his restless head against my shoulder. It seemed to me that Master looked on not with anguish for his son or even gratitude for my nursing, but with the face he'd shown across the crowded station after Master Phil left. There, as I'd stood with Master Phil's hug still warm upon me, his face showed dismay. Now, in the darkness, as I in turn held my young Master, the dismay hardened to disapproval. When he saw that I had seen him, he turned away.

'Ada,' murmured Master Phil, his eyes flickering and sliding from the doorway to my face, 'are you an angel?'

'No, sir,' I said, slipping from him, laying him back against his pillows, stroking the hair from his forehead. 'Rest now.'

Outside Cradock House, life moved on.

A new waiting room was built at the station for all the people who would need to come back to town now the drought was broken. And the number of trains increased until it seemed that the shunting and whistling never stopped from dawn until night. Along with the trains came more people living across the Groot Vis to work on the railway and on the road that would one day go straight to Johannesburg where there was gold to be dug out of the ground and riches to follow it. Auntie's business did well out of all the extra washing that needed to be done.

Then there was talk of something called a boom, on account of the money to be made from wool taken off sheep in a curly coat. But there was also discontent in the township beyond Bree Street; the boom had not paved the roads or strung wire to bring light to the tiny houses or pipes to take away their waste like it had in the white part of Cradock.

In the midst of this boom, diphtheria fell upon the Karoo. It showed no bias about whom it attacked. Your throat turned white and you couldn't swallow and then you died. I worried that Master Phil might catch it in his weakened state, and so I didn't mind that he stayed in his room while the diphtheria caught those who went outside. Some people thought such a disease was caused by the drought, others thought it was caused by the rain that ended it. Life and death didn't choose sides in a way you could predict, my mother Miriam said. It was a matter of luck and the influence of ancestors – not weather or fortune – that decided whether you would live or die.

Cradock House would never die, I told myself as I polished the banisters with oil and scrubbed the *stoep* with soap and water where it had become stained during the drought. No disease, no war, could shake its thick walls or shift its place in the brown Karoo earth. Yet – I stopped and listened – its passages were quieter now that Miss Rose was gone and Master Phil lay in darkness upstairs. And I realised that a house is more than stone and foundations and a roof. A house needs sound and activity to keep it alive. I think only Madam and I understood this.

So I sang as I worked – 'We'll meet again' – and Madam played for an hour each morning to get the day underway. Scales rushed through the house as before, although a little more quietly on account of Master Phil. And when we were not making our own music, Madam was careful to keep the radiogram playing.

Master did not seem to notice the emptiness we tried to fill. Perhaps he welcomed the silence of the day, after the cries of the night. He continued with his usual job of reading his papers in the study. Lately he also spent time looking at his new car in the garage that had been built on to the side of Cradock House. The car was black and had large headlamps that shone in the darkness like the night eyes of spooked animals. Master used the car to go to meetings in the town hall, so Madam was often at home on her own in the evenings, when the only sound was the creaking of the tin roof. When he got home, it was often too late for Madam to play for him as she used to. But it didn't seem to matter any more.

And he didn't seem to need to touch Madam like he used to during the war. My mother said it was because Master had a lot on his mind, especially young Master Phil's illness, and so there was no time for touching.

I still read Madam's book on her dressing table.

Letters have been the currency of our betrothal. Can we meet in Cape Town on the day of our marriage and pick up where they left off?

Edward says I write well. And I know I do, giving him a twist on all the Bannock news and a sprinkle of gossip about those he remembers. But is it a mistake to allow outside news to carry such weight? To avoid the personal in favour of the general?

And what if words – of any kind – dry up when we're face to face?

Will we find things to say that won't need to be written down first? That won't need the safety of prior thought?

Every day Master Phil stayed upstairs in his bedroom. He even took his meals there. Mama made his favourite hot sponge puddings but he was never very hungry. Master would look in in the mornings before he started work, and stand in the doorway and ask Master Phil how he was, and adjust the chain on his waistcoat.

After morning cleaning, I would change my sweaty overall for a fresh one and go upstairs to read to Master Phil because his eyes were no longer good. They had been good enough to take him to war, but now they were too weak for peace. I read from books that Madam chose and that I didn't really understand. But Master Phil listened and sometimes he took my hand in the way that he liked to do, and held it against his thin cheek and explained what I couldn't understand, like he'd told me about war and the place called Sidi Rezegh. But none of the books we read had anything to do with war, for Madam did not want him reminded of it. The books helped Master Phil. Like the piano for me, they took him to a new place.

'We all have something of Pip in us,' he murmured one day, of a book called *Great Expectations*. 'Don't you think so, Ada? Dickens makes us look at ourselves as well as worry about Pip . . .'

'What part of Pip do you have, sir?'

He looked across at me in surprise and was silent for a while, watching me where I sat on the chair with the book open in my lap. It was late afternoon and the sun, where it squeezed through the drawn curtains, was growing dim. Our voices were the only sound in the house.

'Ada,' he whispered, his voice slowing over the letters of my name, 'you already know.'

But I didn't know and he must have seen it in my eyes for he turned away and closed his, as if my not knowing was too heavy for him to bear.

But this was the only time of difficulty; mostly we talked easily. Almost as easily as we'd talked when we were children and he had shown me numbers and the purpose of a bank and the long wait I would have for a future to arrive. Madam said I was the only one who could make young Master Phil forget his illness. Master never said anything to me, and avoided my eyes, but sometimes I caught him speaking in a low voice with Madam and shaking his head, and I know it had something to do with how much time I was spending in caring for young Master Phil. I don't think Madam agreed with what he was saying because she would often walk away. I still don't know what I could have done differently. Perhaps Master's disapproval was not just because Master Phil had once hugged me in front of white crowds or because I had lately comforted him in my arms; maybe it was because Master Phil treated me as a member of the family, and touched my hand, and sometimes smiled at what I said. Perhaps that was the part Master did not like.

During all this time of Master Phil's illness, and the emptiness in Cradock House, and the restlessness of the townships, Miss Rose never came back from Jo'burg. She sent postcards with pictures of tall buildings instead.

Chapter 10

I was now seventeen years old. My world revolved around young Master Phil. I hardly went out any more, the gardener posted Madam's letters to Ireland at the post office on Adderley Street as I used to do before. I had, in any case, found all the words I would ever need and surely read all the possible signs in the shop windows that there could ever be. I also knew how to write down the words that I saw. I have always been better at writing English words and English sentences than words in Xhosa, Mama's language.

Cradock had by now left me behind. The few young girls that I knew, daughters of maids like my mother and Mrs Pumile and her cousin who worked at the bank, all found young men and had babies. They went to live in the townships, or they stayed with their babies in *kaias* like Mama and I did while their husbands went far away to work. Sometimes, when Master Phil was sleeping, I stood on his toy box and looked out over the town like I used to do as a child and saw some of these girls with babies on their backs, walking down the street. They looked tired but proud. There would be no young men left for me. Mrs Pumile used to shake her head and mutter to Mama that it was time for me to find a young man because I was pretty now but I may not be pretty in a few years' time. Whether she was right about me being pretty, I can't say, for prettiness was what Miss Rose had with yellow hair and slate-blue eyes and a voice that teased men.

My hair was dark and curly and although Mama often said approvingly that I had kind eyes, I don't think eyes are enough where prettiness is required. In reply to Mrs Pumile, Mama said that there was no time for prettiness or boys while my young Master lay ill in bed. But I was not downhearted, I was honoured to care for Master Phil instead. My life was filled with love for him and for Madam and Master and Mama, and for Cradock House where I surely now belonged – daughter of the house, Madam had said – and for the piano that was my special joy.

The doctor came one day in his new black car while I was sitting with Master Phil as he slept. He used to get frightened if he woke up and I wasn't there. The room was dark except for a stripe of sunshine that fell across the floor from a gap in the curtains. Dr Wilmott looked across at Madam and Master, then at me, then back at Madam and Master.

'You may speak in front of Ada, Doctor,' murmured Madam, laying a hand on my shoulder. 'Ada cares for Philip more than any of us.'

The doctor had a stern face, rather like Master's. My mother said he was the same doctor who had delivered me at Cradock House.

'We can't expect . . .' he began with a disapproving look at me. Perhaps he had forgotten that I, too, belonged in Cradock House.

'Ada keeps Philip alive,' came Master's voice quietly, from behind the doctor.

No one said anything. I felt a hotness in my face that I hadn't known before.

'Very well.' He reached down for Master Phil's wrist and held it for a while near his wristwatch.

I slipped off the bed and went to stand near the cupboard. The curtains stirred in the breeze, shifting the stripe of sunshine on the floor. Master Phil stirred too.

'Good day, Philip. How are you today?'

Master Phil stared at them. Then moved his neck painfully and looked at me.

'Time you were up and about,' the doctor said in a loud voice and unbuttoned part of Master's pyjama top to place a round metal thing on Master's chest and connect its tubes to his ears. 'Breathe deeply.'

Master Phil breathed, his thin chest rising and falling, the ribs clear to see against the material of his pyjamas. No one said anything. A dog barked and growled outside and my mother Miriam shouted at it from the kitchen.

'Your chest is clear.' He took the tubes out of his ears. 'The wound,' he opened the pyjamas further and probed with his fingers over a red scar, 'is fully healed.'

The doctor sat down on the bed and looked at his hands.

'There's nothing further that I can do for you, young man. Physically, you're fine. The rest . . .' he stopped and looked up at Madam and Master, 'must come from you.'

No one spoke.

'Thank you, Doctor,' said Madam into the silence.

A fly buzzed between the window and the curtains, freed itself and fell on to the floor. The doctor opened his bag and put away the round thing with its tubes. The Master turned away, his shoulders low. Madam clasped her hands hard behind her back, the knuckles white. Madam had very strong hands from the piano; she could twist caps off jam jars that no one else could shift. The curtains swayed again in a fresh draught from outside, bringing outside things – the F sharp whistle of the midday train leaving the station, the smell of Mama's lamb stew drifting out of the kitchen, the raised voices of Mrs Pumile and her Madam next door – into the dark bedroom.

'You don't know!' Master Phil's voice rose in a scream. He reared up in the bed. The covers fell back to show bony legs below his pyjama trousers, like the branches of the thorn tree by the *kaia*. 'You never saw what I saw!' He covered his face with trembling hands, as if they could block out the guns and the blood and the sand of the desert. I made to go towards him but the doctor shook his head at me before turning back.

'Get on your feet, young man,' he boomed. 'Find a job!' He shot a look across at Master. 'Work for a living! That will banish the ghosts.'

'But—' I blurted out in shock, turning to Madam and then Master, who shook his head strongly at me. Wars didn't contain ghosts! Master Phil himself had said so, that day under the washing line when he talked of being afraid. And in any case how could men fight ghosts? Ghosts were mostly ancestors, or maybe an evil spirit like the *tokoloshe* . . .

'I'll see you out, Doctor,' Master said quickly, sending a fierce look at Master Phil's weeping figure.

'Oh, Phil.' Madam knelt by the bed and took him in her arms. His fair hair, lately sprinkled with strands of grey, lay against her shoulder, like it had the night he'd eaten too many ripe apricots. The dog barked again on the street outside and I heard my mother Miriam's footsteps going to investigate. 'Dear Phil, learn to forget. We need you well, you're all we have now.'

Master stopped at the door, frowned, and beckoned for me to leave. I followed him and the doctor out of the room. It would not do to risk more disapproval from Master, or to ask about ghosts right now. Master Phil needed to cry. And Madam needed to cry with him. Maybe they both needed the Master there as well. But grown men like the Master don't cry. They only stand at the door and watch. My mother Miriam says men have no patience with tears.

And yet for all Madam's tears, and Master's impatience, and the unsettling mention of ghosts, I found myself filled with hope. The doctor's instruments had told Master Phil that he was cured, and so the doctor had told young Master Phil to get up. I was sure he would do so. And when he did, the world at peace would welcome him back while the memories of war and the cruel Sahara would fade. His fallen comrades would find their own place and would surely leave him to rest at night. And then he could find a job – perhaps in the Master's office writing letters? Or perhaps in the bank, where I had still not been, on account of Mama keeping her money under the bed in a shoebox.

This would be the start of Master Phil's full recovery. I was sure of it. So I ran downstairs and hugged my mother in the kitchen over the lamb stew and told her that Master Phil would soon be up and about. And then I played a quick scherzo to rejoice in what would surely be.

The day after the doctor's visit, I got out young Master Phil's clothes from peacetime and laid them on the chair. They were a little big for him but still good quality on account of having no one to wear them for so long.

'It's a good day, sir,' I said, drawing the curtains back slightly, 'not too sunny for your eyes.'

And he dressed himself and felt his way downstairs – holding on to the banister, so uncertain compared to the headlong rush of boyhood – and stood swaying in the kitchen as Mama clapped her hands and Madam smiled with tears in her eyes to see him up and about.

At first he walked around the garden, hesitant, as if he'd never seen such a place before. He seemed surprised at the beetles rasping in the hedge and the bokmakieries calling to each other from one end to the other. It was as if the desert had swept away all memory of plants in bloom and grass underfoot, and all memory of sound save for the whine of bullets.

'Was it always like this, Ada?' he asked, his hand sometimes touching my arm for balance, his tall frame stooped as if to protect the inside wound. 'This beautiful?'

'Yes, sir. Even in the drought.'

He smiled then, and reached out to pick a leaf and stroke its velvet underside.

'We could walk into town, sir,' I said, keen to cement his progress. 'There's no dust now the roads are tarred.'

Adderley Street was crowded on the day Master Phil went on his first outing. If the garden had been a surprise for him, then the town was surely even more so. Much had changed since he left for the war. Motor cars now outnumbered horse carts and, as they edged along, they blared their horns and revved their engines and made exploding sounds that startled passers-by.

'Ada!' Master Phil gasped, clutching at his ears, 'No, no—'

'Come, sir, we'll go somewhere quiet,' I said hurriedly, taking his arm because his legs did not seem to work that well any more. 'We can look at the bridge – at the Groot Vis.'

We took a back road towards the iron bridge and I didn't talk in order to give his ears a rest. It was the exploding cars, I realised; the sound of war. But if he couldn't face the world and its noise again, how would he ever find its beauty? If he kept his curtains closed, how could he see the Karoo shimmer in the midday heat? Or spot the orange aloes glowing like candles against the scrub?

He kept his arm in mine as we walked further, our footsteps matching. From a hidden back garden came the shouts of children playing. Purple bougainvillea tumbled over a fence by the garden gate. I picked a flower and gave it to him. He examined its papery petals as if it was a rare jewel and smiled at me. I remembered the first time I had met Master Phil in town, when he was in his uniform, and how uncertain I'd felt about being a black girl walking beside a white boy. Then, I had held back and followed behind him, and felt in turn behind me the disapproval of the white lady he had been talking to.

Now, I walked at his side, his arm through mine.

Maybe I was foolish to believe I could do so, for no one else walked like this, so openly, with such boldness. The white people we passed murmured to each other but I didn't care. Master Phil getting well was more important than anything else. Madam would understand this. Some of the passers-by were people I knew should recognise him, should value the miracle of his recovery, but even so they never said a word on account of me, and walked past with their faces pointing away from us, like Master turned away in the night when he saw me comfort his son.

But I felt only joy. Joy that Master Phil had come this far, joy that he had found a way past the wounds that did not bleed, joy that I might have helped him in some small way. Up ahead, the bank sloped down to the river where mimosas dug for water and women like Auntie washed clothes on the far rocks. Swallows dived down to the shallows and wove upstream, navy streaks against the brown water.

'I love you, Ada,' murmured young Master Phil, leaning against the trunk of a tree, his pale eyes finding mine, his thin hands clasped together like Madam's hands had clasped that day when the doctor came and told us he was cured. 'I've always loved you—'

'I know, sir,' I broke in, gratitude almost choking my voice. 'You're my family.'

But I didn't know. And when I later realised what he meant, it was already too late.

Can I ever repay Ada for all she has done?

It was Edward who said – with rare candour – that Ada was keeping Phil alive, and he is right. Ada has poured devotion, patience, and warmth into our Phil to the point where he has begun to believe he can be well again.

Families, I have learned, are not static but fluid things. They evolve, and so they should. Members circle, or take centre stage, or leave altogether. Ada has found her place, and we are all the better for it. But what has evolved within our four walls is not normal outside.

And I must confess I love Ada like the daughter I wish Rosemary was.

Chapter 11

Young Master Phil died on a Monday. I wasn't with him. I was down in the garden, hanging out the clothes on the line, feeling the slap of wet sleeves against my arms and sniffing the white jasmine as it drifted over from the pergola. From the other side of the hedge came Mrs Pumile's voice, talking loudly to a friend in the *kaia*, while her Madam was out.

Upstairs, Master Phil slept in darkness filled with the smell of medicines and floor polish. But there was hope, now. We had had several outings. Master Phil was starting to eat downstairs more often, too. Madam and Master were talking about taking him on holiday, perhaps to visit Miss Rose.

I bent down to pick up the next shirt and pegs. There was a thud and a scream and, as I turned, I saw Madam rush out of the kitchen and fling herself down over a bundle on the ground that was Master Phil. My mother Miriam ran out and took my hand and pulled me into our bedroom and stroked my face before she rushed out again. Mrs Pumile shrieked through the hedge. I heard the sound of motor-car tyres on the gravel, the urgent voices of the doctor and my Master, and the endless, quiet sobbing of my Madam as I stood waiting behind the curtains that Mama had pulled shut before she left our room.

It was some time before Mama came back into the room where I waited. It was hot with the curtains closed and I felt the sweat gather on my neck and a pain build behind my eyes.

Cars came and went and people's voices rose and fell and the bokmakieries called from the end of the garden, just like they did every day. I wanted to peep, like I used to do from the door when Madam and Master were in the lounge, or when Madam was playing the piano. But this was somehow different. I did not want to disobey Mama at a time like this, so I stayed sitting on the bed as my heart cried out, wondering why Master Phil had been at the window, why he had leant out so far, why he had not called to me in the garden below, how I could have been so wrong about him getting better . . .

'Ada,' Madam said the next day, her green eyes more sore than on the day Miss Rose had left, 'Ada, you will sit with us in church.'

'Yes, Ma'am.' I tried to keep my voice steady but it was hard. My mother hadn't been well lately and I didn't want to leave her but Master Phil was going to God the Father, and I must support Madam and Master. Especially as Miss Rose couldn't come.

The funeral was at St Peter's, the cream stone church on Bree Street, with the bell that rang across Cradock every Sunday morning. I had been to St Peter's before, of course, but never to the front of the church. I used to sit at the back when the children were at Sunday School, listening to the sound of the organ, which was the best part of going to church.

Madam gave me a skirt and a blouse and proper shoes to wear instead of my uniform for the service. It must be because I will sit with the family, I thought to myself, rubbing the good-quality cloth between my fingers and slipping on the new shoes that I had never had before. That is why Madam is giving me special clothes. Like Master Phil, Madam believes I am part of Cradock House and so I must look respectable when the Lord takes my young Master. When I said this to Mama, she replied that I should remember that the shell chairs on the *stoep* had only ever been for Madam and Master and their children and that nothing – not even the death of our beloved young Master – would change that.

It was a cold but clear day for Master Phil's funeral. The sky was of a blue that was darker even than the eyes of Miss Rose who wasn't there. The *koppies* drew close, like guards over the church, their ironstone tops caught by the early sun. I walked to the front behind Madam and Master in my new clothes. People murmured. The organ played gentle Brahms that Madam and I had chosen. I was pleased to be able sit down so I could no longer be easily seen. Madam and Master sat very still, I don't know how they managed it. My heart was so sore I wanted to run away but I must stay to show respect.

'Let us pray for your servant Philip,' the minister said, folding his hands against his smooth white robe and bending his head.

I tried to think of other things, like Mrs Pumile's niece who worked for the minister and his family. She would have ironed the robe. Mrs Pumile herself was standing at the back of the church in her Sunday hat and carrying a large shiny handbag. Mrs Pumile had liked young Master Phil because he had better manners than Miss Rose. Mrs Pumile said she was sorry for my Madam and Master and that they hadn't deserved for Master Phil to die the way he had. I wasn't sure what she meant and I asked my mother but she said we should not speak ill of the dead and that God had taken young Master Phil in the way He saw fit.

'At rest now, after years of suffering.'

The people behind us murmured.

I wasn't used to sitting in the front of the church like this, alongside Madam and Master. Some of Madam and Master's friends were also not used to me sitting alongside Madam and Master. I could feel their eyes on my neck. They would not look at me when I had been with Master Phil in town, but now that he was gone, it seemed their eyes never left me. Or the skirt and blouse that I wore instead of my uniform.

'Let us pray.'

Madam shuddered beneath the black net that came down over her nose. Her dress was black, too, with a heaviness to it so different from the lovely, light day dresses that I washed and ironed each week. Her strong hands were hidden inside black gloves. Master sat without moving in his black suit and tie. I don't know if he approved of me sitting alongside. I think he probably did not, but agreed out of love for Madam. I hoped he might touch her, like he had in the war, but he didn't.

'Let us pray for his family, united in grief: Cathleen, Edward and Rosemary.'

'Amen,' murmured the people behind us.

What of me? I cried inside, pressing my fingers hard into Mama's old black funeral coat folded on my lap. Please pray for me, too. I loved young Master Phil. He was my brother. I have lived in Cradock House all my life, I am not from the restless township at the end of this road. Am I not part of the family now? Madam felt for my arm with her gloved hand and squeezed it. She knew I was thinking of what the minister hadn't said.

We sang *Abide with Me*, and the organ wept over the tune and the stone walls trembled and crowded in upon me in the front row. Madam couldn't sing, and Master couldn't sing. I tried but my voice was empty and all I could do was listen to the tune and imagine young Master Phil's soul floating up slowly but surely to God the Father in time with the music. And then the tears came and ran down my cheeks and there was no way to stop them. Madam and Master had been so brave, so dignified, and I was ashamed of my tears – but still they wouldn't stop. I fought to make no sound, like my young Master had made no sound when he cried, like soldiers learn to cry quietly in war so as to make no sound to give away their position to the enemy.

Madam put her arm about my shoulders. I could hear the whispers of the people behind as they guessed my silent weeping, and wondered among themselves how it could be that a maid such as me should cry so hard for her young Master.

Afterwards, the congregation shook hands with Madam and Master. There were some of Master Phil's friends from the war, with their wives and young families, and they gripped Master's hand and kissed Madam on the cheek and brushed tears away from their faces. No one said anything to me. I wiped my face with a handkerchief and stood with Mrs Pumile among the gravestones and I saw how people looked at my new skirt and blouse and then looked at one another and I knew that however much I hoped to be part of the family, it might only ever be within the walls of Cradock House.

Then I ran home, for there was work to be done. I had to get water boiled and fire up the stove because there must be tea and fresh scones with Madam's homemade apricot jam for the people who'd been in church. My mother was not well enough to help so I'd rubbed the butter into the flour before church and just needed to add the egg to make the dough. The wind from the mountains was cold and made tears come again in my eyes as I ran across Church Street past the signs that I could read and some that I couldn't. My new shoes were uncomfortable so I pulled them off and ran the rest of the way in bare feet.

It took Madam and Master a while to get back, with all the handshaking. The scones were made and cooling on a rack, their peaks lightly crisped the way Madam liked. I laid out the best cups and saucers and linen napkins in the dining room and there were fresh lemons from the garden to be sliced for the visitors who didn't want sugar. My hands knew what to do to make everything right, which was just as well as my eyes could not see for the tears.

The long handshaking meant I could go up to Master Phil's room while the tea was drawing and stand in the centre of the room where the sun used to reach through in a narrow beam on to the floor, and feel him close to me one more time.

Chapter 12

I have written nothing for days.

The letters back to Ireland seemed to drain the last of my strength. The minister insists that we do not blame ourselves, but I do.

Rosemary's absence has been inexplicable.

Now I am son and daughter. Not to Master, who once more doesn't notice me very much, but to Madam, who walks through her empty house with her head on one side as if listening for Miss Rose's radio with its dance music, or Master Phil's noisy clatter down the stairs. I play the piano for her every day – cheerful pieces only, no Chopin's *Raindrop* with its single notes that can undo my heart. For, like Madam, my heart is undone. Master Phil has emptied it by dying when I thought he would live.

Where I was once sad that I no longer went out, and that other young women like me were settling down and having babies, now I had no wish for such things. No calling, no activity seemed worthy of attention now that Master Phil was gone. Even Mama lost the will to scrub and iron as fiercely as before, and jam sponge puddings disappeared from our meals.

'I can't, child,' she would say to me, her head bowed beneath its *doek*, her thin arms set on the kitchen table. 'God rest his soul, I can't.'

It was the piano that saved Madam, and saved me.

Madam carried on teaching at Rocklands School, even though I overheard Master say that she didn't need to do so.

'But I must, Edward,' she whispered with quiet intensity, as they sat opposite each other in the evening, her hands restless in her lap like Master Phil's had been, Master's busy with his newspaper. Madam wore grey in the evenings now, rather than green. And at her throat she pinned a brooch that Master Phil had worn on his uniform collar. 'Teaching keeps me going.' She would press one hand to her forehead, get up and go over to the piano and touch the keys, but then return to her chair and pick up the library book that she never seemed to finish.

For Madam, playing the piano at school was a kind of medicine but playing at home – into the passages and rooms that had once echoed with Miss Rose and Master Phil – proved to be far harder. So she mostly left it to me to make the music that rushed out of Cradock House every day and into Mrs Pumile's *kaia* next door.

'You're a good girl,' Mrs Pumile said to me when we met on the street, for I was soon pressed into my old duties of posting letters and collecting parcels downtown, to save Madam the trouble. 'And so smart, too.' She nodded approvingly at the skirt and blouse that I now wore outside of Cradock House. 'Your Madam is lucky to have you, after that Miss Rose.' Mrs Pumile sniffed and drew her brown paper bag bulging with sugar from the bank beneath her chin. 'That Miss Rose should be ashamed of herself!'

'Because she doesn't come home?'

'Of course because she doesn't come home,' hissed Mrs Pumile, looking round to make sure no one could overhear. 'Playing up in Jo'burg while your Madam and Master mourn – it's a *skande!*' She spat out the word, the Afrikaans for scandal, a word that I knew meant something too bad to be ignored by the world.

'So you must play piano, Ada,' she commanded. 'Play for your Madam and Master and for your mama. Then there will be life in that place!'

And so I did. Every morning it was my scales rather than Madam's that rushed through the house and down the garden. Every evening it was my lively scherzos that broke the silence while Master read and Madam pretended to do so, and Mama crocheted in her chair by the window. Just as I had learnt that musical notes could say different things to the heart depending on their sequence and their length, I now learnt that musical notes could speak to the body in ways I had never understood before. My tunes, echoing through the quiet, finally stilled Madam's hands in her lap.

Once, the doctor who had promised that Master Phil was cured, came to see Madam and Master and stared in surprise when he saw it was I, and not Madam, who was playing.

'Ada is wonderfully talented,' said Madam with a kind touch on my arm as I made to slip away. 'More talented than any of my students at school.' She cast a quick glance at Master as she spoke, and I remembered Master not being keen on me going to school because of trouble later on.

'How are you both managing?' I heard the doctor say as I left. I didn't wait to hear their replies. I knew that whatever Madam said, it would not be the truth. Even though she now wore again the cream day dresses that spoke of a normal life, the real truth lay inside her and was not for showing, or speaking about, or writing in her book, or in the letters that I posted once more. The truth lay in what she could never say, in the sentences of love and loss she would carry forever inside her.

And what of me?

My mother Miriam was less strong these days, and needed to turn more of her duties over to me. And with the piano-playing necessary to fill Cradock House, and the trips to town to fetch groceries and post letters, my days were busy from dawn until dark. Such busyness was just as well, for I soon discovered – as Master Phil could have told me – that those who die are never truly gone. Master Phil was beside me everywhere I went. He whispered words in my ear and he watched me with his light eyes as I dusted and polished. Sometimes I even thought I saw him in the garden beneath the red-flowering kaffirboom, standing pale and thin in his soldier's uniform. 'Come,' he seemed to be saying, holding out his hand, 'let's take a walk. We'll go down to the Groot Vis . . .'

If I had been idle, there would have been no escape from the tears that came along with his voice in my ear, and his light eyes upon me. But my work came in between and there was no time to cry. Instead, I fought to carry the best of him with me – the young Master who had clattered about Cradock House as a boy, the lean soldier who'd hugged me in front of white crowds at the station. When the world confused me, I repeated to myself what he'd taught me about numbers and the Sahara, about banks and cricket, about the nature of war. And also about things that hadn't needed explanation, like kindness and honesty, whatever the world thought.

And I thanked God for the privilege of knowing him, even though my heart ached. For there was something that I didn't understand, something that troubles me still, something that perhaps only a minister of the church can explain.

Why did God the Father do what He did?

Why did He choose to take Master Phil so soon? Why did God take Master Phil when there was such a long world ahead of him?

Chapter 13

Miss Rose got into trouble in Johannesburg. Perhaps that was why she never came to her brother's funeral?

What sort of trouble I do not know, but trouble it was. My mother said it might have been to do with a young man but there was no baby which is usually what happens when girls get into trouble. It also made me think again of the trouble later on that Master had been afraid of if I went to school. I spent some time wondering if Miss Rose's trouble and my possible trouble were in any way connected. Perhaps it had something to do with being away from home? Both the mission school where I would have gone, and Johannesburg where Miss Rose was, were far from Cradock House. I began to understand that it might have been the loneliness of being far away that would make Miss Rose – and maybe me – want the comfort of a baby, however shameful that would be without a proper husband.

Mrs Pumile from next door said that the fact of no baby did not mean that there had never been one. Girls in places like Johannesburg, where there were riches in the ground and all manner of doctors above it, would find a way to get rid of a baby that they didn't want. Mama would let me listen no further to Mrs Pumile, and shooed me away from the hedge through which Mrs Pumile talked. Auntie from the township across the Groot Vis simply shook her head while she scrubbed clothes on the riverbank and said Miss Rose was a bad girl to bring disrespect to her family, especially since Master Phil – God rest his soul – was dead.

After the first anxious telephone calls, and talking in low voices between them – Madam shakily, Master with a frown and tight lips – Madam and Master said very little about Miss Rose. It was as if she was no longer theirs; it was as if God had taken her in life like He had taken young Master Phil in death. I knew this was hard for Madam. She spent a lot of time writing to her sister in Ireland and I once discovered her weeping over her book in the dressing room.

'What can I do, Madam?' I asked, reaching a hand towards her but not touching. 'Is it Miss Rose?'

Madam sat up and felt for her hanky with the lace edges. 'Such a wilful girl,' she said, fighting the tears, 'I really tried . . .'

I found the word 'wilful' in the dictionary that Madam had bought me, and it said headstrong. I decided it was a good way to describe Miss Rose. She followed whatever her own head said and never took account of other people's head thoughts.

In the matter of talking, it was sad that Madam and Master never spoke of Master Phil at all as a way of forgetting Miss Rose's troubles. There seemed to be no comfort for them in remembering him, as there was for me. I could think of his laughter and his lost buttons and his light blue eyes and how he showed me numbers. I could remember how handsome he was in his uniform before he went to war. These thoughts became a way to stop the tears for me. Perhaps, though, when it was your own child, the remembering became a torment rather than a comfort. Perhaps any accident to your children was a nightmare so great that the only remedy was to try to forget not only the bad times but the good as well. It certainly seemed to be that way for Madam and Master. Maybe they talked in private together, but there was nothing in the evenings between them as there had once been in the past, just Madam's hands straying from time to time to Master Phil's military brooch pinned to her dress.

I knew this from watching through the crack in the door, my heart hurt by the silence. Madam would work on her sewing, although there was very little these days, or write letters to Ireland that I posted in town, or look at a library book. Master would sit behind the *Midland News*. The light of the lamp shone on their bent heads. Sometimes she would play if I was busy with supper and Master asked specially, but her fingers were no longer eager. And when she practised, her scales whipped the piano keys as if she was punishing her fingers for not keeping Master Phil alive and Miss Rose out of trouble.

A season later, Miss Rose came home for a short holiday. It was the first time she had been back since she left that day in the blue dress from Anstey's Fashions and the red lipstick from Austen's the chemist. She was just as beautiful as before, perhaps even more so now she was properly grown up. But there was no sign of a baby, either with her or in the way her body looked. She arrived by train, wearing a yellow dress with a tight waist and a full skirt that stood out about her legs. No one in Cradock had ever seen such a dress – and others like it that she wore – and Miss Rose was followed by people's eyes wherever she went.

'Doesn't it crease?' asked Madam, fingering the folds of soft material.

'Ada can iron it for me!' Miss Rose said with a merry glance at me as I brought tea on to the *stoep* for the family. 'You still iron, don't you, Ada?'

'Of course, Miss Rose,' I replied. 'I do all the ironing.'

Miss Rose was not at all changed by her life in Johannesburg. 'Not on the bed, in the cupboard, Ada!' she snapped, like she used to, as I brought a pile of clean washing into the bedroom. Then, glancing away from the mirror on the dressing table where she'd been powdering her face, she looked me up and down, noticing the navy dress that Madam encouraged me to wear instead of a uniform, and said, 'You've grown up, haven't you? Quite pretty for a black girl.'

I caught sight of my face in the mirror – round, smooth, not unattractive – yet Miss Rose's words, unlike Mrs Pumile's, carried no compliment. And it was clear she thought I should still be wearing an overall. Anything better would mean that Madam thought of me not as a servant but as a part of the family.

There were soon several young farmers, and one older town councillor, who began to call for Miss Rose while she was at home. She went out dancing or taking rides in their motor cars to nearby farms. I often wondered what she did there, for Miss Rose had never shown an interest in animals or the veld. My mother and Mrs Pumile disapproved.

'No shame for that trouble in Jo'burg,' sniffed Mrs Pumile through the hedge, 'and still no manners.'

'Out every night, no time for Madam and Master.' My mother shook her head.

And it was true. Miss Rose spent very little time with her parents. It was almost as if she'd forgotten that she was their last remaining child. Forgotten that she had a duty to be a daughter, a daughter in a house that had lost a son.

But Madam was hopeful, I could tell. She began to talk again in the evenings to Master.

'She could make a fresh start,' Madam would say. 'She just needs a steadying influence.'

'Rosemary will never settle here,' Master would mutter and flap his paper in annoyance, 'not when she's seen the bright lights.'

But Madam refused to be discouraged and would jump up and give us a Strauss waltz or some lively polka, listening all the while for the sound of Miss Rose's return with her latest young man and any hopes of a suitable marriage.

But no marriage came to pass. My mother said Miss Rose was too late, as all the good young men had been snapped up soon after the war. Mrs Pumile said Miss Rose had indeed received some offers – she wouldn't say how she knew this, but maybe it was through her cousin who worked at the bank and had access to extra sugar, and also had very good ears. Anyhow, Miss Rose had refused them all, hoping for better prospects with the older councillor. But the councillor turned out to have a previous understanding with a well-known widow who'd inherited a large farm in the Tarkastad area.

Madam and Master said nothing, but when the veld became crisp with frost in the mornings, they put Miss Rose back on to the train in one of her swirling dresses the colour of kaffirboom blossoms and waved her goodbye once more.

'I'll be up with you soon!' called Madam, holding on to her hat as the smoke billowed round the engine and Miss Rose waved out of the train window.

'Lovely,' cried back Miss Rose, her head disappearing inside the carriage before the train had chuffed its way out of the station.

Chapter 14

Mama died while she was cleaning the silver. The doctor said it was a weak heart, that she wouldn't have lived longer anyway, even if the clinic had noticed that she had a weak heart. Madam was upset that Mama might have died because she was working too hard, but Master said she should not feel that way because I had already taken over most of Mama's duties. But Madam still wept into her handkerchief and I guessed it was about losing someone she had known since she came from Ireland. Mama may not have realised it, but she was Madam's longest friend.

I have put the disappointment of Rosemary's visit behind me.

But now Miriam is gone . . .

I could not – and still cannot – bring myself to write about Phil. Sometimes even Ada's glorious playing overwhelms me and I need to contrive a visit downtown or an urgent task at the furthest extent of the garden.

Miriam knew this, and many other things beside. She would say nothing, but was always there when I returned: faithful, practical, discreet. Such words to describe a life lived for others seem so paltry, so insufficient. Maybe her best legacy is simply Ada herself.

The doctor was the same one who had delivered me and attended Master Phil, but he was kinder to me this time and put his hand on my shoulder. Master put his hand on my shoulder as well. The doctor leant over my mother's tiny body and brushed his fingers over her face, closing her eyes. He pulled a white sheet that Madam had given him over her face. Mama had gone. I pray there is a place in heaven where Mama will see Master Phil and walk alongside him like I once did.

Madam took me in her arms and hugged me against her. Her cheeks were wet. She smelled of flowers, not the strong flowers I was used to in our Cradock garden, but gentler ones, maybe like those she'd known from across the sea, those that grew in songs I'd played on the piano as a child. Lilac, primrose . . .

It was just as well that Madam didn't come to Mama's funeral, because KwaZakhele was not a place for a lady like her and in any case Master said no.

'I won't allow it, Cathleen,' I heard him say as I listened in the corridor through the crack of the door. 'It's not safe. And remember, my dear, these people have their own beliefs at a time like this.'

'But Ada knows none of that,' broke in Madam in a low voice. 'Why, she's taken on our values, our beliefs.' She stopped and then went on, 'Have we been wrong to encourage that?'

I peered past the door hinge. Was this another one of those times when I couldn't understand what Madam was saying? Another time like the one when she said the school was deaf? Master Phil had later explained to me that this was a way of saying that something would never be allowed. At the time, I didn't tell him that it was my schooling alongside him and Miss Rose at the town school that would never be allowed.

I watched as Madam moved to sit on the chair at Master's side. She didn't often go and sit beside him; she usually chose the chair opposite. The tortoiseshell comb in her hair caught the lamplight. She still wore grey for Master Phil, and perhaps also, now, for Mama. I can't show how I mourn by means of indoor clothing; all I have is Mama's funeral coat.

'I'm afraid for her, Edward,' Madam went on, twisting her hands like she'd done over Master Phil. 'How will she manage?'

'There'll be other relatives,' Master Edward said, and picked up his newspaper. 'There always are. Especially as we're paying for it.'

Mama did not want to be carried over the river here in Cradock, she wanted to be buried with her ancestors. So I put her black funeral coat on, took my identity Pass and pinned it to the inside pocket, and went by train and then by donkey cart with her coffin to KwaZakhele. Madam pressed pink roses from the garden into my hand for Mama's grave.

The light was not yet up when I caught the train from Cradock with Mama's coffin beside me in the carriage at the back. Mist hung over the tracks and mixed with the steam from the engine so that we moved along inside a cloud until the sun came up and burned it away. It was my first time on a train. I stared out of the window and wished that Mama could rise up out of her coffin and see the veld unfolding before us in yellow waves. Halfway through the journey I had to change to another train. Two old men going the same way saw me struggling with Mama's coffin and helped me to lift it out of the first train and into the next one.

No one came with me – Auntie couldn't afford the train fare but promised to pray at the outdoor church on the *koppie* – and I found no relatives in KwaZakhele who had heard of her even though the Master was paying. I had never been to KwaZakhele before. It was far bigger than the place where Auntie lived, or the township at the end of Bree Street. Many thousands of people live there, in rows of tiny houses or in shacks packed close to each other with no spare ground in between. Even though KwaZakhele gets more rain than Cradock, there were no trees. Instead, smoke from cooking fires hung over the place all day.

After a long time of searching the narrow dirt streets – it was frightening for me with so many strangers shouting and so many dogs barking and hundreds of shacks stretching as far as I could see, and me worrying about Mama waiting in her coffin on the platform back at the station – I found the church that Mama had attended as a child.

'Excuse me, sir,' I said, leaning tiredly against the door round the side that said 'Vestry, knock first'. 'My mother has died and wishes to be buried in your churchyard with her ancestors.'

The minister looked up from his desk and ran his eyes over me in Mama's black funeral coat.

'Where are you from?'

'I have come from Cradock today, sir, with my mother's coffin on the train.'

At first the minister said he was too busy to help and that he did not know of any living relatives at his church with our name. Once I said that I could pay him from the money Master had given me, he agreed to bury Mama. I had to be careful with the money, for it had to cover the cost of the coffin, the train fares, the donkey cart from the station to the church and then from the church to the cemetery. I could never repay Master for his kindness, but at least I could show that I was grateful by giving him back what was left over.

The minister put on a creased white robe – why did he not have someone to iron for him? – and sat alongside the driver.

I squatted in the back, holding on to the coffin to stop it slipping off the back of the cart. It took a long time to get to the cemetery. I felt sorry for Mama being jolted so hard along the uneven roads. I clutched Madam's roses and looked out over the head of the minister and the driver and the horse. The sea was out there somewhere, as blue as the sky, and I longed to see it with ships on it like I had read about, and that had carried our piano to Cradock House, but the land in that place was flat and the township stretched beyond the horizon and no one can see further than the horizon.

Unlike where Master Phil was buried, this cemetery had no grass and the wind threw grit from the bare ground into my face. But I believe God the Father does not think any less of His children if they have a poor funeral with no congregation. It does not mean they are less worthy than those buried in a cathedral with crowds watching and an organ making the walls shake. Mama served other people all her life. God would be pleased with her, I was sure.

There could be no service like Master Phil's, of course, but the minister and I sang *Abide with Me* over the hole that had been dug where the coffin would go, and where I placed Madam's roses, delicate and beautiful against the broken earth. Although the wind stung our faces, it also surely carried our voices up to heaven where God – and I hope Master Phil – were listening. I gave the minister some extra money and he said he would put up a sign with Mama's name so that I could find it if I visited again. Even so, before we left, I tried to fix in my mind where Mama's grave was amongst the many hundreds of mounds. It lay in line with a distant shack with a tin roof like the *kaia* back in Cradock, except that there was no bony thorn tree but a straggly creeper over a piece of fence. In the other direction was a tall light – taller than any light I had seen before – that shed an orange glow even although it was still the day. Where the two directions met, was Mama's grave. Behind me, in the rutted street alongside the cemetery, a lively group of children kicked a ball, their voices rising into the air with Mama's soul.

By the time I got back to the station, the last train of the day had already left and so I sat on a bench through the night, holding on to my leftover money, closing my ears to the shouts of drunken men in the dark beyond the dim platform light, until the first train of the next day appeared through a grey dawn. It started to rain. Other passengers appeared out of the bush beside the railway line. The vast township hid behind a veil of low cloud. I got on to the train stiffly and went home.

Chapter 15

I miss Madam, so I read her book every day. I wonder why she left it on her dressing table when she knew she would be away for a while? It isn't like Madam to be so forgetful of something so important to her. What will she write on in Johannesburg?

The company on board ship is charming. In particular one Colonel Saunders, on his way to rejoin his regiment in India. Mrs Wetherspoon, my chaperone, is quite captivated. And so is he – with me!

How strange that I should spend five years serving my betrothal in Ireland and just when I am allowed to go to Africa to marry Edward, I find myself waylaid by another suitor. It is flattering, of course, but I give him no encouragement. And he, to his credit, is most proper.

In order to fill Cradock House with sound, I play the piano every evening after I've done the dishes. Madam would have wanted it so. I don't put on the lights – I don't need to see my fingers – I just slip into the alcove where the piano is, and begin. At first, there's some light from the sunset, a silky purple rather than the bright yellow stripes of Master Phil's bedroom. Then even that fades, and I play in the dark. I play for myself, and for Mama, and I play for Master Phil who never leaves my heart.

Sometimes Master is in the study writing to Madam visiting Miss Rose in trouble in Johannesburg and he opens the door to listen to me. Sometimes he's in the lounge, behind his newspaper. I notice that he never turns the pages while I play. And often the lamp next to his chair isn't on. Perhaps he likes the dark too. I know he always wanted Madam to play Chopin, so I play Chopin. I hope it gives him comfort in Madam's absence. And then I play Debussy as well, slippery tunes that wander round in your head for days afterwards.

He usually says, 'Thank you, Ada,' when I've finished, although sometimes he seems to find it hard to speak and has to cough before he can start.

Then I say, 'Good night, Master,' as I close the piano. For a while, that's all he says and all I say.

And I know that I am playing for him as well, and for the loneliness that's inside us both.

When I look back on it now, after many years, I know that it came out of the loneliness. Not Master Phil's frenzied sort of loneliness – where fallen comrades give you no peace – but rather a shadow that settles about you with sly weight. Madam knew about loneliness, and the difficulties it can cause, so perhaps that was why she decided to go to Johannesburg to be with Miss Rose, her remaining child. To chase away Miss Rose's loneliness and in this way keep her from more trouble? But loneliness taken away from one place looks for a home somewhere else. And trouble taken from one person will surely search for a new lodging.

I made lamb chops and potatoes and peas and served them to Master, on his own at the head of the table in the dining room.

I ate my supper in the kitchen. Then I washed and dried the dishes and hung up the tea towels on the line outside. It was one of those evenings when the Karoo has a strange, warm light and the stone *koppies* brighten from brown to pink, holding their glow for longer than you think possible, before fading to navy. I wondered if Mama could see the strange light from where she was with God the Father.

I turned back to the house and then stopped for a moment, remembering Master Phil lying on the grass that now bent soft beneath my feet. His skin was golden in the sun, his eyes pale as the lightest evening sky. If I called his name he would surely answer . . .

I went back inside. I took off my apron and hung it behind the kitchen door. Master was in his usual chair in the lounge. I slipped into the alcove and started with *Clair de Lune*. Pink light came through the window and rested on the piano, and followed my hands on the keys. Then I played the *Pathétique*. Master did not turn the pages of the paper. I was used to that by now. Slowly the flush of evening faded and I played the last Chopin nocturne in darkness. Master sat in the darkness as well, his newspaper on his lap.

'Good night, Master.'

'Thank you, Ada. Good night.'

I washed and put on the nightdress Madam had bought me at Badger's, and prayed by the side of the bed for the souls of Master Phil and Mama.

'Dear Lord, make Mama rest now, and give Master Phil peace from the war.'

It was when I was reading my Bible verse for the day that I heard Master's footsteps, not going upstairs but rather heading into the kitchen. Maybe he wanted a drink? Some tea? I put my feet into slippers, ready to go and help him, but the footsteps continued beyond the kitchen, along the corridor, and stopped outside the room my mother Miriam and I had shared since I was six years old.

I waited.

The steps did not continue. He must be ill. He must be worried about having to wake me up. Should I go out to him?

A light tap sounded on the door.

I rushed over and pulled it open. 'Master,' I said. 'Do you need me, sir?' The curtains billowed at the window in the sudden draught.

'Ada,' Master said.

Master didn't often look at me, but he was looking at me now. I thought how tired he had become since young Master Phil had died, how grey and thin his hair was, how faded his eyes were. He was still in his suit and he was fingering the gold chain on his waistcoat.

'Ada?' he said again and looked beyond me into the room as if he hadn't seen it before. He reached out the hand that was not fiddling with his waistcoat and put it on my shoulder.

'What can I do, sir? Do you need some tea?'

But he didn't seem to hear and his hand stayed on my shoulder. I could feel its warmth. I could feel his fingers tightening through the material of my nightdress. This was different from the way young Master Phil had touched me.

I stepped backwards. His hand fell from my shoulder.

We stared at each other, the Master and I.

There had been a young man once, on Adderley Street, when I was taking Madam's letters to the post office, who'd looked at me in the same way. Who'd looked at me as if I could truly be called pretty. He said his name was Jacob Mfengu and he asked me mine. He was well dressed and polite and he worked at the Cradock butcher's and often saw me going down the street. He

said he wanted to call on me if my father would allow. I said I
had no father but that he could speak to my mother. He nodded
eagerly and said he would and we shook hands and his touch
made me feel hot like the Master's hand was making me feel hot
now. I waited and hoped but he never called and when I was
brave enough to go into the butcher's and ask for him by name,
the butcher said he'd left suddenly to go back to his family in the
Transkei.

The Master stepped into the room and closed the door
behind him. And he came towards me where I stood in front of
the bed and this time put both hands on my shoulders. The
hotness grew.

I began to shake. He must have felt it, for he said, 'I won't
hurt you, Ada.'

He reached down and untied the top of my nightgown. I
didn't think to protest. After all, who was I to refuse the Master
who had cared for my mother Miriam and me? How could I
refuse someone who had given me a home and food and the gift
of music? Who had paid for the burial of my mother?

How could I say that I waited for a young man who had once
pressed my hand on Adderley Street, but had never returned?

How could I say that it was Madam's face that I saw as I
looked at him? I reached down and pulled the nightdress over
my head and stood before him, naked.

*The colonel declares himself in love with me, he wishes to marry me.
'Stay on board, Cath,' he urges. 'Come with me to India. We'll marry as
soon as we dock.'*

*And I could if I wished. For he is charming and considerate and not
a rake, and he knows my grown-up heart better, I daresay, than does
Edward. I confess I am more than a little in love with him . . .*

But how can I?

How can I abandon Edward, who has worked so diligently to provide a home for me – even a piano?

The Master came to me three times. We never spoke a word. His footsteps down the corridor, turning from the kitchen, were the only signal I had.

Earlier, each evening, I would still play the piano. I had wondered whether to stop but then thought he would find it strange if I did. It seemed to me that the darkness chased away the sunset too quickly on those nights, bringing with it a terrible gloom that seized my fingers, made my playing forced and filled me with uncertainty over whether he would come tonight.

'Good night, Master.'

'Thank you, Ada.'

When I heard his steps, I would take off my nightdress and lie down on the bed that I'd once shared with my mother Miriam. He would tap on the door and then enter, turning off the light as soon as he came in. He would come to the side of the bed and stand there for a while and then reach one hand down and touch me.

And the next day I would wash the sheets and sweep the floor and make him breakfast and dinner as if nothing had changed. And he would work and eat and read the newspaper and write to Madam – oh, Madam, forgive me, God forgive me – in Johannesburg with Miss Rose who was in trouble.

Chapter 16

I used to wonder what it would be like with young men, the ones who caught my eye on the street when I went to the post office or when I walked with my mother to visit my aunt on Thursday afternoons off. They were bold, though, these young men. Especially when they came back from initiation – *abakwetha* – and they wore their new clothes around town, looking out for a wife.

'Don't look at him!' my mother Miriam warned when I cast teenage eyes at one particularly promising boy in well-pressed khaki trousers on the corner of Market Street. 'He will find out who you are if he wants to.'

But he never did. And once young Master Phil was back from the war, my life was confined to Cradock House anyway, and the young men who might have taken the trouble to pursue me cast their eyes elsewhere. Except for Jacob Mfengu from the butcher's. And he was not bold, but respectful. I had hoped that this was my chance. But I never heard from him again, although the touch of his warm hand stayed on my skin for many seasons.

And then my mother became ill and I needed to nurse her and take on her duties in the house. The possibility of a young man, the possibility even of marriage, had to be put aside.

'You needn't do everything yourself, Ada,' Madam said, finding me drooping over the ironing board one day. 'I can get Mrs Pumile from next door to help out.'

'No need, Madam,' I said, straightening up. Mrs Pumile would rob Madam before the first day was over. 'I'll be finished soon.'

When young Master Phil died, I still had Mama. But when Mama died, I had no one but Madam and Master. And when Madam went to visit Miss Rose in Johannesburg, I had only Master. And after that I had shame. It stayed out of sight at first but then it grew within me and began to swell my body. And it followed me every day for the rest of my life.

Tomorrow I disembark.

Tomorrow I marry Edward in the cathedral on the slopes of Table Mountain.

My wedding dress is ironed and laid out ready, the embroidered skirt double-hemmed to manage the uneven streets of the port. My short veil – a gift from the village school – hangs over the chair.

Mrs Wetherspoon has promised me a bouquet of fresh pink roses, although we do not know if it is the season for them in the Cape. Reverend Wetherspoon will give me away in morning dress and dog collar.

We are all rising at dawn to see the mountain appear over the horizon. When I see it I will know that there can be no turning back.

I have refused Charles Saunders, and he understands that I must do my duty. But I shall always wonder how it might have been.

How it might have been to marry a man with whom I felt a quickening such as I've never known before . . .

At first, of course, I didn't know what was happening. My work dress tightened, my body felt tender. The natural cycle my mother Miriam had told me about stopped. In Johannesburg,

Miss Rose remained in some sort of trouble, Master said. His eyebrows drew together, his lips tightened and he turned away to go into the study.

So Madam stayed away.

Madam, who could have told me what was happening to my body, but who would never have needed to do so if she'd remained in Cradock. Madam, whom I had betrayed. Madam, from whom I could never receive – or deserve – forgiveness.

I couldn't go to Dr Wilmott who had delivered me, who had treated young Master Phil, who had closed my mother Miriam's eyes in death. He would have to tell Master or Madam. So, on one of my Thursdays off, I put my Pass in my pocket and walked across the iron bridge over the Groot Vis to my aunt in the small township by the Lococamp.

'It is my body,' I said, sitting with her in her one-roomed shack. My aunt was old by then, older than my mother Miriam would have been, and she had seen girls like me before. She leant over and put her hand on my stomach.

'Which boy did this? You must marry him!' she said, heaving the pot of hot water for tea off the fire. 'You got no family, so he won't have to pay bride price.'

But I said there was no particular boy.

And she slapped her hand against her *doek*, then she slapped me a little for being with more than one boy and having no shame. She said I was no better than Miss Rose in trouble in Johannesburg. I took the beating and said nothing. She told me of a man who dealt with babies and pushed me out of her shack and left me to walk the dusty alleys until I found the man she talked of. It was getting dark by then and the streets had no lights and gangs of boys roamed around and thin dogs followed me. Smoke from cooking fires hung over the shacks and made the sky grey long before it would have been grey over Cradock

House. It reminded me of KwaZakhele when I had buried my mother Miriam. So I prayed as I walked, prayed to calm my fear of the darkness and the rough people who jostled me. And I prayed to Mama to tell me what to do. But Mama did not answer me, and God Himself was silent for I had sinned with my Master and for that there was no forgiveness.

The doctor, when I found him, was a kind man. He wore a stained white coat, but he also carried a tube with a metal disc like the one the doctor had used on young Master Phil and so I trusted him. There was a queue of people to see him in his tiny two-roomed house. They sat all over the floor inside and spilled out on to the bare earth outside. Wounded youngsters spilling blood, mothers nursing crying babies, old men with terrible coughs.

It was late by the time the doctor had treated all of the wounded, crying, coughing patients but even though he must have been tired, he was still kind. He told me that I was going to have a baby. He also told me that I should tell the father of the baby because I was a fine young woman who would bear many more babies for my fine young man.

'It is not a fine young man, sir.'

'An older man can be just as fine,' he reassured me with a weary smile. 'He can provide more for his children.'

'It is my Master.'

He sat down on a bench against the peeling wall. His shoulders slumped and I wondered why.

'Then you will need my help.'

'To help the baby get born?'

'Oh, child.' He shook his head where he'd leant it against the wall. 'You should not be having this baby.'

'But why, sir?' What was this? Was he a *sangoma* – a witch doctor? Did he see things that I could not see?

'The child will be cursed with a pale skin, paler than yours and mine,' he pointed at his own black arm, 'but not as pale as your Master's.'

'He will be coloured?' I cried.

I knew coloureds. They lived halfway between Madam and Master's people and halfway to black people. They were not one, and they were not the other. Only during the war, when they became soldiers and fought alongside white soldiers, had people been proud of them. But nowadays they belonged nowhere.

I had not known about inheritance. I had not known that this was how coloured people were made: that black people could be diluted and that white people could be darkened and the result would be a boy who belonged nowhere. And why did I think it would be a boy? A boy for the Master in place of young Master Phil? How could anyone replace a firstborn son?

And this child would be coloured. He would not belong to the Master, and he would not belong to me. I would have to tell him that his father had left before he was born, just like my own father. Perhaps that would draw us closer, this pale child and me.

But whereas my own father had disappeared never to return, this child's father was just across the iron bridge over the Groot Vis, a short, dusty walk away. I would have to see to it that he never knew this. I would have to see to it that he, like me, never found his father.

Chapter 17

There are many things in my life that I have not understood at first but then come to understand later on. Like places and people that would not hear of things but were not deaf. Like a future that you could not buy, that always seemed – like the sea – to be just beyond the horizon. Like war that caused a shortage of food and cake tins, and made soldiers die and ships sink and young men never recover from wounds that no one could find. Like Master Phil's love for me that I did not understand until it was too late.

As I grew up I learnt that sometimes these things could be explained by the different moods that words took. Other times the things I didn't understand turned out to be new for the world as well. A new thing of this sort rose up in the 1950s: the creeping fear of skin difference, whispered at first, then shouted, and made real as the child who would be coloured grew within me.

'Apartheid!' Mrs Pumile spat out the word that described this thing, like she spat out tea with too little sugar.

It was a new word for me. I had never seen such a word on the signs in the shops or on the boards outside the newspaper office that had said 'It's War' all those years before. But although the word was new, I understood where it came from. Here was the thing that had worried me about walking with my young Master in town, here was what made white people turn away from me, here was Master's dismay at his son's dependence on a servant. Here was one word that could hold all of those fears.

'It will make us move,' Mrs Pumile hissed at me through the hedge, 'across the Groot Vis, or to the township past the jail on Bree Street, with all those *skollies* and drunks. Be grateful to the Lord, Ada, that your mother never lived to see this day.'

'But what can we do?' I asked, glancing back at the house where Master worked in his study while Madam remained with Miss Rose in Johannesburg.

'I will go back to my family in Umtata,' said Mrs Pumile with a satisfied smile. 'There is a man there who will marry me if I return. But you,' she peered though the hedge, 'you should find a husband quick-quick. You're still pretty enough. There'll be no place for girls with no man to protect them. Coming, Ma'am,' she turned and yelled over her shoulder at a voice calling from the kitchen door. 'Just digging vegetables, Ma'am.'

It had been two weeks since I had visited the doctor in his two-roomed house across the Groot Vis. After he explained about inheritance, he told me that it was too late to get rid of the baby even if I had wanted to. He also said I did not need to pay him because he received money from the mission to do his work. The same mission that gave schooling to black pupils like I once might have been. It was very dark by the time I walked back and I kept up a fast pace and stayed near the light of street fires where people cooked. Men called out to me from the shadows and dogs nosed around my legs for scraps and the stars were hidden behind smoke and the fear of looking up. Was Master Phil judging me as I hurried along so fearfully? Did he understand that it had been my duty? Or did he feel betrayed by what I had done with his father? Like I had betrayed my beloved Madam . . .

I slipped into Cradock House by the back gate and the unlatched kitchen door. Master had had a dinner meeting at the town hall and had not needed food. The garage was empty and I heard his car later on as I lay in bed holding on to my stomach with its burden of child that I longed to love but was afraid would not love me. Not when he saw the difference of skin. Not when he saw he was inferior to white, but also – shockingly – to black as well. What would become of us, this child who fitted in nowhere and me?

'Ada,' said Master, as I served him his scrambled eggs at breakfast, 'the Madam is returning next week.'

I stood next to the table, feeling a hotness stain my face and the child stir like a butterfly within me.

'Miss Rosemary is better now and Madam doesn't need to be away any longer. She is looking forward to coming back. We must make the house especially perfect for her.'

He looked up at me briefly, and then down at the eggs cooling on the plate in front of him. His hands flexed in his lap, then stilled. 'I want Madam to see that nothing has changed since she went away.'

He stopped, lifted his hands and reached for the linen napkin that I wash and iron each day.

'You understand, don't you, Ada?' he went on, addressing a spot on the table in front of his plate.

'Yes, sir,' I said. 'I understand. Everything will be the same as before, just as Madam likes it.'

Edward brought me roses as well. I combined them with Mrs Wetherspoon's. Edward is somewhat changed, as I'm sure I am for him.

More serious, thinner lipped, but ever polite. Too polite, and my fear that we would find no words between us was renewed but then thankfully postponed; what with the Wetherspoons' friends and some local Irish folk who've hosted Edward in the past, there was enough cheery talk to cover the reticence between us.

And now I write this from the train which will carry us to Cradock and our life together. The roses lie beside my coat in the luggage rack above, still breathing their perfume. Edward has gone to reserve a table for dinner in the dining car, giving me the chance to write these few words.

Dear Mother and Father, dear Ada and Eamonn, what would you make of this?

What would Father say of the rich soil and the hordes of dark labourers to work it? What would Mother say of the fine ladies in light-coloured dresses – surely as smart as India? And Ada and Eamonn? Wouldn't they gasp in wonder, as I did, at the vast mountain with its ever-tumbling cloud? 'Take me with you, Cath,' Ada had pleaded before I left. 'I'll be no trouble at all!' And now Edward returns . . .

Chapter 18

I realise that I am doing things for the last time.

I am washing these shirts for the last time. I am fetching bread from the bakery for the last time. I am walking down Church Street in my blue uniform. I look into the butcher's for a sign of Jacob Mfengu but he is not there behind the swinging haunches of meat; he is never there.

Cradock House is sparkling. There are vases of Madam's favourite pink roses on the mantelpiece and in the alcove by the piano where she can smell them when she plays. The brass doorknobs have been polished, the *stoep* has been newly scrubbed. The windows have been cleaned and the beds are freshly made up as if Miss Rose and Master Phil are about to arrive as well. But it is only Madam who arrives tomorrow on the midday train.

I have prepared cold chicken and a potato salad for her lunch with Master. There will be a lamb stew on the stove for dinner, and an apple pie in the larder for dessert. I will even lay out the best cups and saucers for afternoon tea and leave the lemon sponge cake under a glass cover on the dining-room table. I have placed Madam's special book on her dressing table, next to a

spray of mimosa in a glass she brought all the way from Ireland.
I have read from the book for the last time.

*We arrived in Cradock this morning. I must confess that the train journey
from Cape Town was testing. So little privacy, so many hours of baked
earth and sky.*

*Edward has been attentive and careful with me, which normally I
would have welcomed, but with Colonel Saunders' gallantry so recent in
the memory, I have instead found his reticence a little disappointing. But
there can be no regrets. I am grateful to have a settled future.*

*I have now seen our house, a fine sturdy place equipped with plain but
solid furniture and a shy young woman called Miriam who is the
housekeeper. Edward has done well. I hope Miriam and I can be friends,
for we must be of similar age, although Edward says I must not fraternise.*

*I pray it is not too long before we have a family of our own, as I miss
Ireland sorely. When we are at the table, I confess I look out of the window
and imagine it is the stream over Bannock cliffs that I hear, not the dull
brown rush of the river they call the Groot Vis.*

I wash and fold up my spare blue overalls and what I think of
now as the 'white' clothes that Madam gave me: the smart blouse
and skirt for Master Phil's funeral, the navy dress that I wore
instead of an overall. I leave them in a neat pile on the bed for
the new maid that Madam will need. I take my towel and flannel
and the nightdress that Madam bought me, and put them into
my mother's cardboard suitcase.

I take Mama's shoebox from under the bed. I have only put a
small amount of money into it each month because Master and
Madam send most of my wages to the bank on Adderley Street.
Madam explained that I can ask for it back whenever I want it.
She showed me a book from the bank that proves how much
money I own. There is more money in it than the amount I

expect. Madam says that the bank has added extra money to say thank you for lending them the money in the first place. This seems strange to me, someone giving you money without you having to work for it. Of course, I don't have this special book. It lives with the family's papers in Master's study. So that means that I don't have the money either. I will have to manage with the small amount left over from my mother's wages in the shoebox and from the coins that Madam gives me each month for personal items.

I put my identity paper – my Pass – into the suitcase as well. I have no other documents, no references to prove that I worked at Cradock House, no words to say if I was a good worker, nothing to show a new employer for the years of dusting and polishing and washing. I play the piano for the last time, gentle sonatas, the Mozart in C major, Beethoven's *Moonlight*. I take the score for the *Raindrop* prelude and slip it into the bottom of the case where it won't be creased. I don't think Madam will mind.

'Ada?'

'Yes, sir?'

It is the day of Madam's arrival. Master is in the study, standing behind his desk. I wait in the doorway. He doesn't look at me and so I search with my eyes for the bank book among his papers but it is not there. I have looked for it on Master's desk for the past few days but it is never there. I am careful to replace Master's papers exactly as I found them so he will never know, like I used to turn Madam's special book back to the place where she was writing so that she would never know. 'I'm leaving to fetch Madam. The train may be early.'

'Yes, sir. Lunch will be ready for Madam and Master when you return.'

'Thank you, Ada.' He is wearing the dark suit that Madam likes. He still doesn't look at me and turns his grey head away to pick up the keys to the car with the headlights like the eyes of night animals.

As soon as he is gone, I check the dining-room table for the last time to make sure that lunch is set as Madam likes it. Then I put my mother's old funeral coat over my uniform and tie my hair into a blue *doek*. I go upstairs and stand in Master Phil's room one last time, and touch the bed where he lay, and stand beside the curtains that were always drawn to keep out the war, and feel the sun as it warms my back through the glass. I go downstairs and close the door of my room where I waited while he died outside. Then I take up my case and leave by the kitchen door, taking care to latch it, and go through the back gate. I can hear Mrs Pumile talking to herself in her *kaia* next door. I don't want her to see me, I don't want anyone to see me.

I must hurry. I will keep to the side of Dundas Street where there are the most trees and I will keep my head down all the way past the shop signs that I used to use as word practice. Some of the shopkeepers know me but I hope they will not recognise me with a suitcase and covered by my mother's coat. I am now like one of the girls I used to see from Master Phil's toy box, hurrying down the road, only without a baby on my back. Can I ever come down this road in the future with my baby on my back? People will see the child's colour is different from mine and they will know my shame. But will they know that I am not a bad person? Will they understand that the child came from my duty to the Master in his loneliness?

Can Madam ever know this? Can Master Phil?

What I did – how can it be both right and wrong?

Church Street is busy and there are motor cars hooting and dogs leaping about their master's heels and donkey carts lurching along with piles of wood. Master Phil would have hated the noise. Over there, beyond the red tin roof of the magistrate's house on Achter Street, stands the tree near the Groot Vis where he told me he loved me.

This is where my escape becomes dangerous. The iron bridge leads not only to Auntie's small township by the railway camp, it is also the way to the railway station. At any moment, Master and Madam could see me as they drive past in the black car with the eyes of night animals. But I have been listening for the train and so far I have not heard its whistle. There is still time to get across and then turn left off the road and head for the cramped community of huts where Auntie lives.

There are many people going my way now, towards the iron bridge. Their bare feet making a soft slapping sound on the tar road. They murmur amongst themselves, they have friends in the crowd. I have no friends, I will have to manage with this new loneliness and try not to get into any further trouble because of it. Some of my fellow walkers carry cases like I do, some have their goods wrapped in colourful blankets on their heads, some have babies on their backs. I shift the case to my other hand, turn my head away from passing cars and hurry across the bridge and over the brown river and away from Cradock House that was once mine. Away from the bony thorn tree that I was nearly born under, away from the furniture that I have polished all my life, away from the people – some alive, some with the ancestors – that made it my home too.

Chapter 19

Ada is not here. But has left lunch on the table. I can only assume that there is a reason for her absence. Perhaps Mrs Pumile knows. I will check with her once I have unpacked.

Edward is pleased to see me.

'Why you think you can come here?' Auntie demanded angrily, standing in her doorway with arms folded over her broad chest while I waited outside on the dusty street.

'I got no space, you can see I got no space!' She looked down at my swelling stomach, then back up at me. 'And I got no money for an extra mouth.' She turned and went inside.

'It's just for a short time,' I said, leaning against the sloping wall for I was tired from the walk and the strain of getting away, and the child seemed to be swelling hard inside me. Auntie squatted on a thin, striped mat that covered part of the mud floor. 'Then I will find another place to stay.'

'What with? You got money?' asked Auntie from the dimness inside. Auntie was a shrewd woman. She knew that places to stay didn't come without money. And she knew that I had money in the bank.

'You have to pay me for the place.' She pointed at the mat she was sitting on.

My eyes began to see more clearly into the hut. I had never taken much notice of it before, when I visited with my mother. After all, I had the comfort and shelter of Cradock House. I never thought of Auntie's shack with its outside latrine as a place to stay. And Auntie was right: there was no space. Against the wall stood her narrow bed on bricks, sagging in the middle and covered with a faded blanket. Next to it was a rusty paraffin stove and a chipped enamel basin with a bar of soggy green soap. A bucket and a calabash stood ready for carrying water from the communal tap at the end of the street. Nails hammered into the mud walls held Auntie's overall and a towel. String bags piled on the floor held washing waiting to done. The only part of the floor not covered was the mat in the middle, and that was not even as long as my body. I had never slept on a floor before – the evil *tokoloshe* would have no trouble finding me and my baby.

Auntie's hut was no place to bring up a child, but there would be little chance of finding any other place with the sort of child that I would bear. Nobody wants to help a girl who has sinned with a white man instead of her own people. I turned my head, for there it was, a whistle in F sharp, the sound that meant Madam's return.

'I will help you with your washing business,' I said, forcing my voice to be cheerful. 'I have a lot of experience with washing. And I can cook, too.'

Auntie looked up at me, suspicious.

'Why you don't get another job over the river?' She sniffed and gestured towards the Groot Vis. 'There's families that want girls like you that have been maids before. That Madam you talk about so well, that Madam will give you references.' She stopped and stared at me hard. 'Unless you stole from her? Please God your mother never knew this!'

On the street behind me there was a shout followed by more shouts. A woman was being chased by a man who was striking her on the back of the legs with a stick. A small crowd looked on.

'Will no one help her?' I cried. The crowd turned to look at me, then turned back to watch.

Auntie hadn't even come to the door and was instead lighting her paraffin stove.

I turned away too. I told her that I hadn't stolen from Madam, but I didn't want to be a maid any more. I told her I was tired of big houses with furniture that needed to be polished and cakes that needed to be baked for fine tea parties. I told her that I wanted to bring up my child among people like me. Like her. And I told her one other thing that wasn't true yet, but might become true soon enough. I told her that this new fear of skin difference made it hard to live across the river these days.

Auntie shrugged, and checked her stove, and heaved a battered kettle on to it and made tea and gave me half a piece of old bread and told me that I could stay on her floor for a short time but that I must pay her for the piece of floor. When I said that my money was hidden at the bank by the Master and Madam for my own good, she shook her head. But when she saw my face she said I could pay for the piece of floor by washing with her every day down on the banks of the Groot Vis, on account of the fact that I had experience with washing and would be better at it than some of the other girls she'd tried. And when the baby was born, I could put it on my back and carry on washing. Any other needs that I had must come out of the money that was hiding in the bank. Money was no use unless you could buy things with it. Money was no use just sitting in a bank.

I would have to learn how to get it back.

There are two kinds of loneliness. One is loneliness on the outside and one is loneliness on the inside. I am not lonely on the outside any more. There is no room to be lonely. Auntie's hut is full with just the two of us and the child grows inside me and pushes into the space between Auntie and me. And then there is the washing. The hut overflows on good washing days. There is dirty washing, and there is washing that is clean and wet, and washing that is clean and dry, and dirty washing that is needed clean today, and dirty washing that can wait for another day to be done.

I am not lonely beyond Auntie's hut either, because there are any number of people who rush to and from the huts about us. I try to learn the names of those that rush by regularly, so that I don't feel I am spying on the lives of strangers. From my place on Auntie's floor, I can't help hearing them call out in the night, I can't help jerking awake when their children cry. I hear husband and wife arguing, and I later recognise their voices in the street and know their disagreements before I recognise them by their faces or their names. Old men cough in my ear like they did at the doctor's house; I even hear someone snoring in a nearby shack. The only person I heard near to Cradock House was Mrs Pumile, and she lived across a thick hedge at the bottom of the next-door garden. Yet here, far closer than the *kaia* of Mrs Pumile, there is Poppie from the shack alongside and her grandchildren Fulesi and Matthew who are the ones that cry in the night. But Poppie is quiet and she greets me kindly and asks after the baby more than Auntie does. And, further in the matter of learning names, there appear Sophie and Beauty and Pushi and Lindiwe and other women, too, who compete for business in the washing trade down on the banks of the Groot Vis. Some of them live on Auntie's side of the river, but many more of them live across the Groot Vis in the sprawling township that swallows the far end of Bree Street. They wash on their side, or they come across the drift below Cross Street to our side where the washing rocks are better and the river runs easier for the purposes of laundry.

There is also no time to be lonely. Our day starts at sunrise, like it did at Cradock House, but here in the township there is no milk to fetch from the gate. We dress in the dimness of the hut – Auntie doesn't waste candles on morning darkness – and eat our breakfast of black tea and maybe some bread or leftover porridge. I find the mornings hard; the floor hurts my back in the night and the child would like to sleep longer. But there is no time to lose. Even before the first rays of sun pick the *koppies* out of the shadow we are on our way, balancing loads on our heads or in our arms, pushing through with the early, grumbling crowds, Auntie deaf to all in her rush to claim the best washing spot.

I thought I knew about washing but I learn that outdoor washing in the Groot Vis is very different from the washing I used to do in the laundry at Cradock House. For one thing, there is no ironing. But Auntie's customers still want their clothes and sheets smooth. This means we have to be very careful about how we drape the wet washing over the bushes on the riverbank. These are not the sort of shrubs that lit up Madam's garden with their colourful blooms – they would have been too soft to take the weight of wet clothes. No, these are tough Karoo bushes, like the stunted kind that you see at the edge of town where the veld stretches to the horizon. Here, on the riverbank, the bushes can dig down to the Groot Vis for spare water so they grow a little bigger and that suits Auntie's business.

'People come to me,' Auntie murmurs with satisfaction, while the other women fling their washing about with less care, 'because I can make clothes look ironed without ironing. Look.' She demonstrates, flapping a pillow case in the breeze and then deftly letting it drop over a bush, pulling the damp material tight and smoothing it out like icing over a cake.

'Then you got to fetch it before it's dry,' she wags a finger to make sure I am listening, 'and then you fold it and it will dry out into the good folds – just so.' She smoothes the pillowcase and adds it to a pile. 'Also, if you fetch it before it's dry the *skollies* take someone else's pillowcase first.'

Under her strict eye, I learn to stretch and smooth the washing, and to choose the best bushes to dry it on. White washing goes on bushes with the smallest leaves so it doesn't get stained, dark washing goes on whatever is left over. The wind blows in a particular way on the riverbank, and I must make sure each piece is anchored to its bush by bending twigs or thorns like pegs. I learn to shoo away the goats that like to chew up the bushes and the washing on them.

I learn to look out for strangers on the riverbank who might be there not to wash but to steal. For if a customer's washing is lost, Auntie not only loses that customer but also many coins that she – or I, if it is my fault – must pay back for the loss. As I patrol the drying linen, I realise it is not just about the money. Auntie is as proud of her almost-smooth pillowcases as I used to be of Madam's perfectly ironed cream day dresses, or Miss Rose's difficult pleats or Master Phil's well-creased cricket whites. I can understand this pride. And it makes me forgive Auntie's impatience with me just a little bit. There is one further thing that I learn, which is not something that Auntie teaches me. I learn to position myself among the other women even if it means settling for a lesser rock, and I start to wear a *doek* like they do. Like Mama used to. I become one of them. Anyone passing near the river will surely not recognise me now.

I tell myself I am growing up. I tell myself that loneliness can be banished if you train your mind on washing, or on recognising neighbours, or on separating out the sounds that make up the background noise of township life. And here is an unexpected thing: I never thought to find music in noise, but it's there if you search hard enough. Shouts, singing, goats bleating, metal clattering, odd drumbeats . . . Without trying, they each find a place and squeeze themselves into a shifting, vibrant counterpoint. I christen it 'Township Bach'.

At the end of the day I sit down against the mud wall of the hut, let my arms and shoulders fall by my sides, and rest my aching hands on my stomach where the child kicks and turns inside me. I put aside the matter of washing, and I close my eyes to the rush of passers-by. Are you there, Master Phil? Are you watching me, sir, in this crammed place? Have you forgiven me?

'Bread?' a street trader shouts out, his bare feet shuffling along in the dust. He hauls out a loaf wrapped in brown paper from the bag he carries on his back. 'One or two slices?'

I would rather close my eyes again, but it is my duty to buy a slice for Auntie and me from the dwindling amount of Mama's shoebox money.

'Where you come from?' he asks, squatting down beside me, his breath smelling of tobacco and drink.

'Why do you want to know?' I ask, nervous about telling who I am. It must never get back to Madam and Master that I am here, just a short distance from Cradock House. So close that the evil hadeda birds that flap overhead every afternoon could carry my voice – if I speak too loudly – along with them and drop it on Cradock House as they pass.

'You look different from the girls round here,' the street trader says, looking at my still-smart overall. 'That uniform cost white money.'

'I come from KwaZakhele,' I say quickly. 'That's where I worked before. That's where my family is from. But I'm here to be with my auntie.'

He nods, distracted by the arrival home of Poppie and her grandchildren. 'Bread?' he croaks, getting to his feet with difficulty. I notice that he charges me more for my slice than he charges Poppie.

So the daylight hours leave no time or space for loneliness to gather. It is the nights that I must guard against. The nights are when inside loneliness could strike. But perhaps God the Father is being kind. The crying, arguing, coughing neighbours disturb me less and less. I start to fall asleep quickly when otherwise my heart might turn to Cradock House. To Mama and Master Phil and Madam that I miss so much – oh Madam, forgive me – and to the house that I hope has not forgotten my cleaning of it, and the piano that I hope still remembers my touch.

I stood in the garden this morning with an uncontrollable urge to cry out Ada's name to the Karoo sky, to the koppies, to wherever she is.

I confess that I am frantic with worry. Cradock House is her home, the only home she has ever had. We are her family, surely?

Where could she be?

Chapter 20

The child within me grows. I no longer fit into my uniform and Auntie lends me an overall of hers that I can use until the child is born. I allow myself no wondering about how it will be, what he will look like, who he will look like. Auntie does not ask me any more about the father of this child and for that I am grateful. I have at least a few months to prepare for the questions that will come when she – and the other women that I have met on the riverbank – see the pale colour of the newborn and turn away from me, as I know they will. For the moment I am just like any other girl who gets into trouble with a boy who does not stay. Like my mother. Like Miss Rose?

There is a shame to this, but for most people it is an every-day shame. Girls fall in love. Boys leave them. A child is a blessing whether or not the boy stays. But it will not be like this for me.

There are some coloured families nearby, but they keep to themselves and I stare at them and see that the whole family is the same colour. There is no extra paleness or extra darkness between the children or their parents. All are the same shade. It is strange that at a time when the new word 'apartheid' is forcing blacks and whites away from each other, I should bear a child whose colour falls between the two like the brown water of the Groot Vis.

I go to see the doctor once more on a quiet washing day. There is a little boy crying on the ground from a sore on his knee and I squat next to him and comfort him and try to keep further dirt from his wound until the doctor can see him and clean and stitch up the hole. I am reminded of Master Phil as a youngster, his missing buttons, his many scraped knees.

'Do you know nursing?' asks the doctor when he gets to see me.

'A little,' I reply. 'I cared for someone when they were dying.'

It is the first time that I have admitted to myself that young Master Phil was in fact dying all the while I cared for him. That the wound with no blood was far more dangerous than the wound of the boy the doctor had just fixed. That it is the inside wounds that never heal, that eat away at the good flesh until there is nothing left. If I had known that, I wonder what I could have done. Are there ways to cure inside wounds? Are there doctors who know about such things?

'He was the son of my Master,' I say, as the doctor feels my stomach. He looks at me quickly, wondering. 'He was in the war and when he came back the outside wounds healed but the inside ones stopped him from getting better.' I find tears on my cheeks, then, and the doctor helps me to sit up. Women waiting their turn on the floor murmur among themselves. One calls out something gently in a language that I don't understand and the others nod and sway against each other.

'I did my best,' I say through the tears. 'I made him laugh, I read to him, I played the piano for him, I loved him the only way I knew how but it was not enough.' The tears drip down on to Auntie's spare overall, like they dripped on to the smart clothes Madam gave me for the funeral. I take a deep breath and the child settles within me. 'What makes such illness? Is it the work of ghosts in the war, making wounds that no one can see?'

The words come out of me like a fresh discovery. Why had I not thought of it sooner? Ghosts causing invisible wounds? If men did indeed fight ghosts in the war, then perhaps the wounds they suffered would be invisible too. And yet young Master Phil had told me that war was not about ghosts. But maybe he was wrong about that, like I had been wrong about him getting better. Even Dr Wilmott seemed to think that ghosts from the war were chasing Master Phil. He'd seemed to say that work was the only thing that would frighten them away.

I start as the doctor places a hand on my shoulder. 'You mustn't think of such things at this time, child. You must save yourself for the baby; he will grow more from love than from sadness.'

'But are there doctors for such silent wounds?'

The doctor nods. 'I believe so. But it takes a special training to cure a soldier such as your young Master. Now try to drink some milk to make the baby's bones strong and yours, too. Come back and see me when you feel the child dropping within the womb.' He smiles. 'You will have a fine baby.'

I meet his eyes and I know that he is saying this to be kind. He knows what I will face when the baby is born. He knows that this baby is also like an inside wound.

'*Uhambe kakuhle*, go well. Next, please.'

'You play piano?' One of the women pulls at my shoulder as I rest on the ground outside the doctor's house before setting off for Auntie's hut. This talk of ghosts and silent wounds has troubled me. I rouse myself to look up at her. She, too, is being kind. She has left her place in the queue to come and talk to me.

'Yes, I do.'

She is an old woman. She wears a faded blue dress, much mended. I glance at her hands, they are twisted and the knuckles are swollen. The fingers do not look as if they could play. I am too troubled to talk much about music right now.

'There is a piano at the school,' she says, turning to point with a gnarled finger but somehow she gets the direction wrong. The school, the only building in the township, is the other way. 'But there is no one to play it.'

My heart leaps from its trouble at her words. Madam's face rises up before me. A piano! The child kicks strongly and I gasp.

'Go there,' urges the old woman, her hand fumbling down from my shoulder to shake my arm, 'go there and play.'

'Do you play?'

'Once,' the woman says with a smile that is neither happy nor sad and exposes blackened teeth in an expanse of gum. 'When I was young.' She bends towards me again. I realise she is not looking at me, she is not focused on my face. 'If you have a gift,' she says, milky eyes staring at where she believes my face to be, 'then it must be shared.'

'I will go,' I say, shaken by her blindness, and my own selfishness. 'I will find a way to go there and play for the children.'

A younger woman comes out and takes the woman's hand to lead her back inside. Before they step through the door, the old woman turns back.

'Tell me what you play.'

'Chopin,' I say. 'The *Raindrop* prelude.'

She closes her empty eyes and lifts one hand for a moment

over imaginary keys and then feels with her slippered feet for the entrance and shuffles inside.

I get up to go.

It's getting dark – Auntie allowed me off only after I had finished my share of the day's washing – and darkness turns the township into a place of danger. It offers cover for the robbers that hide during the day. I must choose a route that avoids the *shebeen*, from where men stumble red eyed and mad from drink. They will make no allowances for my condition. Sometimes the police come and raid the *shebeen* and chase everyone out of the place with their truncheons. Then they overturn the barrels of beer so that the brown liquid runs on to the street. The next day, the *shebeen* women begin brewing again because – like Auntie with her washing – that is their only way to make a living.

Smoke from cooking fires hangs in a ribbon above the alley I hurry down. I smell simmering maize meal, a smell that never bothered me before, but since the baby its sweetness makes my stomach feel ill. I turn my nose away from the fires where people are cooking, and I turn my thoughts away from robbers and ghosts and young Master Phil who I loved but could not heal, and I look up and out over the huts that surround me. In the distance is the iron bridge over the Groot Vis. Beyond it, the sky is clear and painted with orange streaks above Dundas Street and Cradock House.

I want to report Ada's disappearance to the police but Edward will not allow it. He says we must give it time.

He does not understand.

He does not realise what I have lost.

It is not only my family that I miss. My fingers miss the piano and my heart misses music. My eyes miss words and my head misses reading. All I have is the score for the *Raindrop* prelude but that contains only musical words to tell your hands how to play the tune. Even so, I touch it every day where it lies at the bottom of my cardboard suitcase for the feel of the paper under my fingers.

Yet if I had a book, I would need to find time to read it because we wash all day, and at night I am too tired and I would have to buy extra candles to have enough light to see the pages in Auntie's dim hut. But I don't want to lose my reading, so I ask the man who sells bread to pick up any thrown-away newspapers that he can find on his trips into town. This he does, and each day I fold a single page under a stone above the riverbank and whenever there is a free moment I go up and sit under one of the mimosas and prop the page on top of my growing child and read every sentence. Sometimes there are new words in the newspaper, and I struggle with them as I have no one who can help. Auntie's language is not good and most of the women I work with cannot read.

My reading tells me a lot about what is happening across the Groot Vis. It is strange, because I realise that I am learning more about the town now than I ever knew when I lived in the middle of it. I learn about elections for the mayor – the man who wore the gold chain that I saw at the meeting in the town hall before the war – and I wonder if Master still goes to meetings and leaves Madam on her own at night. I read about the Reverend Calata from the township beyond Bree Street who begs the town council to continue giving soup once a day to hungry people in the townships and the council says no. I read about new rules that say you cannot go to certain places if you have a black skin like mine. It does not say what rules there are for coloured people with skins that are the same as my child will have.

'What does it say, your newspaper?' one of the women,

Lindiwe, always asks when she sees me reading. Lindiwe is small and round but very strong in her smallness. She sometimes helps me lift heavy bundles of washing on to my back.

'Today they talk about the price of wool,' I say, pointing to the sentence I am on. 'And if it's a lot, they call it a boom.'

Lindiwe is young, like me, but she has lived in the township beyond Bree Street all her life. She never went to school but I think she is clever because, although she lives on her own, she knows a lot about people and why they do things. Lindiwe always makes sure to find out what other people think of a problem that she is thinking about at the same time. In this way, she is the opposite of Miss Rose.

'Can you teach me to read like you, Ada?' Lindiwe is saving her money to buy an iron and an ironing board so she can start a business offering perfectly ironed laundry. She whispers this to me one day, and I promise not to say a word because Lindiwe could put Auntie out of business.

'I need to know this reading, Ada. I will pay you for the teaching of it when I am rich!' She giggles and rubs her fingers to denote endless amounts of money. 'I will be so slow at it that you will become a wealthy woman!'

And so we start.

Just like Madam taught me my letters, I will teach Lindiwe. Just like Master Phil told me their meanings, so I will tell Lindiwe.

'*TomorrowIsailforAfrica.*'

We try to do one letter a day.

Slowly she begins to recognise letters and then the words that they form, just like I did. Then we start to make sentences out of the words. I show her how words can have different meanings even though they look the same. And then how those meanings change again when words gather themselves into groups.

Like me, Lindiwe is learning about a world that she thought might be there but until now could never be touched.

It makes me sad to think how much I owe Madam that I can never tell her.

Chapter 21

I still cannot understand why Ada left.

Edward says he has no idea, he says she worked so hard to get the house ready and then simply disappeared. He says: 'That's why you can never trust them, you can educate them and pay them well and take care of them, and they will just go off and leave without a word.'

I am not so sure. I think something must have happened. I feel I know Ada as well as Miriam did, perhaps even better, for Ada had surpassed Miriam in some respects. And yet, in others, Ada was less experienced than her mother. She'd hardly been in the outside world. I worry for her. What can have made her leave? Is she ill? How can I find her? Surely I must try. The new maid is unsatisfactory. I think I will get Mrs Pumile in for the ironing and manage the rest myself. There's only Edward and me, after all. And I will look for Ada . . .

'Ada! Ada!'

I jump. It is Auntie, from further down the riverbank where she is gossiping with a friend. 'Go fetch the next lot!'

I squeeze out the sheet I am rinsing and get to my feet – the child makes this hard, he does not like to be interrupted at his rest – and find a bush to stretch it over. Then set off to Auntie's hut to fetch the next bundle of washing. The bank is slippery with gravel and steep in places where the feet of washerwomen have worn a path between the rocks and the bush. The sun burns down directly from overhead and that means there is at least one more session of scrubbing that can be done today and be ready for folding by evening. I have started to measure the day in loads of washing.

But Auntie is fair to me. She sometimes finds a small amount of milk to give me to help strengthen the baby, like the doctor said it would. And she takes me with her on Sundays to the church by the *koppie* outside the township. The people there are welcoming to me because I am related to Auntie. Some of them are neighbours and I know their names. They ask no questions about the baby and the lack of a husband. Auntie, though, is still troubled by this lack. I think that is why she brings me with her. She prays that I will be saved despite my mislaid husband.

Even so, I like going there. Not to be saved – for I already believe in God – but for the space, and the lack of pushing people, nosing dogs, smoky fires and cooking maize meal. Also, it's a part of the Karoo I've somehow always known, even if I could only see it from a distance. Beneath my feet is the hard thirsty land that I used to stare at from Master Phil's toy box, as it stretched to the mountains where there is snow in winter. Now, though, it is the end of summer, and all about me the earth is clothed in waves of fragile grass with golden paintbrush tips. From where we stand in their yellow tickling midst, I can look straight up at the *koppie* and watch the sun wander across the brown stones and make them shine. I spot a single thorn tree at its base, like the bony tree that overhung the *kaia* at Cradock House. Wherever I go I seem to find something to remind me of Cradock House and those that I have loved there.

The minister wears a robe – better ironed than the minister in KwaZakhele – and stands on a large boulder and tells us that

God the Father wants us to be brave and to show mercy to others even though they do not show mercy to us. He talks about skin difference and the word 'apartheid' that Mrs Pumile first told me. He says that we are being tested in a fire and that the time will come when we will be free to take our place alongside all other free people in the world. Several of the men shout out words that the congregation pick up and shout back. This church is more lively than Master and Madam's church.

It is a war, he calls out at the end of his sermon. A war of liberation!

'Amen!' the congregation roars.

I will need to find a dictionary to look that up. I have heard this word 'liberation', but I don't think it means the same as peace. I've had difficulty with the meaning of peace before, like when I asked Miss Rose why there was still fighting during peace. Perhaps liberation holds the same difficulties?

I look at the people around me. To my surprise, they are smiling and clapping. I feel a clutch at my stomach that is not the child. They surely cannot want a war like the one I remember. A war with bombs and fires that made Master wring his hands and Madam weep? A war of ghosts that took young men and wounded them like young Master Phil was wounded? Black people were not trusted enough in the matter of guns to fight in that war. They did not pay its price. They do not know the pain of it. If they did, they would not smile and clap. But if such a war does come, I tell myself as the baby turns within me and I rub my stomach to make him rest, I must be prepared. I must harden my heart, I must choose sides carefully. I must be prepared for the enemy-in-waiting.

The people chant and clap and Auntie sways against me and closes her eyes and lifts her arms. The women in their blue and white dresses send their swooping hymns up past the *koppie* and towards the horizon. I feel the same trembling that I used to from the organ in Madam and Master's church. For the moment, there is no war, there are no enemies-in-waiting. The sun is warm and the air shakes with our voices for I, too, join the singing and it lifts me and the child up and lets us fly away.

It is raining, the first rain for many months. The Groot Vis has come alive. Brown water races beneath the iron bridge, carrying trees and animals and perhaps people, too, that have been caught in its path. The rocks where we scrub are hidden beneath foamy waves. The drifts are closed. Children stand on the bridge and jump up and down and throw sticks into the water and watch them carried off in the torrent and they scream at the shaking of the bridge from the force of the water. The sky pours, the township streets become rivers too, and carry their own load of rubbish and lick at the opening of Auntie's hut. There will be no washing today. I hold a towel over my head and tell Auntie I am going to see Lindiwe.

The streets are almost empty, but on high ground outside each hut sit buckets and tins and calabashes normally used for transporting water or keeping beer or sour milk – anything to catch the spare rain and avoid a trip to the communal tap. Auntie put out hers overnight.

The school is quiet. I am relieved. I hurry across the bare playground, my feet squelching in the hard earth that has now turned to mud. No one comes to send me away. I knock on the door but there is no reply. I knock again, then push open the door and go inside and shake out my towel and wipe my feet on the linoleum floor. I have never been inside a school before. A long passage stretches ahead of me, with doors on each side. It is dark but I can make out pictures taped to the walls and there are also rough drawings scrawled on the walls and over some of the pictures. Each door has a small window at head height and I look inside but all the classrooms are empty. At the end of the passage there is a door with no window and I knock.

'Yes?' comes from inside. I push open the door.

'School is closed,' a black man says, looking up, frowning, from a laden desk. 'You must come back tomorrow.' The man is about Master's age, but his hair is a dark fuzz and he wears a shirt that is grey with washing. The points of his collar curl.

'I am sorry to disturb you, sir, but I am not a student,' I say, clutching my towel. He waits. I take a breath and battle to remember the sentences I have been practising. I think the baby is stealing some of my memory because I don't remember as well as I used to. 'I play the piano. I know about music. I am looking for a job, sir.'

He looks me over, his gaze stopping on my swollen stomach before returning to my face.

'I met a blind woman and she said that you had a piano but no one to play it, no one to teach the children about music.' My words come out in a rush, and they are not the words that I practised.

'Where did you study?' the man asks.

'I was taught by my Madam. I can play for you, sir, you will see I speak the truth.'

He gives a little smile. 'Where have you been teaching?'

'This is my first time to be a teacher.'

He raises his eyebrows and gets up and comes round the desk. He is tall, taller than Madam or Master or young Master Phil. 'You will have to prove yourself . . .'

'Take me to your piano, sir, and I will prove myself.'

My heart is pounding and this man must surely see it in my neck and in my throbbing temples. He must also think I am very bold. But this is my chance. This is my chance to earn a living doing something I love. This is my chance to break free. Free from the longing for Cradock House and its people, perhaps even free from the poverty I find myself in with Auntie. I once had a chance – a different sort of chance – with Jacob Mfengu from the butcher's, but it came to nothing. This chance, this time, I must not fail.

'We will see,' he says, leading the way out of the door and striding quickly down the passage.

He goes through a door that leads to a second passage and then through another door and we are suddenly in a hall, not as big as the town hall on Market Square, but still bigger than any other room I have seen on this side of the river. There is a row of windows high up on one of the walls, and a small raised stage at one end. It is dark. It is also hot from the closed windows, and there is a smell that comes from when a place needs to be aired. As my eyes start to see better, I see red curtains drooping from rails on each side of the stage. They are missing curtain rings and some of their bottoms drag on the floor and some of their hems are undone.

'There is the piano,' he says, pointing through the gloom towards a brown upright pushed against the side wall.

I walk over to it, the child for once still within me, and open the lid. My hands come away covered in dust, and I wipe them on my towel. I look down at the piano for a moment, remembering Madam's beautiful Zimmerman, the creaminess of its ivory keys, the satin shine of its wood. I touch a key. It feels spongy and gives off a flat tone. I pull out the stool and sit down. It wobbles on uneven legs.

This piano will not be in tune, I tell myself, for it is old and no one has taken care of it and no one has played it for a while. But it still carries music within it – as all pianos do – and if you play it with love, it will give you the music you're looking for.

The tuning and the broken keys mean nothing. Play for Mama. Play for the child. Play for Madam. Play for Master Phil. Play for a job.

So I lift my hands. The tune rises in my head. My fingers reach for the keys and find the opening notes, and I begin. It was as I thought; the sound was flat and tinny, the pedals didn't depress properly, some of the keys no longer worked. But I encouraged the piano and I played all the way through and in the hot, dusty silence of the empty school, it was the most beautiful 'Raindrop' I had ever played.

'What is your name?' he asks, when I have finished and the last chord has faded away.

'Mary Hanembe,' I say, a name that I have made up. No one will connect a young woman called Mary Hanembe who plays the piano and who has a coloured child with the Ada that once lived at Cradock House. But I do not have a Pass with that name on it – my Pass identity paper says Ada Mabuse and I keep that folded at the bottom of the suitcase next to the *Raindrop* prelude score – and I must hope that he will not ask for one.

'What will you do, Mary Hanembe, in your first lesson? When there is noise and shouting and the children misbehave?'

'I will play a march, sir, or a polka, and I will let them sing and dance. And when they are tired I will tell them about the man who has composed the music and why it is special.'

'We do not have much money for a music teacher.'

'I will take whatever you can give, sir.'

He glances at my stomach where the child swells beneath Auntie's overall, and nods. And so it is done.

He says I can start the next week and he names an amount of money that is a little less than what I used to earn with Madam and Master but will be enough to pay Auntie for her piece of floor and have something left over. Auntie will be angry to lose me from her washing business but her anger will be reduced by the money I will pay for rent. And she will become used to this arrangement so that by the time the baby arrives, the money may even make her look past the colour of the child and let me stay.

'Where do you come from?' the man asks, as we walk down the passage past the scrawled-upon pictures. 'Your English is good, you will help the children by speaking such good English.'

'KwaZakhele,' I say quickly, 'but my family is here in Cradock.'

He nods, but doesn't ask me how it is so. Perhaps he suspects that the Madam who taught me the piano also taught me good English. He does not ask me why I no longer continue with that Madam. He does not ask about the coming child. I have prepared answers for those questions, but he does not ask them. He also does not ask for references. A maid like me without references means only one thing: that such a maid must be untrustworthy, must have lied or stolen from her Madam and been sacked for her wickedness. I have no easy answer for my lack of references. I would have to lie. I would have to say, perhaps, that my Madam became ill and went away, that I could not get references before she left.

'My name is Shepherd Dumise,' he says, instead of questioning me further. 'I am the headmaster. You were lucky to find me; the other teachers might not have been interested.' He smiles. His face is kinder now, since I played the piano. I smile back.

'What was the piece you played, Mary?'

'The *Raindrop* prelude, sir. By Chopin.'

We have reached the front door. A strip of linoleum is curling away from where the floor runs out and Mr Dumise presses it down with his shoe. He tells me to arrive early for my first day, so that I can be ready to play a march while the children arrive for something he calls assembly. He tells me that I will be the first music teacher that the school has ever had.

'Thank you, Mr Dumise. I will be here early on Monday.'

I step out of the door and into the playground. It is still raining. The Groot Vis rages beneath the iron bridge. I wish I could run for joy, but the child is too heavy and the headmaster still watches me, so I will walk in the rain and it will soothe me and calm the child and make a song like it used to on the *kaia* roof beneath the bony thorn tree.

'What do you think, Master Phil?' I whisper with hidden excitement to the sky, and to the swollen clouds that race across it. 'Are you proud of me for this?'

Chapter 22

'You think you can come and go when you want!' Auntie shouts over the rush and roar of the Groot Vis. 'Go find another place to stay!' She turns her back on me and disappears into the dimness of the hut. Poppie's grandchildren stand in their doorway, fingers in their mouths, noses dribbling, and listen to the river and stare at me until Poppie pulls them away.

'But I will pay you instead for my place,' I say from the entrance, wiping the rain off my face. 'I will pay you a good sum for the place. And I will wash with you when I'm not at school.'

Auntie looks up at me from where she is sitting on her bed. The floor is piled with bundles of dirty washing. I can see she is reconsidering. 'How much?' she asks.

I tell her what I can afford to pay that will leave a little money left over from my wages. I have also taken Lindiwe's advice about what such a place on a floor should cost.

'It is not enough,' says Auntie, turning away again.

'I would pay more if there was a bed,' I say.

Auntie snorts and reaches for her kettle to make tea. 'A bed! Where you think I can get a bed?'

I wait outside. A couple slosh past, ankle deep in a furrow of dirty water that swirls down the middle of the street. Rubbish

– paper, tins, waste – crusts the edge of the flow. The couple look at me and wonder why I and the child stand in the rain outside a hut when we could go inside for shelter.

I say nothing. I remember young Master Phil explaining that talk about money between people is called 'negotiation'. He said there was a time for talk in negotiation, and a time for silence.

'Maybe you can stay till the baby comes,' Auntie mutters after some time has passed. 'I do this only for the sake of your mother.'

'I have a chance to be a teacher, Auntie. Why are you not pleased for me?' I struggle to keep my voice steady. 'Mama would be pleased.'

The roar of the river reaches a new crescendo. I remember Madam and I playing the opening to the Grieg piano concerto. I remember she said it was the sound of the stream tumbling over cliffs near her home in Ireland. But the Groot Vis is not Grieg; it is Beethoven, grand and heavy and a bit frightening.

Auntie sniffs and roots about for her tin of tea. 'Come out of the rain.'

I don't have a dress that fits me, and the shoes that I wore at Cradock House have become scuffed from walking on dirt roads and up and down the riverbank. I do not have any polish to make them shine.

But I must make the best of what I have got. I will wash and stretch Auntie's blue overall to get it smooth, I will arrange my hair with neatness and I will see if Poppie or Lindiwe have any shoe polish that I could borrow until I get enough money to buy some. And maybe the children and the teachers will be satisfied by my music and will not notice the poorness of my clothing and shoes.

Ada left her clothes behind, ironed and neatly folded on her bed. The house was immaculate. She set out a full lunch for Edward and me, and even had a stew on the stove for our evening meal.

It was a departure perfectly calculated to cause us – to cause me – as little inconvenience as possible.

But why did she not say goodbye? Even in a note to me privately? Left here, on my dressing table, beside my diary?

What event can have taken place that so unnerved her as to make her unwilling to say goodbye – and yet leave the house in perfect order?

This is what I cannot understand.

While Auntie sleeps, I keep myself awake at night and practise the fingering for the march that I will play on the first day of school. Perhaps it will be a *marche militaire*, or perhaps a *military polonaise*. I call up their melodies in my head and my fingers follow where they lead. I wonder if the baby can feel my fingers over his body, I wonder if he can put together the notes that I play to make a tune in his own head?

I am excited. I fall asleep with the music and the heavy Beethoven rush of the Groot Vis in my ears.

Chapter 23

On the day I started as a teacher, something changed.

It was a cold day. The river was no longer angry and racing beneath the iron bridge, but rather making a mist that curled around the bluegums and dissolved into the hard blue of the sky as it rose. Our neighbours had been up since dawn to fetch water once more from the communal tap since the rain had dried up. Paraffin stoves were lit, crying children were fed their porridge. It was the same day as it was every day, and yet somehow different. Auntie left for the riverbank with the first bundle of washing. She said nothing as she went. She had said nothing to me for some time. I told myself that it was still part of negotiation and that I must not weaken.

I walked to school in my carefully smoothed overall, and the shoes I'd tried to clean with spit and a cloth. It was as I pushed through the crowded streets that I felt the newness rise up in me like when the child first touched me like a butterfly from within. I stopped for a moment against the elbowing tide, and looked about with fresh eyes, but little appeared different from what I'd come to expect. The streets still reeked of uncollected rubbish, the faces in the crowd were thin and struggling, the maize meal turned my stomach, the latrines overflowed. And yet . . . among the filth and the struggling was there an opening? A way past the loss that had lain on my heart since I left Cradock House? Could this rising newness, this fresh calling, in fact be the future that young Master Phil had said I would have when I grew up?

I pressed on. The 'Township Bach' swelled. The river ran quietly beneath it. Miss Rose said I would never have a future unless I went to school, so there. Other white people said you needed money in order to have one. But maybe my future was different. It was possible that white people were wrong when they insisted on a connection between money and a future.

'Miss Hanembe! Miss Hanembe! Mary!'

I turned quickly. I must be careful to remember I am now Mary Hanembe. The noise and the bustle of pupils was making me dizzy and forgetful. I wanted to go away and sit down somewhere quiet but the headmaster was standing further along the passage, impatient, waiting for me. He wore the same clothes as when I had seen him before. His shirt collar still needed proper ironing.

'Yes, good morning, Mr Dumise.' I fought my way to his side past a surge of children in every sort of tattered clothing. I need not have worried about my overall and my scuffed shoes; I fitted right in among the pupils.

'We're about to begin in the hall,' he said hurriedly. 'You must go in and start playing. Liphi,' he tapped the shoulder of a barefoot boy talking in a group nearby, 'take Miss Hanembe to the hall.' The boy broke away from his friends, looked me over, taking in the baby, pointed a thumb down the passage and headed off. I followed him. And that is how my teaching future started.

The hall was already filled with more boys and girls than I had ever seen in one place. I hesitated, but the boy Liphi disappeared and no one took any notice of me so I pushed through the crowd and went over and opened up the piano and sat down on the wobbly stool. There were some teachers talking in a group on the stage beside the drooping curtains but they also paid me no attention. The windows high up had been opened and the musty smell was gone and a cool breeze touched my neck and made me feel better. I rested my hand on my stomach for a moment to quieten the child's kicking, and thought of Madam with her hands on either side of mine, encouraging me, and then I began.

A *marche militaire*.

The piano was still tinny but I remembered which of the keys were broken so they didn't bother me, and I used extra pedal to make up for their lack. Strangely, as soon as I started, a great silence came over the hall and the notes echoed off the walls and over the heads of the teachers on the stage. I looked up quickly, worried that they did not like what they were hearing. But I kept going and played the march a full three times through. By the third time, I could feel the floor and not just the stool shaking, as hundreds of feet jumped in time with the music. As the last chord died away, they began to clap – even the teachers on the stage – and I felt my face go hot and I knew that it would be all right.

The headmaster held up his hand for them to stop and said I was the new music teacher and they clapped and whistled once more and the headmaster joined in as well. He also said a few other things about what was to happen that day at school – I later learnt that this was what an assembly was for – and then sent them off to their first lesson. He looked down at me and nodded and I started to play again, this time a Chopin *polonaise*. The youngsters chattered and danced their way out of the hall. The teachers came down off the stage and stood around watching me play. Once I had finished, they came forward.

'What a surprise,' said a woman in a blue dress with long sleeves that rode up her thin arm when she reached over and shook my hand. She said her name was Mildred.

'Well done,' said another, a man this time, with thick glasses and a jacket with holes in the elbows. 'Do you play jive?'

They seemed not to notice my faded overall with its weight of child, or my broken shoes, and they wished me luck and said it was the first time many of the children had ever heard a piano.

I wish I could say that it went easily from then on, that the clapping and whistling in the hall meant it was going to be a good future, that I and my child might find a place here to work and be accepted by my colleagues and stay out of trouble. But another challenge had lately arisen – the matter of birthplace. Proof would soon be required, the headmaster said wearily to his staff, to show that all teachers had the right to live and work in Cradock.

'But why?' demanded an excitable man called Silas, who was the deputy head and taught history. 'We must go where the work is. This is not a crime!' Several teachers sitting on low benches clapped. We were on the stage in the hall at the time, in a loose circle around the headmaster. Behind us, the drooping stage curtains gave off a smell of mildew. From outside came the din of rough sport in the playground.

'In Johannesburg they call for us to burn our Passes!' hissed the man keen on jive. His glasses reflected in the single light that hung over our heads. Some of the older staff exchanged nervous glances and muttered amongst themselves. The noise level rose to muffle the shouting from outside.

'That's wild talk,' said Mr Dumise loudly over the upsurge, from his position in the centre of the stage. 'If we keep our heads down, they'll forget about us. Reverend Calata at St James School is sure of this. If we cause trouble,' he shot a warning glance across at the deputy, 'then we call attention to ourselves.'

'I say we ignore their stupid rules,' retorted a young woman named Dina, who wore a different coloured turban on her head each day.

The circle splintered into groups, each taking a particular position. I realised this was a debate, and it occurred to me that debate was altogether different from negotiation, but that both involved trying to be on the winning side.

I kept quiet. They no doubt had papers to prove their background and their work history. But when the time came to gather such proof, what would the authorities do to me – a girl with no family, no training, no references and no Pass document in the name of Mary Hanembe? It was already a surprise that Mr Dumise had not asked to see my Pass. I lived on the edge of discovery. Yet why should the matter of skin be subject to rules? And what would Master Phil have made of this alliance between skin and the law?

My pupils gave me no time to dwell on these latest developments. After the excitement of that first assembly, they proved to be as rough as Mama and Mrs Pumile had warned. Many of them lived on the street and had no parents and were always hungry. That made them fight, like they saw men fight outside the *shebeen*, or fight over a woman, or over ownership of a goat. On the street, disputes were only ever settled by fists or knives, and so it was at school. I learnt to shrink back against the wall to protect myself and my child from their rampaging. This was passion such as I'd never felt before. And fevered air such as I'd never breathed before.

Mr Dumise said that the poor behaviour was because we had more street children on our side of the river than Rev. Calata

had at the strict St James School in the township past Bree
Street. And that criminals hid from the law on our side of the
river and set a bad example. It was true that our township was
not as well organised as theirs. And we did not have a township
leader like Rev. Calata, a man respected even by the white mayor
at the town hall. Perhaps, I thought to myself, it was also the
presence of the nearby jail that made the St James children
behave better.

In the matter of teaching, I was luckier than my colleagues
because my subject offered respite in the midst of turmoil.
Music both settled my pupils down and gave them wings. It
helped them forget, for a moment, all the things that made their
lives so discordant. Just as music had shown me a world beyond
Cradock House, so it let these young ones fly away from the
township to a new place where there was no hunger or blood.
Each day they leapt into the hall eager to escape their lives – and
the harder subjects of numbers and words – and demanded
more jazz and more syncopation every time. In the first weeks of
my job, I played every lively piece I knew. 'More township jive,
Miss H,' they would shout, ignoring everything I tried to teach
about the music I was to play. 'More jive!' They forgot their
hunger and their disputes, flung off their thin jackets and danced
and stamped their feet in time and tired themselves out as much
as I tired my fingers out and the child inside me. It was glorious.
I reasoned that if I gave them everything they wanted now, then
at a later stage they would be prepared to listen to what I wished
to say if they wanted me to play for them again. It was, I suppose,
a sort of negotiation, but without money. I think Master Phil
would have approved. But the noise from the hall must have
been a severe trial for teachers in nearby classrooms.

'You are more tired with this teaching than with my washing,'
Auntie said crossly, breaking her silence after the first few days

when I returned to the hut and lay down on my piece of floor in the middle of the afternoon.

'It is true,' I said, feeling my eyes droop and sleep approach.

'You must think of the child,' Auntie muttered.

I tried to hold back a smile. It was the first time that Auntie had taken the part of my child against me. Dear Lord, I told myself, wait until she sees the colour of this child that she defends!

And then I slept.

Does Ada remember us?

I think of her every day as I write this diary.

Did we drive her away by some form of neglect of which we were not aware?

Was it that she missed Miriam so much she had to be among her own people? This is Rosemary's view, from Johannesburg, but I don't think it is correct.

Has she gone to KwaZakhele? I have asked the maids of my friends but none of them has heard of her whereabouts. Even Mrs Pumile has no idea where Ada is, although she said Ada did not look well the last time she saw her. On the other hand, Mrs Pumile has benefited from Ada's absence; she now earns a tidy sum ironing for us.

Edward says that after all we did for Ada and Miriam, even if she comes back we must never employ her again. He is most insistent upon this. He also insists that I forget about trying to find her.

The school was the first place where I met black men and women who had learning. At the start I was nervous, although Lindiwe said I should not be. But they had been to school and I had not, I said to her. They were trained to deal with children in a classroom and I was not. They may be suspicious that the headmaster, Mr Dumise, was willing to spend some of the school's small amount of money on me instead of on books for more important subjects.

'No matter,' Lindiwe said with finality, shouldering her latest load of washing. 'None of them can do what you can do on the piano.' If Lindiwe had been Miss Rose, she would have added: 'So there.'

But the teachers didn't complain, or look on me with suspicion. Instead they accepted me, they ignored my poor clothing, they didn't look down on my lack of schooling and training, they seemed ready to take my piano playing as a good enough substitute. And they also didn't complain – at least not to me – that my arrival had raised the noise level in the school to even greater heights. What was more difficult to deal with was their curiosity. Curiosity about where I came from, how I learnt the piano so well and – they didn't ask this but I saw it in their eyes – whether I had a father for this baby that I was carrying.

'How did you learn to play like that?' asked the numbers teacher, a quiet and serious young man called Sipho Mhlase who had been silent during the debate about the right to work in Cradock.

'Who was your teacher, child?' This from Veronica, an elderly lady with a craggy face like Auntie's, who had shaken her head at the jive man's comment about burning Passes. Veronica took the younger children for reading when not busy calling from the classroom window to her chickens that roamed the back yard of the school. The same bad people that stole washing off bushes at the riverbank would steal Veronica's thin birds if she relaxed her guard.

'Where do you come from?' The pretty young teacher, Dina, attacked the matter of my pregnancy from the angle of geography. She leant on the piano as I finished playing the morning march one day, and took in the swelling of my stomach beneath Auntie's overall.

I hesitated.

'You don't have to say, Mary,' she glanced down at my swollen belly again, 'but people wonder . . .' Dina was the closest to my age on the staff. She was wearing a different coloured turban again and the boys followed her with their eyes, like men had followed Miss Rose with their eyes. But she wasn't selfish like Miss Rose and sometimes offered me bread and jam from her own lunch.

'I come from KwaZakhele,' I said hurriedly, closing the lid of the piano and heaving myself up off the wobbly stool. 'I worked for a Madam in Port Elizabeth who taught me to play.'

There was a beat of silence in Dina, like a rest in music.

'You don't need to call people Madam and Master,' she said in a quite different voice. 'Just because she taught you doesn't put her above you.' She stared at me. I could see the clever folds on the top of her blue turban. 'We take what whites teach us and use it to get ahead. But we don't grovel to them.' Her eyes flashed at me. 'We don't grovel!' I remembered Mrs Pumile saying the word 'apartheid' to me with the same heat through the hedge at Cradock House.

'One day, Mary,' she pulled my arm through hers as we left the hall, 'we'll call white people by their names – yes,' she nodded as I gasped, 'just like they call us by our names. And there'll be no shame in it.'

'How could I call Madam "Cathleen"?' I murmured to myself.

'Cathleen? So . . .' Dina's turban nodded.

The child kicked again and I felt a dizziness that made me sink to my knees on the linoleum. No one must find out! No one must look for a Madam who knows the piano and is called

Cathleen! Pray that the hadeda birds do not hear gossip from Dina and bear it back to Cradock House . . . I tried to rise but the walls crowded upon me like in church when young Master Phil had gone to God the Father and the organ had wept and Madam and Master had not touched one another for comfort.

'It's OK,' Dina whispered, crouching down beside me and putting an arm round my shoulders.

'Miss Hanembe? Dina?'

'I'm sorry, sir.' I breathed deeply to still my fearful heart. Mr Dumise's concerned face swam into view. 'It won't happen again.'

'Take Mary home,' said Mr Dumise to Dina in a low voice. 'She can rest and then come back when she feels better.' He turned away and went back into his office.

I waited till his door closed. 'I can go on my own,' I said, not wanting Dina to see my poor circumstances at Auntie's hut or to learn more about me than I had already given away. What if Auntie was there and addressed me as Ada?

But Dina tossed her turbaned head and took my hand firmly and led me out of the school and across the playground. The Groot Vis rushed gently in the background, still carrying spare water from the floods.

'You are kind,' I said to Dina when we got to Auntie's street. 'I will go on myself from here.' But Dina ignored me again and waited until I led her right up to the open doorway of Auntie's hut.

'I have no milk to give you tea,' I said, squatting down on my mat while offering Auntie's narrow bed to Dina. She stayed in the doorway, her eyes slowly adjusting to the darkness inside as mine used to do when I came to visit with Mama all those years before.

'That is not your husband's bed?'

'I have no husband.'

She looked at me, then looked at the rusty paraffin stove, the hooks for my towel and Auntie's towel, the piles of washing, the dented kettle.

'I will see if I can get you some jam. You need to be strong for the baby.'

Chapter 24

'Auntie,' I gasped, 'wake up, Auntie, it is the baby!' I cried out as the agony rose from my stomach and wrapped itself round my back.

I had been lying in pain for some time, thinking that it would go away, but now it grasped me too firmly to resist and I felt the gush of my waters breaking beneath me. It was night. I could hardly see Auntie as she struggled into her overall and felt about for the candle next to her bed. She struck a match, lit the candle and her face floated towards where I lay on my place on the floor.

'I will get the doctor,' she said hoarsely, stepping over me. 'Hold this to your face.' She pulled a cloth from the wet washing pile and pressed it across my forehead.

I lay on my side and watched her stumble out of the hut. Through the open doorway loomed the shape of nearby huts and above them the prick of stars. I remembered seeing stars at Cradock House when hanging out the dishcloths after supper. You don't normally see stars in the township because of the smoke from cooking fires, so it must be very late at night or very early in the morning. Another spasm of pain caught at me and I twisted on the floor. The stars blurred.

'Hush, hush,' whispered a new voice and a hand stroked the cloth over my forehead, like I had done with young Master Phil. But this wasn't young Master Phil. The Master never approved of me caring for young Master Phil like that . . .

'Poppie?'

'Yes, child. The doctor comes soon.'

'I did what I thought was right, Poppie.'

'Hush, child, hold my hand.'

'It was my duty,' I said, the loneliness of Master's face appearing in my mind, the sound of *Clair de Lune* playing as the sun set and the purple light following my fingers on the piano . . . 'Will I be forgiven, Poppie?'

'Shhh, shhh, turn on your side.'

'Madam must not come.' I struggled to sit up and Poppie pressed my shoulders down again. 'Is Madam here?' I stared out of the doorway, expecting to see Madam at any moment in one of her cream day dresses, perfectly ironed.

Then the doorway filled and it was not Madam but the doctor who had been kind to me and he knelt over me and turned me on to my back and felt my stomach.

'Boil water,' he said to Auntie, who had also reappeared. She and Poppie busied themselves with the paraffin stove. 'Give me a fresh sheet for Ada to lie on.' Auntie hesitated, then pulled a folded sheet from the clean washing pile. The doctor rolled me slowly to the side, slipped one part of the sheet under me and then rolled me to the other side and spread it fully beneath me.

The pain seemed to have stopped for a moment and I could see Auntie and Poppie's lined faces in the candlelight. Poppie saw me looking at her and took my hand again and began to sing, like the women on the riverbank. I tried to push the pain away and think about the tune that she sang, the key – maybe

D minor – and the length of the notes and the rests between them . . .

But soon the pain was back and I found myself crying out and twisting on the floor again.

'Will I be forgiven?' I gasped and caught at the doctor's hand. 'Does God understand?'

'Think only of the child,' instructed the doctor, passing my hand to Poppie and turning from her questioning eyes to busy himself with hot water and cloths. The candle smoked, plunging the hut into shadow. Auntie scratched for another one in the tin under her bed.

'Madam,' I moaned as a strange feeling began to take hold of my lower body. I felt the pressure of the child moving down and wanting to be born. The doctor moved my legs and nodded to Auntie and Poppie.

'The baby is coming.'

Auntie squeezed around behind me and lifted my shoulders to rest against her. Poppie held my hand and murmured her song. The doctor knelt between my legs and I felt the pain press down through me and I found myself crying for it to end. Madam's scales rushed like the wind from Cradock House all the way to the township, and I saw Master's car with its lights like the eyes of night animals peering into the hut.

'Go away!' I cried.

Auntie hissed at my shoulder. The doctor was saying things I couldn't hear, and Poppie was fetching something more from the clean washing pile. Auntie would not be happy at this disturbance to her business.

'Almost there,' the doctor said. Poppie wiped my forehead.

I panted with the pain and the pressure and my body seemed on fire and I felt I should be torn apart until suddenly the doctor moved his hands and the pressure eased and there was another gush and he was gathering a little red bundle from between my legs. 'A fine girl,' he said with a quick smile, holding the child close to me and then wrapping it in one of Auntie's clean cloths. The pain was going away from my body, the roar of Madam's scales was fading, the night animals were disappearing from the doorway.

The doctor laid the baby in my arms and I looked down. Her tiny face was indeed pale, as the doctor had told me it would be, and her eyes were the colour of milky early evening sky. She opened her mouth and gave a healthy cry. I traced a finger down over her nose and her mouth and felt the little lips seeking my finger. The doctor nodded encouragingly and got to his feet. Auntie and Poppie remained where they were, mouths open, eyes wide, staring down at the newborn child in silence.

It was only the presence of Poppie and the doctor that stilled Auntie's tongue on the night the child was born. She hunched at the edge of her narrow bed as the doctor packed his bag. Poppie hovered by the door, her eyes darting between Auntie, myself and the child.

'Nurse often,' the doctor said, touching me gently on the shoulder, 'that will bring the milk to your breast soon.'

'Thank you,' I said, on the edge of tears. 'Thank you for helping me.'

He nodded, then gathered his bag and bent through the doorway. Auntie pushed herself to her feet and followed him out. I could hear the mutter of their voices. I looked at Poppie. She gave an uncertain smile. Her eyes slid down to the baby in my arms.

'Will I be forgiven, Poppie?'

She hesitated. Still the doctor and Auntie talked outside.

'Only the Lord forgives, child. You have to ask Him.'

The child stirred in her cloth and I lifted her closer. The eager mouth sucked at me, the velvet cheek nestled pale as tea against my breast. I prayed she would find a way to love me even though I had given her this pale skin.

Auntie returned and began noisily to clear up the cloths that the doctor had used, her back firmly to me. Poppie crept out with a murmured goodbye.

'Who did this?' Auntie demanded, turning on me then, and thrusting the bloodstained cloths towards me as if they were to blame for this birth, this child who would belong nowhere. It was getting light and I could see her face better now than in the candelight. Her eyes blazed at me, her hands holding the cloths shook with rage.

'It doesn't matter any more,' I said, gathering my voice, knowing this was the first of many battles. 'The child's skin cannot be changed.'

'Have you no shame?' she hissed, like she had done when I cried out during the birth. Perhaps, even then, she suspected something.

'I felt shame for many months. It cannot get worse.'

She snorted and flung the last cloths together. 'You don't know how bad it can get. Praise the Lord Miriam never saw this day.' She hauled the bundle over her bent shoulder and pushed out of the doorway.

I was on my own for an hour or more as the township slowly woke around me. It was hard to know how much time was passing and I cried a little, on account of being alone and having no one to share the birth of the child with, unlike my mother who had had Madam with her when I was born. I lay with my child in my arms and remembered many things from when I was growing up. Things that made sense, and some that didn't. Master Phil pulling me to stand by him at the opening of the new bank, Miss Rose leaving for Johannesburg when she ought to have stayed behind, Madam teaching me the letters of the alphabet, Mama crocheting in her chair, head bent, eyes turned away from mine when I asked about my father . . .

What would you do, Mama, if Master came to you when Madam was away? If he stood before you with faded blue eyes sore from the loss of young Master Phil and lonely from the absence of Madam? If he reached out and touched your shoulder and promised not to hurt you?

Would you turn him away?

Mama understood duty and loyalty. But in this matter, duty to Master and loyalty to Madam could never be on the same side. Allowing one meant betraying the other. Mama would have had to make a choice, like I did. But what would she choose? And if she chose to turn away, would she lose her job? Her home?

The child of my choice slept in my arms, making snuffling sounds and pursing her tiny lips. After some time I became thirsty and inched over the mat to the stove. There was some water left in the kettle that was now cool. I drank it all. I must go and fetch water from the communal tap to make up for the water Auntie had given to the doctor during the birth of the child. Then I must learn to carry the child in a blanket on my back so I can go back to school tomorrow and face the headmaster and Dina and Sipho and Veronica and my students and, later, Lindiwe and the washerwomen from the riverbank. I will hold up my head and I will bury my shame, like I am learning to bury my days at Cradock House and my debt to Madam lest it be misunderstood. And I must hope that Mr Dumise has found me worthy enough to let me stay.

162

I laid the child down and reached for my overall. My body felt stiff, as if it had been stretched in directions it was not used to. I longed for the warm water of Cradock House to clean myself and to run over my face and through my hair as I used to do after morning cleaning. And then I would change and go upstairs to read to Master Phil and imagine he was getting better . . .

If I collected a full bucket of water then there would be enough left over from drinking and cooking for a simple wash. But I should go soon in case Auntie returned and threw me out before I had the chance. I put my overall on and wrapped the child in another cloth – there was no way to disguise her pale face, it shone above the covering for all to see – found my cracked shoes and took up the bucket. My body ached from where the baby had been born.

It was still early, this first morning with my daughter. The moon hung luminous in a grey sky streaked with rising smoke. Shadowy figures moved along the streets. A rim of sunrise showed orange on the horizon. I walked along the road, holding my child in my left arm and the bucket in my right. A girl child, not a boy.

I would call her Dawn.

I have almost given up hope of finding Ada now. It's been six months and still no sign of her.

People – among them Edward – say it is foolish to feel responsible for a maid, especially one who has disappeared. And yet I do, and have done so since the day I lifted her as a newborn out of Miriam's arms.

After much difficulty and many letters, I have found the correct church in KwaZakhele where dear Miriam is buried. The minister wrote back to me. He remembered Ada, but said he had not heard from her since. He mentioned that he had put up a small sign on Miriam's grave.

Although Edward will not allow it, I would like to visit the cemetery where Miriam lies, almost as a way of paying my respects and love to Ada who was like a daughter to me.

I shall find a way.

Chapter 25

What did young Master Phil see as I walked down the dirt road in the half-light? What did he think of my sin? And of the pale child I held against my chest? Would he turn away from me? And from his father? Yet this was not a question he'd ever have had to answer. For if he'd been alive, Master would not have come to me in the night, even if Madam had been away in Johannesburg. It was Master Phil's absence, together with Madam's absence, that led to the footsteps down the corridor, and the knock on my door, and the shame that would walk by my side forever. Yet if Master Phil had lived . . .

And then there was the matter of skin. When I look back on it now, when I look back at the girl on the dusty road carrying a newborn baby and a bucket, I now realise I knew nothing about skin. Skin touched me only lightly within Cradock House. It was only beyond its walls that the world divided itself so strictly between black and white, with coloureds falling awkwardly in between. Yet I thought I understood those grades of colour. I thought I could manage even under the new word called apartheid that Mrs Pumile spat through the hedge. Only once I came to live across the river did I realise that I was wrong. For there was something deeper. Something beneath the surface division into black, white or coloured. Something that reached beyond myself and my child, for which there was no word that you could find in the dictionary. It came down to the mixing of blood within a single family.

It grew a life of its own. It reached out to people we knew and forced disputes amongst them. It divided old friends from one another, it split families in half, it turned strangers into enemies. It would do its evil work on others however hard I tried to appease it. It had terrible power, this difference of skin between mother and child.

It became for me, I suppose, a war. Maybe not the kind that had taken young Master Phil, and maybe not the kind that the minister on the *koppie* had talked about, but a private war that spilt over into those around us. A war with no winning side. Nothing prepared me for this. For now, though, as I tramped along the uneven gravel road to the water tap, I couldn't help crying out to God the Father: where do You stand in the matter of skin? Do You believe that what I did with Master was a sin because our skins did not match, or was it a sin because I betrayed Madam?

'Ada! Ada!'

I looked up from Dawn's tiny face. It was light now, and the smell of cooking maize drifted on the cool morning air. It bothered me less than it had when I was newly expecting. The water tap was just a little further, at the end of the street, but my stiff legs were finding the walking hard, like Master Phil's legs had once struggled.

'Ada!' Lindiwe's strong hand grasped my bucket arm and stopped me. She thrust a bundle of washing over one shoulder. 'The baby!' she gasped, craning to see.

I nodded and lifted Dawn towards her and watched her face. Lindiwe's face – her sharp, knowing eyes, her forehead creased or smooth – always told me exactly what she was thinking. When we were learning new words, Lindiwe's face would tell me if she understood, or if I had not explained well enough. Lindiwe's face was my first guide as to what made a good teacher.

She stood beside me now, legs planted apart to anchor herself beneath her heavy load. As her eyes devoured every feature of the tiny baby on my arm, I both longed for and feared her reaction. Around us, the township stirred with the first cries of the day, for there was never a moment that passed without struggle or loss. Women pushed past us to queue at the tap, and in the distance came the F sharp whistle of a train leaving the station.

'Oh, Ada,' Lindiwe breathed, and her face fell into lines of fear and dismay and the fight not to step away from me and be on her way. 'Ada,' she searched my face, 'why?'

I looked around me. A man chased his goats in front of him, washerwomen headed down to the Groot Vis – I was keeping Lindiwe from a favourable scrubbing rock – and a group of boys huddled over a waning fire. At Cradock House, Madam's new maid would be fetching the milk from the gate.

'It was my duty,' I said.

'But who had such power to make it so?' Lindiwe's tone was suddenly fierce.

'I can't say.'

She stared down at Dawn who slept quietly, her lips moving in her first dreams, her skin the colour of the Groot Vis.

'What will you do?' she murmured.

'I will stay here and teach.'

Lindiwe sucked in her breath and I could see her mind working through the difficulties. 'Your auntie did not know?'

'No. I'll find another place if I have to.'

She shook her head and it was only when she dropped her

hand that I realised she had been squeezing my arm all the time. 'Go well, Ada,' she said finally, finding a gentleness towards me, her voice sinking below the rising tide of people about us. She shifted her bundle on to her other shoulder and made to go on her way.

'Are you still my friend?' I asked.

Lindiwe looked away from me as if there was something across the road that had caught her attention, rather like Madam used to look out of the window for Ireland when she disagreed with Master. A barefoot youngster darted past, bumping against my bucket as he went by.

'Careful!' I cried, clutching Dawn harder.

'I knew there was something wrong,' Lindiwe murmured, 'when you never talked of a boy . . .'

'But are you still my friend?' I asked again.

'I am still your friend.' She turned and hurried towards the river and, after a moment, her stocky figure dissolved into my tears.

I stood in line at the tap, holding Dawn's face against me so others would not see her skin this first time, and filled my bucket. No one took any notice. Several women had tiny babies on their backs. When I got back to Auntie's hut I would practise tying her into a blanket. Then I would wash as best I could and gather my few possessions together in case the money I was paying for my place on Auntie's floor was not enough for her to overlook the colour of my child. Perhaps the doctor might know someone who would show me kindness, who would understand that what I did came out of duty, not out of spite or looseness.

I must get into a clean overall, lift Dawn in the blanket on to my back and go to school. It would not do to be absent even for a day. But what if Mr Dumise said I was no longer welcome as a teacher? What if my attempts to prove my worthiness had failed, and skill in music was not enough to cover the discrepancy in skin between my child and me? I was surely a poor example to my students. I myself would not condemn anyone for feeling that way.

I lifted the heavy bucket and headed back. It was hard getting back to Auntie's hut. The bucket was heavier than Dawn's weight and dragged my right arm down. I had to stop halfway to swap over. I fear that I spilt some water on the way.

Chapter 26

I gathered my courage and knocked on the headmaster's door, as I had done the first time I came to school. Mr Dumise worked long hours. He would be there.

'Come in.'

He looked up from an open file. But he was not alone. Sitting opposite him and gesturing into the air was Silas, the deputy head.

'Mary!' At the sight of the blanket tied around me they scrambled to their feet.

'It must be a boy,' cried Silas with enthusiasm. 'Only a boy could survive all that noisy music!'

'No, sir. It is a girl. I have called her Dawn.'

Silas clapped his hands and then grasped mine and began to pump them up and down. The headmaster came around his desk and grinned. These were the first true congratulations I had received, apart from the kind doctor's. 'What a fine name,' he said. 'Enough, Silas! You must rest, now, with your family.' He was a kind man, Mr Dumise. I had heard that his wife died some years ago. That must be why his shirts were so poorly ironed. Silas skipped behind me, keen to examine Dawn in her blanket.

'The students can wait a day or two till you're stronger,' Mr Dumise went on, still smiling.

I heard the intake of breath behind me and felt Silas's eyes on my neck and then on my face.

'Mary!' He grabbed my arm. 'How could you? To betray your own people!' He made to shout something else but instead flashed a glance at the headmaster, snatched his hand off my arm as if he'd been burnt and rushed out of the room, letting the door bang behind him.

Mr Dumise stared after him, mystified, then back at me. I must harden my heart, I said to myself. This is the enemy-in-waiting. This is my private war.

'I have something to say about the baby, sir.'

Mr Dumise still had not looked at Dawn. He still had not seen her face and felt the divisive power of her skin.

He hesitated, then said, 'It's not necessary, Mary.' Perhaps all he suspected was that I had no husband. Perhaps he had been told so by Dina, after her visit to Auntie's shack. I wished that was all it was. I wished I could nod, and leave it at that. I wished I could be an ordinary girl whose boy left her with a baby and no prospect of marriage. Like Mama. Like Miss Rose?

'It is not the lack of a husband, sir. It's a matter of skin.'

He stared at me for a moment, confused by me, confused by Silas, then walked reluctantly round to look at Dawn's small head poking out of the blanket. I stayed looking forwards. I did not want to see his face; I did not want to witness the disgust once again.

The papers on his desk were in neat piles, just like Master's desk at Cradock House when I looked for my bank book. Timetables were pasted on to the wall behind his chair and a brown jacket with a frayed collar hung from a tarnished brass hook. Through the window Veronica's chickens strutted and pecked in the back yard. He walked back to the desk and sat down. He clasped both hands in front of him and stared at the papers before him. I felt Dawn stir and move her head against my back. In the space between her snuffling and the bent head of Mr Dumise hung my chance for a future.

'I know it is a sin, sir, and I pray that one day God will forgive me. But I ask you please . . .' The words rushed out of me like on the day I had asked to be a teacher.

He looked up.

But instead of the anger I had feared – as with Silas and Auntie – there was only pity. I'd been preparing myself for anger, steeling myself for it, holding myself upright even though my mind and body were weary and longed to rest. As I stood there, his sympathy began to bend me, to make me want to crumple on to the floor and reach for some understanding, some comforting arms. The hours since Dawn was born had been consumed only with survival.

'There's no need to beg, Mary,' he said quietly. 'If it was only up to me your job would be safe. But as teachers we must set an example. There are those who'll want you to leave.'

He saw me struggle with weakness and came round the desk to ease me into the chair against the wall. I sat there, leaning forward to protect the precious bundle on my back, and waited until my heart steadied itself, like I used to wait for Dawn's kicking to subside.

'Is there anything more you need to tell me?' His voice was gentle.

I looked up, bewildered. What was this now? Did he want to know who the father was? I dare not tell anyone, in case it got back to Cradock House and Madam.

He leant against the desk. 'What I mean is, will there be

any . . .' he frowned and searched for the right word, 'difficulty? With the father?'

'Oh no, sir,' I said, relieved to have an answer that would satisfy. 'The father will never know.'

He looked at me uncertainly and I could tell he was wondering about the circumstances of this baby, wondering if I had fallen in love across the 'colour line', or whether I had been taken against my will.

I pulled myself to my feet. For all his sympathy, Mr Dumise could not guarantee my job. It would be up to my fellow teachers, and how they viewed a black woman who had sinned with a white man – whatever the circumstances. I must go back to my classroom. I must give them no other cause for my dismissal. The child on my back is innocent, but even so she will expose me, and challenge those around her into acceptance or rejection of us both. And then divide them by their choice.

'I will go to my class now, sir.' I clasped my hands together and felt their roughness from outdoor washing. My heart must grow a similar hide.

'Are you feeling strong enough?'

'Yes thank you, sir.' I looked across at him, at the worry on his face above the shirt frayed from too much washing. I hesitated, then asked, 'Will it be all right with the other teachers?'

He shook his head and moved some papers around on the desk. 'I don't know, Mary. That's a battle you will have to fight.'

I wonder if Ada still plays.

I remember her Chopin – the Raindrop *– and her Debussy. Where I could impart gaiety, Ada could show brilliance. Where I aimed for gentle melancholy, Ada found heartbreak . . .*

I will be going to KwaZakhele.

By dint of quiet manipulation, I have arranged for our minister's wife to lead a pastoral visit to our sister worshippers at a church outside Port Elizabeth. We ladies will be escorted by the minister and his parish council. The aim is to build ties and find ways in which we can support the many poor women and children at that place.

Edward, after a private visit from the minister, has given grudging consent. I don't imagine I will learn anything more about Ada from the trip, but I will see Miriam's grave and I will pray for Ada's well-being.

For I am convinced she is alive.

And when I return, I intend to widen my inquiries.

Chapter 27

'Out!' shouted Auntie, waving her arms at me when I arrived back at the hut. Her *doek* was awry, her overall creased from bending on the riverbank. 'Take your things and go!'

She had dragged my suitcase to the door. She had rolled up the mat that I had lain on for the months since I had arrived in the township. Poppie watched from the gloom of her own hut alongside but did not intervene.

'I will go,' I said, 'but first I need to feed Dawn.'

I bent over and untied her from my back with shaking hands. She was crying, her eyes tightly closed, her mouth wide open as if in protest at Auntie's harsh words. I pushed the overall aside and lifted her to my breast. The eyelids flickered, the tiny mouth pursed and latched on to me and I felt the tug of her gums and the answering response of my body. I am not sure she received much nourishment what with Auntie's rage and my own nervousness, but the doctor had said I should let her nurse often to encourage the milk to flow.

'Who is the father of this child?' Auntie stood over me with her hands on her hips.

I remained silent. If I said that Dawn sprang from duty, she would surely conclude that my Master was the father. There were no other white men to whom I was bound by duty. Auntie was shrewd in such matters.

'If it was by force, then it must be said so. A girl who is raped gets more sympathy.'

Still I remained silent. Dawn's sucking filled the air between Auntie and me, as she had filled up the space between us when she was inside me.

'I want you gone when I come back,' Auntie shouted finally, heaving a pile of dry washing on to her hip for delivery to its owner.

Dawn was falling asleep, her lips were losing their grip on my breast. I lifted her up and patted her back, then wrapped her once more in the blanket and lifted her on to my back. Once she was secure I knelt down and opened the suitcase to check that my spare money and my Pass were still at the bottom. My hands were shaking so much that the paper creased and the money would not stay in one place. Then I pulled my towel from where it hung alongside Auntie's and put it in the case. There was nothing left here for me now.

'Ada?' It was Poppie. She peered through the gloom at me. 'I have brought you some nappies.' She offered a pile of worn but clean cloths.

'Oh, Poppie,' I whispered, clasping her hand, 'you are more kind than I deserve.'

'Where will you go?'

'I have a friend,' I said, taking up my case, speaking with a strength I did not feel inside. 'I must hope she will be kind too.'

Poppie hesitated, then said, 'Come back and see your auntie in a while. She will see she has been too quick.'

And so it was that I found myself once more walking the length of the township on the day Dawn was born. My legs were tired, and my arms ached from carrying the cardboard suitcase and my back was not yet used to the weight of my child. But I must not complain, for this was the easy part. The danger came in crossing the Groot Vis to get to the township at the end of Bree Street where Lindiwe lived. If I was lucky, the river would be low enough to take the drift below Cross Street. If not, I would have to take the iron bridge that I'd vowed I would never cross again. And if I ended up living beyond Bree Street, I would have to make that trip every day, for Lindiwe's hut and my school lived on opposite sides of the Groot Vis. The river would have to be crossed if I and my child were to survive.

I found myself remembering the very first long walk – when I left Cradock House with my suitcase in my hand and Dawn growing within me and little prospect of a future beyond washing for a living – and the fear of discovery rushed over me again, and made me turn my face away from passing cars in case Madam and Master should drive by.

By now it was late afternoon and the streets were thronged. The press of strangers troubled me less than it had that first day, and I found myself listening for the rough 'Township Bach' to bear me and the child and my suitcase onwards through the tight crowds. Ragged children wove past, bowling uneven hoops of wire before them. Who would Dawn play with when she was their age? Who would be prepared to be her friend?

I was lucky with the river that day. The drift was open. I sat down on the riverbank to take off my broken shoes. It would not do to get them wet – they were the only shoes I had. The brown water of the Groot Vis slipped smoothly over my feet as I waded across, cool as the water on my neck from the tap in the laundry at Cradock House.

Lindiwe was not at home when I arrived, so I sank down with my suitcase outside her hut, grateful for the chance to rest.

The hut was not far from the strict St James School, and from there came the sound of a choir singing *Panis Angelicus*. Then an African song with chanting and clapping. I should form a choir, too. I should help my children to sing and not just to dance to my piano.

Lindiwe's hut was newer than Auntie's, with a good thatch roof that seemed thicker than Auntie's and one small window cut in the side with a square of glass propped within its uneven edges. This meant the inside of the hut was lighter. Perhaps, I thought through my weariness, I could pay Lindiwe not only money for rent but also teach her to write without her needing to worry about paying me. That is what I could say to her when she saw me sitting outside her door. That could be my plan. A negotiation, I murmured to myself. Before I learnt the word from young Master Phil, I never realised how much of life seemed to revolve around negotiation.

Some barefoot boys in crumpled shirts and grey school shorts ran past, staring at me curiously, wondering why I sat clutching my child on the bare earth outside Lindiwe's hut in the growing cold of evening. A man and woman lurched away from the youngsters' path, and yelled after them but their voices were thick with drink and hardly carried. I looked away.

The choir-singing had stopped and the sun was moving down past the huts now, casting long shadows that painted the ground black behind them. The creeping shade took me back to the darkness of young Master Phil's bedroom, broken only by the bar of yellow sunlight that used to wander across the floor from the gap in the curtains. Once, when we'd been reading *Great Expectations*, the sunlight came and fell across his bed and he stretched his fingers into its yellowness and said I already knew what part of Pip he had inside himself. At the time, I never thought too hard about what he meant. I never felt it was my right to know. But maybe I should have done. Maybe if I had thought more deeply, I could have saved him.

'Oh sir,' I murmured, too tired to guard against the welling loneliness, 'forgive me.' Yet what risk would I have run to know such things? Even after all this time I cannot bring myself to accept what he might have meant. It is too dangerous, it takes what I did out of duty with Master and recasts it with Master Phil as something altogether different.

'Ada?' Lindiwe stood before me, shoulders bent under a heavy load, the muscles standing out on her arms and neck like thick cords.

'It will only be for a short while,' I said urgently, struggling to my feet. Dawn cried into the blanket on my back, then fell silent. 'I will pay you. And I will teach you everything I know for free.'

'Oh, Ada.' She slung down her load and sat down. I levered myself down beside her. This time she didn't avoid my eyes and I could see that hers were no longer uncertain, merely weary. 'How could I turn you away?' She motioned inside the hut. 'But it's so small.'

'Thank you,' I gasped and took her hand. 'God bless you! I will try not to be a burden.'

The tears that had stayed away since the early morning suddenly came back. And then Lindiwe leant against me and wept too, saying that she had hated herself all day for the manner in which she had greeted Dawn that morning.

'I don't know if I can do this,' I said, tears and relief mixed together. 'I have sinned against someone I love and I have made God the Father angry.'

'Hush,' murmured Lindiwe, stroking my arm. 'That is past. God will forgive if you serve Him through the child.' She paused and her forehead creased and I could tell she was searching for the right words like she used to during our lessons. 'God is not like the white man. He does not hate Dawn because of what you did.'

I thought about this for a while as darkness gathered about us and my body began to stiffen, and the sky deepened to an inky blue. It was what I hoped too. While I myself was perhaps forever flawed, I could still serve Him through Dawn. And whatever happened, God would not punish the child. But what of Madam? Even if I found a measure of forgiveness through Dawn, I could never receive it from Madam.

Candles began to flicker from nearby huts. A woman was singing to her child, *Thula thu'*, like Mama used to sing to me, like I would one day sing to Dawn. Back towards Bree Street, Cradock's electric lights beckoned through the bluegums and the pepper trees in front gardens. Madam would be sitting down in the lounge opposite Master. The light would be shining on the brooch she wore at her throat, perhaps the green one, perhaps – still – Master Phil's military badge.

'She's beautiful,' said Lindiwe, holding down a fold of the blanket and examining Dawn's sleeping face closely. 'One day you will be proud.'

Before Dawn was born, I was in the midst of a negotiation with my students. It was not a negotiation about money, like with Auntie, but about lessons. I needed to find a way to teach that went further than playing every noisy piece I knew. But I proceeded slowly, as young Master Phil had told me. Negotiations, even about things that don't involve money, take time. So I played and played, and waited for the day when they would be prepared to give me some quiet at the start of each lesson to talk about what lay behind the tunes they loved to dance to. That was the negotiation: a little teaching, in return for more jive.

But, as it turned out, I had no need for such tactics. Dawn proved to be the ultimate silencer. One look at the child's pale skin and all riotous behaviour ceased. 'Have you heard of a man called Beethoven?' I asked into the unexpected hush, playing the first bars of the *Eroica* symphony. They stared at me, they stared at one another, they peered furtively at the new baby on my back, and then they listened. They discovered that Beethoven had been deaf and yet still managed to make beautiful tunes. They also discovered that many musicians were as poor as they themselves were, and experienced hunger like they did, and found joy in music as they did. Many were outcasts among their own people. The colour of Dawn – herself an outcast – was somehow a backdrop to the stories I told, and to the tunes that brought the class alive at the end of each lesson.

So while I had feared jeering, it did not come about. Instead, Dawn provided both the lull and the spur to take my teaching to a new level. Now, I taught first and played afterwards – to a rapt audience. They accepted the new arrangement without objection.

After this success, I went further. Since hearing the St James choir, I began to play tunes that could be sung to. I would write the words on the blackboard before the children arrived in class, and leave them to sing along if they wished. Rousing pieces, like *Ode to Joy*, or lilting songs like the ones Madam used to sing about Ireland. At first they only danced. Then, later, they began to sing too. Roughly, wildly at first, then with more under-standing, even though, like me, they'd never seen the places we sang about.

'Oh Danny boy,' they crooned, discovering tenderness amidst the school's clamour, 'the pipes, the pipes are ca-a-lling . . .' The human voice is every bit as able as the body to take us to another place.

I was under no illusions. There was certainly gossip about me and some laughter behind my back. But in the classroom, where I could hold their attention, music occupied us more than the shame of a teacher who had sinned with a white man rather than with one of her own. As long as I could keep their interest with my stories and my playing, they overlooked the colour of the child. If only it had been so with Auntie. And with my colleagues on the staff.

The first year of Dawn's life coincided with a lack of rain. This took on a new meaning for me, beyond the brown dust and the shimmering heat and the worse-smelling latrines and the longer queues for water at the communal tap.

It meant that the drifts were open.

It meant that my journey to school from Lindiwe's hut in the township beyond Bree Street could be made across the Groot Vis at the drift. It required only for me to take off my shoes and wade across. It meant that although I now lived on the same side of the river as Master and Madam, there was little risk of them seeing me. I could stay well away from Bree, from Church Street where it ran down to the iron bridge, and Dundas Street beyond that, where Cradock House lay with its apricot tree that once carried me in its sap, and its wooden floors that once shone back at me as I polished them each week.

Yet even as I stayed out of sight, there was nowhere to hide my black skin. For around the time that Dawn was born, the people who ruled my country began to make many new laws in relation to skin. Some of them I knew about, like the ones that said black people were less important than white, and that you had to be born in a place or have lived there a long time before you would be allowed to stay. One law that I didn't know said it was illegal for a white man and a black women to lie together.

I already suspected that such a lying together was not right in the eyes of God but I learnt only later that it was against the law of the land and that, if discovered, you could go to jail. I wonder if Master knew of this law when he stood in the doorway of my room at Cradock House and said he would not hurt me? If so, why did he take such a risk? Was the loneliness in him so great that he was prepared to risk even the white man's jail – and the shame that would fall on him and on Madam? Perhaps, therefore, it was a good thing for him that I left.

Mama had always said that jail could reach out and take you even if you had done no wrong. As I grew up I used to doubt if that was true, but perhaps Mama was wiser than I realised. She knew what was coming. For with these new laws, jail now had the right to do so. You did not need to be a bad person to be sent there, you did not even have to do anything wrong, you just had to be someone of the wrong colour. The policemen that cruised the township in their vans knew this.

The arrival of Dawn with her coloured skin amidst such new laws presented a dilemma for my fellow teachers. It was bad enough that black people were beaten for the smallest offence, and suddenly forbidden to enter certain places or sit on certain benches – there were now 'Whites Only' signs in the Karoo Gardens – and unable to move away to work just because they wanted to. But now they faced the difficulty of having to take sides over a mixed-race baby. Our once happy staffroom became divided territory. Silas would arrive early, turn his back on me and gather about him those who agreed I should leave rather than advertise my betrayal of fellow blacks daily via the pale child. Into my corner, however, strode the colourfully turbaned Dina – after initial dismay – and the quiet Sipho Mhlase who taught numbers. Dina was sure I must have been the victim of a wicked man. I had shown courage in not pleading for help – shades of not grovelling – therefore I deserved support. At the worst of this time, I wondered if it might be best to stay away from the staffroom altogether. It was Lindiwe who talked me out of it.

'You have to fight!' she said to me in the candlelight of her tiny hut as we ate soup one night. 'Hold your head up and they will respect you.'

Through this difficulty, Mr Dumise trod a careful path. He had no grounds to dismiss me because my teaching was popular and I was never absent from school.

'But look at the example she sets for our students!' retorted Silas.

'Have you no pity?' I heard the headmaster say softly. 'She was no doubt raped.'

'She deceived us!' Silas went on heatedly. 'She should have said she was having a coloured child when she applied for the job.'

Chapter 28

I played the Raindrop *today and it brought back memories of Ada.*

As I expected, there was nothing to be found about her on my trip to KwaZakhele, not from the minister, or from the site of dear Miriam's grave in a cemetery of the utmost starkness.

Such was the poverty and deprivation of the place that I came back determined to do something – not in KwaZakhele, for that is too far away – but here in Cradock. We sit across the river from a township where the people must be equally wretched. Unlike KwaZakhele, they do not even have a church. I believe they meet outdoors on Sundays at the foot of a koppie.

And as for Ada, I still feel she is alive. I sense her every time I play. But as the months turn into years I am less hopeful of seeing her again.

The township beyond Bree turned out to be different from Auntie's Lococamp community. It was not a jumble of huts and a tangle of alleys with no order to it. This place had been laid out with roads that were intended to be straight, and schools and playing fields that encouraged healthy minds and muscles. Good behaviour comes from such a combination. At St James School the children wore their uniforms proudly, and played football, or sang in the choir I'd heard that first day. This township had pride. Even the mayor sometimes listened to Rev. Calata when he spoke out against the police that careered along the rutted streets and threw residents in jail for no reason other than the matter of skin. Indeed, Rev. Calata used to say, why should such a place not think of itself as part of Cradock, subject to the same laws and benefits? In contrast, Auntie's township over the Groot Vis had grown up on its own and knew itself to be separate and unworthy.

But sadly, at the time I arrived, I could see that much of what had been planned was falling into the kind of disrepair I knew so well from across the river. The straight roads reeked from overflowing latrines. Rubbish that was once collected now piled up to attract flies, and illness followed toddlers that played in it. Paint peeled from the impressive walls of St James School, and the grass on the sports grounds withered from missing care and water. The soup kitchens that used to feed the poor were manned less often now, and I even heard talk about the taking of money from the *shebeens* into the bank account of the town council to pay for white services, instead of black. I wondered if Master knew of this, if Master approved of such theft. There were also signs that the well-behaved children were starting to run wild like the youngsters across the river.

Down on the riverbank, the women that I thought were my friends now steered clear of me – probably warned by Auntie – and tried to turn their backs on Lindiwe as well. Their views were a mixture of what I faced at school. Like Silas, they believed I had deceived them – and, more importantly, Auntie – by keeping quiet about the colour of the coming child. Like Veronica and Mildred, some would not condemn me to my face but rather avoided my eyes and took their washing to a distant rock. Others never spoke to me again. The low singing that I loved now came from further away.

Lindiwe even had to reassure some that I would have nothing to do with their washing. I could tell she was worried and I used to ask her at the end of each day if she had had enough business and whether she wanted me to leave.

'Stay,' she would say with a weary sigh as she stretched out on her bed and closed her eyes for a rest before our simple evening meal. 'It will be all right.' Between those of her customers who stayed faithful and the money I paid to her in rent – I willingly gave her more than I had paid Auntie – she kept going and after a while there were no more questions of Lindiwe, although I myself was never particularly welcome on the riverbank.

As the washerwomen turned away from me, so did others. There was no invitation to return to the church on the *koppie*, where vibrant singing swept over the polished stones and far into the Karoo veld. I could go to St James Church now, with its disciplined choir and its carved cross above the pulpit, but I still missed those Sunday mornings outdoors – I even missed the minister with his wild talk of a war of liberation, and the joyous chants of the congregation in response. Joining their soaring hymns had bound me to a new family. Not since Cradock House had I felt such a sense of belonging – even though some of what they said frightened me – and such a sense of escape.

For this new belonging was indeed a kind of escape. As I sang, it lifted me out of the township, it freed me to roam across the veld in my mind, like I used to imagine from Master Phil's toy box on the top floor of Cradock House. It showed me the brown desert floor rearing up to the mountains where there was snow in winter, it let me trace the first shining trickles of water that fed the Groot Vis. It even flew me to another desert where Master Phil lay beneath the palms of an oasis. To belong – and yet to be alone under a seamless sky – surely this was a gift from

God? A gift to replace the house and garden of my childhood? A gift to replace the people who were once my horizon?

When I missed this belonging-yet-aloneness, I would put Dawn on my back and walk out of the new township towards where the sky met the earth, for the pleasure of being on my own and yet part of a company with the birds and the small animals that scurried about us. When the sun was at its highest, Dawn and I would squat in the bony shade of a thorn tree and I would describe to her that other thorn tree I'd first met as a child. The air trembled not with the outdoor church's massed singing but with the heat of the veld as it stretched into watery mirages far ahead.

'Look, Dawn,' I whispered, pointing into the distance, 'the land is melting.'

In the township beyond Bree I learnt that there were times when it wasn't possible to run away. I learnt that there were times when violence had to be met with violence. I'm not proud of this knowledge; it's something I wish I had never learnt. For once you let it in, it's possible you may use it without reason. And what God the Father thought of this knowledge, I do not know. But then, I do not know what God the Father thought about the random cruelty of the white policemen that patrolled our streets either.

This knowledge concerned men in particular. I learnt to be especially careful with men. I got to know the alleys where men lived who assumed – because of the difference in colour between my child and me – that I did not care who I lay with and would do so again for money or under threat.

When I confessed my fear to Lindiwe, she pulled something slender and pointed from beneath her bed and held it out to me. It was a sharpened bicycle spoke. I didn't want to take it.

'No,' I whispered, horrified by its evil thinness, the intent of its pointed end.

'Like this, Ada.' Lindiwe ignored me and demonstrated in the dark of the hut. 'Thrust inwards and upwards for the heart.'

'I can't.'

'You must.' She held it out to me. 'Take it. I have another one.'

At first I wouldn't carry it. I didn't think I had the courage to use such a thing. I feared that God would not forgive me a second sin. But then one day I saw a young woman dragged away before my eyes and I ran back to the hut to fetch it from where it hid beneath my sleeping blanket.

In my old life on Dundas Street I could never have imagined defending myself like this but here, with Dawn vulnerable on my back, I knew I wouldn't hesitate.

For times when bicycle-spoke defence was not needed, Lindiwe had contacts. These contacts, I discovered, were good for all sorts of things. The bread seller that she used – unlike the old man who sold to Auntie and Poppie – could supply milk as well, and at a price that allowed us to buy one bottle a week. It meant that for half the week we could have milk in our tea. Then there was the woman that stacked shelves at N.C. Rogers General Dealers on Market Square. She often found spare maize meal that she sold to Lindiwe for less than the *spaza* store in the township charged. Sometimes a twist of sugar appeared in the same packet as the meal. Lindiwe gave this woman a very good washing service.

Lindiwe explained that you did not need to work with money in order to make a living. You just needed to find people that had goods that you wanted, and then offer them goods or services in return. The hardest part was deciding the value of each side of the trade. How many loads of washing should

Lindiwe give for a five-pound pack of mealie meal and a tin of tea? Tea was also spare at the store, it seemed.

Lindiwe also had a brother. At first I was not sure what he was good for – other than words – but he never arrived empty handed. Often, though, what he said made you forget about what he had brought. This was unusual in the township where outside goods were highly prized and far more valuable than words.

'This is Jake,' she said to me one evening when a short man stepped silently through the door as we were practising her reading. They hugged and murmured together before he shook my hand in the African way and stared at Dawn in her wash basket. He was some years older than Lindiwe and wore a tattered jacket over trousers held up with string. He had his sister's bright, inquisitive eyes. Like hers, they were also able to see inside people.

'Lindiwe says you teach. It must be hard.' He glanced across at Dawn's pale face above her blanket.

'Yes,' I said. 'Some teachers understand, some want me to leave.' It was odd to hear myself speak with a stranger so soon about something so important. But that was what Jake did. He didn't waste time on matters that others spent hours upon. And he took you along with him in his manner of speaking.

'What will you do?' he asked, as if he had known me all my life and not just a few minutes in the hut of his sister.

'I shall stay,' I said, relieved to find I could say the words strongly, 'as long as they let me. They like my teaching. And I fill in when other teachers are absent. Our school is not as big as St James.'

'You're reliable.' He nodded. 'We need reliable people.' He glanced across at Lindiwe, then pulled a brown paper bag out of his pocket and handed it to her. She unwrapped it quickly, her fingers eager, like Madam's fingers used to be eager to play the piano before young Master Phil went to war.

'Where did you get this?' She gasped and showed me four sausages nestling in the bottom of the bag. She sniffed. 'And so fresh!'

Jake smiled. Lindiwe looked at him with suspicion.

'I found them,' he said, grinning. 'They were spare at the butcher.'

'The butcher on Church Street?' The words were out before I could help it. The bright eyes of Lindiwe and her brother turned on me. Lindiwe believed I had come from KwaZakhele. I had always said that I did not know Cradock well.

'I once walked past that butcher,' I said, shrugging. 'On my way here from KwaZakhele.'

It was only a small lie, just like the ones I had told Auntie when I said I was tired of working across the Groot Vis. Or when I lied to Mr Dumise about my real name. It was just one more lie to protect myself and Madam and Master, especially since the law meant jail if you were caught.

'It is a good butcher,' said her brother, watching me carefully. 'The white man there charges a fair price.'

I could see them wondering, as Mr Dumise had wondered, about the father of my child, as anyone who met me seemed bound to wonder about the father of my child. Any white man – even a butcher – was a possibility. I wanted to say: it's not what you think. I do not even know that man! When I asked for Jacob Mfengu – Jacob Mfengu who might have married me – I asked the black man who is his assistant. I do not even remember what that white man looks like.

'Ada?' Lindiwe put her hand on my arm, sensing my panic. 'Let's cook the sausages now, while Jake's here.'

'Yes,' I said, getting up hurriedly to light her paraffin stove. 'Yes, I will do that while you and Jake talk.'

Even with Lindiwe who had remained my friend, who had taken Dawn and me into her hut and shared her life with us, even with Lindiwe I must guard what I say. One careless word about my old life and it would suddenly find me. And find the shame that I carried with me.

The sausages hissed in the pan and gave off glistening beads of fat. I warmed some leftover maize meal alongside them, letting the sausage juices mingle with the stiff meal and crisp its edges. Lindiwe and Jake talked quietly but sometimes fiercely in the candlelight – several times I saw Lindiwe shake her head at something he said. I thought of what he'd said about me being 'reliable' and that 'we' needed reliable people. Usually I understood what black people meant when they spoke. They did not use words that took different moods upon themselves. But Jake was not talking about my dependability as a teacher. He was talking of something else, some cause that lay beyond my work. Something that lived underground and drove men like him to meet in secret to plan what they called a Revolution.

I'd only ever heard this word since coming to live in the new township, and so I looked it up in the dictionary at school and found it was related to liberation. Liberation – what the minister at the outdoor church said would happen once we'd been through the fire and found freedom. I already knew that this liberation did not always mean peace. Revolution, I discovered, was not so unsure of itself. Revolution was liberation with blood. Revolution didn't care for any half measures. And it was not concerned with what came after.

'Be careful,' said Lindiwe when it was time for her brother to leave.

'Good luck, Ada,' he said, taking my hand in the African handshake. 'I will see you again.' He turned to hug his sister.

'Be careful,' repeated Lindiwe, watching him as he stepped through the doorway and melted into the darkness of the township streets. Jake was always quiet like that. You never heard him arrive and you never saw him once he was beyond the door. I wonder if he was the one who taught Lindiwe how to use a sharpened bicycle spoke.

Chapter 29

I am the black woman with the coloured child. Everybody knows me, even in this place where I am a newcomer. Even so I am lonely. Such loneliness, I have discovered, does not yield when a future beckons. The birth of Dawn meant I was up at night to feed her, and in the dark of the hut a hollowness plucked away at me. If only I could heal my heart, if only I could tell someone about Master Phil – and what might have happened if I'd realised his love for me was not that of a brother towards his sister . . .

The only time this loneliness faded was when I played for my students and let the music carry me away. But then, cruelly, it lay in wait for my return and tricked me into remembering once more. The 'Township Bach' narrowed into the whoop of an owl outside Master Phil's bedroom, or the sweet soprano of Madam as she sang notes for me to find on the piano. When I walked with Dawn through the Karoo scrub I saw, instead of the crouching plants, Madam's favourite pink roses in a vase on her dressing table and smelt their perfume as clearly as I could read the pages of her special book. Memories never fade, they simply hide, only to emerge greater in number and intensity, and fresh as when I first made them.

I also don't belong here yet. And those who don't belong can find themselves used by those who do. If you have stepped out of your place in the world, if you have sinned against your fellows, you must expect to be a target. You must expect to be used by others for their own purposes, for their own causes. In this case, the protest against Passes. I myself had only ever been asked for my Pass twice on the streets of Cradock, but in Johannesburg – maybe on account of all the gold in the ground – it happened all the time. Maybe it was to do with money. Maybe white people in Johannesburg felt there was not enough gold to go around and so they wished to send some black people away and keep the riches for themselves. Maybe the business with Passes was just an excuse. Maybe riches from the ground were for a white future only.

Whatever the case, I was very nervous of anything to do with Passes, given my lack of one in Mary Hanembe's name, and the fact that the one in my own name had not been signed since I left Cradock House. There were more police in the new township. More police with shorter tempers and growling dogs that strained at their leashes. More police to ask to see your Pass and throw you in jail if it was missing, or unsigned.

Silas wanted to protest against Passes.

'We'll march from the school across the Groot Vis, up Church Street to the town hall!' he announced, waving his arms during teatime. 'We'll show strength in numbers! The St James teachers will join us – the choir will be there.'

The town hall! The Karoo Gardens where I used to sit on a bench beside the aloes, warming my feet in the sun! But it was too far, there would be too many eyes watching.

'And after we're at the town hall?' asked someone.

'We hand in a petition about how we hate the *dompas*, then march back the same way,' Silas said, searching through the staff with a determined eye. The jazz man waved his fist in the air like the congregation on the *koppie* had done. Mr Dumise frowned.

'What about you, Mary?' Silas's smooth tone caught me. 'Where do you belong on this?'

The room turned to look at me.

I wanted to say that this was not a matter of belonging, but rather a matter of singling out. Of finding another means to show that I didn't belong at the school, and never would. And that it had less to do with a march about Passes, and more to do with punishing me for lying with a white man.

Silas waited, as all enemies do, with a smile on his lips.

'Members of staff must make their own choice,' came the voice of Mr Dumise, quietly but clearly from his position at the teapot. 'It is a personal matter.'

'Then let's hear Mary's personal opinion,' interrupted Silas on a rising note.

I could tell some of my colleagues thought Silas had indeed pushed into a place that had nothing to do with Passes. Hold up your head, I told myself sternly, remembering Lindiwe's words. Hold it up and maybe they will respect you for that.

'I will not put my child at risk,' I declared, forcing my voice to be firm.

Silas hesitated, then turned away with a flash of irritation and called for a show of hands in favour. A few arms went up, but only reluctantly.

'No matter,' he said defiantly, making a fuss of slapping the back of the jazz man and the few others in favour. 'We'll go ahead anyway. We'll show the marchers from St James that we're united!'

I met Mr Dumise's glance across the room. Church Street and Market Square was a boundary I dared not cross.

My lessons finished soon after the meeting. I set off for Lindiwe's hut through the usual packed streets and then across the drift at Cross Street with the water cool on my bare feet.

'Ada?' A small man suddenly appeared at my shoulder, from the shade of the mimosas. He walked just behind me, alongside Dawn in her blanket. It was Lindiwe's brother, Jake.

'What did they decide?' he asked into my ear. His rough jacket brushed my arm.

'What do you mean?'

'At your staff meeting. What did the staff decide?' Dawn shifted on my back at his voice. Dawn loved Jake, for he swung her over his head, or sometimes brought her a tiny toy he'd carved himself. Dawn was not the only one he treated kindly. Sometimes he brought me an apple, or the latest newspaper.

'How do you know about the meeting?' I stopped. He fell back into the hurrying masses and motioned for me to go on.

'What did they decide?' he repeated, when I had carried on walking.

'There weren't many in favour,' I said. I looked round for him but he was gone, swallowed up. I wished he would stay for once, and talk about normal things. I liked Jake, and I think he liked me.

I pushed on, my head filled with thoughts of Passes and divided staffrooms and Jake, who knew other people's business before they knew it themselves. A woman who was the mother of one of my students nodded to me. I smiled back. Increasingly, there were some who were prepared to know me to my face. I'd come to value every tiny nod or half-smile even if they never went so far as to speak to me.

It was a start. One day they would know me for what I was. One day they would see past the difference in colour between my child and me. If God the Father could not bring it about, then I would make it happen on my own.

Dawn became ill and stopped drinking from me. Not in the way young Master Phil was ill as a child, after eating too many apricots from the garden, but in another way where she coughed and shook in her wash basket on the floor of Lindiwe's hut and her normally pale cheeks turned red. I held her in my arms and rushed across the drift – not bothering to take off my shoes – to the kind doctor's tiny house. From further up the river I heard someone shout my name, and from even further away came snatches of women singing over their washing.

'Please!' I pushed past the queue and called out to him where he tended to an old man. 'Please help me.'

He nodded and pointed for me to sit on the floor alongside several other women with babies. I squeezed into a space. Dawn cried and coughed, her skin fiery to the touch. My shoes oozed river water. The women looked at me, and stared at Dawn's skin but said nothing out of sympathy for the child's condition. If only I could go somewhere and not feel I had to apologise for her. For me . . .

He was gentle with her when he got to me. He used the round metal thing that I had seen Dr Wilmott use on young Master Phil. He looked inside her mouth and I remembered the sickness that happened at the end of the drought when people's throats turned white and they died, and I prayed that God the Father would not punish Dawn like that for my sin.

'Do you have money?' he asked, pulling her vest down gently over her chest when he had finished.

'Why, sir?'

'She needs special medicine,' he said. 'I don't have such

medicine but I can write a letter for you to get the medicine at the chemist in town. But it will cost money.'

'You have no medicine for her?'

He looked at me. 'None of it is strong enough.'

Dawn coughed and coughed, her tiny chest heaving, her eyes streaming. The women around me murmured and shook their heads. More patients peered through the door.

'Write me the letter,' I said, fighting tears. 'I shall find the money.'

He handed Dawn back to me and began to write.

'Will they give me the medicine if the child and I have a difference of skin?'

People gasped, but the doctor put a hand on my shoulder as he gave me the paper for the medicine. 'They will give it. Be brave. Next, please.'

I ran again along the dirt streets and again across the Groot Vis. Below the drift, the river narrowed into a brown channel between shallow pools. Holding Dawn's hot body against my shoulder, I thrust past people and goats and women like Lindiwe with loads on their heads or shoulders. Some shouted at me. I listened to no one. Back at Lindiwe's hut I laid Dawn on the floor. Then I pulled open my case and grabbed all the money that I had hidden at the bottom – money from my wages that I was saving to buy Dawn some shoes one day, or to buy a new overall, or to pay Lindiwe if her business suffered on account of me. Dawn screamed, my hands shook, my heart seized with fear of going into the chemist where someone might see me, where the man who made the medicine might refuse us after all.

I pulled a cloth from Lindiwe's washing to wind over my hair and forehead and partly across my cheeks, and an extra nappy to cover Dawn's face, then ran down Bree Street past Madam and Master's church and then to the place where Bree joined Church

Street and changed its name to Dundas, where my child and I would be plain for all to see. It had been more than a year of Dawn's life since I left Cradock House. To my left, down on the riverbank, the mimosas and the bluegums still dug for water where Master Phil and I had once walked. Further away, the iron bridge still shuddered with fine motor cars coming and going to the station, and with the quieter footsteps of black people carrying suitcases and babies on their backs as they had done more than a year ago. I kept my head down, and pressed Dawn into my shoulder. Yet her cries rang out, and people – white and black – turned to stare at me and whisper amongst themselves. Cries that must surely carry to Cradock House and give us away. Pray, I told myself fiercely, pray that no one turns round and knows who you are. Pray that Master and Madam are at home, pray that Master is seeing to his papers in the study, pray that Madam is practising on the piano and does not hear . . .

The chemist was the same one where Miss Rose had bought red lipstick before she left for Johannesburg and the trouble that would find her there. There was now a separate door where black people queued and the two women already waiting hissed at the sound of Dawn's coughing and allowed me in front of them. The separate door might save me, I realised, for it led into a room closed off from the rest of the chemist and only contained a small window into the place where the chemist mixed his medicines. A white person in the main part of the shop would not see me where I stood.

It took some time before a man appeared in the window. He was wearing a white coat and I remembered him from a time when Madam had asked me to fetch a parcel for her. I'm sure he did not know me. He had a strong face, this man. A face that would show exactly what he thought, like Lindiwe's face always showed intent, like Master Phil's face showed war and love.

'Yes?'

I handed him the letter. He looked at the covered bundle that was Dawn coughing in my arms. Her face was hidden beneath the cloth and he could not have seen the difference in skin.

'Do you have money to pay?'

I felt in the pockets of my overall and pulled out all the coins that I possessed and laid them in a heap on the small counter beneath the window. Some of the coins were rubbed smooth and I wondered if coins wore out and if he would find them too old to exchange for medicine.

'I hope this will be enough, sir,' I said, trying to keep my voice and my hands steady. 'It is all that I have.'

He did not count it but just ran his eyes over the pile and then over me. 'It will be enough. Sit down,' he motioned to a low chair in the corner, 'and I will make it for you.'

When he returned, he brought a bottle and a spoon with him. He explained that I needed to give Dawn a spoonful of the medicine in the morning, at midday and in the evening until the bottle was finished.

'If you don't finish the medicine, the child will become sick again,' he warned. Then he said he had another medicine that he would give Dawn now that would help her until the first medicine started working.

'For the same money?' I asked.

He nodded. 'Yes, for the same money. Now unwrap the child,' he said.

I stared at him. Unwrap her? Then he would see her face fully, then he would know my shame and he might refuse to give us the medicine after all.

'Sir,' I said, slowly taking the cloth off Dawn's face and unwrapping the blanket from her hot body, 'the child is innocent.'

The chemist stood on his side of the window and I stood on mine, holding my coloured child between us. Dawn had lost weight and her pale legs, once free of the blanket, kicked only feebly. He looked with his strong face from me to the child, then picked up the spoon and filled it with red liquid from a large bottle he took down from a nearby shelf.

'This will bring down her temperature.' His voice was quiet, like young Master Phil's used to be quiet when he talked in the darkness of his bedroom. 'It will calm her so that the other medicine can do its work.'

He leant forward and I held Dawn out to him. Carefully he tipped the liquid into her mouth in stages, waiting for her to swallow each dribble. I stroked her arms and whispered to her and she fixed her blue eyes on the spoon as it approached her mouth. Her chest shuddered from past crying. Then the chemist shook the first bottle with Dawn's medicine and gave her a spoonful of that as well.

'Now,' he said, 'listen carefully. The next spoon must be tonight.'

'I understand, sir. And then three times each day until it is finished.'

He tightened the cap on the bottle and turned away to rinse out the spoon in a basin. Then he put the spoon and the bottle into a brown paper bag and gave it to me.

'Your English is very good,' he said, like Mr Dumise had said when I asked for a job.

I looked away from him and down at Dawn. I wanted no talk of where I had learnt such English. Dawn's eyes looked back at me, calmer now, and these days no longer milky with babyhood but made of a clear, blue light. The eyes of young Master Phil. Also, I realised suddenly, the eyes of her father as a young man.

'I am grateful, sir, for your help. Do you need all of this

money?' It was still lying in a heap on the counter. The chemist spread it out with his fingers and took some of it.

'No,' he said, clearing his throat. 'There is some change.'

I stared down at what he had left. He had left some of the more valuable coins for me to take back. I looked up at him and in that moment I think he knew. Knew that this child sprang from one of his patients, someone he knew, a home where I had been taught English, a family that I had run from. Knew, also, that this was all the money I had in the world.

'Thank you, sir.'

'The child will be fine in a few days,' he said, watching me.

I could feel his eyes on my neck as I left, like the eyes of the congregation on me when I sat at the front of the church beside Madam and Master for young Master Phil's funeral. But the chemist's eyes were kinder than the eyes of the congregation. He had seen my sin but did not condemn.

Chapter 30

Maybe there was more to Dawn's escape from illness, and my escape from being seen in town, than powerful medicine and good luck. The minister on the *koppie* always said that God the Father had a plan for each of us, however much we disappointed Him. Sometimes I thought I could see a part of it just out of reach, like the mirage I'd show Dawn as it hovered across the veld at midday. Even though I'd sinned, it seemed He still cared for me and protected me, especially where it touched Dawn. Her survival therefore required my own, and perhaps this was the plan. And so when Dawn was better, I put her on my back, waded through the drift, and gratefully returned to the piano that was my refuge, and to the demands of my students who had missed their daily ration of jive and Beethoven.

Slowly the days began to settle into a steady, though savage, rhythm. I let the good things in, and fended off the bad as much as I could, for apartheid was closing its vice upon the township and making men on both sides do things that God the Father surely disapproved of. It was becoming a war, and like in all wars there are shortages of love and food but not of smoke and blood, and there are friends that might turn out to be enemies-in-waiting. Sometimes I thought I saw Jake near where baying youngsters threw stones at the police, or in the shadows by the beer hall, or with groups of older men around a street fire at night. I never called out to him, and he never showed that he saw me, even though he would appear at my side in daylight near the Groot Vis and pull faces to make Dawn laugh while the river rippled about our feet. This was the future: from the dangerous streets that bore me from hut to school and back again, to the 'Township Bach' whose clashing strains accompanied me wherever I went. It was messy, it was spirited; it must be seized if God's plan was to work. This was His gift to me. But these words don't tell of the unspoken need to be on guard for my child's life throughout each hour of the day. Trouble lurked at every step, and avoiding it could only be achieved if the threat was spotted early enough. One hand on my child's shoulder, one hand on the bicycle spoke in my pocket, both eyes alert to the unexpected move. I am ashamed to say it was not always easy to think of it as a gift.

So I turned my head away from the actions of those like Jake and Silas who wanted not just liberation but revolution as well. There could be no place for me in that kind of war if I was to serve God the Father by keeping my child safe. I began to set aside some coins once more from my wages to save for Dawn's first shoes now that she was almost walking, although my most urgent task was to train her to sit quietly by the piano while I played for daily assembly.

'This is a special day,' announced Mr Dumise one morning in the months after Dawn's illness. The staff on the stage nodded to one another and leant sideways to look past the curtains into the wings.

The high windows were open and I could hear familiar shouting on the street outside and, from further away, the sudden moo of a cow. There were a few cows in the township, brought there with difficulty by workers off farms, but they struggled to survive on the harsh scrub and usually died.

'From time to time we receive money for books from generous supporters of our school. This is one of those times.' He held up his hand to stop the enthusiastic clapping. I put a finger to my lips to hush Dawn into silence. She loved to clap along with the children. She stared up at me with huge blue eyes, and put her thumb in her mouth.

'We are honoured to have with us today the person who has led this donation.'

He turned aside and motioned someone forward. Mr Dumise was very good in this respect. He often invited visitors to the school, ignoring the sighs of Silas who thought our needs would be better met by noisy demands rather than quiet persuasion. Mr Dumise said it was to do with raising something he called a 'profile'. I had looked up the word but I was more used to it in its other form, where it meant a picture of you sideways on. It was a good word, I thought, for me to add to Lindiwe's list of words that took different moods.

I glanced up.

It was the cream day dress that I saw first. Then the slender arms and strong hands that I remembered so well and the soft brown hair in a bun. Madam stood tall and dignified against the drooping red curtains, and smiled down at the youngsters. Mr Dumise said more words and there was more clapping. I reached down with urgent hands and pushed Dawn between the legs of the piano stool.

Oh Madam, please look away, please do not see me, or the child! Please don't hold Cradock House in front of me once more . . .

'Miss Hanembe! Miss Hanembe, the march!'

I stared at the piano, my fingers frozen into a hardness to

equal the stained ivory keys. The tentative, hard-fought rhythm of our lives, the fragile hope of a future – even the many deceptions – hung ready to be torn away.

But it would not do to show this in front of Mr Dumise and the staff.

And Madam.

Once again I must harden my heart, I must hide what I feel, I must hide as much as possible. I reached for the tune in my head and forced my stiff fingers over the keys and began to play. The piano heard me and poured out its music. The children streamed out of the hall, the staff followed them. I kept my head down and played Chopin's *Military Polonaise* and my fingers followed what they knew for my eyes were blind with tears. I played it again and again until the notes echoed through the empty hall.

'Ada?' she called over the music.

I stopped and looked up. She was standing on the bare stage next to Mr Dumise. Her cream leather shoes, I could make out from my place at the piano, were rimmed with dust from walking through the scuffed earth of the playground. They would need polishing.

She held out her arms and said once more, 'Dear Ada.'

Mr Dumise looked from Madam to me and I saw understanding in his look – and something else I could not quite read – and then he turned quietly and left the hall.

I got up off the stool and stepped up on to the stage where Madam put her arms around me and hugged me like the time she did when Mama died and the doctor closed Mama's eyes in death. Over the smell of the mildewed curtains I picked up the old scent of flowers on Madam's skin, and felt the familiar softness of her dress against me.

'Why, Ada, why? Why did you leave us?' She was laughing a

little now, through her own tears. She had not yet seen Dawn. She had not yet found out that her husband had sinned and that I had sinned. 'We've missed you so!'

I couldn't find any words. I have always liked to prepare sentences for important times, like when I asked Mr Dumise for a job, although sometimes I forget what I have learnt and say more than I intend. But now, with Madam looking down at me with such kindness and with such misplaced relief, I found myself with no words at all.

'Mama?'

It was Dawn who found the words.

It was Dawn who told Madam what she didn't yet know.

Dawn had pulled herself up on the side of the piano stool and stood there unsteadily, perfect pale skin gleaming, the blue eyes of her father wide and questioning.

I watched Madam.

I heard her gasp, I saw confusion in her face, then shock, then I saw the recognition wash over it in waves, like the rising waters of the Groot Vis in flood. Her pale skin flushed. She turned back to me and I could see her fighting what she feared was the truth.

'You must leave us.' I found my voice. 'Please, Madam, you must leave us here and say nothing.'

It was the first time that I spoke to Madam as one woman to another, rather than as a servant or a pupil. And I saw her recognise it.

'But Ada—'

'It is better this way.'

She stood before me and I could see her tallness begin to wilt, like I'd longed to bend on the day that Dawn was born and Auntie had thrown us out. I could see the awful truth begin to make itself at home in her and I prayed that God the

Father would comfort her, for I never meant her to be hurt like this.

Oh God, forgive me.

Madam, forgive me, although I know you never can.

If only I could find a way to say that I did what I did out of duty.

I reached out and took her arm – I had never touched Madam in this way before – and led her to one of the hard chairs on the stage. She sat down and folded her hands in her lap, the knuckles as white as on the day the doctor saw Master Phil and told him that he couldn't do any more for him. Her hair was no longer completely brown but had flecks of silver at the temples. Young Master Phil's military brooch gleamed at her throat. From down by the piano, Dawn began to whimper.

'You must go home, Madam.' I bent down to her urgently. 'You must forget this day.'

'It's your home, too.' She looked up at me, eyes sore and weeping.

'I am grateful for everything you taught me, but it's better for me here.' My voice shook as I lied once more.

I turned away from Madam who I loved even more than Mama, and went down the steps and gathered Dawn in my arms and left through the side door.

Chapter 31

The march to the town hall had taken place while Dawn was ill. Jake told me this when he appeared through the doorway one night with an egg for Dawn.

'It was a start,' he said, with a shrug. 'We must organise better next time.' He touched Dawn's cheek as she lay sleeping, then squeezed my hand and was gone.

Dina said afterwards that only about half the staff had taken part, on account of the sirens echoing across the river at the time the march was to start. I'd heard them as well, from Lindiwe's hut where Dawn slept from the medicine that was making her better. I heard, too, the noise from St James School, as their group were broken up by the police before they could get along Bree Street. The screech of car tyres on gravel, the barking of dogs, the brave chants dying in the Karoo air to leave a loaded silence that hung over the township all day.

'Even the St James choir,' muttered Dina. 'The police stopped the choir and arrested the choirmaster!'

Several of our teachers began to drift away as Silas's small group headed across the Groot Vis and up Church Street.

'We went fast, for the streets were empty,' Dina said with a toss of her turban, 'but they were waiting for us at the town hall.'

Silas had planned a speech and then the handing over of the petition, but it never happened. Instead, several large white policemen piled out of their vans and began slapping their truncheons in the palms of their hands. Silas tried to enter the town hall but his way was barred. At this, the remaining staff took fright and ran back to school. Only Silas and the jazz man left at walking pace, Dina sheltered between them.

Dina said many white people watched. She said it was only the presence of the white people watching that stopped the police from using their weapons. I did not meet her eyes when she said this. It made no difference. Madam now knew where I was. She had seen Dawn, she knew my shame. And I had left her alone with this knowledge on a dusty stage in an empty hall with mildewed curtains. I am not proud of that, and I cried inside as I carried Dawn away, but what could I do? The pain for Madam would be far greater if it became known that her maid had lain with her husband and borne him a child with pale skin and his own blue eyes. If Auntie shrank from the knowledge of a relative that was not black, if people on the streets of the township turned their faces away, how much worse would it be for Madam – and Madam's friends – to accept a child that was not white? Dawn fell in between. She pleased no one, she was at home nowhere but with me, and one day she might even reject that. I had been foolish enough to bring a coloured child into a world where black and white were the only alternatives. In the white world, she could even be used against Master to send him to jail. Did Madam realise that?

But if she did as I asked and went home and said nothing, she could escape the shame. She could even fool her heart into thinking it was a dream, or a nightmare – like my fear of Dawn being seized by the car with the eyes of night animals. She could pretend she never saw me, that the brown upright piano with the bad keys remained silent, that the child with the coloured skin and the blue eyes did not exist. She could instead take comfort in Cradock House. It would not fall, it would stand as sturdy as it had ever been. The apricot tree that once carried me in its sap would bloom and make fruit for jam, the red tin roof would thunder with hail every year or two, the beautiful Zimmerman would sound to the music of Grieg and Debussy, and Madam would continue with Master as before. Only her diary might know the truth.

I have learnt many things in my life and understood only some of them: inside wounds, a future that arrives unexpectedly and cannot be bought, words that mean different things when grouped together, trouble that leaves one place only to search for a new home. All these things, it seems to me, gather themselves into a greater knowing or unknowing that cleverer people than me call wisdom. What wisdom I had found told me that Madam should turn away and go back to Cradock House, and I should turn away and go back to Lindiwe's hut. That would be the end of it.

It has been a month since I found Ada.

There are many truths that I have had to accept and suppress – for the moment.

The worst of them are hard even to write down.

I must record at the outset, though, that I believe Ada has been an innocent victim. Edward took advantage of a sheltered young woman for his own pleasure. Witness his insistence that I stop looking for her.

And the outcome of his guilt lies in the innocent eyes of a child. And such eyes – the eyes of Edward as they once were, the eyes of my beloved Phil who is no more.

In the time since, I have wandered the house. I have endured tea parties. I have been civil to Edward. I have sent cheerful letters to Rosemary in her latest crisis. I have played our piano and wept at the memory of Ada fighting through Chopin on an instrument so battered she had to improvise around defective keys.

And I have visited the library.

I have read up on the laws of parliament: the Immorality Act, the Mixed Marriages Act. I am discovering that what I feared years ago when I was refused a place for Ada at the children's school on account of her colour has come true.

We have allowed the creation of a divided land. And Cradock House lies along its fault lines.

Chapter 32

Madam came on a hot afternoon.

The latrines smelt bad, flies settled on rubbish in the streets and the heat rolled over the township in pressing waves. Down at the Groot Vis, women struggled to find space to wash in the idle current. Across the river I imagined dogs panting in the shade of covered *stoeps*.

I had just fed Dawn and was singing to her *Thula thu' thula bhabha* like Mama used to sing to me in our *kaia* at the bottom of the garden beneath the bony thorn tree. Dawn was sweaty and I fanned her with a cloth before laying her down on the foldout bed for a rest. She was too big, now, for her washing basket. At night she slept in a broad cardboard box that I found in the school yard.

'Ada!'

A slender figure blocked out the harsh sunlight where it fell through the doorway on to the mud floor. I jumped up, horrified that she'd risked the dangerous streets, the surging crowds. Master should never have allowed this.

Dawn pointed. 'Ndwe!' she shouted. 'Ndwe!' Dawn couldn't say Lindiwe's name so called her Ndwe.

Madam stepped carefully inside. She was wearing a pale

green dress with a sweeping skirt, and a straw hat with a broad brim angled well down over her face to protect her from the sun. She stood there for a moment, disconcerted by the lack of space, unsure how to greet me in such a place, for she had surely never been inside a mud hut before.

'How did you find us?' I blurted out, forgetting my manners, feeling the same clutch at my heart as when I saw her on the stage at school, the same clutch as when I heard Master's steps coming down the corridor and then stopping outside my door. 'Why have you come back?'

But she didn't reply straight away. Instead, she took off her hat and fanned herself for a moment. Then glanced again at the cramped space between the beds, the paraffin stove in the corner, the uneven window, the bare earth floor under her shoes, as if now seeing the narrow parts of this life properly. I realised she was looking for a chair, but seeing none – and no space for one anyway – she gathered her full skirt beneath her and sat down on the end of the bed as if it was as perfectly made as her own back at Cradock House. Then she smiled at Dawn who stared up at her with curious eyes made large by the gloom of the hut. Dawn was used to skin darker than her own, the only person she had seen with skin paler than hers was the chemist who gave her the medicine that saved her life.

'I wanted to ask you to come home.'

There it was.

I got up and went to stand by Lindiwe's bed. I wished the hut was bigger; it was hard to tell lies in such close proximity.

'I can't do that, Madam,' I began. Dawn, sensing something was wrong, cried and lifted her arms to me. I reached down and gathered her in, holding her soft body close, this child who I loved and who I hoped would always love me even when she discovered the price of the skin difference between us.

Madam looked at me and she looked at her husband's child. Her eyes were clear, not sore and weeping as they had been when she was at the school, or on the day Miss Rose had left or the day young Master Phil died. Perhaps all the weeping had already been done.

'Let there be no misunderstanding between us, Ada,' she said quietly, leaning forward to stroke Dawn's tiny foot, 'only acceptance and the need to go forward.'

What of forgiveness? I wanted to say. Can you ever forgive me for doing what I thought was my duty? Surely that was beyond us, surely that was too much to ask. 'I have sinned,' I said, unable to meet her eyes.

'The sin is not yours alone to bear,' she said firmly. 'Look at me, Ada.' She leant forward, forcing me to look at her. 'Listen to me. Edward is responsible for this. You and the child should not suffer alone and . . .' she glanced around at our poor circumstances, 'I will not allow it to happen.'

I felt the walls of my heart that I had hardened for so long begin to loosen, but I could not weaken yet. There was more to consider than the sin against Madam herself.

'It is against the law,' I said. 'Master could go to jail.'

I saw fleeting surprise on her face, as if she hadn't expected me to know such things. She shook her head. 'No he won't, as long as we're discreet. Those laws are not pursued in Cradock to the same extent as in larger cities.' She paused, then added, 'I have made some inquiries, Ada.'

I sat down on Lindiwe's bed. A silence fell between us. Dawn kicked her feet. Madam started and half rose from the bed, her hand reaching for her throat, as shouting burst out on the street.

'There are other matters that lie beyond the law,' I ventured, ignoring the noise outside. I had never talked to Madam like this. My school teaching and my outcast status in the township had made me brave. In any case, I had nothing left to lose. 'What of your friends who will see the child and know where she comes from? People will turn away from you,' I stopped and caught my breath, 'as they have turned away from me. Even strangers turn away.'

For the first time, I saw her control falter. She lifted a hand and wiped her forehead, shielding her eyes from me in the process. The hut was very hot, I could feel a channel of sweat trickling down Dawn's back where she sat pressed close to me.

'If they turn away,' she murmured, more to herself than me, 'then they are not worth knowing.'

'But it is so hard,' I cried out then, willing her to understand, feeling the heavy air tremble with my words. 'You don't know how hard it is! They will make you feel a stranger in your own place, they will never forgive you! And what about Dawn? She belongs nowhere, but in the township there might be other coloureds for her . . .'

I tried to stop myself shaking. Dawn twisted in my lap and stared up at me, the beginnings of fright puckering her tiny face.

'Ada, dear—'

'And I will be in fear of Master,' I muttered.

There it lay, beneath everything, hidden even from me. Would I ever sleep peacefully again under the same roof as Master? Would Madam, if I was there?

'Ada!' came a cheerful call from outside and Lindiwe swung through the doorway with a load of washing on her shoulder. 'Oh, excuse me, Ma'am.' She stared at Madam, who had risen to her feet. Lindiwe looked at me and I saw that she had already guessed who this was. She slung the load down on to her bed. I did not know what to say. I should have introduced Lindiwe straight away but my head and my heart were confused and slow.

'How kind of you to be Ada's friend,' said Madam, seeing my distraction and holding out her hand to Lindiwe. 'I owe you a debt I can never repay. And,' she paused and glanced at me where I sat, 'I want you to help persuade Ada to return to work for me.'

'But Ada has a job already,' said Lindiwe swiftly, glancing from Madam to me. 'Ada does important work teaching. She must pass on her cleverness to others.'

'Yes,' said Madam, 'I agree. Ada should continue to teach. But she could live at Cradock House and we would support her and the baby in return for a little light housework when she can manage.'

I stared at Madam. Lindiwe stared at Madam. I could see Lindiwe calculating my good fortune. Wages from school, food and clothing for Dawn and myself, books to read, shelter under a roof that did not leak, water that did not need to be fetched. All for a little work on the side.

But I did not think of those things. I thought simply of the quiet of my old room. Of the smell of jasmine as I hung out the washing. Of Madam's companionship. Of Mama and young Master Phil who lived most strongly for me within the boundary of Cradock House. I thought of music, I thought of new melodies waiting for me inside the Zimmerman, and old familiar tunes ready to fill my heart once more.

And I thought of temptation. And how the need to belong was a temptation so hard to resist.

I stood on the iron bridge today after Madam left. I stood upright, not hiding from the cars or the passers-by that might recognise me. There was no need to hide any more. I went there because it was cooler than Lindiwe's hut and also because it seemed the right place to be. I stood in the centre, with white

Cradock on one side and black Cradock on the other and the brown water of the Groot Vis – brown like Dawn's skin – creeping beneath me.

What should I do, Master Phil? I whispered. If you were here now, what would you tell me? Master Phil, who had loved me and yet touched me only with respect. Master Phil, who knew the price of skin difference long before I did . . .

I could turn away now, away from the crowds, away from the women washing on the riverbank, and walk to Cradock House and back into the rest of my old life. Or I could turn the other way, and pin my chances and Dawn's chances on a township future. With the first I would find the private belonging I sought, with the second I would continue to battle for partial acceptance. With the first I risked exposing Madam to shame and to the law, with the second her life and Master's life would go on as before.

Master Phil would have told me to write down all the best and worst things about each side and then choose. But some of those things could only be whispered, they could never be written down. And some that could be written down could never be decided upon until they had been tried. Would the presence of Dawn and me tear Madam and Master apart, would it poison the air in Cradock House and taint the memories of all that had gone before? Was it no longer possible for Cradock House to be home?

Where did Master himself stand in all this?

And while I could imagine a life ahead that drew on the best of Cradock House and the best of the township, would it be so for Dawn? Wouldn't she be better off in the township where the turning away hopefully went no further than an insult or a jostle on the street? She would miss Lindiwe, and Jake's sudden visits. I would miss them too. If we returned to Cradock House wouldn't Dawn find herself – wouldn't I find myself – isolated and perhaps at risk from the law as well?

Lindiwe looked only on the practical side. Apartheid might be building barriers between black and white, but when it came down to survival there was only one way to go.

'Such an offer!' she cried when Madam had left, stepping carefully out of the doorway in her beautiful dress, to be escorted away by a young man from St Peter's Church on Bree Street who had been paid by Madam to find me.

'You will still be able to teach, and just think,' Lindiwe flung her powerful arms wide within the cramped hut, 'you will have your own *kaia*, your own place!'

I nodded. Yes, I would have my own place. Maybe not my old room in the house, because of the laws that stopped whites and blacks living together, but at least the *kaia*, where Dawn could stand in the doorway and watch the water pooling at her feet when there was rain, or listen to it beating through the bony thorn tree on to the tin roof.

'There will be food!' Lindiwe went on keenly. 'And medicine for Dawn if she gets sick. Ada,' she grasped my hand with her own hard one, rough from washing, 'the revolution is for angry men like Jake. You have a child to bring up.'

'But Master is the father of my child!' I blurted out, the first time I'd said the words since I told the kind doctor and then learnt the burden of inheritance. I looked quickly across at Dawn, but she was fast asleep in her cardboard box. Dawn hadn't even heard those words from me when I talked to her at bedtime of my inside loneliness. Master is the father of my child. I know it, Madam knows it and now Lindiwe knows it.

'I know he's the father.' Lindiwe glanced at Dawn as well.

'How do you know?' Panic rose once more. How could she know? Who else knew? Had someone at the school found out?

'I guessed it.' Lindiwe reached for my hand and pressed it gently. 'And I saw it in your eyes just now. Ada,' she squeezed my hand again and spoke slowly, 'this time it won't be your duty.'

I stared at her and felt the edge of tears.

'Unless you wish it to be so?'

'No!'

Yet there it was, even from Lindiwe. The suspicion that I had wanted the Master's attentions, that I had sought him out to lie with me. Did all women who were taken by force or who succumbed to duty have to bear this? Did Mama face criticism that she had thrown herself at a young man with no thought of the consequences? That it was all her fault? Had such criticism come from Master, said or unsaid, when she was expecting me?

'Are you afraid he will want you again?' Lindiwe's voice was low, for such thoughts could indeed only be whispered.

'The law will not allow it,' I said, strangely relieved that such a law existed even though it must cause pain for those who truly loved someone of a different skin. 'And this time I would be brave. This time I would say no.'

I listened as the word I should have said fell into the quiet space between us. It was cool inside the hut now, but the thatch roof lost its heat silently, unlike the tin roof of Cradock House that kept you awake at night or interrupted your talk with its creaking.

Why didn't I say no the first time? Why did I believe that duty was my only option? Even though duty and loyalty are often on opposite sides it does not mean that one has to be sacrificed for the other. And if my duty and loyalty had been to God the Father – as it should have been – then I would not have had to make such a sacrifice, I would not have had to choose between Master and Madam. I could have chosen God's way instead, and He would have told me to say no. Yet even without God's way, why did it take such time and pain for me to learn that I had the right to say no for myself as well?

Even if saying no might have meant losing my job, my home . . .

I am learning, I am learning.

I lifted the kettle off the stove and poured tea into two cups for Lindiwe and me. We still had a small amount of milk left and I smelt it to check it was fresh before stirring it into the tea.

'I think your Madam is a clever woman,' Lindiwe murmured after a while, sipping from her cup in the gathering darkness. 'She wouldn't offer you a place unless she was sure your Master would leave you alone. And the only way she could know this is if they have decided so together.'

I stared at her.

Lindiwe's insights always took me by surprise. She could read minds and uncover hidden desires like no one I had ever known. She had taken the measure of Madam from just one meeting.

'It would have been a negotiation?' I wondered out loud. 'A negotiation without money . . . a trade, like offering free washing for flour and sugar.' I leant forward. 'But what would Madam use to enforce such a trade?'

'Why, Ada,' Lindiwe said with a twist to her smile as she lifted her feet and rested them on a pile of dirty linen, 'you talked of it just now. She would threaten him with the law!'

I gasped and set down my cup on the earth floor with trembling fingers. 'Surely it would be too shameful for Madam to do such a thing? If he went to jail she would lose everything, her family, her friends, her place at tea parties—'

'But she would get sympathy,' Lindiwe interrupted, 'whereas your Master would be disgraced forever.'

I got up and went to the doorway. Thin clouds mixed with smoke swam across the face of the moon. From the hut opposite came the sound of a guitar being violently strummed and a voice began to sing off-key.

'And if they made such an arrangement,' I turned back, 'what benefit would it have for Madam?'

'Your return,' said Lindiwe simply, 'with Dawn. This Madam is a fair woman, she feels responsible, she wants to give you and Dawn a better future. And,' she hesitated and I motioned her to go on, 'perhaps she's lonely, as you are.' She gave me a gentle smile, Lindiwe always knew my heart. 'And there can be little left between her and your Master now.'

I gazed at Lindiwe, seeing the further loops of cleverness play out in her mind, how she'd calculated the consequences of Madam's negotiation, how she divined its outcome despite knowing nothing for certain.

At first Edward denied it.

Only when I wept and said the child had his eyes – and the eyes of dear Phil – did he pass a hand over his face and admit his part. He said he would understand if I wished to ask him for a divorce. But we are both too old and settled in Cradock House to throw away what we have built here. Edward is not a bad man, merely misguided and foolish, as I have learnt men can be. And I must confess our regard for one another has always been based on fondness rather than passion, although that is no excuse for his behaviour. Maybe five years apart before marriage is not conducive to success . . .

Having achieved a tentative accommodation, I allowed some time to pass before telling him my plan.

He is deeply disturbed, but I have been insistent about his – our – responsibility.

He said we put ourselves at risk harbouring a coloured child, and I agreed we would need the inattention of the authorities – not to mention the blind eye of friends – to get by. However, without saying as much, I led him to believe that if he refused to support Ada and her child, or if he behaved towards them in any manner other than the most honourable, then I could not guarantee that his adultery would remain secret.

Tomorrow I go into the township with a young man from St Peter's who says he knows where Ada and her coloured child are lodging. I pray she will agree.

As yet, I have written nothing of this to Rosemary.

Now that it is almost upon us, I wish I could say I am confident but it isn't so.

How will Edward react? Will he look upon this child as anything other than the potential agent of his downfall?

Will Ada and Dawn find comfort here or just another form of isolation? Can I ever forgive Edward?

Am I doing the right thing?

Chapter 33

I did not write down a list in favour of returning to my old home, and I did not write down a list in opposition to it. When it came to Cradock House, the temptation of food and shelter for Dawn, and music and Madam for me overcame all else. Such advantage clearly outweighed anything opposing the move. And surely God the Father would not have brought Madam to me unless it was part of His plan for me to return? But I am not used to such decisions, or the sensible way to make them, or whether God does test us in the making of such choices.

It was another hot day when I returned. Swimming youngsters competed with the washerwomen for space down at the Groot Vis and threw stones at yellow-eyed dogs nosing in the shallows. Lindiwe had delayed her departure to see me off and she wiped Dawn's sweaty face with a wet cloth before we left and promised that her hut – or one of the huts she planned to build as a landlord – would always be there for us if we needed to return. God was truly kind when He gave me Lindiwe as a friend. Her strength has become my strength. Even so, tremors shook my body as we said goodbye.

'It is the right thing to do,' I said, looking into Dawn's trusting face set with the eyes of Master who would surely not want me back. I should have listened to Master Phil's voice in my ear, I should have—

'It will benefit Dawn.' Lindiwe heaved a load of washing on to her back.

'Ndwe!' Dawn heard her name and held out her arms. Lindiwe leant down and nuzzled her nose against Dawn's in a familiar game.

'This is your chance.' She straightened up with difficulty beneath the load and squeezed my arm hard. 'There are many who long for such good fortune.'

I never thought to make the journey back again. Only the emergency of Dawn's illness had forced me into town. Yet here I was, my pale child in my arms, the 'Township Bach' fading at my back, returning to what was once my home and might be yet again. Women with similar bundles and babies on their backs pushed past, wondering what luck – or cruelty – had fallen upon me to make me go this way. And then God the Father came upon me as I walked, and the newness I'd felt on my first day of teaching began to fill me and overflow into the heat of the day. It sparkled off the brown water, it rose in the song of the washerwomen. I clutched Dawn tighter with fierce hope. This must be the plan: a new future.

Madam was sitting on the *stoep* of Cradock House in one of her cream day dresses, waiting for me. Nothing had changed. Jasmine twisted through the pergola above her head in thick ropes, wafting its perfume through windows left open to catch any breeze that might come by. The old house with its pale stone walls and its red tin roof watched me as I came up the path with Dawn on my hip – she was too heavy for the blanket – and my cardboard suitcase in my other hand. I wondered if the place remembered me, as I hoped in the dark township nights that it would. Whether the apricot still carried me in its sap, whether the stairs and the doorknobs remembered my polishing of them, whether the piano held special music in store for me to play. Whether the souls of Mama and young Master Phil were smiling on me as I walked up the path through the heat towards Madam. Whether I was the only part of it that was changed. Or – I trembled again – whether I was making the biggest mistake of my life since I took off my nightgown and lay down with Master. After all, I had work in the township, I had shelter with Lindiwe, I had found rhythm in the noise.

'Big!' crowed Dawn from my hip. 'Big trees, Mama!' I put down my suitcase.

'Ada!' Madam rose and came down the steps. 'How wonderful!'

She embraced me and I smelt her flowery perfume that I'd been close enough to smell for the first time on the day Mama died. She turned to Dawn with a sharp intake of breath, as if taken aback once more by the sight of the child's family likeness. 'Will she come to me?'

It was strange, that first time of seeing Madam with Master's daughter in her arms. I could sense the love in her for my child, but also an immense sadness beneath, like the crying that lay beneath laughter when soldiers left for war. Dawn stared at her with Master's eyes and then reached for Master Phil's brooch that Madam wore at her throat.

'Pretty,' she said. 'Toy for Dawn?' I'd only ever spoken to Dawn in English, like Mama did with me unless she was angry. Good English, I had reckoned, would be Dawn's passport out of the township.

'Careful,' murmured Madam, swaying gently and capturing Dawn's tiny fist in her own hand. 'Don't prick yourself. We'll soon find you some toys to play with, won't we?'

We did not move back into our bedroom in the main house on account of the laws that said whites and blacks should not mix in that way. Instead, I carried Dawn past the apricot heavy with orange fruit, past the kaffirboom guarding the washing line, past the boundary hedge where unseen beetles rasped, and set her down in the *kaia* at the bottom of the garden beneath the bony thorn tree.

The *kaia* was newly painted and Madam had moved Mama's old bed and rug in there, along with a cot for Dawn like I had seen for sale in newspapers for large amounts of money. Although there was no hot water – we used the downstairs bathroom in the main house for bathing – there was a basin with a cold tap. There was also a proper toilet with a chain that pulled and made Dawn's eyes widen with excitement, and the floor was smooth concrete polished to a red shine. Madam had worked hard. She had even put up curtains for us. Dawn ran to finger them, and patted their folds and hid behind them. Dawn had never seen curtains before.

The *kaia* was bigger than Lindiwe's hut in the township. It was just for Dawn and me. It was riches such as I had never expected to see again.

'Thank you, Madam,' I said, sitting on the soft bed, letting the old harmony steal over me. I'd forgotten what it was like to have such a refuge, and such kindness given so freely. No harsh din in my ears, no smoke in my throat, no press of strangers staring at Dawn's skin, no fear of robbery and the need for sharpened bicycle spokes.

'Don't,' said Madam with a catch in her voice. 'You and Dawn deserve it. Now,' she went on more briskly, 'I think it's time to dispense with "Madam". I'm sure you can find another way to address me.'

Master Phil had once told me not to call him Master, but I

never managed to call him Phil except to myself. Dina said that one day we would call all whites by their names – after a war of Liberation had swept the country. But now, it seemed, a small liberation had taken place within Cradock House.

I would find a new way to address Madam. Something that fell between Madam and Cathleen, something that showed respect but also admitted the moment in the school hall when she and I met as women for the first time. Perhaps I could call her Mrs Cath.

'You're free to come and go as you like, to accommodate your teaching.'

But what of Master? I wanted to say. For all Lindiwe's persuasion that Master and Madam have come to an arrangement, how can I be sure? Will my township strength hold fast if he tries to touch me?

First, though, before anything else, there was the piano. With Madam holding Dawn, I ran into the lounge and opened the Zimmerman and brushed my hands across the keys and felt their resilience after the sponginess of the school piano. Then sat for a moment, and waited for the piano to remember me, and for the music to find me once more.

'Come, Ada, some Chopin!' said Madam gaily. 'The *Raindrop* prelude?'

So I began, and I could tell Madam approved, for the single notes fell into Cradock House as sweetly as they ever had. Yet for me, the school version played in the quest for a job outdid my playing here for it spoke with a passion I could never match. And I realised that music – and maybe life – depends less on the quality of the instrument or the player than it does on the commitment with which it is played.

Mozart's lively Turkish rondo, then a Beethoven sonata, then a Debussy arabesque . . .

Dawn responded to the music the only way she knew, clapping and wiggling her tiny body like she'd seen my students do back at school. I was briefly worried that Madam might be offended but she pressed her hands to her cheeks and stifled her laughter at the little one's cavorting, and then bore Dawn off to the kitchen for some milk and rusks. And still the music rose and fell under my joyful fingers, and I played until the sun began to dip behind the hedge where the beetles were now silent.

Madam did not expect me to step back into the kitchen as I would once have done. Indeed, she had prepared a meal for us that evening and said we would share cooking duties in the days ahead. And that I had no need to wear aprons or overalls unless I wished. So when Master arrived, I was not cooking but walking in the garden with Dawn, listening out for the bokmakieries that she'd only ever known from stories in the gloom of Lindiwe's hut.

'Where are they, Mama?' Dawn's hand in mine stiffened with excitement.

'You have to be quiet and listen.' I bent down to her. 'Some things can't be seen, they must be listened for, and maybe they're in their nest already.' And then, as if the birds themselves understood, the calling and answering rose from opposite ends of the garden.

'We stay here all the time, Mama?'

He came with Madam down the kitchen steps and past the apricot tree, his back rigid and straight as it had ever been. I stood waiting, holding Dawn's hand in mine, restraining her from dashing off in search of the birds that had now fallen silent, but in reality clutching her in case he was coming to snatch her away.

It was Madam who stepped in with the right words, Madam who found the courage to make the introduction, Madam who had always softened him.

'This is your daughter, Dawn,' she said quietly. Her face was pale, perhaps she'd used more of the powder that sat on her dressing table than usual.

Master's stern gaze swept past me and fastened on Dawn. He did not move. I stared at him, searching for the shame that had followed me but only recently found its way to him as well. To my horror – for I am not a vengeful person – I found rage churning within me like the Groot Vis in flood, because maybe he felt no shame, maybe he cared little for how he'd hurt Madam and used me to avert his loneliness for her.

But then I saw it.

I saw how he had withered within his uprightness, how his body was lost inside the dark suit with its chain across the front. How his side-parted hair had turned completely white, and his blue eyes were washed out, like Madam's eyes used to look during young Master Phil's illness or Miss Rose's troubles in Johannesburg. Shame had destroyed his body like it had almost destroyed my mind. This faded man, I realised, was a shell. He had no claim on me any more; I would have no trouble in refusing this man. I loosened my grip on Dawn's hand.

'Mama?' She looked up at me, uncertain as to why we were standing in the garden like this, standing and staring at one another with no words between us.

'I have agreed to support Dawn, Ada,' Master said distantly. Even his voice was thinner. 'Provided she is not told of it. And there must be no talk about this among your friends.'

I glanced at Madam but she remained silent. The bokmakieries started up again, one on the roof, one in the hedge.

'Mama!' Dawn cried, pointing, and turning her head back and forth to follow their calling. She wasn't used to songbirds. She'd only ever heard hadedas in the township at evening, or seen crows squabbling over rubbish in the streets.

'I shall say nothing, sir. But I cannot hide Dawn.'

There was a pause. Then he said, 'She could attend the mission school.'

'But, Edward,' Madam interrupted, putting out her hand to him, her eyes darkening with anxiety, 'you never said—'

'That is the school you thought of for me,' I found myself breaking in, the anger rising once more, 'but Mama wouldn't let me go so far away.' I looked at Master squarely but he wouldn't meet my eyes, he wouldn't see the mother of his child. 'I won't let Dawn go that far away either. She can go to the township school with me.'

'Up, up!' Dawn lifted her arms and I bent to pick her up. Master looked at me properly, then, as if noticing someone who up till that point had been invisible. It was the first time I had talked back to him; the first time I had spoken with my own voice and not as a servant.

'Of course she can,' resumed Madam swiftly, glancing at Master with a passing coldness that I'd never seen in her before. Perhaps Madam is stronger, too, than she was before. 'That would be for the best.'

'As you wish.' He inclined his head and turned away.

I felt the clutch of Dawn's arms as she wrapped them round my neck. 'Thula thu', she began to sing, as if to join the birds in their chorus, 'thula thu' . . .'

'Sir?' I managed, but he was already walking away.

Will you not greet your daughter, sir? Even if she may never know you're her father, will you not greet her? Will you not see she is a fine child? That I have cared for her well?

Madam touched me briefly on the shoulder, and followed him inside.

I suppose I was foolish. I should have expected he would distance himself from Dawn as much as possible. After all, there was the law to consider; it made sense not to reveal himself to her as her father. Yet something else struck me in Master. Something behind his shuttered face, something beyond his unwillingness to greet his child, something besides the withering that had so reduced his body. It took me a while to understand what it was. It worried me through dinner – which a chattering Dawn and I ate in the kitchen while Madam and Master dined in uneasy silence next door – it worried me through the washing-up, it worried me through the pegging out of the cloths on the line in the familiar soft purple of evening.

It came to me later as I lay in the *kaia* and listened to the tap of the thorn tree on the tin roof and watched Dawn finally asleep in her smart cot and waited for the hoot of the owl in the kaffirboom, and wondered if I had made the right decision to return. It was a thing that I had grown used to in the township but never seen in Cradock House before.

It was disgust. Master looked at Dawn with disgust: that worse version of dismay that he had shown towards the bond between his son and myself. Disgust like Auntie showed, like Silas showed, like those in the street who turned away from the evidence of my sin. Madam did not see it. She did not recognise it on Master's face. And I am grateful, for it would have hurt her even more than she was hurt already.

How was it that a man could look upon his own child – his own blood – in the way that a stranger would? How was it possible that there could be no stirring in his heart for his own daughter? Then I remembered what Lindiwe had said to me on the day Dawn was born. She said that God was not like the white man. He did not hate Dawn for my sin. So I should have expected that Master might do so. I should have expected him to turn away from his daughter. I should have expected his disgust.

For white people, the dividing power of skin is clearly greater than the closest ties of blood.

Chapter 34

Briefly:

Ada has returned with Dawn. The first meeting with Edward was strained but we managed.

The child is tremendously appealing, and having Ada back is, for me, the return of a beloved daughter.

Will the law leave us alone? And what of our friends?

I must take each day as it comes.

I cannot write of this to Ireland.

'Ada! Ada!' Mrs Pumile waved a hand through the hedge as I stepped out of the *kaia* that first morning after a sound night's sleep for both Dawn and me. A soft bed, no unnerving shouts from nearby huts, no trek to fetch water at first light with Dawn heavy on my back.

'Where you been? Your Madam has been so worried!'

'I have been away,' I began.

'Mama?' Dawn crawled down off the step in front of the *kaia* and ran to the hedge to see where the talking was coming from.

I waited. For once Mrs Pumile could find no further words. I could see her eyes bulging through the hedge, I could see her mouth wide open. I could see her head trying to get around what was before her eyes. I could see her throat swallow and her tongue run round the edge of her lips.

'Is it,' she pointed towards the house, 'is it?'

'Yes,' I said.

'Did you?'

'I am a teacher, now, Mrs Pumile. In the township.'

She stared at Dawn, seeing the skin pale as tea and the eyes blue as early-morning Karoo sky.

'Not Ndwe,' called Dawn, pointing through the hedge.

'No,' I said, scooping her up in my arms. 'This is Mrs Pumile.'

'Umile,' said Dawn, with a smile that showed two teeth.

As with every friend faced with the evidence of my shame, Mrs Pumile swung for several moments between condemnation and sympathy.

'Your Madam asked you back?' This I could see was causing her great difficulty. That a white Madam could be forgiving enough to welcome back the black person with whom her husband had sinned . . .

'Yes,' I said. 'She wished to give Dawn a good future.'

'Your Madam,' observed Mrs Pumile after a pause, 'could teach many Madams how to be. Welcome back, Ada,' she thrust her hand further through the hedge to grasp mine, 'but do not parade the child about!' She leant forward and hissed, 'This apartheid never leaves us alone. Keep the child out of sight, away from visitors.'

A call came from her kitchen. Mrs Pumile straightened her *doek* and yelled over her shoulder, 'Just coming, Ma'am.' She turned back to me and wagged a finger, 'Keep her out of sight, Ada, out of sight.'

But it was not possible to keep Dawn out of sight. Each day I walked down Church Street and across the Groot Vis to teach at school. Each day Dawn came with me, either on my hip or skipping alongside me. Yet the reaction that I feared most – arrest for my sin of lying with a white man and bearing him a child – did not happen. Policemen lounging outside their station near Market Square took no particular notice of the discrepancy in skin between my daughter and me. And whereas Dawn's skin caused much talk and insults on the township streets, in white Cradock very little was said. People noticed but looked away quickly. I realised it was a part of a pattern I knew well: they didn't want to see Dawn's skin. If they didn't see it, then it wasn't really there. Like if they looked away from Master Phil and me walking side by side and stopping beneath the tree for him to tell me that he loved me, then it didn't really happen.

The shopkeepers on Church Street whose signs I had read, the post office where I had posted Madam's letters for so many years, the butcher where I collected the family's meat – and where I still looked for Jacob Mfengu – all these saw us and turned their gaze away. They never responded when Dawn smiled and waved at them. It was as if she didn't exist. For her part, Dawn loved to enchant strangers and must have wondered, in her baby way, why she was ignored. For Dawn had no idea that she didn't belong. She had no idea that she fell in between, like the brown water of the Groot Vis divided black from white. Dawn, as a child, was happily colour-blind.

Master's ignoring of Dawn within the walls of Cradock House was equally fixed. I never expected him to embrace her, but I hoped that there might be a softening, or the odd kindness. But there was not. Dawn was a constant reminder of his failure, the living expression of his disgust. An inside wound that would eat away at him, like the memories of war and ghosts had eaten away at young Master Phil until there was nothing left of him. I wonder if Master recognised this wound in himself. I wonder if he knew its hunger.

I could see this injury in Master, but he kept it well hidden from Madam. Most evenings she sat upright in her chair opposite him and never saw it in his face or heard it in what he said, for their talk was of ordinary things. From the crack in the door I overheard them discussing Dawn from time to time, and Master did so with detachment, as if it was young Master Phil's ability on the cricket field they were talking about, or Miss Rose's reluctance over piano lessons, or my schooling from many years before that might lead to trouble later on. Madam managed to respond to his control with a clamp on her own feelings. She did not ever weep, she did not ever accuse, she did not look out of the window for Ireland. The time for tears and accusations had gone. What was left between them was an emptiness. An emptiness worse than any that had gone before. An emptiness that I believe would have struck even if I'd remained in the township, and Dawn had never been before Master's eyes each day – for a betrayal such as his can never be undone.

And afterwards Master would pick up his newspaper, and Madam would go to the piano and play safe nocturnes; quiet, deliberate pieces that stole through the house but didn't echo in your mind the next day. Instead, matters beyond Cradock House occupied our heads, though we never spoke of them out loud.

Chapter 35

Apartheid announced itself in heavy black letters like those used during the earlier war. It filled the *Midland News*, and dominated the posters outside the newspaper office. For me, it spoke in the words of brave Rev. Calata fighting for his people, and the minister under the *koppie* calling for liberation, and the feel of a bicycle spoke under my shaking fingers. For Master it spoke in the face of a coloured child, and in the fact of breaking a law and ending up on the wrong side of a war.

Mrs Pumile was right. This apartheid would never leave us alone. We were caught up in it, all of us, whether we wished to be or not. Failures committed in the past could now rear up again, at far greater cost. Master's inside wound was not just about disgust; it was also about fear.

'You are lucky, Mary,' observed Dina, leaning over the piano as I finished the morning march, 'to find someone to give you lodging and also let you teach.'

'Yes,' I said, reaching for an answer that I had prepared. 'This Madam knew my first Madam.'

There was no choice but to lie once more. One day Dawn, too, would see through such lies. One day I would have to tell her. I laid a hand on her head as she played at my feet with a toy clown of young Master Phil's that Mrs Cath – as I now called her – had given Dawn. 'This Madam doesn't need much house-keeping from me.'

Dina raised an eyebrow and straightened up. 'You seem to find the only generous whites in the world,' she remarked.

'Jam?' said Dawn, grabbing on to Dina's skirt. 'Deen got jam?'

'Not today, monkey.' Dina laughed, but with an edge. 'Ask your new Madam!'

Dina did not intend to be mean or jealous. She was simply suspicious, suspicious that I had fallen upon such good fortune. A *kaia* of my own, a Madam that supported Dawn and me and asked for very little work in return, an escape from the teeming township that Dina herself would secretly have prized, for all her contempt of Madams and servants and the grovelling she believed was required between them.

Mr Dumise, too, was suspicious.

'You are well, Mary?' he stopped me in the corridor one day, looking over the new skirt and blouse that Mrs Cath had laid on my bed in the *kaia* one day. The skirt was dark blue and the blouse was white – she had bought two – and they were the first truly grown-up clothes I had ever had, apart from the clothes for Master Phil's funeral. Even Miss Rose might have been prepared to wear such clothes.

'Yes, sir,' I replied. 'I have been lucky as well.'

He nodded and glanced down the passage as if checking to see it was empty. 'You are not in further trouble?'

I stared at him for a moment, wondering whether to explain everything, the connection to Mrs Cath, the name of Mary instead of Ada. Yet how much did a name matter? It was only a small deception compared to what I had already done in hiding the colour of Dawn until she was born.

'I am not in trouble, sir. Mrs Harrington has given me shelter.'

He looked at me, and I could tell he was reviewing all the facts that he knew about me: my arrival at school while expecting, my explanation of who taught me music, the subsequent colour of Dawn, the lack of a husband. To that he added the shock of Mrs Cath when she saw me in the hall, followed after a while by the improvement in my circumstances and dress. Everything pointed towards her family being not only my lifelong employers but also the home of Dawn's father.

'Shelter?' he repeated back to me.

Mr Dumise was a good man. He wanted to make sure I had not been forced into a relationship with Dawn's father once again. He wanted to make sure that the clothes and the *kaia* were not a bribe.

'You are kind, sir,' I said, holding my head up and feeling a hotness in my face, 'but there is no longer anything for me to fear.'

'Then take your luck, Mary,' he said quietly, 'and hold on to it. Such advantage comes rarely.'

Lindiwe said I should give no explanation to the staff about my change of circumstances.

'Why do they need to know?' she asked, shrugging. 'They turned away from you over Dawn, they have no right to say what is right or wrong.'

Jake, coming upon me suddenly on the iron bridge over the Groot Vis one day, surprisingly gave no opinion of my move. Perhaps he had been warned by Lindiwe not to. I was relieved, I had worried he might disapprove of my new life. I didn't want to lose Jake. But he did say that going back to live at Cradock House was one way of getting something he called 'compensation' for what had happened.

Later, I looked this up in the dictionary and found it meant payment for a loss or an injury. If this was so, then the return to Cradock House was all the payment I needed, although nothing can ever compensate Dawn for a father who does not see her and a skin that is neither black nor white.

'But there are risks,' Jake said, lifting Dawn on to his shoulders where she squealed with delight.

'Higher, higher!' she insisted, grabbing his hair. 'Dawn can reach the sky?'

Passers-by hissed at us. A man spat on the ground as he hurried past.

'I know about the laws,' I said to Jake, relieved that I could talk to someone instead of hiding behind my tangle of lies. 'I could go to jail. Master could go to jail. But Mrs Cath said if we were discreet that wouldn't happen.'

I had already thought of the possibility of imprisonment. It was something I considered before leaving the township. If I was ever arrested, then the best place for Dawn would indeed be with Mrs Cath at Cradock House, where she would be taken care of.

He touched my arm. 'More chance of him than you.'

I stopped. He stopped as well.

'Look, Mama! Look how high I am!' Dawn bounced on his shoulders, calling and waving to people all about us who ignored her. Beneath our feet the Groot Vis trickled in the summer heat and the washerwomen keened a low accompaniment.

'But why?' I asked. Surely the risk would be equal or perhaps even greater for me? The law might assume I had tricked Master into lying with me.

'Ada, dear Ada,' Jake murmured, 'the white man's sin is greater because it is more public. The white man falls further than the black woman.' He grimaced. 'The newspapers make more of his fall.'

I had not thought of it like that. I thought that if the law struck, it did so evenly. Both Master and I would be punished. Mrs Cath would escape. It did not occur to me that Master might be the only one to suffer. The compensation that Jake spoke of and that I had accepted could turn round and send Master to jail and leave me untouched.

Had Mrs Cath truly understood that when she offered me a home again?

The past is never enough if you are searching for a future. I now needed to graft the best of the township – my lively students, the music I taught them, Lindiwe and my few friends – on to the refuge that was Cradock House. And it was music that bridged the two parts of my life, as it has always done. The singing and dancing of my wild students, and the 'Township Bach' that enveloped me each time I crossed the Groot Vis, nudged alongside classical pieces that challenged my fingers and wandered around in my head for days afterwards as if rejoicing in their own homecoming. I began to shift the boundaries, to play jive at home, and more Debussy – despite the piano's defects – at school. Mrs Cath put her head round the door and smiled at me with her eyes and laughed at Dawn who clapped her hands and boogied in time with the beat.

Dawn's love of music was not expressed through any instrument – she showed no interest in the piano – but through her pliable body and dancing feet. The township became her stage. Whilst I returned to Cradock House each day with gratitude, my child looked back over her shoulder at what she was leaving behind. However much she enjoyed her new home, Dawn danced to the beat of 'Township Bach' as if it was her essence, rather than simply half of her inheritance. But there can be no regrets, as Mrs Cath often says to her book. God's plan for me was to keep Dawn safe until the evils of apartheid were swept away. I did what I thought was right. I have learnt that the only thing to be gained from past wrongs is the wisdom not to travel the same route again.

And Cradock House has indeed welcomed us back. The bokmakieries call from opposite ends of the garden in the freshness of morning, the hadedas flap overhead in the waning heat of late afternoon. In the warmth of the kitchen, I feel Mama on my shoulder, while from the pages of books that I once read to him, young Master Phil's voice rises. Mrs Cath and I resume our secret conversation through her diary while downstairs music of all kinds tumbles out of the piano and into my fingers: scherzos and pavanes and études and the African jazz of Miriam Makeba and the Skylarks. I am sure Phil hears it and is happy that I am home – just as surely as I know he loves Dawn from the place where he is now.

If the world had been different, if skin difference had never mattered, Dawn could have been our child.

Chapter 36

So far, the law has left us alone.

But it has not left my students alone. Across the Groot Vis, and in the township beyond Bree Street, many youngsters have been thrown into jail, some of them those that I teach. The only way I know this is when they are absent from school.

'They were taken,' the remaining children cry, and dance with frenzied energy to cover their fear that it will be them next time.

There is talk of boycotts. The dictionary says it means refusing to do business with a place or a person. It occurs to me that it is what Master does to Dawn and me. But Jake says it's a tool for blacks to use against white shops in town. For we may be poor, but there are many more blacks than whites in our country and if each one stops buying white goods then there will be white hardship. Jake says there are many different ways to make a revolution.

The matter of Passes fed this revolution. Beneath the music and the rhythm of my new life it lurked, like the *tokoloshe* of my childhood, or an illness you do not see until it is too late. The Pass defined who you were, and where you were allowed to stay. It was a piece of paper that proclaimed skin colour as the most important part of you. Since the failed marches, the police showed even less patience. No Pass meant instant arrest. The township complied with sullenness, but hissed its hatred of the men with their truncheons and their dogs, and their convenient jail.

'Will there be war over Passes?' I asked in the staffroom one day as we drank our tea and Veronica called, 'Kiep-kiep', out of the window to her chickens in the yard.

'It's happening already,' said Dina with conviction. 'Look at this.' She gestured to a week-old newspaper that showed reports of Pass burning and policemen beating the burners, in a township near Johannesburg many times bigger than KwaZakhele where the huts stretched beyond the horizon.

'Will there be a war, Mrs Cath?' I risked asking her one day as we bottled apricots in the kitchen. Dawn dropped the stones one by one into a metal pot counting, 'One, two, three!' and giggled at each clatter.

'A war over Passes?' She stopped for a moment from writing labels in her sweeping style, the branches of the 'A' in apricot extending above and below the rest of the letters. I did not often ask her about matters beyond the house, I was careful to say nothing that could cause her to regret my return, or the forgiveness that she had somehow found in her heart for me. Yet I wished to know more. It was time to know more.

'I hope not,' she began. 'The government should see sense and abolish them, but . . .'

'But what, Mrs Cath?'

'Some people say they want a war, a confrontation. I can't believe they'd be so foolish, but I've learnt men can be like that over many things.' She picked up her pen and began to write more labels. 'It won't affect us, Ada. Not here in Cradock.' She looked across at me and her eyes softened. 'You'll be safe here.'

'It won't be like the other war?'

'What's war, Mama?'

'Have you counted all the stones?' I asked her, ladling the fruit into the labelled jars.

'Will I do it? Will I do war?'

'Oh no, dear,' Mrs Cath said, slipping Dawn a peeled apricot half. 'War is only for soldiers.' She turned away for a moment, her free hand reaching for her throat. She no longer wore Phil's military brooch every day, but couldn't help reaching for it even when it wasn't there.

'I'm so sorry, Mrs Cath,' I murmured to her back.

She turned back and reached for the jar I'd just filled. I watched her tighten the lid with hands made strong from the piano.

'Will there be bombs?' I asked.

Mrs Cath looked at me across the glistening jars and smiled with her mouth, like young Master Phil had smiled that day in the garden when he confessed he was frightened of war but tried to cover it up. 'There's nothing to worry about, Ada. That was a war between countries, this would just be a disagreement within our borders. Not the same at all.' She reached over to touch my arm. 'I will protect you and Dawn.'

At the mention of her name again, Dawn looked up, her fists full of apricot stones, and grinned at us. 'Protect Dawn!' She giggled and jumped up, flinging the stones back into the pot. 'Protect Dawn! Protect Dawn!' She began to dance and slap her hands against her thighs like the youngsters did on the rough streets across the Groot Vis. Mrs Cath and I stopped our bottling and watched her elastic body, and separately marvelled at her ability to cross the divide as if it was no more than shallow water.

So Mrs Cath would be on our side if such a war did come? Was it just the side Dawn and I were on or was it the side on which all black people lay? And what about Master? Master who believed that black people should stay in their place, yet Master who had broken the laws of the land to lie with me. I knew how important it was to pick the right side in a war. In the last war, Master and Mrs Cath and I and Miss Rose and Master Phil had been on the same side. Their enemies – the people across the sea who had made our piano – had been my enemies. Their worry had been my worry.

But in this war, who would be enemy and who would be friend? Were Master and Mrs Cath already on opposite sides?

I have rescued some money from the bank. I asked Mrs Cath to take me there so that I could understand how banks work and how I could get my money back if I wanted to one day. She did not know I intended to take some money out of the bank at the same time.

Mrs Cath went into the study and found the bank book that I had searched for in vain before leaving Cradock House. I waited in the doorway, as I had waited on the day Mrs Cath was to return from Johannesburg. I could still see Master sitting behind the desk, in the dark suit that she liked and the shirt I had starched and ironed, telling me he was leaving to fetch Mrs Cath as the train might be early. He never looked up, he never once lifted his eyes to meet mine. It was as if his lying with me had never happened. Like the white people on the street who looked away from Dawn so they didn't have to accept that she existed.

I took the small ridged book from Mrs Cath's hand and said I would keep it safely in the *kaia* under my mattress, along with the Pass that I now carried every day on account of the extra attention that Passes were getting.

'But why, Ada?' Mrs Cath straightened up from Master's desk to look at me with anxious green eyes. She knew that important papers could be stolen. She knew that *kaias* could be burgled. Mrs Cath didn't know I had made a slit in my mattress that was invisible to the eye.

I put my hand into my pocket and felt the book under my fingers.

'I needed money one day – Dawn was sick.' I felt the fear in my heart as I remembered her coughing, and the agony of wondering whether my coins would be enough for the medicine at the chemist. 'I couldn't go to the bank to get it.'

Auntie had been right in that respect: money was no use just sitting in a bank. Money was only valuable if you had it in your hand. I never again wanted to be without the means to get hold of it. If anything happened to Mrs Cath, I would have to appeal to Master, and I didn't want to do that. I didn't want to be in a position of asking him for anything. I had also decided that, since it was my bank book anyway, it should be my choice about where to keep it. See how my township life has made me strong?

We went one afternoon after school, when Dawn was playing under Mrs Pumile's uneasy eye in the garden next door.

'Watch her,' I warned quietly, 'she'll be off and into your Madam's house before you know it!'

'I'll keep her out of sight, poor child.' Mrs Pumile still found Dawn's skin a worry. 'And ask my cousin why she keeps all the sugar for herself.'

It was the first time I had been inside a bank. There was a long wooden counter with ladies and gentlemen sitting behind it with papers in front of them. The place smelt of linseed oil and floor polish. I looked out for Mrs Pumile's cousin, whose job it was to polish the floor, but she wasn't there. Perhaps she was making tea that she wheeled around on a trolley, along with the sugar that the bank seemed to order too much of. Large ceiling fans creaked slowly overhead and sent cool breezes against your neck as you stood in line below. The school hall in the township could have done with such a fan.

Mrs Cath explained to the lady behind the counter that I owned the money described in the bank book.

'I would like to have some of it back,' I spoke up, showing her my Pass to prove that I was the same Ada Mabuse as the one who owned the bank book.

'Ada,' Mrs Cath ventured, exchanging a glance with the lady, 'your money is safer here, you might be robbed if you carry it round with you.'

'But I needed money when Dawn was sick,' I repeated, 'and I had no means to get hold of it.'

'I understand,' Mrs Cath nodded, putting a hand gently on my arm, 'but that won't happen again.'

The lady behind the counter was watching us. She wore a pink blouse with puffed sleeves that are difficult to iron, and a matching hairband. I could see she was surprised by my English, and by the way Mrs Cath and I spoke as if we were equals. She stared when Mrs Cath touched me.

'Please, Mrs Cath,' I said, calling on the boldness I had learnt in the township. 'I need to have some money in my hand.'

Mrs Cath inclined her head and smiled. 'Of course. It's yours to do with as you choose.' She turned to the lady in pink. 'Can Ada withdraw two pounds, please?'

The lady raised her eyebrows and counted out the money. I rolled it into my handkerchief and pushed it deep into my pocket. When I got home I would slip the book and my Pass and the money deep within the hiding place I had made in the mattress. Mama had kept her money in a shoebox under the bed, but I knew that robbers looked under things – under mattresses, under beds. Lindiwe had taught me that. But they don't look inside them.

Chapter 37

Dawn was growing as fast as the granadilla creeper that Mrs Cath tended for its purple fruit. Alongside her growth in length, she grew two ways of behaving.

The first was reserved for Cradock House, where she minded her manners and learnt to help with the dusting and polishing as I had done under my mama. But each day as we walked across the Groot Vis, where the washerwomen sang and the brown water flowed sluggishly, Dawn changed from the daughter I knew into one who was a stranger. She did not seek out the few coloured children in the township – the small community where I had hoped she might find a home – but instead ran with the toughest black youngsters she could find, as if her skin was goading her into proving herself worthy of a greater blackness than she had been born with.

At the same time, men like Jake began to talk not of war or revolution, but of the Struggle. A struggle where Passes still burned, but so too did the huts of blacks thought to be uncommitted. The house of the kind doctor who wrote the letter for the medicine that saved Dawn was burnt to the ground as a warning that even missionary money was tainted. Jake himself no longer appeared out of the crowds to swing Dawn off her feet, or stepped through the doorway of Lindiwe's hut with spare sausages from the butcher. Or sought me out down by the river.

'He is part of it,' Lindiwe whispered to me over an early bowl of soup before I hurried home in the light. 'He says he must leave the country to learn about guns – guns, Ada . . .'

'Why don't you find different children to play with?' I would press Dawn, while suppressing my fears for Jake. 'There is Lindiwe's niece Nomse, or Bongani who learns the piano with me.'

But Dawn would toss her head and laugh at me with her light blue eyes and tell me not to worry and then run off to her wild friends for another day of troublemaking.

'You don't understand, Mama,' she would insist whenever there was some particular upheaval. 'You need to be tough to live here.'

'But you live in Cradock House too, Dawn. How can you behave so differently between the two places?'

'Because I'm two people, Mama!' she responded gaily, and I had no answer to that.

Mr Dumise, grey haired now, was as diplomatic as ever and overlooked Dawn's skirmishes. Of all the staff, only Dina was able to reason with Dawn, for Dawn loved Dina's glamour and her colourful turbans and her determination to fight the white man's government and not grovel. But even Dina battled to temper Dawn's wilfulness.

'Where does she get this?' Dina said in dismay, after failing in another attempt to stop Dawn's fighting.

'It is her skin that drives her on.'

Dina looked pained and then nodded in agreement and took my arm as we walked back to class. I remembered Mrs Cath describing Miss Rose as wilful. And I wondered again about inheritance and how much of Dawn came from myself and Master, and if it was possible for her to have gained an extra dose of wilfulness from Miss Rose. And how much came from the surroundings in which she found herself.

'Why do you fight so much, Dawn?' I asked as we lay in the darkness of the *kaia* at the end of the day.

'Because I'm different from you, Mama.'

I sat up and looked at her where she lay on her back in the new bed Mrs Cath had recently bought on account of her increasing length.

'I'm sorry every day for giving you the skin you have.'

'Hush, Mama.' She leant over and kissed me on the cheek. 'I don't know if it's the skin, but I love the township!' Her eyes sparkled in the gloom. 'And I want to belong there.'

But how can you, my precious child? I wanted to cry out to the *kaia*, to the bony thorn tree, to the apricot that now surely carries you in its sap. I have tried so hard to give you a future here – the future that God the Father wanted for you, and spared me for. I have protected you, I have saved you from washing for a living, or illness caused by foul latrines. I've shielded you from drink and the violence that goes with it outside the *shebeens*. Your wild black friends will tire of you, they'll turn on your pale skin one day and want nothing to do with you. This I know. These things I have seen.

'Mama!' Dawn sensed my fear and leant over to hug me, her pale skin smooth against mine. 'I will find my way, just as you have.'

But at what cost, I wanted to say, what price will have to be paid? I felt tears, then, futile tears like those that had come upon me at Master Phil's funeral.

'I'll always come back, Mama,' Dawn went on gently, for she had as much capacity for tenderness as she had for trouble. 'I love you and Mrs Cath and Cradock House, I'll always come back.'

Miss Rose has had a baby. Mrs Pumile says that is hardly surprising given the amount of trouble Miss Rose has found and that sooner or later this always means a baby.

Mrs Cath only came to hear of this baby a while after it was born. It seems that Miss Rose wished to keep the news quiet for as long as possible. Like I kept quiet the fact that I would be having a coloured baby. But in the matter of colour, Miss Rose was luckier than me. Her baby was white. But there is one thing that we both share: neither Miss Rose nor I have a husband to go with the babies we have borne.

'She's coming to stay,' said Mrs Cath breathlessly, hurrying into the kitchen one day clutching a letter. Her hair had escaped from its bun and fell about her shoulders like it did when she was in Master Phil's bedroom comforting him in his war nightmares.

I lifted my hands out of a bowl of flour that I was rubbing butter into for scones. 'Does Miss Rose know?'

I had never asked Mrs Cath if Miss Rose knew about Master and me and that I had had his child. How do you tell your daughter that her father has sinned in such a way? Nor did I know if Mrs Cath had told Miss Rose of my return to Cradock House. How do you tell your daughter that you have accepted a sinner back into your home? Perhaps Miss Rose didn't know. Perhaps this was the reason for Mrs Cath's particular disturbance.

'I wrote to her a while back,' Mrs Cath began, reaching a hand to tuck her hair back into its arrangement and avoiding my eyes. 'She was,' Mrs Cath hesitated, looking in her mind for the right word, like Lindiwe used to do, 'surprised.'

I kept my eyes down as well and returned to the scone

mixture. Surprise was surely not what Miss Rose felt. Anger, yes. Betrayal – for Miss Rose regarded Master as her particular property, to be charmed at will – almost certainly. Indifference? Perhaps. If I was lucky.

Edward wants to find out who the father is, why he has not done his duty by Rosemary and married her. I have refused to fan this particular fire. It's true that folk will gossip, but we have been down that route before, and I have learned that the only course is to hold up one's head and go forward. It is interesting to realise that I have learned this from Ada. She has steeled herself against isolation and disappointment by only looking forward.

So we welcome our new grandchild with open arms, and I pray that Rosemary will now settle down to motherhood, and abandon her waywardness. But I have no confidence that she will, for I've long since acknowledged that where my daughter is concerned, I am without influence or understanding. How hard it is to admit such a failure with one's own child!

My immediate concern is her reaction to the presence of Ada and Dawn.

Chapter 38

'This is Dawn, she's almost ten,' said Mrs Cath, her cheeks once again pale, as they had been when she introduced Dawn to Master.

'What hair!' exclaimed Miss Rose, pointing to Dawn's tight curls and stroking the fair waves of her own daughter, Helen.

'Ada, would you bring the tea?' Mrs Cath forced a smile at me and patted Dawn reassuringly.

The family was sitting on the *stoep* in the shell chairs I'd longed to sit in as a child but had been forbidden to do so by Mama. I returned with the tray. There were fresh scones with our homemade apricot jam. We had worked hard to make Miss Rose's homecoming special. A roast leg of Karoo lamb was in the oven, there would be butternut squash steamed with brown sugar and cinnamon, and Cape brandy tart with dates from the desert where Phil had fought in the war.

As I poured tea, little Helen played on a blanket at Mrs Cath's feet. Dawn ran down to the *kaia* and returned with a toy rabbit Mrs Cath had knitted for her years before.

'No,' said Miss Rose, reaching over and taking the rabbit from Helen's hand and tossing it back at Dawn. 'She has her own toys.'

And that is the way it went.

Each day Miss Rose put on a new dress – no more full skirts now, but dresses that clung to her hips and narrowed themselves at her knees – and sat on the *stoep* and called for tea or walked down town to do errands. Sometimes she took Helen in the pram, but mostly she left her with Mrs Cath, along with strict instructions that Dawn's company was not welcome for her child. For Mrs Cath, this was a great trial. She understood Miss Rose's anger and hurt, as she herself had been angered and hurt, but the labelling of Dawn and me as unworthy and the rejection of our company as being unsuitable for her grandchild was a shock she found hard to bear. I could see all this in the tightness of Mrs Cath's back, I could hear it in the forced gaiety of her piano playing. We had a lot of polkas and mazurkas during that time, but none of them caught fire.

'Shall we make lemon meringue pie for dessert, Ada?' she said, her eyes sore, her hands keen to be busy to avoid the awkwardness of sitting with Miss Rose while having to shoo away Dawn.

'Of course, Mrs Cath,' I replied, and we would go about our whipping of egg whites and squeezing of lemons with none of the talk that usually rose between us.

Dawn, after early enthusiasm for Miss Rose's stylish clothes and city manner, soon chafed at her alienation. While she often seemed happiest among her gang in the township, I knew that Cradock House was her respite, even if she never wanted to admit it was so. Miss Rose, with her cutting words and her thoughtless actions, was threatening the only quiet place Dawn had ever known.

'She hates me,' Dawn muttered early in the visit, after another incident of being slighted. 'Why does she hate me, Mama? I haven't done anything to her.'

'Miss Rose cares only for herself.' I looked up from the piano, where I'd been playing Gershwin. Dawn loved Gershwin, loved to twist her body to the offbeat rhythm of the *Rhapsody in Blue*, loved to dance for little Helen. 'She sees no need to offer kindness elsewhere.'

And another time, in the quiet of our room, 'Why is she so different from Mrs Cath?'

I smiled and glanced out of the *kaia* door. The kaffirboom leant over the lawn, its leaves painting shadows on the grass where Master Phil had once sat. How many times had I asked myself this question? How could a mother as caring as Mrs Cath be rewarded with so selfish a daughter?

'Only God the Father knows, child. It was like this even when we were children. But,' I turned back and stroked her pale arm, 'Miss Rose has the affection of Master. And Master gives us shelter. So she must be treated with caution . . .'

'*Andikhathali* – I don't care!' Dawn hissed from her township self. 'She means nothing to me!'

With Master, Miss Rose charmed and flattered as before, knowing that he still found her hard to resist. But she trod carefully. After all, Master sent her money every month. I knew that. From the crack in the door, I'd overheard him talking to Mrs Cath about how much Miss Rose was costing them to live in a smart flat in Johannesburg while finding no means to support herself.

'She ought to find a job,' Master would say. 'There's surely something she could do.'

'But what?' Mrs Cath would shake her head. 'She's qualified for nothing, she didn't want to teach, or nurse. We hoped she'd marry one day.'

And there they left it.

But on this visit there was another side to Miss Rose's

dealings with Master. A side that she kept well concealed from Mrs Cath. She found a way to ally herself with Master that went beyond the tricks of flattery. She found common ground that they alone shared.

She cast them both as innocent victims. Two souls taken advantage of by unscrupulous lovers.

I doubt that Master agreed with Miss Rose's position, but it was surely comforting for him to bask in her uncritical charm when there was such a dearth of it elsewhere in his life. Miss Rose with her yellow hair and her vivid dresses and her teasing manner – and now with a beautiful blond baby, even if no husband – was a burst of sunshine. I could see it was so. And I did not have the heart to disapprove. After all, Master was a shell of what he had once been. He might deny Dawn even the smallest recognition, but he'd held to his bargain of giving us a home and a future. Across the Groot Vis, blood and fear were rising with the passing of each season. Even Lindiwe despaired. Her latest hut had been burnt down before it could be occupied. We will make this place ungovernable, said the people who drove the struggle. We will tear down and burn up this place until there is nothing left but the bare Karoo earth.

Miss Rose kept up her strategy of charm-plus-victimhood for some time. But one evening, as they sat together on the *stoep* while Mrs Cath played the piano and I finished making dinner and the hadedas listened as they flapped by, Miss Rose made her move. She told Master that he was unnecessarily generous in giving Dawn and me a future within Cradock House.

'Pay her off,' I heard from the hallway, where I passed on my way to the dining room. 'Don't keep her here. She'll leave anyway, as soon as it suits her.'

There was the clink of a glass being replaced heavily on the tray. And the sharp strike of a match for Miss Rose's cigarette. I waited. Another enemy. Dawn and I would never be without enemies. Even in Cradock House.

'I've promised Cathleen,' came Master's voice. From the piano rushed a lively scherzo, as Mrs Cath searched for cheerfulness in advance of the evening meal. I waited, my hands clasped against my blue skirt.

'You owe her nothing more,' hissed Miss Rose. 'You have your own family to take care of. And it's not safe.'

There was a pause. I heard Dawn's footsteps behind me. Since Miss Rose's arrival, I'd encouraged Dawn to spend more time in the *kaia*. Now I turned and put a finger to my lips. Dawn shrugged and returned to the kitchen, resigned to her exclusion.

'There haven't been any prosecutions in Cradock...' Master's voice trailed off.

Mrs Cath had switched to a Bach air. D major. I crept closer to the door.

'No prosecutions yet, you mean,' I heard Miss Rose say. 'But who knows how long that will last?'

I understand revenge.

Revenge is when you attack someone for the wrong they have done you in the past. Revenge draws upon stored bad blood. So now I think I understand a part of Miss Rose. She has taken revenge upon me for being better at the piano than she was, for being the daughter to Mrs Cath that Miss Rose herself should have been, and for, so she thought, luring Master into my bedroom.

Before she returned to Johannesburg, Miss Rose went to the police. Or she said enough to make someone else go to the police. I now know this. It has been reported to the police that my wickedness has resulted in a child that Master and Mrs Cath are being forced to support for fear of being exposed by me.

It was a banging on the *kaia* door at midnight that first told me about Miss Rose's revenge. I had heard about this sort of thing, but I never thought it would happen here in Cradock House. But then I must remember that I do not live in Cradock House, I must not sit on the shell chairs on the *stoep*, I am not part of the family even though Mrs Cath treats me as if I am. Therefore I – and my daughter – do not come under the protection of the house in the matter of midnight visits by the police.

'*Waar is die kind* – where is the child?' a thickset policeman with a black truncheon shouted when I opened the door a crack. Here it was, what I had feared for so long. Here, coming out of the soft night like a single clap of thunder, was the possibility of jail for Master and myself. Here was the possibility of humiliation for Mrs Cath. The possibility that Dawn might grow up alone.

He pushed me aside roughly. A second white man in plain clothes followed him. They swept their torches over the inside of the *kaia*. I heard their heavy breathing, as if they had been running, as if this was a hunt and we were prey.

Or an ambush, like Phil under the guns at Sidi Rezegh.

'Don't touch her!' I screamed, pushing myself between them and Dawn, where she lay blinded, crumpled with sleep, in the harsh light of the torch.

'*Ja*, just look at it,' the first man said with satisfaction, elbowing me aside to press the torch closer to Dawn's pale face. '*Hotnot* for sure!'

Understanding and then anger flared in Dawn's light eyes at the insult. She knew about policemen. We hid from them in the township, these angry men with snarling dogs and vans with grilles into which they flung anyone without a Pass. Since she was a child, I had warned her about them. I had warned her to keep her anger in check and her fists by her side with such men.

These were not township ruffians that could be taken on. These men had truncheons, they had guns. A cool head is the only defence against such men, I used to urge. Wait and pick your own moment to fight back.

'Ada?'

I heard a cry from outside and then Mrs Cath was there, hair undone from her bun, dressing gown with its embroidered flowers trailing about her bare feet. She had run out of the house without her slippers. Her feet must be icy, for it was a winter night with the chance of frost. In the background I heard the kitchen door slam.

'What do you think you're doing!' she gasped at the men.

Taking advantage of their distraction, I flung myself over Dawn's body, shielding her with my own, and scrabbled beneath the mattress. If I'd been in the township, if I'd been in Lindiwe's hut, the sharpened bicycle spoke would be in my hands—

But it wasn't.

I forgot it lived across the room in a drawer with my Pass, ready to go into the township each day. I thought we were safe in the *kaia*, I thought there was no need for such a weapon by my bed.

Could I still reach it? Could I push past the two men? Was it a time for a cool head or a time for fighting back?

The heat rose in my face. My body tensed, ready to spring.

But Mrs Cath was there in her bare feet and her soft gown, Mrs Cath who had no knowledge of bicycle spokes and their desperate uses. I should not bring the blood of the township here to stain my floor unless there was no other choice.

The first man twisted round, his torch swinging wildly. 'Who's the father of the kid?' he demanded.

Mrs Cath hesitated.

The bony thorn tree creaked and scraped against the *kaia*

roof. Mrs Cath's eyes were black in the shadowed room. They flicked to me, then to Dawn, then back to the men, the second of whom was smiling in a way that held no humour.

'Ada!' Mrs Pumile's voice shrieked through the hedge. 'Ada?'

The men exchanged glances, annoyed at the possibility of further interruption.

'I don't know who the father is, Sergeant.' Mrs Cath drew herself up and spoke with slow assurance. 'It is of no concern to us. Now,' she drew breath and went on calmly, 'my husband is a member of the town council. He is ill at the moment, otherwise he'd be here. If you give me your names, please, he will follow this up with your superiors.'

The policemen looked at each other. This talk of superiors was not what they wanted to hear. They were used to being obeyed – even if it was with resentment – not deflected with smooth talk of superiors. The first man, who seemed to be in charge yet always looked across at his colleague for approval, swung his torch again around the walls, as if there were other pale-skinned children to be flushed out.

I felt my nails biting into my palms as I sifted Mrs Cath's lies, and wondered how it is that women can lie so easily. And I realise that it is because we have borne children, and once you have done so, a child's life is worth far more than the telling of a few untruths.

'We had a report,' said the first man sulkily, lowering his torch, 'that there was a case of immorality here.'

Mrs Cath moved around the two men and extended an arm graciously, gesturing for them to leave, as if all they had ever been were guests at a tea party who'd stayed a little too long. 'There must have been some mistake. I'm sure my husband will not press charges. You were only doing your duty.'

The first man shrugged and turned his torch off. The *kaia* plunged back into darkness, Dawn's pale skin and furious eyes disappeared into the night. Mrs Cath edged towards the door, still holding out her arm for them to leave. The second man hesitated, watching me coldly.

'Come on,' said his partner.

The second man followed, deliberately swiping his truncheon on the door frame as he left. The blow splintered the wood and I felt Dawn shrink back on to the bed. Mrs Cath ignored it and nodded formally to me. 'Good night, Ada.'

And I realised that Mrs Cath's lies had not only driven the policemen away and saved us from arrest this night, they had also saved Dawn from learning what we'd concealed from her so far: that her father was not some unknown man who took me by force – as I think she believed – but the Master.

Dawn was awake before I was the next morning. She had quickly fallen asleep after the men left – the young live only for the moment – whereas I lay for hours in the pressing darkness, hearing the wind worry the door within its damaged frame, and reaching over to touch her every so often to make sure she was still there. It was only as first light began to creep around the curtains that a fitful sleep came.

'Who is my father, Mama?'

I roused myself and sat up. She was on the side of the bed, arms wrapped round her knees, light eyes meeting mine in accusation. Her words wheeled about us within the *kaia*, like the torch of the men chasing around the walls.

Who is my father?

And who is mine? I wanted to ask. She is asking me as I asked my mama. I have given up knowing but it haunts me still. Is ignorance worse than knowledge? Will Dawn find more comfort in knowing, for all the shame it might bring? At least my unknown father and I shared the same skin.

Dawn's eyes – light as Master Phil's – never wavered from mine. In their depths I saw the conflicting sides of my child: the biddable one at Cradock House, the wild girl of the township. I had thought it was only her skin that goaded her on, but maybe I was wrong. Maybe this second Dawn was forever in violent, unknowing escape from her father. Maybe it was the secret of his identity that drove her away from me and from white Cradock, and towards the explosive streets. For driven away she increasingly was. I feared where it might end.

'Ada?' There was a knock on the door.

I nodded to Dawn and she went to open it, picking her way over a splinter of wood from the truncheon blow of the night. Mrs Cath had not slept either, I could see that. Her green eyes were swollen, her hair fell about her face in a cloud as it had once done at the time of Master Phil and the apricots. She reached for Dawn straight away and embraced her. I watched as Dawn's dark head lay for a moment against Mrs Cath's shoulder, like young Master Phil's had lain as a sick child and as a tormented man.

What should I say, Phil? I asked him, as Mrs Cath whispered words of comfort to my daughter. And what would we say if Dawn was your child and not Master's? But if that was so, then surely we would have found a place where we'd be welcome despite the difference in skin between all three of us? Perhaps in Ireland, where you once said we might go . . . Or is such a place unheard of in the world? And such a skin discrepancy never able to be overcome?

Mrs Cath had not even dressed before coming out to see Dawn and me. Mrs Cath normally never appeared downstairs in her nightclothes.

'I'm so sorry, Ada,' she said hoarsely, meeting my gaze over Dawn's head. 'I'm so sorry.'

'Will they come back?' Dawn asked, breaking free of Mrs Cath's embrace. She was tall now, taller than me, but not as tall as Mrs Cath yet. In a few years she would be a woman, a beautiful brown woman.

Mrs Cath gathered herself after Dawn's pulling away, and chose her words carefully. 'I don't think so, Dawn. I will ask Edward to make sure it doesn't happen again.'

I opened my mouth to protest – surely if Master went to the police it would make matters worse?

'Why did they come?' Dawn persisted, looking first at me then at Mrs Cath. 'Did they think they would find my father here?'

'Oh no, child,' I rushed in, before her words could gain any import from the pause between Mrs Cath and me. 'It was a mistake, just as Mrs Cath said.'

My reply hung on the air, too swift in denial, too ready with the lie.

'You don't want to tell me, do you?'

I stared at her, this lovely, fierce girl with the dancing feet that had somehow sprung from Master and me, and I could not tell her. Not now. Perhaps not ever. If I told her, everything that we had built for her at Cradock House would collapse into the brown earth. She would be angry with Master, she would be hurt for the sake of Mrs Cath, she would disapprove of me for not having had the strength to say no. For Dawn, there would never have been a conflict between duty and loyalty. She would have made her choice of her own free will; she would have shut the door on Master if she so wished. Even as a girl, my daughter has the strength and determination of a grown woman.

'I can't tell you,' I said firmly over my quaking heart, reaching for my own hard-won township strength. 'There are some things that are best left alone. I must answer to God the Father for what I've done.'

I held myself straight, as I'd done when I showed her pale face to Mr Dumise and to Silas on the day she was born.

'It doesn't matter.' Dawn shrugged. She turned away to pick up the sack she used for her school books.

'What do you mean, Dawn?' Mrs Cath spoke then, clasping her hands so that the knuckles showed white.

'I can always go and live in the township.' She lifted the sack over her shoulder. 'Then there'll be no one for them to find when they come looking for *hotnots* again.'

Chapter 39

I fear that God may become angry with me. So far, He has allowed me to go unpunished for my sin provided I raised my daughter in a godly way. This was Lindiwe's view, when she first comforted me over Dawn: God will forgive you if you serve Him through the child. God will keep you safe so that you can keep the child safe for His later purposes. And over the years – like when Dawn was ill, like when Mrs Cath found me in the township – I believed that God was indeed protecting me, offering me a future in order that I should protect His child. This was God's plan.

But now Dawn sought to leave my protection. She wished to take her chances beyond my ability to keep her safe. Did that mean that God would now have no further use for me? Or had I raised her well enough to be granted His long-lasting forgiveness?

We have fixed the *kaia* door frame. Mrs Cath said she was sure we would have no further night visits. Master said nothing, not at breakfast when I saw him that morning, not when he walked past me in the kitchen later that day, not when I laid a pile of folded washing in the linen cupboard opposite his open study door. It was as if it had never happened. Like his lying with me had never happened.

In fairness to him, I decided that Mrs Cath had probably ordered him to stay inside when the police came, reckoning that they might pick up the family resemblance if he was present, but even so his lack of the smallest sympathy towards us filled me with contempt. I opened my mouth to say something and then closed it again. Master has given us shelter so far. I must be grateful for that. I must not expect more.

For Dawn, the midnight visit was the catalyst she had been waiting for. From the time when the policemen came, I knew it would not be long before she left. But her reasons for going had nothing to do with a fear of being arrested. She was going because she preferred to be somewhere other than Cradock House. When I tried to understand this, the fact that my daughter wished to go back to the place from where she had been rescued, I could not do so. For me, the only place that made sense was Cradock House. The only solace that there was lay in the piano.

Each afternoon, on our way back from school, Dawn and I grew silent as we approached the house, expecting to see a police van in the driveway and rough men swaggering on the lawn. But everything was quiet – everything except my heart and, no doubt, Mrs Cath's, for we both knew the police were simply biding their time before the next attack.

I played a lot of Beethoven in the weeks after the midnight visit. Its grandeur and certainty – unlike the wanderings of my beloved Debussy – became my anchor. With Beethoven you knew where you were going. Even minor keys stood up for themselves. There was time to steel your fingers, and your heart, for the crescendos.

'You play more Beethoven these days, Ada,' Mrs Cath said, coming into the house with fresh roses from the garden, for the rains had come to feed the flowers and swell the furrow with brown river water, and Mrs Cath was filling the anxious days with gardening. 'You used to prefer the romantics.'

I ran my hands over the gleaming keys, my fingers hesitating for a moment where the bad keys would have been on the school piano. B flat, G. 'I like his tunes because they're clear, Mrs Cath, and sure of themselves. You can be certain what they mean.'

She nodded and lifted the roses towards me. 'Smell. Aren't they glorious? Isn't the joy of music what we read into it? What isn't certain? What we open ourselves up to hear?'

'But she will leave, Ma'am!' The old word slipped out before I could stop it. I struggled to keep my breath.

Mrs Cath put a gentle hand on my shoulder and leant down to look me in the eye as she'd done when teaching me my letters. 'Yes, one day she will. You need to be brave.' She straightened and turned to the window like she used to years ago, looking for Ireland and the family she'd left behind and the place she'd called home where the land was soft and green and the stream fell over the cliff to the sound of Grieg. And I realised Mrs Cath had travelled this route more often than me, firstly when she was the one doing the leaving, and then when Miss Rose left, and then our dearest Phil. I remembered the many days when she wore grey dresses and reached for his badge at her throat and whipped her fingers through her scales, and I knew that I had much to learn in the matter of leavings.

I have become inured to partings, although this one was particularly poignant. It happened when Dawn was thirteen.

I'd seen it coming for some time and I knew we were powerless to prevent it. Dear Ada did her best but Dawn possesses a quantity of her father's stubbornness and was utterly determined. She hopes to find her way in the township but it is a tough place and I fear she will falter. Poor child, she is very confused by her mixed race and who are we to say that we would manage any better? The ramifications of Edward's folly will resonate long after we are all gone.

Rosemary – from Johannesburg – says it was inevitable and seems to suggest that Ada herself should relocate too. She says the prosecutions for immorality are rising in the city and are sure to reach even our little dorp.

Edward is much reduced in stature over all this. He finds it impossible to engage either with Ada or his daughter in any way whatsoever. He leaves it to me to provide the cohesion between the two halves of our lives – Cradock House and the kaia.

I do the best I can, although I, too, am reduced.

There are no dinner parties. Our friends are tentative with us.

I take pleasure in the small things: the blue flash of Dawn's eyes, the perfume of roses, the majesty of Ada's Beethoven.

Chapter 40

I know that Lindiwe is lonely. She misses her brother. Even though Jake inhabited the shadows and only appeared rarely, she still felt protected by him. I miss him too. But now he has gone. And in Johannesburg, in a place called Sharpeville, the war on skin difference has entered a dark place. Police used their guns to kill sixty people who gave themselves up for arrest for not having a Pass.

I found Mrs Cath in tears over it in the kitchen.

'What have we done?' she whispered. 'Some were children – shot in the back.'

'In the back, Mrs Cath?'

'They were running away.'

The townships mourned, and raged. My pupils arrived at school with their pockets weighed down by stones, ready for hurling at the police vans that prowled the perimeter of the playground. Blood stained the school's corridors once more from their skirmishes, for the truncheons were never far away and the hard Karoo earth is not kind to young arms and legs. In class, the quiet songs I'd introduced no longer satisfied. It was fighting songs they wanted, liberation songs, songs whose words cried for power and freedom – and revenge.

'*Amandla!*' they shouted in the school hall, drowning Mr Dumises's pleas for calm. '*Amandla!*' they shouted on the streets, in defiance of the lurking police.

Amandla ngawetu! Power is ours!

The townships were ringed with soldiers in riot gear. They fired gas in the air that made you cry. Dawn stumbled into Cradock House one day with streaming eyes.

'Here.' Mrs Cath rushed on to the *stoep* where Dawn sat weeping, and set down a bowl of cold water and soft flannels. 'Gently now.' And together we bathed her eyes, and wiped her face.

'I hate them!' Dawn screamed, hands raking at her swollen face. 'What have I done to them?'

Mrs Cath and I exchanged glances. Master was in his study, he would hear her. But he never came out.

In the township beyond Bree Street, Lindiwe's new hut – a hut built with her own carefully hoarded money from washing – was torched the day it was finished. You would think that mud walls and a corrugated-iron roof would not burn, but burn it does if petrol is thrown upon it. The walls crumble, the carefully beaten floor melts. The iron roof tilts and its anchoring stones slide off, then it falls down and is stolen the moment it is cool enough to handle. Lindiwe does not feel targeted herself, because those that set fire to things do so randomly, but she does not like to dwell upon it. And she speaks of Jake only when asking me to check the newspapers for his name where they write about arrests and protests and the new word, terrorism.

I remember when apartheid was a new word.

It seems to me that words can give birth to other words that might never have come about on their own. This new word has been born out of apartheid. These burned huts and dead children and streaming eyes have been born out of apartheid.

Lindiwe has once again proved to be a faithful friend to me. Of her three huts that survive, one has a spare place with a bed. This, Lindiwe is prepared to give to Dawn for free so she can live in the township one day, as she is determined to do, despite my fear for her, despite the children her age that died in Sharpeville, and those that goad death on our own festering streets.

'I can pay you when the time comes,' I insisted to Lindiwe one afternoon when I was visiting. It was winter and the light was fading fast. Cooking fires were already burning. I would need to leave soon to make it out of the township in daylight. The dark was not just for robbers, now, it was for the police too. 'And Dawn must help you with washing – it will occupy her outside of school.' I was determined Dawn should contribute. There is nothing to be gained without work.

Lindiwe shook her head impatiently. 'I don't wash any more, Ada, I look after my huts!' She thrust a muscular arm towards the rough streets now milling with the unemployed. Without jobs, all that was left was loitering and setting fire and robbery. Even honourable people were driven to it by the emptiness in their bellies and the lack of a place to stay. 'After the fire, and with so many squatters looking to steal a place, I must guard my huts every day.'

I nodded. I knew it had become so. Unless you defended your possessions in the township, they would be stolen off your back, or from under your bed, or from over your head. There is no limit to what people will do if they are desperate.

'Now,' Lindiwe lifted her kettle off the paraffin stove and poured hot water into her aluminium teapot, 'what has happened that makes Dawn want to come here? Is it your Master?' Lindiwe has always felt that it would only be Master who would break the arrangement under which Dawn and I lived at Cradock House.

'It is not Master. It is Dawn's skin that drives her.'

It was what I had told Dina at school years before. Dawn might be in flight from her father as well, but in the end it came down to skin. It was ordained from the moment I lay with Master. Any child with a skin that does not belong, that is neither one thing nor the other, will always rush to extremes in an effort to find a true home.

Lindiwe laid a hand on mine. 'When the time comes, I will see she goes well. I'll be her spare mother.'

And so it was done. And when Dawn came to me one day and said she wanted to leave, I would not weep and forbid her. I would keep my tears in check and tell her that she could go provided she stayed in the hut that had been organised for her. It wasn't a true negotiation, but more of a trade. I will let you go, my precious brown girl, provided you stay where you will be safe. For I know that I cannot keep you here. I know that Cradock House is not the refuge for you that it is for me. You need to find your music elsewhere.

'I'll be fine with Lindiwe, Mama.' Dawn sat cross-legged on the bed in the *kaia*, her books in her sack, her clothes packed into my old cardboard suitcase that had once carried my few possessions across the Groot Vis to a township future.

'Stay away from *tsotsis* that throw stones, and come back often,' I managed, holding on to my breaking heart. 'To see Mrs Cath, to eat . . .'

'To see you, Mama.' She leant forward and put her young arms round me and I rested my head on her shoulder, like Phil had rested his head upon my shoulder in the darkness of his bedroom. Dawn has always had tenderness bound up within her wildness. In some ways, it is the tenderness that I fear for the most.

Since she has moved, Dawn has promised that she will meet me in the hall before assembly each morning. Sometimes she doesn't come, and I struggle to play the march, imagining what might have happened. Every night, alone in the *kaia* with its fixed door, I worry that she may never reappear. The dead youngsters of Sharpeville haunt me.

'Dawn! At last, child – but look at your clothes – what have you been up to?'

'Dancing, Mama!' She twirls around in front of me, slender brown legs flashing, hands flying. 'How is Mrs Cath? Can I borrow your pencils? I've lost mine.'

It takes a year or more but slowly I get used to her disappearances and my heart lifts whenever she returns from whatever it is that she does, for it's not always dancing.

'Are you careful with boys, Dawn? Don't lie with them till you're older,' I warn, as I have warned her since childhood about boys and the trouble they can bring, for she is beautiful now in her wildness; a pale exotic against the blackness all about her. She must not fall, she must not do what I have done or what her grandmother did. She must be clever and wait until she finds a man who will stay. A man with matching skin.

'I know, Mama. I'm careful, I know what can happen.' She leans down to me at the piano, gaiety melting into tenderness, and rests her cheek on mine.

But I do not ask what she does or where she goes. I do not wish to know. I think I am becoming like those white people I despise: if I don't see something, or don't hear something, then it has never happened.

'How is Dawn?' Mrs Cath asks nervously each day I return home. Mrs Cath reads about the stone-throwing youngsters, she smells the smoke rising across the Groot Vis, she has seen the tear-gassed face of Dawn. But she does not dwell on it. Neither do I. If we don't talk about it, then maybe the stones and the smoke and the sirens will not engulf Dawn.

'She is well, Mrs Cath,' and Mrs Cath nods with relief and hands me a pretty handkerchief or a bottle of our homemade apricot jam and tells me to give it to her when I next see her. I cannot tell her that I don't see Dawn every day.

Master never asks after his daughter, but then he never saw her when she was living here, so there is no difference to be made of the fact that she is gone. I always said to myself that I would speak to him about the not-seeing, I always said I wouldn't let it lie. But when Dawn and I were in the *kaia*, I never wished to risk him throwing us both out. Now that she is gone, there is no reason not to speak. And the words have grown stronger within me rather than fading with the passing years. They want to be said. They are like an inside wound borne for too long, eating away at me, demanding to be released.

I took courage one morning when Mrs Cath was out and Master was in his study with the door open, listening to my piano. Elgar. *Chanson de Matin* – song of the morning. It was early summer, and in the back garden the hedge beetles waited for the full force of midday heat to start their rasping chorus. The *koppies* on the edge of town glistened in the yellow sunlight. It was too beautiful a day to have a confrontation, but it wasn't often that I was alone in the house with Master. I left a sonata unfinished and appeared in his doorway before he could close the door.

'You never ask after Dawn, sir. Even after the tear gas.'

He still wore a chain in his waistcoat and he still did not meet my eyes.

'I am sure she is well,' he said distantly.

He bent over his papers. Still he did not look up. He should be made to face what he did. It was too late for apologies, but I needed some release from the feeling that it was all somehow my fault. I'd waited a long time to say these words. I'd prepared them many years ago, and practised in the night until I knew them off by heart so there was no danger that I would forget them, or say more or less than I intended. Maybe God the Father might disapprove, but I could not help myself. I had been quiet for too long.

'She is well enough, but her skin gives her no rest. It will always be this way.'

He said nothing.

'I did what I thought was my duty, but you knew about inheritance.'

Still he said nothing.

'You knew about the law. I did not.'

My words struck him like stones flung on the township streets. He flinched. I felt a trembling in me, like I had trembled at Phil's funeral when the white congregation watched the back of my neck. But this was not a trembling born of fear or sorrow; this was a trembling born of many years of waiting, and many years of stored injury. It was, I'm ashamed to say, a kind of revenge. I waited. The space between us grew cold.

'I made a mistake.' He looked up briefly. 'You were—' Something flickered in his washed-out eyes for a moment, then shut down.

'You have never greeted Dawn or me since.'

'I supported you instead!' He was suddenly possessed of rage and slammed his hands flat down on the desk. I felt myself take a backward step.

'I let you come back for Cathleen's sake. God Almighty! The police could return any day.' He clutched his head, disturbing the white hair where it lay carefully combed from its side parting.

'Don't you understand, Ada?' He looked at me fully now. His hands were shaking. 'We could go to jail if they decide she's mine. It'll be all over the papers.'

I thought of Jake.

'They make more of the white man's fall,' I murmured to myself. Master did not hear me. An F sharp whistle sounded from the station. Once upon a time, Phil hugged me there in front of white crowds and Master saw it, and hated it, but when Phil was gone he took me for himself anyway.

'Please leave me.' Master stared down at his papers once more, the rage spent. 'Please leave me alone.'

I watched him and I tried to be angry, but all that was left in me was pity.

'I think she left Cradock House to spare you from the law,' I said softly, wondering if it might indeed be true. Dawn has never said so, but maybe she knows, maybe she has always known. Maybe I am the ignorant one.

'What?' I heard him gasp as I turned away.

Maybe she left Cradock House to spare me, too.

Chapter 41

I have been asked to arrange a concert.

It's become known there is a young teacher at the school across the river who is a brilliant pianist. Because of my fund-raising connection with the school – and of course my music – I have been asked to contact her and invite her to play. It's an attempt, in these fraught times, to defuse tension.

No one, it seems, knows that the teacher concerned is Ada.

Where in the past I have been so assiduous in my championing of our black community, now I'm afraid of what I have unleashed. What will happen when I reveal Ada as the teacher, our Ada, with her coloured daughter who has Edward's eyes?

So far, within our circle, there has been a tacit, though awkward, accommodation. No one has ever mentioned the fact of the coloured child under our roof. And the police have left us alone after that one horrific night. But this public exposure may well precipitate what Ada was afraid of when I visited her in that desperate, cramped hut: that we will be ostracised. And the police may choose to act once more.

And yet I have no choice. Ada deserves the right to perform. Her ability is truly extraordinary. She deserves to be heard in every way.

Something special happened for me soon after Dawn left. I was invited to play the piano at Mrs Cath's school. Such an invitation was no ordinary thing, for this was the school that would not hear of me attending it when I was young, even although the laws at that time were not so exact. This was also the school, according to Master, that would lead me to trouble later on if I went there. I am old enough now to smile over this – surely it is not possible that I could have found any more trouble than I have found already!

But no matter.

It was also no ordinary thing because at the time of the invitation the laws of skin difference were at their most fierce, and the dead of Sharpeville lay like a weight between black and white. Different skins were not allowed in the same place at the same time, particularly if they were enjoying themselves. The law insisted that such enjoyment should be had at separate skin-matching venues. Whites should have fun with whites, blacks should have fun with blacks, and so on. I'm not sure how Mrs Cath and her school managed to get past this but somehow they did.

I think it was a matter of finding the right words. Words can be persuaded to take on meanings that you don't expect. Words can even outwit those who believe they own all their possible meanings.

'Ada!' Mrs Cath put her head around the *kaia* door one afternoon, not long after my confrontation with Master. There had been no change since that talk. Master remained detached, and I don't think he said anything to Mrs Cath, for her attitude to me never wavered from its usual kindness. 'May I come in?'

She sat down on the bed next to me. Mrs Cath saw no shame in sitting with me in this way. 'There's to be a concert at my school. I've been asked if you will play. There'll be singing from St Peter's choir,' she ticked off the items on her fingers, 'and the school orchestra is to do Strauss.'

I waited for a moment, confused. 'Why do they want me?' I asked. 'There must be whites as good as me?'

'Oh, Ada,' her forehead creased, 'how sad you should even say that.'

'I don't mean to be ungrateful, Mrs Cath. But black people aren't allowed at your school. I know these things.'

She glanced at the door for a moment, where Dawn and I had repaired the frame from the midnight truncheon blow.

'I'll tell you, Ada, I'm not sure myself how this has been done. But,' she leant towards me, 'it seems they wish to reach out, and they have permission.'

I looked down at my hands that had played so many hundreds of pieces but only ever at Cradock House or in the township. Even music obeyed the laws of skin. Mrs Cath continued to speak but I found myself struggling to hear her. My head seemed unable to accept what she was saying and it came to me only in fragments.

'People have heard of you . . . The first music teacher in the township . . . I spoke to Mr Dumise . . .'

'You spoke to him?' I felt the familiar shiver about names and Passes and the tangle of lies under which I worked across the river. What would he say? What would my fellow teachers say? Would accepting such an invitation be thought of as a betrayal of the struggle? I'd already betrayed my fellow blacks by lying with a white man.

Mrs Cath placed a hand on my arm. 'Ada?'

'This is a new thing for me.'

Her green eyes softened. 'I know. You don't have to decide straight away. But Mr Dumise is keen for you to play. And I'd be,' she stopped for a moment to find the right word, 'honoured, yes, honoured, Ada, if you would.'

No one had ever said such a thing to me. No one had ever

considered me worthy of such a thing. Only Phil – and Mrs Cath herself – have ever valued me for myself and for what I could do. Yet maybe, I wondered, as I stood with suddenly tearful eyes at the *kaia* door and watched Mrs Cath go back into the house, maybe this was a sign from God the Father that I am to be forgiven. Maybe the anger that I feared would fall upon me once Dawn left has been stayed for good.

And so I said yes.

Boldly, without consulting anyone in the township, without dwelling on the consequences of a black woman playing for a white audience, I said yes. And, like the arrival of Miss Rose back at Cradock House that caused the world to change, so another change took place when I played at the school on the white side of the Groot Vis.

It turned out that I was not the only black person there. The organisers of the concert had been clever in more than the matter of getting past the laws governing blacks and whites under the same roof. They had also invited Mr Dumise and several township community leaders.

This helped me.

When I had said yes to Mrs Cath, I knew that such an invitation might not be well received in the township. If my old enemy, Silas, had still been at school, he would have found a way to prevent me taking part in this sort of white event. But when Mr Dumise announced to the assembly one day that I had been invited to play across the Groot Vis, my students forgot their resentment and the stones in their pockets, and shouted with delight. Any doubters on the staff kept their feelings to themselves. I thought Dina might call it sucking up to the white man but she didn't. Dina had much else to occupy her, for she had recently married and was occupied in the making of babies with her new husband.

'Just show them!' she threw over her shoulder while rushing off to her hut after lessons. 'Show them that blacks are as good as whites!'

Sadly, certain of the black community leaders refused to come, for the invitation was indeed regarded with suspicion, such was the divide between black and white at the time. But mostly it was taken to be a small gesture on the part of the white school involved, and a welcome one. There had been few such efforts made in the past.

The other person who did not come was Master. I was not surprised. Master had not been well lately. And it was better that he should not come, because otherwise people would look at him and would look at me and there would be no way for them to look away from the truth.

Dawn didn't want to come, much as I wanted her to.

'They will stare, Mama,' she said quietly, her buoyancy for once stilled. 'They will stare at you because of me, not because of your music.'

'I'm so sorry, child—'

'Don't be! Play well, Mama!' She hugged me tightly. 'It'll be your night!'

So it was that I found myself crossing the green lawns of the school that Miss Rose and Master Phil had attended. The school building was painted white and there were flower beds set against the pristine walls. All the windows had glass in them. It was early evening and groups of children in ironed uniforms and polished shoes stood about on the grass, talking to each other and not playing rough games as they would have across the river. The last hadedas of the day flapped overhead, no doubt surprised to see me in this new setting. I was wearing my white blouse and my navy skirt and a pair of lace-up shoes with heels from Cuthbert's Shoe Store. They were the first shoes I'd ever bought with money from the bank. How proud I felt to be able to afford them! Such shoes will last me for the rest of my life. I had never worn heels before, so I practised on the piano at Cradock House in them so that I would have no trouble managing the pedals on the night.

'Mary?'

I turned, and there was Mr Dumise, in one of his threadbare shirts, smiling at me but looking a little lost among the neatness of everything. Mr Dumise was used to running a school where just keeping the toilets working was a triumph. The possibility of green grass and unbroken windows was beyond his imagining.

'Mr Dumise. My name is not Mary, at least not on this side of the Groot Vis.'

He nodded and I think I saw a sparkle in his eyes. 'I shall try to remember. But we're very proud of you, whatever your name is.'

'I hope I don't let you down, sir,' I said, 'for there are others that play as well as I do.' The school knew Mrs Cath's playing; I couldn't compete with her.

'Ah, but you bring something from the heart,' he said, touching his hand to his chest. 'Play tonight like you played when you first came to school.'

I nodded, feeling once more the heat of the closed-up hall on my neck, and the dust on the piano keys beneath my fingers. In the background, the Groot Vis rushed in flood. Dawn stirred heavily beneath my overall.

Play for Mama, play for the child.

Play for a job . . .

'Ada? Mr Dumise, how good of you to come!' It was Mrs Cath, wearing the green satin dress she used to wear for dinner parties many years ago. She was paler than usual, but perhaps it was face powder.

'Ada, come, my dear, we're about to start.'

⟨⟩

The school was the smartest building I had been in apart from the bank. The corridors smelt clean and the floors were freshly polished. There were hooks down one side to hold blazers. There were untorn pictures and maps on the walls. It was the way that a school should be.

In the hall, there were paintings of severe ladies wearing black gowns with satin and fur upon them, and flat black caps with tassels. They were the smartest ladies I had ever seen. And the stage curtains did not drag their feet on the ground.

As I waited for my turn alongside Mr Dumise and the community leaders, it was a little like sitting in church with Master and Mrs Cath at young Master Phil's funeral: once again, people's eyes were on my neck. This time, though, there was a difference. Most of the eyes seemed to be curious, some even friendly, particularly the children in the audience who whispered and craned their necks to look at me. It was surely a novelty to see a black woman in their school who wasn't a cleaner. And these white youngsters probably never met black children of their own age. It was against the law.

The evening began with the church choir singing selections from the *Messiah*. Mrs Cath sang in the sopranos and conducted the choir from the piano. The singing was different from the singing I was used to down at the Groot Vis. Here, the choir kept a firm grip on their pitch. No swooping up to the note was allowed.

And then the school orchestra arrived, and there was some noisy rearrangement of chairs and uncertain tuning of instruments. Finally the youngsters gathered themselves and bounced their way through the *Blue Danube* under the conducting of a man with a large moustache. I found myself itching to move with the beat. Some of the audience swayed gently to the music and clapped politely afterwards, but mostly their reaction was tame compared to what I was used to. It seemed that white people liked to stay in their seats when listening to music. But maybe it was only because they had seats? There were no chairs in the school hall that I came from. Such an absence was clearly an advantage in the matter of enjoying music. I stole a glance at Mr Dumise and wondered if he was thinking of our township students and their wild jiving. I longed to gather up both groups and let them make music together – for surely music breaks through boundaries, and should have no colour?

'And now, ladies and gentlemen, we welcome our guests from across the river. Headmaster Mr Shepherd Dumise, and community leaders Phillip Skoza, Daniel Maludi and Peters Schwaba. And,' the headmistress paused while the audience clapped, then held up her hand for quiet, 'and from the same school we welcome our soloist tonight, Ada Mabuse!'

I felt my heart contract and I looked across at Mrs Cath. She nodded. Alongside me, Mr Dumise touched my arm in encouragement and murmured something I couldn't hear. One of the community leaders leant forward and gestured for me to go. The stage was a long way off from the front row where I'd been sitting and it was all I could do to walk there in my new shoes without tripping. I dared not look back at the massed audience but rather concentrated on the piano gleaming on the stage. Mrs Cath had assured me that its keys were as good as the Zimmerman back home.

I sat down and touched it gently, and waited for a moment. Every piano has its own heart, every piano deserves to be given its due if you want it to recognise you and give you its music.

Mama came to me, and Phil came to me, and then Mrs Cath came to me, and finally my pale Dawn. If only she could have been here . . .

I lifted my hands and the tune rose into my fingers.

The *Raindrop* prelude. By Chopin.

The first liquid notes rang out, and then the tender melody drifted into the hall, hovering and falling, and rising up again in its own time. I forgot who was listening, and I forgot where I was, and I played for those I had loved and they listened and gave my fingers wings.

When it was over there was silence. Then I became aware of feet drumming on the floor. For a moment I was back in the township on my first day as a teacher; the youngsters were stamping to the *marche militaire*, they were dancing to the beat, they were flinging their bodies this way and that as if bewitched . . .

But it wasn't the township. It was the school that I hadn't been allowed to attend. It was white students and their parents who were clapping and calling for more, more music.

And so I gave them more. I gave them some grand Beethoven, and a little sinuous Debussy. Still they clapped and wanted more. I looked down at the audience and I saw no one but Mrs Cath, wiping her eyes. And then I took a chance. I gave them what my students loved to dance to. What Dawn loved to dance to. Township jive, like Miriam Makeba's *Qongqothwane* – the Click Song – with its vibrant rhythm and its offbeat base. *Pata pata*. The African jazz of the Manhattan Brothers. Hugh Masekela's golden trumpet . . .

Mr Dumise was beaming in the front row, the invited black leaders were staring about them uneasily but clapping nonetheless. The smoke, the crowded streets, the baying police dogs were gone. Then, from the back of the hall came the familiar slap and slide of bare feet on floor and I glanced up quickly from the keys. It was Dawn.

The audience turned around in surprise.

The clapping faded, then intensified as my daughter, hair

flying about her face, slender arms above her head, danced behind the back row. I heard them murmur as they wondered to each other who this pale, barefoot girl in the short skirt was. Where she had come from. Why she was here. Who she belonged to, with a skin that was neither black nor white, and eyes light as an early Karoo sky.

And still she danced, in an ecstasy of grace and energy. Danced as if her life depended on it. Danced as if there was no tomorrow.

Danced for me.

This time the police did not pound on the *kaia* at midnight, but knocked on the front door of Cradock House in the lazy, beetle-rasping heat of afternoon.

'Ada!' Mrs Cath rushed into the kitchen, green eyes enlarged with fear. 'Quickly, please go to your *kaia*!' She grasped my arm with fingers hard from the piano. 'Stay there.'

As I hurried past the apricot, past the hedge, beneath the kaffirboom, I felt the same tears that had welled in my eyes as I left the stage to embrace Dawn at the back of the hall. Some of the pupils were drumming their feet on the floor. Some were standing up, craning their necks to see my pale daughter.

'You came! Oh, Dawn, you came!'

'No one plays like you, Mama!'

'Stay, child,' I said over the uproar. 'Have tea and come home for the night.'

'I can't, Mama.' Her slender chest heaved from the effort of the dance. 'I only came for you, I only danced for you – not these others.' She gestured at the audience, on their feet now and still clapping. Some of the children were standing up on their chairs to get a better view. Others left their places and began to crowd around, captivated by Dawn, her lithe body, her exotic face, her wildness.

With a final touch of her cheek against mine she was gone, bare heels flashing, the door banging behind her, out into the darkness and back to the township beyond Bree Street.

There was no way to deny it. They saw she was my daughter in every way except for her skin. And her eyes. The eyes of her father, my Madam's husband.

They asked to see Edward alone but I would not allow it, so we sat in the lounge across from each other. I did not offer tea. They said it had 'come to their attention' that Edward had fathered a coloured child.

'It's true,' I said, taking the initiative (I remember the conversation verbatim), for Edward appeared totally shrunken and unable to respond. 'We do not deny it. But the child lives elsewhere. And my husband fathered her before this was a crime.'

This wasn't strictly speaking true, for I'd done the research. The Immorality Act was just in force when Dawn was born, but I have found that when dealing with local officialdom, an appearance of assuredness can go a long way.

'We'll need to interview the girl,' the one in charge said, 'and the mother.' He was a tall man, more refined than the louts that broke into Ada's kaia. But just as menacing. 'Then the state will assemble its case for prosecution.' They began to speak of witnesses, of procedures, of the statutes involved.

I stood up.

They looked at me, opened their mouths to say more but I pre-empted them. 'I must ask you to leave now. Thank you for informing us. We will, of course, be engaging legal counsel.'

They shrugged, as if nothing we could do would make any difference, gathered their papers, and left.

I waited in the *kaia* until I heard their van leave. Then I went back to the house. Mrs Cath and Master were sitting opposite one another in the lounge. I watched from the crack in the door. The clock ticked. They said nothing, although Mrs Cath seemed to be expecting Master to speak, and glanced across at him from time to time. I waited. A sudden breeze rattled a window. Still they sat. It occurred to me how much time they spent together in silence, bereft of words or touch. Through Phil's illness, and Miss Rose's troubles. It is the opposite of what I expected married people to do. Yet maybe this is what happens in a long marriage: husband and wife turn away from intimacy, retreat into themselves, particularly if they are split by different views of the world. Or maybe it is a sign that there was not enough between them from the start.

I lifted up my hand and tapped on the door. It was time to step out from my usual hiding place.

'Come in, Ada,' Mrs Cath said, turning away from Master and nodding at me, as if she'd known I was there all along. Master stared down at his fingers. The newspaper lay on the floor beside his chair in an untidy heap.

'What do they want, Mrs Cath?'

She hesitated for a moment, then said firmly, 'They want to prosecute Edward.' It was the first time she had called Master by his name in front of me. Like the moment at school when we saw each other not as madam and servant but as women, now Mrs Cath was treating me as an equal in relation to Master.

'And prosecute me?'

'They want to interview Dawn first.'

'Dawn?' My heart went cold.

'Only to talk to her,' Mrs Cath hesitated, glancing at Master, 'for evidence. But, Ada,' she added swiftly as she saw the horror on my face, 'Dawn herself won't be charged with any crime, you mustn't worry.'

But I did. For Mrs Cath had no idea what went on in the township, or the side of Dawn that lived there. Her fierce will. Her desire to prove herself, to be more black than she was, to be part of the inferno – liberation, struggle, revolution, war – that was engulfing us all.

I didn't care what happened to me, it was Dawn who mattered, Dawn who must be protected. If they found her and took her away for questioning, Dawn would resist. I knew she would. She would fight, and protest, and kick and scream even though she herself might only be a witness or a victim, someone not to be charged with any crime. And at the end of it she would be forever damaged.

'Ada! Ada!' Mrs Cath rose, but I was already out of the room, out of the back door, down the garden, out of the back gate that I'd passed through with my child growing within me, down Dundas Street gasping for breath, across Church Street with my chest heaving, down Bree with a sharp pain in my side from the running, past the jail and into the township on desperate feet, even though it would soon be dark.

Chapter 42

'Stay out of sight, Dawn. And watch your tongue if they find you!' I begged, as Lindiwe, Dawn and I sat in the gathering darkness of Lindiwe's hut, with only a candle on the floor for light. The naked flame threw trembling shadows on the mud walls. From outside came the noise of men making their way to the nearby beer hall, their weekly wages in their pockets. It was a Friday. I strained through their shouts for the sound of police sirens coming for my child. I said nothing about being prosecuted myself.

'But why, Mama? I've done nothing wrong.'

Lindiwe reached a hand across and touched my arm in sympathy and then turned to Dawn. 'No, you haven't, but your mama gave you a skin that makes you do wild things. This is what your mama fears if they come and take you to the police station – that you will fight back.'

'They have no right!'

'They can do what they like, child!' I cried. 'It's not a matter of rights at all.'

Still I had not admitted that it was Master who was her father. Still I tried to keep to the fiction that an unknown white man gave her the skin she bore, that the police were confused, that their pursuit of us was a mistake. Yet she surely knew. After all, had she not left Cradock House partly to save us from the law?

Lindiwe got up to lift her kettle off the paraffin stove. 'Let us think what would be best,' she said quietly. 'What will keep Dawn safe.'

'I must leave,' Dawn murmured, her anger disappearing, the tenderness returning as she reached across and wrapped her young arms around me. 'Then there'll be no evidence any more. No brown skin that they can find, wherever they look.'

'No, child,' I wept against her cheek pale as tea. 'We can manage. Maybe Mr Dumise, or the Reverend Calata will speak up for you.'

'Oh Mama.' Dawn drew away and looked at me with sadness. 'Anyone who helps me will be under suspicion. It must end with me.'

'But where will you go?' Lindiwe, always practical, returned with mugs of strong tea that she placed on the earth floor before us.

'To Jo'burg,' said Dawn with certainty, eyes gleaming even in the darkness of the hut. 'No one will find me there.'

'Jo'burg!' I gasped. Jo'burg, the place of trouble like Miss Rose found, like Sharpeville with its dead children. 'So far away!' How could I help her if she was so far away? And if I was in jail?

'I'll find work.'

'Doing what?'

Dawn had yet to finish school, the only thing she knew was what I knew: polishing, dusting, ironing. I'd taught her English and sent her to school so she could go further than just housework.

'I'll dance!' she said then, with a quick smile. 'Look how they loved my dancing the other night!' She got up and began to twist and bend in the candlelight, moving to unheard music, to a rhythm that was hers alone.

'If you answer their questions with politeness, they will take your answers and let you go,' I tried again, desperate to reach the dancing figure before us. 'But if you resist, if you argue . . .'

Dawn struck a final pose and then dropped down to the floor, her supple limbs crossing beneath her like sleeves tucked into a folded shirt.

'Don't you understand, Mama? I came to the concert specially for you,' she asserted through the gloom. 'I danced for you, Mama. I was going to leave one of these days anyway, even if the police hadn't come.'

'Dawn!'

'The Karoo's too small, too small, Mama,' she coaxed, trying to make me believe. 'The future will be better in Jo'burg. More brown skins like mine, they say.'

The future will be better in Jo'burg, Miss Rose had also said, as she waved goodbye in the blue dress and the red lipstick from the chemist. I looked at Dawn, this girl-woman who fell in between, like the colour of the Groot Vis, and I knew that nothing I could say would make any difference. From the moment I learnt about inheritance from the kind doctor whose house is no more, I knew she would never belong with me. The first raid on the *kaia* had strengthened her desire to leave Cradock House; this latest crisis was giving her the reason to shake the Karoo dust from her feet altogether.

Yet who was I to judge? I myself had returned to Cradock House out of a desire to belong somewhere.

She scrambled up and stood in the doorway, as Mrs Cath had once stood in the doorway to Lindiwe's hut when she found me. 'I'll fetch my things and come back. Will you stay here, Mama?'

She took a quick step back and leant down to grasp my shoulder. 'Stay here tonight? The train goes early.'

'I knew it was Master,' she whispered later, as we lay in the darkness on the floor together, 'when Miss Rose started to hate me.'

I took her hand where it lay next to me and pressed it against my face, feeling the rough patches on the knuckles and the smoothness of the palm, inhaling the sweet youth of her. Beyond the outline of her head with its smoother-than-African hair, unexpected stars peered at us through the open doorway.

'I thought it was my duty,' the words came out of me in a rush, 'when he came to the door – can you forgive me, child?'

She turned to face me. Her blue eyes glittered black as coal.

'I won't forgive Master,' she said with quiet heat, 'and I won't forgive Miss Rose.'

I felt the chill in my heart deepen, for although such strength might help her survive, it might also drain the tenderness from her being. Tenderness that still laced her heart despite daily injustice. I prayed that the world would change in time, so this might never happen.

It was a grey dawn like the morning when my child was born and I'd walked to the water tap with Dawn on one arm and Auntie's bucket on the other. A rim of sunrise showed on the horizon, picking out the purple shapes of the *koppies* where they loomed above the town. People hurried down the street, some with suitcases like Dawn, others with no possessions. It was quiet; the 'Township Bach' had yet to reach its usual pitch, the troublemakers had yet to fill their fists with stones.

'You have the address of my friend?' Lindiwe had checked as we left her hut.

'Yes,' said Dawn, pale but keen in the early light. 'Thank you, Ndwe.'

Lindiwe took her hand and squeezed it. 'You must write to your mama.'

'Yes, I will. I'll write every week.'

'And to me. It will be good for my reading.'

They were trying, I know, to help me. Trying to cover my silence and the weight that was bearing down upon me as each step along the dirt road took us closer to Bree Street, closer to Church Street and the bridge across the Groot Vis, closer to the station that would swallow my child before the sun was up.

A group of youngsters with Afro hairstyles waved at Dawn, their hands falling to their sides as they saw the case in her hand, and Mama's old funeral coat over her shoulder. She didn't stop to talk as she normally would have done, but kept on walking between Lindiwe and me. Even the jail was quiet. Police vans sat in a line outside, silent, waiting to perform the cruel business of the day.

We reached Church Street. Dawn glanced up towards the Karoo Gardens on Market Square, where the benches I used to sit on now said 'Whites Only'. Dawn never knew what it was like to sit on those seats and warm her feet in the sun – the signs had gone up when she was a child.

We turned on to the bridge. Below us the Groot Vis slouched around rocks where the first washerwomen were finding their places. Drooping weaver nests trailed close to the surface of the water. The river was low but we hadn't taken the drift because it would have meant Dawn getting her feet wet and somehow that didn't seem the right way to leave.

I could see the train sitting in the station already. Shunting noises came from further along the track. Above, capturing the first rays of sunlight, was the *koppie* where Auntie's outdoor church had once been. I sometimes saw Auntie in the distance but she never greeted me or Dawn. In this, she had turned out to be like Master – and many other whites: if you don't see something with your own eyes, it doesn't really exist. Like schools that won't hear, and minds that can be deliberately closed to what is just around the corner.

'Mama?' Dawn took my arm and led me up the station steps, for I'd stopped and stared about me as if it was a strange place.

'Yes,' I gathered myself, 'we must get a ticket.'

Lindiwe had kindly offered to pay for Dawn's ticket because in my rush out of Cradock House I had not fetched the money that lay in the slit of my mattress. I will pay Lindiwe back the next time we meet.

'Johannesburg,' said Dawn to the man behind the bars in the ticket office for non-whites. 'One way.'

The man looked her over, noting the cardboard suitcase, the tattered funeral coat, the luminous face against the blackness of Lindiwe and me. He licked his finger and counted the money she gave, then pushed a ticket through the opening and pointed at the waiting train.

'Change at De Aar. Ten minutes,' he said.

There were no crowds on the platform as there had once been. No buglers playing 'We'll meet again', no ladies fluttering lace handkerchiefs, not even any laughter to cover the tears.

The train began to work up steam. I stared at the pigeons on the rafters. And then I felt Phil again, the warmth of his hug, the scrape of his cheek where he'd forgotten to shave. I turned to Dawn, who should have been his child, and took her slender body in my arms and held her as I myself had once been held.

'I'll be back, Mama,' she choked, as our tears ran together.

'Yes,' I managed, 'to see Mrs Cath, too.' I'd said the same

thing when she left Cradock House. The train blew its F sharp
whistle.

'Come now,' said Lindiwe, lifting Dawn's suitcase and
opening the door of the third-class carriage. 'One last hug.'

Doors banged all along the train as the last passengers went
on board. Dawn undid my arms from round her and climbed
the steps into her carriage. She put her case and Mama's coat
down and leant out of the window. Excitement fought with the
tears, for she was eager to go, eager for the good future she
believed waited in Johannesburg. Lindiwe and I reached up and
took her hands. One hand for Lindiwe, one hand for me.

'Go well,' shouted Lindiwe over the snorting engine. 'Work
hard and write to your mama!'

'God bless, God bless!' I tried to say, but the words stayed in
my throat.

With a massive effort, the train began to move amid clouds of
steam. The pigeons took off from the roof beams. I ran alongside,
not wanting to let go until the last moment. Lindiwe shouted for
me to stop. Then the platform ran out and I felt her slip from
my grasp.

'I love you, Mama!' She leant out of the window and waved
hard. 'Tell Mrs Cath I'm sorry not to say goodbye!' She dashed
a hand across her face to wipe the tears.

The train began to gather pace. Dawn's carriage curved away
from us. Another blast from the whistle, this time a shade below
F sharp, and the train struck out for the empty Karoo, first to the
junction at De Aar and then beyond to Johannesburg where
there was gold in the ground and – God protect her – all manner
of trouble above it.

Chapter 43

'Come,' said Lindiwe, taking my arm. 'We will walk together.'

So we walked back across the bridge. Some washing friends of Lindiwe called to her from their rocks and she waved at them. I looked back. The train was just a smudge of smoke against the vast, brightening sky. Then the sun burst over the horizon fully, glancing off the tin roofs on Church Street and washing the stone walls with peach light.

'Will she ever come back?' I found myself saying out loud.

'She will come,' replied Lindiwe comfortingly. 'One day.'

'Like you told me one day I would be proud of her?'

'Just like that – and you are!'

'Why,' I asked, clearing my throat and lifting up my head to face the coming day, 'why are you so good to me?'

'Because I am your friend.'

We stopped on the corner of Church and Dundas. Lindiwe's place lay at the end of Bree Street. My place lay down Dundas. She gave me a fierce hug. Even now that she is a landlord, Lindiwe has lost none of her washing muscles. We agreed to meet later.

Dundas lay cool and quiet under its pepper trees as I walked down the road. The sun hid briefly behind a *koppie* but would strike soon enough and then the street would waken to a sudden heat, like the blast in your face from an open oven door. Dawn used to love the cool of early morning at Cradock House, the dew beneath her toes, the first trill of the bokmakieries, the vygies opening their glossy petals as she dashed past.

It was the car on the road that made me wonder what was wrong. Visitors usually drove up the gravel driveway. And, in any case, who would be calling before breakfast?

I began to hurry. Then I began to run along the verge by the dry water furrow, for I could see Mrs Pumile standing in the road and she was holding her hands over her mouth. Just then, a siren began to howl. Not the dreaded police siren but a different one, a different note, a different beat – and a white ambulance with a revolving light lurched out of the driveway of Cradock House and tore along Dundas Street.

'Such trouble!' Mrs Pumile shrieked, wringing her hands. 'I heard nothing, then the ambulance came! Your poor Madam! The Master on a stretcher – oh Ada, this is too bad, too bad after that rude Miss Rose and the young Master gone – coming, Ma'am!' She stumbled back into the next-door garden as her Madam called with impatience.

The back door of Cradock House was unlocked.

'Madam! Mrs Cath!' I cried but my voice fell into an empty place. I rushed upstairs to her bedroom but it was empty. The bed looked as if it had not been slept in. I went across the passage and knocked on Master's door and then went in. His bedclothes were rumpled, some of them trailing on the floor. There were the usual bottles of medicine sitting on his side table, bottles that I dusted around, like I dusted around Mrs Cath's diary where it lay on her dressing table.

The only thing to do was work. It was a Saturday so there was no school. Once, it might have meant Dawn's return for the weekend and an orgy of feeding her up, but not this time. I went down to the *kaia* and changed my clothes, then wound a *doek* over my hair like Mama used to, and got out the cloths, and tried to calm my racing head. If Master was in hospital, how could he be prosecuted? Did the law take into account illness? Would the law force an ill man into jail? Would the law instead turn its full attention on me?

I went upstairs again, this time to Phil's bedroom, and clambered up on the toy box and peered out over the town, and into the Karoo, and searched with my eyes for a train snaking its way north, but there was nothing to see. Just the vast yellow plains, interrupted here and there by ironstone *koppies* and the occasional dust cloud from an approaching car.

I did the polishing and still no one came home.

Master lay ill, Dawn receded ever further from me. The law waited.

By the middle of the morning I was tired and the house was too quiet so I took off my *doek* and sat down at the piano. I tried a little jazz, like Dawn used to dance to, but it echoed too noisily through the empty passages and too sharply in my heart. So I gave the house a Chopin nocturne instead, the one in C sharp minor that was published only after the composer died. I think it's the best one, the one he kept aside for himself, a gem where each octave-leap surely touches heaven?

'Ada!'

I rushed from the piano. Mrs Cath was in the hallway.

'Oh, Ada.' She dropped her handbag on the hall table and subsided into the small chair we keep by the telephone. Her grey hair was half undone from its bun, her eyes were bruised like they had been when Miss Rose left, and when Phil died. Her soft cream dress had a stain on the sleeve, as if blood had been scrubbed from it without success.

'I saw the ambulance,' I cried, kneeling down.

She leant forward and dropped her head in her hands. I got up.

'Come, Ma'am,' I said, 'let's get you to the sofa, and I'll bring strong tea. Come . . .'

I took her hands – I no longer feared touching Mrs Cath, we'd got past that – and eased her to her feet. She leant on me as we went into the lounge and over to the sofa. I bent down and removed her shoes and lifted her legs up so she was lying lengthways, then covered her with the red shawl she kept nearby.

'Dawn?' she murmured, pressing her eyes closed with her fingertips. 'Is the child safe?'

'Yes, Mrs Cath,' I replied. 'She is quite safe. And I will make you tea.'

I went into the kitchen and put on the kettle, got out the tray and laid an embroidered cloth on it, and found Mrs Cath's special teapot-for-one that she'd brought with her from Ireland and used when she wanted a private cup of tea. I sliced homemade brown bread and buttered it and spread it with apricot jam from our tree, and cut the slices into triangles.

'Oh, Ada, you are kind, so kind.' Mrs Cath lifted herself up. 'Please,' she went on, noting the tray set for her, 'fetch a cup and have tea with me.'

I hesitated, but she smiled and gestured towards the kitchen. I brought a cup, and extra hot water, and poured tea for both of us and sat down opposite her and waited while she sipped, and forced herself to eat some of the bread.

I waited.

When Master came home, who would nurse him? Could I find it in myself to help take care of him? It might not be my duty – but surely God the Father would expect me to show mercy? Master's face stared at me, the faded blue eyes, the carefully parted hair, the fierce lips that only softened for Madam, for Miss Rose. *I won't hurt you, Ada . . .*

'He's gone, Ada.'

I started and stared at Mrs Cath. It couldn't be. Surely it couldn't.

'He had a heart attack. They did all they could but he died on the way to the hospital.' She put the cup down, rattling the saucer as she did so.

I got up from the chair and went to the window. The car that had been outside the house was gone. Perhaps it was the doctor's. Perhaps the doctor went with Master in the ambulance and then came back later for his car. Once Master had died.

My daughter has gone too. She climbed on a train bound for Johannesburg perhaps at the moment that her father fell ill. Without knowing it, she left at the very point when she – and he – would no longer be pursued. The accusations against Master would die with him. Dawn would now be of no interest to the police. She would just be another accident, another mixed-race girl who fell in between. They would take the papers they had collected against Master and throw them away, like rubbish is thrown into a waste-paper bin, and move on to another target.

My daughter had gone for no reason. She went to spare her father, and to spare me, and to seek a better future, a future she might have discovered here after all.

But it may not be over. They may not throw the papers away. They may instead come for me with greater venom now that Master has eluded them.

The floor rose up.

Madam called 'Ada!' and I remember no more.

The funeral was delayed until I recovered from my fall. Mrs Cath had to call Dr Wilmott to the house to bandage my head where I'd struck it on the side of the chair. My arm was sore as well, where I'd fallen on it, and Mrs Cath got Mrs Pumile in to help, for Master's linen needed to be washed and stacked at the back of the linen cupboard, and his clothing packed up for donation. The carpet had to be scrubbed of my blood, and then there was Miss Rose's arrival to prepare for.

Now I am at the front of the church, with a *doek* covering the wound, and wearing my best navy dress and my shoes with heels that I wore to the concert at Mrs Cath's school. Perhaps some of today's congregation were there, perhaps some of them clapped when I played. I once believed that my skill at the piano might provide the means to overcome the colour of my child – for Auntie, for my fellow teachers – but it didn't. So I shouldn't expect that a white congregation will shelve its disapproval, however much my playing might have inspired them. Or however much Mrs Cath might appear to forgive me. I have sinned. Even with Master in his grave, I am still a sinner in their eyes.

But I have proved that I can live with this. God the Father has spared me so far, and no amount of white disapproval can change that. As long as I have a piano, I can survive anything. Even the departure of my daughter becomes bearable while the music soars.

This time there is touching in the front row. Mrs Cath takes my hand and squeezes it. She is worried about me but I make light of my head and my sore arm for they will soon heal. Miss Rose ignores the movement, as she has ignored me since she arrived. She looks straight ahead, her black hat with its broad brim rigid upon her head, her skirt tight about her knees. Mrs Pumile hissed when she saw the shortness of Miss Rose's black skirt. Helen is not with Miss Rose, she is at her boarding school in Johannesburg.

'Receive, O Lord, the soul of Edward, beloved father of Rosemary, devoted husband of Cathleen.'

I feel the intake of breath behind me.

They know, of course they know. Or perhaps – because Dawn is not here – they will pretend that it never happened. That the coloured girl with Edward's eyes, who once lived at Cradock House, did not exist. That the coloured girl with music in her feet and a wildness in her heart was just passing by. They can't see her any more, so she was never there.

Chapter 44

The town council also believe that people who can no longer be seen might simply disappear. So they've decided to move the Lococamp and the Bree Street townships to a new township called Lingelihle that will be built further away on the road towards Port Elizabeth, with only a distant sight of the Dutch Reformed Church steeple. They say it is to reduce overcrowding. They say it is because of hygiene. They are right – but if such matters are the main concern, I wonder why they don't just improve what is here already.

This means that our rough school across the Groot Vis will be demolished. This means that Lindiwe's well-guarded huts will have to come down. Only St James School will be spared, on account of its distance from the white end of Bree Street, and its prominence through Rev. Calata.

They say the new houses in Lingelihle will be made of brick and that new schools will be built and that life will be better and cleaner in the new place, although it is further to walk to town, and the land is higher and the winter winds will sweep colder across it than they did over the old townships. They say it is the law.

There are meetings in the St James School hall where the paint peels from the walls and people wonder, if there is a shortage of paint already, how will there be enough paint for new buildings? There is much talk about compensation for those who will lose their homes, however poor they may be. I know about compensation. It's supposed to be a payment for loss, like Jake said Mrs Cath's generosity to me was a payment for the loss of Cradock House when I left with Dawn growing inside me. But I know that payment in money can never replace what is lost from the heart. Lindiwe's huts may have been simple but they were built from her own muscle and effort, and they sat amongst people she knew and who knew her, and their parents and grandparents before them. No compensation can replace that.

'I don't want to leave my father's house,' said Veronica, my fellow teacher who kept chickens and was nervous of Pass-burning. 'Then the ancestors won't know where I am.'

And then there was the matter of rent.

'You'll be in better houses than you have now,' insisted the Superintendent at one such meeting. And he goes everywhere with a police escort. Today they stand legs astride, arms behind their backs, truncheons clasped in their fists. Two town councillors sit by the side of the Superintendent. They look frightened, they reach for books in their briefcases and page through them often.

'Tell us what the rents are,' a man calls.

The Superintendent consults his notes. 'Three rand sixty-eight for two-roomed houses, four rand thirty-nine for four roomed.'

There are gasps, and then muttering around the hall. The muttering grows to a rumble.

'But we pay one rand fifty-five now, so why should we move?' shout several voices over the uproar.

'What about compensation?' someone else yells.

People glance at one another and then turn round to watch the police at the back of the hall. How far will they let this go? I see there are two more policemen now, they've come in quietly. They don't wear uniforms but they carry cameras. They are photographing the audience, especially those that call out. My head is still sore. It aches when I'm anxious.

'The houses will be better than what you have. And we will try for compensation.'

'There must be compensation.' Lindiwe gets to her feet. Lindiwe's English is very good now. Lindiwe knows about compensation. The cameras click, I lower my face.

'No move!' come shouts from a wilder section of the audience, taken up by the rest. 'No move, no move!' Feet drum on the floor, but not in the way of applause. Several elderly residents get up and leave, covering their faces with their hands. The Superintendent looks towards the uniformed policemen, who begin to patrol across the back of the hall, swinging their truncheons lightly.

It is the edge of chaos.

If Rev. Calata had been at the meeting, he would have found a way to calm the crowd and get what they wanted by quieter means. Rev. Calata believes in negotiation. And there is indeed a negotiation to be made. After all, if the town council wants blacks out of sight then it must pay them or reward them in some way to bring this about. But Rev. Calata has been banned, which means he can't attend public meetings and he can't leave his house without a policeman watching him. This is the way it is. Even his picture has been removed from its place near the stage, leaving a pale square on the wall where it once hung. So it is up to people like Lindiwe to stand up for what they believe is right.

And me?

I glance about. Some people recognise me but some will not do so, for I am the woman who sinned with a white man, and the white man is the enemy. I'm a target, particularly as I don't live in the township. People get beaten for not showing solidarity. It's called black-on-black violence. And I'm also easy prey for the white police. They know who I am, they know my sin, they can arrest me whenever they wish. Be careful, I say to myself. There is no right side in this sort of war.

Yet I'm ashamed of myself for not standing up, I have good enough English and a good enough brain to handle such a negotiation.

'They promised compensation,' Lindiwe insisted later, as we pushed back to her hut through the bad-tempered crowd. I felt for the sharpened bicycle spoke in my pocket. Sirens blared. Impatient young men shouted '*Amandla!*' and reached for missiles among the rubbish on the side of the road. Bricks began to whizz over our heads towards an approaching police van. The crowd surged, dust flew up and choked our throats. My head pounded. Lindiwe grabbed my hand. From behind us rose the frenzied barking of police dogs. We began to run.

'I worked hard for my huts,' Lindiwe panted. 'I won't move till I get it!'

All night the crowds rampaged through the streets, pursued by the police and their crazed dogs. All night Lindiwe and I lay awake in the darkness of her hut, flinching when the chase came close . . . and the shouts, heavy boots and barking dogs thundered by in a wild staccato. Lindiwe kept one hand on her buckets of water, kept full since her first hut was burnt down. Only when the gold of sunrise quivered on the horizon did the madness abate.

The township was quiet that day. Quiet like after a storm has passed, or when waiting for a new one to arrive. For the first time, I am glad that Dawn is not here.

Chapter 45

In my mind I live with Dawn. I wake with her in the grey morning light, I see her as she searches for work among the thousands who've come to find their future among the gold mines, and I watch over her when night comes and the stars are hidden by smoke. Perhaps it is the same for all of us. Perhaps we all live with others, especially those we love. I once lived with Phil, I once heard the whine of bullets over his head, I once felt the sand of Sidi Rezegh beneath his fingernails, I sometimes imagine him and Dawn and me as a family.

Since Master's death, I've come to understand that this kind of imagining is also strong for Mrs Cath. When I am in the township she imagines what I am doing and puts herself in my place as a teacher. When I return home she wants to know what each day has brought. Mrs Cath grasps both sides of my divided life, especially the side that few whites see. And as the fires burn and the struggle rages, she worries for me, and she worries for Dawn whose days neither of us can truly know.

'When will she come back, Ada? She'd be safer here than in Jo'burg . . .' She touches a photograph of a laughing toddler Dawn that now hangs on the kitchen wall since there is no longer any need to hide such things from Master.

I have prepared an answer for this.

'She wants to be where there are more coloureds, Mrs Cath.'

We never speak of the coming together of Master's death and Dawn's departure. We never voice the thought that if she'd waited one more day – if I'd waited one more day instead of rushing into the township – such a leaving might never have happened. But I know in my heart that Dawn was intent on going. If not then, then soon after. This is the answer that I cannot give to Mrs Cath. I cannot tell her that Dawn, like Miss Rose, was seduced by a Johannesburg future.

I also can't tell Mrs Cath that Dawn seems to change her address often, that she doesn't appear to have found a job yet, that her letters are filled with stories of bright lights rather than steady work. I don't tell her that Dawn appears to be following the same brittle path as Miss Rose. In another world, Miss Rose – Dawn's sister, after all – might have helped her find a job, or a place to stay. But Miss Rose and my daughter are as far apart as Ireland is from Cradock, even though they live beneath the same arc of southern sky.

'Dawn will find her way,' Lindiwe says, encouragingly, as we drink tea together. 'Give her time.'

While I have no influence on Dawn's future, I have tried to encourage Mrs Cath to reclaim hers: her white life, and the friends who are part of it. After all, the law has turned its attention elsewhere, and with Dawn gone as well, Mrs Cath's friends have no reason to shy away. The evidence of mixed blood is gone. And it is true that they have tried. They invite her to tea parties and music evenings, they include her in bridge afternoons and farm visits, they call for her in their cars and take her for drives on to the open Karoo plains. She returns with sprays of papery everlastings and bags of purple figs. But I can tell she is unsatisfied. Their company does not fill her.

'A marvellous day, Ada,' she will say, laying aside her hat and seating herself at the piano. 'The Colletts are delightful.' Then it will be Mozart, but her fingers are distracted, and she will miss a couple of difficult passages and stop midway, and start on something else and that will go no better and then she'll say that she is tired and will rather play tomorrow.

Although there is much to be grateful for here in Cradock House, there is a curious limbo in my life.

I thought that with Edward gone I would feel more free. And I do, in some ways, for I can visit whom I chose, I can express myself freely – within reason.

But this country that I have come to love holds me in its vice. Because of apartheid, travel abroad has become difficult and expensive. I still dream that I might go back to Ireland for a visit. It has been more than fifty years since I saw the curl of the waves on the pebbles in Bannock cove. Fifty years since I heard the tripping melody of the stream over the cliffs. I long to embrace the families of my dear sister Ada and my brother Eamon . . .

But they say one should never return to one's birthplace after a long absence. Too much will have changed. So let me rather rejoice in my adopted country, for all its agonies. Let me celebrate the devotion of, first, Miriam, and then Ada and Dawn. They are indeed my family, as I wrote in my diary so many years ago.

I know that I am struggling to fit all these pieces of my divided life into any sort of order, any sort of understanding: Master's death, Dawn's leaving, Mrs Cath's restlessness, the forced removal of my school, the destruction of the townships – these things have come upon me too suddenly. Perhaps it is because my head still aches, even though my arm is healed and no longer bothers me when I'm at the piano. Perhaps my head is weary.

Perhaps this is why I am struggling to follow the voice echoing in my mind, a voice telling me it is time to act. Dawn is not here to require my protection, Master is not here to trouble the law, the police have not come to arrest me. I am free – but afraid of lifting my head after years of seeking the shadows. But it is time to step forward. For if the barriers between black and white Cradock could be broken without the need for violence – then surely I must play my part.

What would Phil say? Would he encourage me to be brave, as I once encouraged him? But this is not a war like the one he fought. There are no bombs dropping suddenly from the sky, there are no tanks crushing men into the desert sand. It is a war of hunger and casual cruelty, a war of suffocation by rules, a war of gradual, creeping death.

In the end, all wars come down to personal survival, and in this I have a choice. Should I help others, or should I save myself?

I have seen the new township and the new houses. They are indeed better, but they are also far away from the centre of Cradock. Even so, many people are willing to move; many hope for a better future even though their ancestors will have to search to find them in such a new place. Those who drive the struggle say the removals are about whites exercising power, and they're right. But if the houses are solid and the schools better equipped – and ways found to teach youngsters the truth – then each day might be a little healthier than the one that has gone before. For most people, that may be enough.

I have prayed to God for many years to tell me what is fair, and whether skins should be free to mix after all. If this is so – and apartheid is wrong – then is war the only answer? And does the struggle and the coming revolution have His blessing? The minister on the *koppie* thought so, but I've never heard God's answer for myself, and I've never known His will.

I've never known if He favours another way apart from war. Until now. It was surely His voice that I heard in my ear at the meeting at St James?

'You know English, Ada. You know about negotiation. This is my plan for you. This is why I have saved you. Not to live through your child, whose path you cannot influence any longer. Not to hide yourself in Cradock House, with only the solace of your music. But to reach out and make a difference.'

The name of the new township, Lingelihle, means 'good effort'.

Surely I must try.

Chapter 46

I have discovered that there is more money in my bank book than I expected from my wages as a teacher. I asked Mrs Cath about this and she said she had not stopped paying me even though the arrangement was that I only receive board and lodging at Cradock House.

'Why, it's for your future, Ada,' she said, looking up from the sweet-smelling roses she was arranging on the mantelpiece. 'For when Edward and I are no longer here. It's your pension.'

I have not thought about what will happen when Mrs Cath is gone, but I have heard of a pension. I've read about it in the newspaper. White people talk a lot about pensions. I suspect it is one of those things for a white future only – like the gold they wish to keep for themselves.

Mrs Cath's generosity means I have more money than I need, yet I am careful to save as much as I can. I send money to Dawn and I buy myself a new shirt from time to time but mostly the money rests in the bank on its own.

'You must keep some aside,' my fellow teacher, Sipho, warned, wagging his pencil at me, 'for if you get sick. Medicine is very expensive. And where will you live when you get old?'

This I know. For all its sturdy foundations, Cradock House might not live forever, or it might pass to a new family that have no interest in me. There is nothing certain in this world. The bank must hold enough money to keep me and Dawn safe on this earth until God calls us. But even so, that still leaves some over.

Jake once said there are many different ways to make a revolution.

So on a day when the Groot Vis was barely a trickle, I stood outside the town hall at eight o' clock in the morning in my shoes with heels, waiting to see the Superintendent. Even at such an early hour, cars were already baking in the sun in their parking places, and stray dogs slunk into the shade of the building. The palms across the road in the Karoo Gardens drooped motionless over where I used to sit as a young girl, warming my bare feet in the sun and watching the long-beaked birds fussing about the orange aloes. But today the benches were empty, not because of the heat – but because their 'Whites Only' signs had been ripped off, and red paint splashed all over the seats. The board outside the newspaper office that had once said 'It's War' in big black letters, now said in slightly smaller letters 'Gdns Shame!'

Black women did not often try to see the Superintendent on their own. Usually they came in numbers, with placards protesting about Passes or uncollected rubbish, or with men who did the talking. The Superintendent almost always refused to see such groups, and the police hovering nearby in expectation of trouble would be quick to swoop.

'You can wait,' the girl behind the counter said carelessly, 'but he might not be able to see you at all. If you tell me what it's about—'

'I will wait.'

'Round the back,' she said, shrugging. 'This is whites only.' She turned to a young man who'd appeared next to her and rolled her eyes. She reminded me of Miss Rose, although she was not as beautiful.

There were no benches or seats round the back so I sat on the ground under a pepper tree, grateful for the shade. My head doesn't like direct sun any more. There was no grass to cover the earth and I worried that my skirt would look dirty when I went to see the Superintendent. People came and went, complaining to each other about the heat. Most ignored me although one man stopped and said that there were no jobs available.

'I don't want a job. I'm waiting to see the Superintendent.' He opened his mouth to say something, then changed his mind and hurried off. It was past midday when the woman came out of the back door and beckoned to me. I had practised the words I was to say until I knew them off by heart, but I wasn't sure I could say them because my mouth was dry with thirst and also with nerves. This was not like trying for a job with Mr Dumise. I couldn't rely on my music to speak for me.

'You'll have to be quick,' she said over her shoulder, and pointed to a door. 'It's almost lunch hour.'

The door was open but I knocked before I went in.

'Yes?' The Superintendent was sitting behind a desk, writing. He didn't look up. A framed photograph hung on the wall, showing a dark-haired young man smiling in a black robe while holding a roll of paper tied with a tassel. The Superintendent's head – bald now – shone under the ceiling light. His hand moved steadily across the page. I recognised him from the meeting at St James School. This time he was alone, no councillors alongside, no police standing guard. On a table in the corner a fan droned, fluttering a pile of papers in its arc. There was a map on the wall. I made out the Groot Vis, and then a series of rectangular grids that spread across the paper from the riverbank. Lingelihle.

'Good morning, sir, I've come about compensation for people being moved.' The words came out of my parched mouth in a rush.

He flung down the pen that he'd been using to write on the paper in front of him and reached up to wipe his broad forehead. Even with a fan, the room seemed empty of air. It reminded me of the school hall the day I played the piano for a job.

'I've told you people once, I've told you a million times, we'll try, but I can't guarantee – understand? *Verstaan?*'

I licked my dry lips. Remember what Phil said, I told myself. Remember about silence in a negotiation . . .

The Superintendent looked at me properly, running his eyes over my white shirt and my navy skirt and sighed, as if disappointed at my silence. 'I can't help it if you don't understand. Just go now – *weg is jy* – I've got work to do.' He waved a hand to dismiss me and turned back to his papers. I wonder why it is that important people don't have anyone to take care of their clothes for them properly. The Superintendent's collar needed starching.

'I have money, sir,' I said. 'I will pay some of it towards the compensation.'

His head jerked up.

'But if you don't need my money, then I will tell the *Midland News* that you have enough already to pay for it.'

'Now, just hang on – *wag*.' He rose from his chair, his face settling into half-angry yet half-amused lines. 'You can't come here and threaten.' He glanced down at the telephone, then at the open door. There were policemen on duty at the front of the building. He only needed to shout . . .

I felt my legs tremble. I held my hands hard at my side. There was no bicycle spoke in my pocket. Only words could save me now; only the sentences I'd prepared might stop me being arrested and thrown into jail, for that is what would happen after the shout for the policemen, or the telephone call to the security guards.

'I have also written three letters,' I said, grasping my courage, reaching for what I'd rehearsed on the hard ground outside the back door of the town hall. 'One is to the *Midland News*, and one is to Mrs Cathleen Harrington of Cradock House in Dundas Street.'

The man gaped at me from where he stood behind his desk, the amusement gone, the resemblance to the smiling young man on the wall behind him now lost. I forced myself to breathe deeply. I wanted to wipe my face. Sweat was starting to gather above my lip.

'If I'm arrested then the newspaper will print my letter. If they don't, Mrs Harrington will show it to the town council. Mrs Harrington's late husband was a councillor—'

My voice cracked as I ran out of breath.

One thing I have learnt is that all white men fear exposure in the newspapers. And the Superintendent was no exception. He rocked forward slightly, steadying himself with his fists on the desk. Then he uncurled and flexed his fingers as if they had suddenly become stiff.

'Your English is good,' he said, addressing the desktop with forced care, like Master had once addressed his desk when he didn't want to meet my eyes. '*Skoon.*' He straightened up and looked at me and my clothes. His tone roughened. 'What about the third letter?'

'It is to a newspaper across the sea.'

'Who are you?' He almost leapt at me across the desk, the

veins standing out in his neck, the hands balling into fists once more.

I swallowed, and called up the rest of what had to be said.

'If you don't need my money then the *Midland News* will say that the town council has enough to pay compensation.' I waited a moment. 'And they will praise you in the newspaper, sir.'

The fan whirred through the silence and he strode across the room and snapped it off.

'You haven't got money for such a scheme! *Nooit!*' he shouted. A bee that had been buzzing against the flyscreen on the window fell to the floor. I reached into my pocket and laid a piece of paper on the desk. I had called in at the bank. They wrote down how much money belonged to me. Not my name, just the money.

'It's all I have,' I said. 'I want to use it to help people if you don't have enough.'

He stared down at the paper with suspicion, then up at me. His bald head was sweaty under the light. The lady had used a rubber stamp to show the bank's name and the date. The ink had spread a little with the heat while I sat outside on the ground, but the numbers were still clear.

The paper certainly did not show as much money as would be needed, but I think it was more money than he expected. I picked up the paper and put it back in my pocket.

'Thank you, sir,' I said. 'I will go now.'

Chapter 47

Ada has done a foolish thing.

She has attempted to threaten the Township Superintendent, a man with a short temper that Edward was never particularly keen on.

I heard about this not from Ada herself, but from our timid Mayor, who came to see me and sat in the lounge twisting his hat between his fingers and jumping when Ada appeared with tea.

Not that he presented it as a clear threat. Instead he seemed to see it as the well-intentioned act of an earnest but untaught woman, worried about the deteriorating situation in the township and imagining she could help. Even the matter of certain letters – he was particularly vague on this – didn't persuade him that Ada was more shrewd than the unworldly soul he imagined. I remained silent, not wishing to contradict this impression. Assumed naivety might save her.

But I suspect that the Superintendent was in no doubt as to her sharpness.

I asked the Mayor if he wished to speak to Ada himself, but it soon became clear that he thought it was I who ought to be doing the speaking, I who should be reining in this maid who, he said with apologetic emphasis, was 'so close' to my family.

It was only after he'd left, when I went up to my bedroom to lie down for a while, that I saw the envelope tucked into my diary on the dressing table, alongside the small vase of geraniums I picked yesterday.

Is Ada well?

Mrs Cath came to sit on my bed yesterday evening. 'No, don't get up,' she said as I made to rise, wondering if she was ill, if there was something she wanted, as I'd wondered what Master wanted . . .

'Dear Ada,' she murmured, smoothing Mama's blue shawl that lay across the bottom of the bed. 'Why did you do it? To threaten the Superintendent – it's close to blackmail.'

I hadn't met the word blackmail before. I thought I'd started a negotiation, although negotations usually try to let both sides succeed in some way, so perhaps it was not a negotiation after all because I had no intention of letting the Superintendent succeed even in part. Later, after Mrs Cath left, I looked up blackmail in the dictionary and it said it was an attempt to get money by threat. And I realised that this was exactly what I wanted, except that the money would go not to me, but to those on whose behalf I had stepped into the town hall that morning.

'I left you a letter,' I said to Mrs Cath.

'I know, I read it – it's very good,' she admitted with a smile that didn't quite reach her eyes. 'I taught you too well, perhaps.'

'I decided this on my own, Ma'am,' the old word slipped out, 'I never wanted to make trouble for you.'

'I know.' Her eyes roamed about the room, taking in the sheet music on the table, my Bible alongside, and Dawn's dressing gown hanging behind the door in the hope of her return one day. 'Would you have done it if Dawn had still been here?'

'No.' I shook my head, then gasped as a new thought struck me. 'Is the Mayor blaming you because of me?' For mayors were surely like Superintendents, with just as much, if not more, power. I should have realised they would try to attack me through those I love – with Dawn gone, Mrs Cath was next in line.

'I will go back,' I said urgently. 'I'll tell them it has nothing to do with you. I'll—'

'No, Ada,' Mrs Cath held up a hand. 'No. You've done a brave thing. Too few people have conviction these days.' She looked down and I caught a glimpse of Phil in her face, for although Phil mostly resembled Master, there were moments when he appeared in his mother's eyes and in her lips – and always in the words she spoke. 'And,' she went on, 'with Edward gone and Dawn away, there's no reason not to.'

She stood up and walked to the table, bent over one of the music sheets, and nodded at its familiarity.

'Are you quite well after that fall?' She glanced across at me, her green eyes settling on the scar at the side of my face.

'Yes, Mrs Cath.' It did not do to complain. And the body takes its own time. I have learnt that.

She turned back and touched a page with long fingers. She was more stooped now, and she needed special glasses to see the piano keys.

'Who would have guessed . . .'

'Guessed what, Mrs Cath?'

'My sister Ada, you know the one you're named for in Ireland? She would have done something like this.'

She closed the door quietly behind her.

Chapter 48

They were waiting for me at the Groot Vis, where Church Street mounts the bridge over the river and then aims for the station and the vast Karoo beyond. They did not come for me at Cradock House – where Mrs Cath might have intervened – or at school, where my students might have proved obstructive. They chose, instead, to wait for me by the river in the cool shade of a pepper tree, as if taking their ease, with the weavers chattering noisily nearby, and the lazy slip of brown water over rocks below.

'Pass!' one of them demanded as I went by. His partner slouched on the far side of the van, chewing something and eyeing the crowd who shied away from the van, heads down. This was an everyday business. I myself had hurried past many such vans, many such inspections for Passes. I fumbled for my document, hampered by my arm which was stiff in the mornings until I'd played the piano. The man barely looked at it.

'Get in,' he said, thrusting the Pass back at me and nodding to the other man to open up the back of the van.

'Why?' I asked, seizing courage, standing my ground. 'My Pass is in order. My Madam signs it for me.'

'It's not about the Pass,' he said. 'Get in.'

This was no random check. They knew enough about my movements between school and Cradock House to know where to position themselves. They'd been watching me, and then they'd lain in wait. It was an ambush, like when Phil had been ambushed by tanks in the desert at Sidi Rezegh. Like when leopards stalk and then pounce on their prey in the veld.

I had broken the law. I had lain with a man who did not share the same colour as me. I had also stepped into the Superintendent's office and tried to trade letters I'd written for the compensation that my fellow blacks deserved. They were right. It wasn't about the Pass.

The back of the van was cramped and I struggled to sit with my knees drawn up to my chest. Dawn, I found myself whispering, Dawn . . . The van made a U-turn and then swung off Church Street and down Bree, towards the jail that Mama used to say could snatch you even if you were innocent. Houses I'd once walked past whipped by in a blur, there was the purple bougainvillea draped over a fence, now came the cream stone of St Peter's Church where I'd first heard an organ, then the jail. The van lurched to a halt.

They hustled me through a rear door and took me to a room with no furniture. There were bars on the single high window. I stood in the centre for a while but no one came, so I sat on the dusty floor with my back against the wall and stretched my legs out before me and watched the sun's rays edge across the opposite wall. My hands would not be still. I lifted them up from my lap and held them out in front of me, willing them either to stop, or to move to an imagined piece of Beethoven, or the single notes of the *Raindrop*. Phil's hands had never stopped shaking with the memory of his dead friends . . .

Should I give in quickly and say I was mistaken to write such letters? That I didn't mean to threaten the Superintendent, that

I am just a simple, stupid woman who believed she could help? If I'm lucky, they will look no further than me, they will threaten me and then toss me out, or beat me first and then toss me out – far from Cradock House and the township and all that I've ever known, sent to a part of the land that I have never been to, like Transkei, where Mrs Pumile always says she is going to but never does. I would be an exile, but I would still be alive. And, if God is merciful, so would my daughter.

Or should I ignore my trembling hands, and the growing fear that they will go after Dawn in Johannesburg, and wait? Say nothing? Wait for the *Midland News* to publish my letter. Wait for Mrs Cath to show hers to the town council. Wait for the newspaper across the sea to take an interest in a black woman from a small Karoo town known for little more than rocky *koppies*, brown dust and a lack of rain.

But maybe I am stupid to imagine that anyone would take notice of me. That the council or the *Midland News* or the paper overseas would feel any need to act upon my story.

The door burst open.

'*Staan op!* Stand up!'

Two men in uniform came in. They had guns in shiny leather holsters on their hips. Behind them came two black men in overalls carrying a table that they positioned in the middle of the room. They went out and came back with two wooden chairs that they placed carefully on one side of the table. The black men did not look at me. The men in uniform sat down on the chairs. I have often been in places where seats were not meant for me.

'You're under arrest for crimes against the state,' one of the men said, opening a file on the table. 'Don't deny it – we have all the evidence. *Verstaan jy* – understand?'

'There will be a trial, sir?'

He slapped through the pages till he came to the one he wanted. The other policeman examined the ceiling.

'You're a member of a banned organisation – *verdomde* ANC.'

'No, sir, I belong to no organisation. I am a schoolteacher. I did what I did on my own.'

'You want to bring down the country. They gave you orders to cause trouble.' Still he spoke towards the table and the file before him, like others have done when they were unwilling to meet my eyes. They do it to show disdain, but to me it speaks of cowardice.

I looked at him, his uniform surely ironed by black hands, and I felt the anger build. Why is it that even when we're hated so much, we're still so useful?

'If you wish to put me on trial, sir, I shall defend myself.'

He looked up then, and his companion tore his gaze from the ceiling to regard me with hostility.

'Your English is good,' he said, considering. 'But there's no need for a trial. The evidence is clear. Finished and *klaar*.'

My head was beginning to ache as it often did these days, but I still understood what they were trying to do. They wanted me to confess. But I have read books, and I have read the *Midland News*. If I don't confess, they can't keep me here forever without giving me a trial. This I know.

'Then I will stay in your jail, sir, until it is time for you to release me. If you wish to keep me for longer, then the law says there must be a trial.'

He snatched the file, leapt to his feet and upturned the table. It crashed to the floor in front of me. I fell back in fright, my body tumbling to the ground, my weak arm crumpling beneath me, my hands – oh God, protect my hands for the piano – jarring on the concrete floor.

I didn't hear them leave, I only heard the door slam and then I was alone. I dragged myself to the wall and lay down against it. The pain in my arm subsided but my legs were trembling and my hands burned and one of my fingers was bleeding where it had slammed into the concrete. My head, surprisingly, was clear.

They don't want a trial; they want a confession.

A trial means publicity, like the publicity around an ANC man called Nelson Mandela, who made his own defence and gave a speech that has resounded from one end of the country to the other. White men don't like publicity about blacks. They don't like such things to be exposed in newspapers.

They left me alone for the rest of the day. I blew on my throbbing hands and stared at the slow march of the sun across the wall and forced my heart not to think of Dawn, making her way in Johannesburg, imagining she was safe. Vans drew up outside and the guttural laughter of policemen reached me through the high window. And then Phil came to sit by my side, and Dawn danced for me with flying hair and heels, and Mama patted my shoulder but shook her head to see where I was. Shoo, child, she seemed to be saying with disapproval, I taught you to know your place, what foolishness has brought you here?

I don't know God the Father very well. I pray to Him often, but He never replies or perhaps I don't hear what he says. There are others who say that they hear His answers every day, but I have only ever heard Him once, when He set me on this course. 'This is my plan for you,' He whispered over the shouting at St James. 'This is why I have saved you'.

But as night came and my body stiffened with the cold and my throat dried up for lack of water, I began to wonder if what I had heard was truly His voice, if what I had done was truly His plan. If only He would come to me now, and tell me so . . .

But maybe I'm being unfair. Perhaps it was He who sent Phil to sit at my side on the concrete floor, and Dawn to entertain me as the light faded, and Mama to remind me of where I came from. Perhaps this is His way with me. To speak to me not directly, but through those I love.

It must have been hours later that the door opened and someone shoved a latrine bucket through, and a plastic cup of water.

They left me for another whole day. I watched the time pass in the wandering of the sun across the wall, and the slow darkening beyond the barred window. They pushed a small amount of maize meal on a tin plate through the door with the cup of water. I ate the porridge and dipped the edge of my skirt in the water to clean the cut on my hand. The material came away brown from the dried blood. I drank the remaining water slowly, holding it in my mouth for as long as possible before swallowing.

No one came.

The night was blacker than any night I've known. Even under the township smoke there is still some light to be found, but here, in this cell that I could walk across in five steps, they had the power to blanket the stars beyond the window, and shroud the moon from where it hung for the rest of the world to see.

'*Staan op!*'

A powerful light – the moon after all? – stabbed my eyes. I tried to scramble away from its harsh beam but it followed me on the floor, trapping me on all fours like the night animals captured in the headlights of Master's car.

'Who gives you orders?'

It was the same policeman, but there was no second policeman, and no table and chair following. My head, from lying on the concrete, didn't want to work. I'm no longer young, it's true, and my head takes longer these days to find its starting point. Perhaps I've become soft and used to my mattress at Cradock House—

'Who? *Wie?*'

I don't know what he wants. I only take orders from Mr Dumise. These are not the orders he means.

'I have no orders, sir. I am a schoolteacher.'

'When did you last see Jake Bapetsi?'

'I don't know Jake Bapetsi.'

I hope God the Father will forgive me for more lies, but I will do nothing to endanger Lindiwe. I will pretend to know nothing of Jake who used to swing Dawn in the air and bring us sausages and talk of the struggle. Jake, who used to meet me by the river, and once smiled at me with fondness. I will say nothing of his plans to go over the sea to learn about guns and bring them back to start the revolution.

The light swept away. Swift footsteps followed it. The door slammed shut. I huddled back against the wall, drawing my legs in, protecting my swollen hand against my stomach. I would like to whisper a message for Lindiwe to the black hand that takes away my latrine bucket every day, but I can't risk it. Everyone knows there are traitors who put white before black. In the township, the *izibonda* – the black policemen – show no mercy to their own people.

The outline of the cell began to emerge as day came, and the sun proved stronger than the policeman's ability to hide the moon and stars from me.

They brought me water in a cup.

'The latrine is full,' I croaked, through parched lips. The black hand came through the door and I passed it the bucket.

I made myself sip the water slowly, running my tongue over

my lips to soften them with the last of the liquid. If only I could put my head forward and feel the cool drip of water over the back of my neck like I used to in the laundry at Cradock House. I began to dream of water. I moved my toes – they have taken away my shoes – and felt the brown river surging over my feet in the drift, and Dawn drowsing on my back in her blanket . . .

At the point when the sun was at its strongest on the wall, there came a rising tide of sirens and shouting from outside the window. I strained to make out what was being shouted but it was white shouting and it was in Afrikaans and I don't know Afrikaans well. Instead I watched a column of ants, somehow alerted to the prospect of food, as they marched in a line from the window and across the floor and swarmed over the tin plate that had carried yesterday's porridge.

Weakness is gathering me in.

I stand up and force myself across the cell to keep my body moving. Five steps forward, turn, five steps back. My arm is hurting again, my hands are swollen and too large for the piano keys.

Five forward, five back.

'Who gave you orders?'

'No one gave me orders. I am a schoolteacher.'

A cup of water on the floor. Sometimes porridge, sometimes nothing.

'Where is the *kleurling* girl?'

'No one gave me orders.'

'We know she left, we can get you for immorality.'

'I am a schoolteacher.'

It is night. I'm an animal caught in the lights.

Chapter 49

I spent all morning at the jail on Bree Street, having finally been directed there by the policeman at the charge office in town. He knew nothing, I think he shifted me to the jail for want of any other course of action. But as it turned out, I have indeed found Ada.

At first they denied they were holding anyone by her name in their cells, but then a young reporter from the Midland News *happened by. He'd been sent by his editor following their receipt of Ada's letter. Apparently they'd also had an inquiry from the overseas paper to whom Ada had already posted the third letter.*

Clever Ada. Foolish Ada.

On the one hand I'm so proud of her, on the other I fear the storm she's unleashed.

Will they track down Dawn? The police might want to make an example of them: immoral black mother, coloured child, illicit activities . . .

'She is a simple woman,' I said, advancing the argument for Ada's naivety. 'She meant well. I will take responsibility for her if you release her now. She's a good teacher. She keeps children in school, so important these days.'

Come back tomorrow, they said.

May I see the investigating officer? I inquired.

What is the status on compensation? the reporter asked.

Come back tomorrow.

My throat is sore from the talking, and I have no energy for the piano. And even if I did, my hands are shaking so much I doubt I would be able to play. There is no one I can talk to about this.

They threw my shoes back into the cell.

'*Staan op!*'

'No orders—'

Hands pushed me from behind. I tried to reach my shoes but they were too far away. Someone cursed, and shoved them at me.

The corridor outside my cell was bright with light. Boots stamped on the floor behind me. A hand grabbed my shoulder and a voice hissed in my ear, 'You make any more trouble, you won't get out of here next time. And we'll find the girl – the *kleurling*. Now go!'

I stumbled to the door through which they'd brought me, not sure if it was a trick, some other way to get a confession.

'Now go! *Voetsak!*'

I stepped out, turned back to see what was to happen next, and felt rather than saw the door slam in my face. For some time I stood swaying on the concrete step, my vision blurring and then clearing. It was night. The river rushed heavily in the background. There must have been rain. Wind stirred the trees on the pavement. The stars that had been hidden now burst from their places in the sky. No one opened the door behind me. I sat down on the step and tried to put on my shoes with my swollen fingers. It took a long time, and all through the struggle I waited for the door to open, for someone to reach out and seize me. My shoulders hunched themselves in anticipation of a blow to my head. Then the shouting, and the questions starting all over again . . .

No one came.

I got up and hobbled on to the road. My feet had also swelled and the shoes began to cut into my flesh so I sat down again and took them off.

I don't remember how it was that I managed to get along Bree Street with my damaged feet, and then across Church, and then along Dundas Street to Cradock House. But perhaps God the Father came to my rescue, not with words in my ear, but with the means to keep me alive. I found myself creeping into the garden of a smart house where there was a tap. I turned it on and opened my cracked lips to the stream of water and drank and drank until the sweet water overflowed from my mouth and wet my shirt and ran down my legs.

It was a long way from the jail to Cradock House. Stones on the pavement cut my feet and I stumbled often. The trees that during daylight gave welcoming shade now cast threatening shadows like men advancing in war, or men waiting in ambush once again, men intent on killing me outside prison walls where they could not be blamed.

The furrow was running with river water. Dogs barked as I made my clumsy way. In one house, a light appeared and a face leant out of the window to check for burglars.

Voetsak, they'd said to me. It's what you say to dogs.

Then, after what seemed hours, there was the gravel drive-way and the sturdy outline of Cradock House. And the footpath leading past the angled spikes of strelitzia flowers – like broken spears in the night. From the back garden loomed the kaffirboom, as if waiting for me to hang washing on the line, as if ready to listen once more to Phil talk of war and the fear of it.

'Mrs Cath,' I croaked, rapping weakly on the front door, 'Mrs Cath . . .'

And then she was there, in her blue nightgown, with her hair floating in a cloud about her face.

'Ada, thank God! Thank God!' She knelt down and embraced me where I lay on the wooden *stoep* that I have scrubbed so often in my life.

'No orders,' I muttered, my vision blurring again, 'nothing of Dawn.'

Chapter 50

I have never sought to be well known. I have preferred the shadows ever since my sin of lying with a white man – and the shame that walks with me every day because of it. But it seems I am no longer allowed to sit on the side. People seek me out now, rough people that I have always shied away from on street corners, people who are part of the struggle, people who live underground lives, people who talk of Mandela, people who see me as a rallying figure.

'You can speak out!' they hiss with excitement, while looking over their shoulders. 'Your name has been in the papers – the police can't touch you any more! The compensation we're getting is because of you!'

But I don't like this. I'm not used to being at the front. And I don't want to preserve what has happened in the jail on Bree Street – I want it to go away. I followed what God said, I tried to make a difference. I tried to show there was another way to make a revolution, a quieter way than with guns and shack-burning and confrontation. I can't say if my way succeeded, I can't say if it made those in power think again, but what it did do was leave me sleepless with the terror of it, and unable to control my body that I once took for granted.

I am ashamed to say that my jail experience has become a badge of honour for others to notice, and the reason for further upheaval, rather than a check upon it. And as for those who think I am safe to speak out now because of my name in the papers, they are wrong. The police can take me whenever they want to. I am being watched again, I see a van on a street corner as I walk by, with a policeman speaking on the radio. The *Midland News* and the paper overseas will care less the next time.

The policeman meets my eye. I look away. I pray they do not find Dawn. I want to get back to my classroom with my wild pupils and play jazz for them, and show them how music can set us free. I want to ease my shaking fingers and my lame arm into some pure Mozart. I want to return to the sweet distraction of Debussy. Only the piano can cure me. Only the piano can help me forget.

In the matter of compensation, it is hard to know if my threat to the Superintendent actually worked. The letters were never published in the *Midland News*, or overseas, and there was no detail of my arrest, although Mrs Cath says the papers printed my name and were aware of why I was in jail, and sent a reporter to check I was alive. Nevertheless, it's true that compensation has now been agreed, and people are moving to Lingelihle to their new homes made of brick, but I can't claim that it is because of me. And somehow it no longer matters, in view of what came afterwards. For, all through the days I spent in bed at Cradock House while Mrs Cath bathed my still-trembling hands in cool water and rubbed them with sheep lanolin, the rain fell and the Groot Vis rose and rose.

Mrs Pumile, looking in nervously from next door – perhaps more due to my new reputation than the rising waters – insisted it was a sign, but she would not say what such a sign meant. The swelling river and its shadow, the gathering revolution, were also on Mrs Cath's mind as she nursed me, but she said nothing. She didn't have to. I heard it in her fingers when she played. Liszt's *La Campanella* taken too slowly, arpeggios lacking bite . . .

I could hear the river clearly through the *kaia* door.

At first it was a brisk eddy, then a howl of demented water that went way beyond the Beethoven rush of my youth, or the tumbling Grieg of Mrs Cath's Irish stream. This flood had no musical equivalent, and it raged at a pitch both higher and lower than anything I'd ever heard on the piano. The drift disappeared beneath angry waves. The washing rocks gave birth to huge whirlpools. The legs of the iron bridge were choked with uprooted trees and the carcasses of drowned animals. Those township residents on the move to Lingelihle had to wade through torrents as the skies poured for days without end. 'It is the ancestors,' I heard Veronica say with a fearful glance upwards. 'They weep because we're leaving our old places behind.'

Despite the rain, Lindiwe came to visit me.

'There is talk of you,' she whispered nervously, shaking out her battered umbrella. 'They want you to speak at a rally at St James.' Lindiwe's face always showed what she was thinking. She feared what I had done, and what it might mean for those around me. She already lived with the possibility that one day the police could arrest her for the crimes of her brother. Lindiwe is no coward – indeed I have never known anyone as brave – but she is practical. She knows that taking a stand can be foolhardy against truncheons and tear gas and jails that starve you to death. She is determined to live through the struggle and not be consumed by it. She wants to get to the other side of liberation.

'They won't leave you alone, now,' she murmured. 'Not after this.'

'You mean the police?'

'No, the struggle—'

'Ada?' There was a flurry of knocks on the door. I felt my hands begin to shake, but these were not blows on the door, it was not night. Mrs Cath hurried into the room, holding Master's golf umbrella at her side. She was wearing rubber boots on her feet, and thick gardening gloves over her strong hands. Red spots stood out on her cheeks.

'Oh!' She stopped, then came forward with a gloved hand outstretched to welcome Lindiwe. 'Good morning, Lindiwe. How did you manage on the roads? Bree Street is flooding! They're calling for help to save the houses. You must be cold,' she went on, seeing her damp clothes. 'Here, wrap Miriam's shawl about you. Ada,' she turned to me, 'there's no time to lose. I'm going to see what I can do. I'll lock the front door but the back will be open—'

'Be careful, Ma'am,' Lindiwe said quietly. 'The river is angry.'

Mrs Cath looked at her, then at me, and nodded, for we knew more about the Groot Vis than she did. We had forded the river and washed in its brown waters, we had learnt how its usual mood of sluggishness could swell to one of frenzy. Like an undercurrent turns a crowd . . .

'Ada.' She glanced nervously at the garden behind her, where the grass was slowly sinking beneath veins of rainwater. 'Cradock House . . .'

'I'll get up, Mrs Cath.' I pushed away the bedcovers and reached for my clothes, ignoring the pounding in my head that came upon me so often these days. 'I'll watch for the water.'

'Bless you.' She managed a smile, wrestled the umbrella open and set off across the soaked lawn. The hem of her dress clung wetly to her boots. I watched her go. Mrs Cath was not young any more, she should not be doing heavy work. It was I who should be going, and she who should be remaining at home.

'You must go too,' I said to Lindiwe, as I climbed into my skirt and an old jersey. 'You need to watch out for your new house.' For the huts that Lindiwe had built with her own hands were already gone, pushed by council bulldozers into the Karoo earth, and all she had was her new place in Lingelihle, and it still waited for glass in its windows.

Chapter 51

They called it the Great Flood.

The Karoo has always been a place of dust and little rain, so when the rain does come, the hard earth is never ready for it and shrugs it off and lets it drain into the Groot Vis, instead of welcoming it into the ground to make the soil soft for planting. During our Great Flood, the water was not content just to surge, but chose to rip out everything in its path. It was this debris that choked the bridge and made the water back up behind it in a vast dam, and steadily rise above the riverbank until with a mighty gush it overflowed into the nearby streets. This made it not just a normal flood, but a Great Flood.

It soon became clear that white Cradock had suffered more than black Cradock. Or perhaps it was the case that white Cradock had more to lose. Many of the houses along Bree Street were washed away or so badly damaged they had to be pulled down. St Peter's survived, but few other buildings. The maps and documents in the town engineer's office floated away. The jail's records were only partly saved. I wondered if the record of my own arrest – so fresh, so likely to be at the top of the pile – was amongst those swept away by the raging tide and, if so, whether I might slip back into the shadows once more. For white people, if there's no paperwork, then it never really happened.

Cradock House, and our end of Dundas Street, somehow escaped the Great Flood. The brown water prowled along the street like a hungry animal but never quite reached the house.

Mrs Cath tried to help save some of the furniture and paintings from the magistrate's house on the corner of Church and Bree. The magistrate himself, returning from a case of stock theft in the Graaff-Reinet district, was stranded on the far side of the Groot Vis and could only watch. The floodwaters were already surging ankle deep through the house when she arrived. Mrs Cath and Mrs Maisie, the magistrate's wife, carried out the Dutch family Bible and the rare books from the library, before rescuing the small *riempie* stools and the fabled Baines painting that hung in the hallway. By then the dark waters were swirling too deeply, and the rest of the furniture – the yellow-wood dining table, the brocade armchairs – had to be abandoned.

'Such a tragedy, Ada!' she gasped upon her return, dress caked with mud and hair plastered to her head from the relentless rain. 'Maisie wept. I wept. The water just kept rising, like the beach as the tide comes in – a tide of mud. We couldn't save the house. Oh God,' she cried, pressing her hand to her chest, 'this is the whirlwind, I know it is.'

'Come,' I said, helping her off with her sodden boots, 'drink your tea, eat some of this date loaf. Then you must rest, Ma'am.'

'You're so good to me. I don't know what I'd do . . .'

In the half-demolished township at the end of Bree Street, many of the huts not already flattened gave up and toppled into the waters of their own accord. If the town council had wanted a means aside from compensation to encourage blacks to move to the new township, nature provided it. My school across the Groot Vis was inundated and the brown upright piano with its defective keys lost to me forever. So, too, the battered desks, the dusty red curtains with their trailing hems, Mr Dumise's cramped office, the yard for Veronica's chickens, the hall where my students sang and danced to their own beat. So, too, the shacks and huts of the lower Lococamp. All of it disappeared under the water and, when that subsided, lay forever buried under a slick layer of dark Karoo mud.

The community across the Groot Vis was gone.

Now there was no choice about whether to move or not. White men and their laws made no difference. My quest for compensation made no difference. The river had spoken. The river had determined the future.

Chapter 52

Mrs Cath stayed in bed. After a week, I walked downtown to Dr Wilmott's surgery. The streets were paved with a black mud that sucked at my shoes. The lamp posts showed the watermark of how high the river had come. Many pepper trees lay on their sides, their roots exposed like dirty underwear. I searched with my eyes for the tree where Phil and I had stood when he told me he loved me, and the tumbling bougainvillea nearby, but both were gone, overwhelmed by a sea of mud and broken branches.

Such was the destruction, the policing of skin difference and its laws faded before the larger crisis. In those first days, police vans went about the business of rescue rather than pursuing blacks for Pass offences. Truckloads of casual labourers were picked up in the township and set to work freeing the bridge of its collar of congested trees and dead animals. White and black technicians scaled poles to restore the telephone cables. The sun shone from a pale, apologetic sky.

'Mrs Harrington is not well,' I said to the lady in the pink dress behind the desk at Dr Wilmott's surgery.

'Mrs Harrington will call us, I'm sure,' she said, turning back to her typewriter and inserting a fresh sheet of paper.

'She does not know that she isn't well,' I said.

Several women waiting to see the doctor looked at one another and then looked down at their magazines. I was not supposed to be in their waiting room. Dr Wilmott had a separate entrance for his black patients, like the chemist that cured Dawn had had a separate entrance for blacks.

'Go and sit in the non-European waiting room,' the lady said without looking at me, and briskly turned the roller at the top of her machine to feed the paper through.

So I did. I waited quite some time until the doctor had seen all the people in the white waiting room.

'Yes, what is it?' Dr Wilmott was old, now, as old as Master had been when he died. 'Why, it's the Harrington maid. What seems to be the problem?'

'It is my Madam,' I said. 'She is sick, sir, but she does not know it.'

He looked at me, and I wondered if he remembered that he was the one who delivered me in Cradock House, and he was the one that closed my mother Miriam's eyes in death, and that I was the one who had borne Master's child.

'She helped during the flood, and she doesn't want to get up.'

'Well then, she should take all the rest she needs. Now,' he made to return to the white waiting room that was filling up once more, 'I have many more patients. The floods, you see.'

I could tell he didn't believe me because in his eyes I was only the Harrington maid. He also didn't know that I was all that was left of Mrs Cath's family, for Miss Rose had never called even when the telephones had started working again, even though the floods had been on the radio news. But I wouldn't let him go. Doctors are not always right. After all, he was the one who believed Phil was no longer ill.

'You must call and see her. Or I will have to take her to the hospital.'

He stared at me, his face reddening, his hands fiddling with the buttons on his white coat, his thin hair standing up on his head as if in outrage at my behaviour, my rudeness, my insistence. My sin.

'You will do no such thing,' he boomed, like he'd boomed at my dear young Master. 'Now leave. I will call on Mrs Harrington during my afternoon rounds.'

'Who is this?' There was no mistaking the quick, annoyed voice. I could almost see her tossing that beautiful yellow hair, rolling those slate-blue eyes.

'It is Ada, Miss Rose. From Cradock. Ada Mabuse.'

'What is it that you want? Where did you get this number?'

I waited for a moment, not for the purpose of negotiation, but to remember the words I'd practised in my head for I am not used to the telephone. I have no need to use it because no one that I know possesses one. I would have no one to call.

'Ada? Just get on with it, please.' Miss Rose's voice was as crisp – and as cold – as the frost beneath my bare feet in winter when I fetched the milk from the gate.

'It's Mrs Cath,' I said. 'She is not well.'

There was a pause from the other end.

'Was the house damaged? In the flood?'

'No. But Mrs Cath helped to save other houses, and now she is ill.'

'Why hasn't Dr Wilmott phoned me? Why does he get the maid to call?'

I flinched at the withering note she put on 'maid'. Mrs Pumile was right. She always said Miss Rose would never grow out of her rudeness.

'Dr Wilmott thinks Mrs Cath will get better.'

There was a pause.

'Then why are you calling? Do you think you know more than the doctor?'

I waited, this time to let some silence grow, and to hope that within its boundaries Miss Rose might wonder if she'd been too quick. Like Auntie was too quick to throw me out.

'Well? Ada?'

'I thought you should know, Miss Rose. Your mama is tired. I have seen such tiredness in others before. It is not something that is cured with sleep.'

I heard her shallow breath in my ear, as if she was panting.

'I'll try to visit. But it's not a good time for me.' Her voice became wheedling, as if I had the power to keep her mother well until such time as it suited Miss Rose to visit. *Will you iron my petticoats, Ada? I'll buy you peppermint creams . . .*

'Thank you, Miss Rose. Mrs Cath will love to see you. And Helen, too.' For Helen must be sixteen by now, and although Mrs Cath had visited her in Johannesburg, Helen had been to Cradock only twice.

I waited. There was a click at the other end. Miss Rose had put down the phone.

Chapter 53

I must fight for the return of my daughter, for this dancing in Johannesburg will only lead to trouble. And I must fight for Mrs Cath. I know Dawn and Mrs Cath are only two souls, rather than the thousands in Cradock that deserve help, but it is a fight that my ailing head can manage, a fight that I can get my arms round, a fight that I have a chance of winning. For my head is struggling to keep up. Or perhaps it is not the fault of my head alone, but the demands placed on it since I left jail.

Speak at the rally, Ada!

Insist the new school gets built faster!

Talk to the newspaper about flood relief, lost Passes, feeding schemes, class sizes, about babies dying from dirty water . . .

It is your duty. It is your struggle now. Your revolution.

'You must,' urged Dina, on my first day back at school. 'You're famous!'

The new school in Lingelihle was not ready, so we had moved to St James, where the young teachers were determined to recruit me. They told me of a new thing called black consciousness, words that I'd never seen paired together before. They spoke of Steve Biko, who taught the idea, and who was drawing supporters away from the jailed Mandela. I am cautious with such new words. They take time to arrive in a dictionary, just as the ideas they describe take time to root in the mind. But this was not the way of the younger teachers. For them, the time for caution had long gone.

'The police are watching me, I can't risk being caught again,' I insisted to those who wanted to use me to further the revolution. 'I can only offer my music.'

'But they let you out! You survived! You're the face of the struggle!'

But it is too much for me. It is Dawn and Mrs Cath that I must save.

From Johannesburg, Dawn writes every week, as she promised.

I am dancing, Mama! They have places here where people come to watch dancing – and I am the best! People ask for me!

I get paid every night by the owners of this place, and I also get paid by the people who watch me.

And what of your studies, child? I write back. Do you study when you are not dancing? When you are too old to dance, you will need an education in order to get a proper job.

I don't need to study any more, Mama. I can earn enough by dancing. Now tell me about the flood. The papers say that Bree Street was destroyed – even the jail. Is this not good news?

Lindiwe says she has heard that Dawn dances not only for black and coloured people, but for white as well. No good can come of this.

Mama was right. However much you might believe you have been accepted and can sit in the chairs meant for whites, it will never be the case. And it is even more the case for Dawn, my child who belongs nowhere, my child who falls in between, like the brown waters of the Groot Vis once divided white from black until the flood tore everything apart.

And Mrs Cath remained in bed.

'I have made butternut soup.' I offered a spoonful to her where she lay against her pillows, gazing outside. She loved to watch the garden beyond her bedroom window, the sunbirds flitting among the orange Cape honeysuckle, the pampas grass waving its feathery plumes.

'We're so lucky,' she murmured. 'I can still see Maisie's ruined place.'

'Have some more soup, Mrs Cath,' I urged, 'then you'll be strong enough to help Mrs Maisie start a new garden.'

She took one more spoon then set it down on the tray.

'We had lilac, back in Ireland. I've never got it to grow here. Edward wasn't interested, you know, Ada. He left the garden to me.'

She glanced at her diary lying on the table next to her bed. Not the red velvet one of my youth, but a slim book covered with soft brown leather, closed with a silver button clasp.

'A little Chopin, Ada?'

And so I began to play the entire set of Chopin nocturnes for Mrs Cath. Twenty-one in all. I think of each one as a jewel, a precious, shining gift. Twenty-one gifts for my Madam as she rests upstairs . . .

Miss Rose arrived today. She arrived by hire car from Port Elizabeth. It is now possible to fly in an aeroplane from Johannesburg to Port Elizabeth and then borrow a car for money, and drive up to Cradock. I fear this will one day mean the end of our railway line.

Miss Rose jumped out of the car and made a fuss of rushing inside, calling to Helen to take out the luggage. Miss Rose was as smart as ever, with a tight striped jersey over a long skirt with a slit down the side. She did not greet me as she went by. Helen, getting out of the car more slowly, turned out to be as tall as her mother, with the same yellow hair, but without the biting tongue.

'Hello, Ada,' she said shyly, reaching for my hand. 'I remember your piano.'

'Welcome, child,' I replied, feeling her young skin, wishing I could hug her as a reminder of my own daughter. 'Your granny will be so happy to see you.'

'Is Dawn here?' the girl asked eagerly, looking about her.

'No,' I caught my breath, 'she lives in Jo'burg, near Soweto township.'

'Oh.' She glanced towards the house where her mother's shrill voice could be heard. 'I wish I'd known. It would be good to see Dawn, and we could send news of her, couldn't we?'

I looked at her eyes, soft as Mrs Cath's, and found myself fighting down sudden tears. I hadn't wept in jail, I hadn't wept when I returned to Cradock House, but with a few words this surprising girl had touched me.

'Perhaps,' I said, recovering myself, 'but the laws don't make it easy.'

'I know,' she whispered, leaning closer to me, not unlike Dawn in one of her intense moods. And then she said, 'I hate those laws. Mum doesn't, but I do.'

I stared at her. We hardly knew each other. She would have heard of me from her mother, and that would only have been unfavourable.

She smiled, awkwardly, and shrugged. 'Mum and I don't agree on much.'

I smiled back. 'I'll tell you a secret: it was the same between your mama and Mrs Cath. Now run in, child.' I nodded towards the house. 'Go and see your grandma. She'll be waiting for you.'

That night, we had dinner in Mrs Cath's bedroom. I made a leg of lamb with roast potatoes and Karoo vegetables to celebrate Miss Rose and Helen's return, and an omelette for Mrs Cath, who found eggs easier to eat. I carved in the kitchen and took their food up on trays laid with cream linen from Ireland.

'Where is yours, Ada?' asked Mrs Cath.

'I was going to eat downstairs, Mrs Cath,' I replied, with a sideways glance at Miss Rose. 'You haven't seen your family for so long.'

'Nonsense!' she said with a flash of her old spirit. 'Bring yours upstairs like you always do.'

It was a strange meal, one that I would have relished if we had been on our own, for the lamb was fragrant with wild Karoo *bossies*, while the vegetables were tender and the roast potatoes crunchy, just as Mrs Cath used to like them. We would not have needed to say much. From beyond the bedroom window came the heady scent of jasmine newly unleashed by the waning heat, and the last bokmakierie call-and-answer of the day, while in the background the Groot Vis dawdled gently, as if trying to convince us of its docility.

Instead, Miss Rose dominated, although she said very little of importance. There was talk about the latest theatre shows, the quality of the shopping in a place called Illovo, the difficulty of getting acceptable help in the home. She asked no questions about Cradock or the floods, or Mrs Cath's life and well-being. As ever, Miss Rose was occupied with what happened to her, rather than what affected others. She didn't appear to notice the good food, or the perfumed twilight.

Helen shrank into her seat and contented herself with her dinner. Mrs Cath gazed out of the window at the growing night.

'Jo'burg is so busy now, there's never any parking when you need it. And I won't go into the city centre, too dirty, too many blacks.'

I ate the last of my lamb. There was a beat of silence.

'Did you see the flood damage on your way in?' Mrs Cath turned from her window and attempted to steer the conversation away from dirt and blacks and how they belonged together in her daughter's mind.

'Oh yes,' Helen put in, quick to pick up the new thread. 'We saw the damage along Bree Street. Were you frightened?'

'Yes, a little. It was so noisy, you see. A great roaring,' said Mrs Cath. 'Tchaikovsky – the *1812* – with cannons.' She glanced across at me. 'Ada likes to think of things in musical terms.'

'We don't get floods in Jo'burg. Our climate's much better, far more stable.'

And so it went on; Miss Rose taking the conversation in her direction, Mrs Cath trying to find a way to return it to the rest of us, Cradock House observing the tussle.

A bat streaked past the window. There are bats in the township, I saw them as I waited for Lindiwe after Auntie threw the newborn Dawn and me out of her hut. Some people say that bats are evil spirits. That they are the dead coming down to spy upon the living.

I brought up the dessert, homemade granadilla ice cream, made from the purple fruits that grow so well on our granadilla vine. Helen ate up her bowl and asked for more, like Phil used to with Mama's jam sponge pudding. Mrs Cath lay back on her pillow, her hands motionless on the covers. She wasn't getting downstairs to play very often. Her fingers were surely lonely for the piano.

Miss Rose paused for a moment in her one-way conversation.

'Thank you, Ada,' Mrs Cath murmured. 'Delicious meal.'

I gathered up the trays. I could see her weariness. Whenever she sees Miss Rose, she hopes it will go better, but it never does.

'I think I'll rest.' Her gaze lingered on her granddaughter. 'We'll talk more in the morning.'

But there was no more talk in the morning. When I went up at seven o'clock with Mrs Cath's tea and buttermilk rusk, she was lying on her side, arms stretched towards the window, beautiful strong fingers curled in her palms. She had used some perfume before she went to sleep, for a faint scent lifted the close bedroom air.

'No!' I found myself crying, as I set down the tea so hard on the dressing table it spilled. 'No! Not yet!'

She did not wake.

And although it was wrong of me, although the dead should only be touched by God, I reached out to her cold hands. I tried to warm them with my own, even tried to pry the fingers open – if I could open her fingers then she may wake up, for Mrs Cath's life is in her fingers – but they remained closed and not even my warmth or my tears could quicken them.

'Ada?'

I started, and snatched my hands away. It would not do for Miss Rose to see me like this, touching her mother as if I had the right. But it wasn't Miss Rose, it was Helen, standing in the doorway, in a pair of pink striped pyjamas, her eyes round with growing realisation.

'She wanted to see you.' I stumbled to where the girl stood rooted to the spot, for my eyes were blurred with tears and the pressure was heavy in my head. 'She wanted to see you, you and your mother, before God took her.'

Helen swallowed. 'Can I look?'

I took her hand and led her to the bed, not too close, but near enough for her to see that apart from the clenched hands, it looked as if her grandmother was simply sleeping. We stood together, Mrs Cath's grandchild and I. Dawn, I cried inside. You never said goodbye. Helen's hand remained tucked within mine.

'Do you believe in God, Ada?' Her voice wavered.

I freed my hand and touched her hair, golden like the grass that springs from the veld in late summer. Surely the work of God, I used to think, as I walked through its waving tendrils with Dawn in my arms.

'I try to serve Him. Child,' I drew her away from the deathbed, it was not the memory of Mrs Cath I wished her to keep, 'your granny served Him the best of anyone I know.'

A door opened along the passage.

'What is it? What's the matter – oh, no.'

Miss Rose rushed into the room, belting her silk dressing gown. Her face, without its usual powder and paint, looked older. Helen dropped my hand.

'Get out, Helen. This is not for you to see. Why did you let her in here, Ada?' Miss Rose rounded on me.

'She wished to say goodbye, Miss Rose.'

Helen, with a last agonised look, turned away and left the room. I waited, halfway to the door. I wondered if Miss Rose could also smell her mother's scent, that faint trace of Irish cottage flowers that she must have sprayed on herself before she fell asleep for the last time. How comforting to breathe a familiar fragrance! If only I could have played for her as well. Our beloved Chopin. The *Raindrop* . . .

Miss Rose bent over her mother, and sighed. I picked up the

cup and wiped the spilled tea with a tissue, and searched for some grief in her face, but it was hard to find. Tears are not the only way to show grief – this I know, for my mama never cried over Phil and yet mourned him deeply – but there was nothing in Miss Rose's face or in her body that suggested sadness.

'Go and call the doctor. Quickly. And the minister. I don't know who's at St Peter's these days.'

'Yes, Miss Rose. God be with you, Miss Rose. I'm sorry for your loss.'

She lifted her slate eyes and looked at me over the body of her mother.

'Thank you, Ada. Now go do as I say.'

I forced myself down Bree Street in the filmy morning light. The Great Flood clean-up still continued. Bulldozers growled through the wrecked houses, lifting great heaps of brick and branches in their jaws and setting them down into waiting dumper trucks. To my right the river ran in plain view because the mimosas and gums that used to dig for water on its banks were gone.

Mr Dumise must be told. Lindiwe must be told. Then I must hurry back, for there would be food to prepare for those calling to pay their respects, and washing to be done. And Dawn . . .

Miss Rose was determined that the funeral should take place without delay. 'It's Helen,' Miss Rose said, with a toss of the head. 'Helen needs to get back to school.'

St Peter's Church sat alone above the debris, its thick stone walls intact but its graveyard a mass of overturned headstones and sagging hedges. The minister said it would be ready for the service. He said there was no flood damage inside, and that they would lay planks across the devastated graveyard for the congregation to walk over.

The house with the tap that had given me water when I stumbled home from jail was gone, swept away. So, too, the place where a dog had barked at me and its owner had leant out of the window, fearing an intruder. The jail was still standing but a greasy line scarred the walls, reaching up towards a row of shallow windows, one of which was so recently mine. Two policemen swivelled out of the doorway, carrying cardboard boxes of papers. They looked across at me, wondering why I was lingering in front of a place that could snatch blacks so easily. I pushed on towards the township and St James School. I prayed there would be no roadblocks today, no Pass-checking to slow me down, no van on a corner waiting for me.

Since the floods, our students had joined those at St James to make a defiant throng. Wherever you looked, youngsters huddled and gathered stones. Rumours flew of uprisings in Soweto driven by young people like themselves, taking on the might of the apartheid state. The fact that St James had been spared – both by the floods and by the council bulldozers – gave them fresh voice.

'*Amandla!*' they roared in their hundreds. The waters have spoken! A new flood has begun! Despite Rev. Calata's once tight discipline, despite Mr Dumise's untiring efforts, despite the encircling police, St James School was beyond anyone's control.

Into this chaos I came on the morning my beloved Mrs Cath died. Mr Dumise had set up a table in a corridor to handle the affairs of his original students, and it was towards this that I pushed my way.

'Mrs Harrington has died.' I shook his arm in the jammed corridor. One of my pupils waved at me. A group of girls jived to their own clapping rhythm. Dawn, I thought, I have to find where you're dancing. I have to tell you in time for the funeral . . .

'What?' Mr Dumise bent his grey head above the frayed shirt collar closer to mine. A bell rang. No one took any particular notice.

'Mrs Harrington.' I cupped my fingers towards his ear. 'She has died. I am needed to help with the funeral, sir.'

'I'm sorry, Ada,' he said, for I have abandoned Mary Hanembe; everyone now knows me as Ada. There is nothing to be gained with a false name any more. I have no secrets any more.

'We will pray for you. Mrs Harrington was a fine woman.'

'Yes, sir.' I tightened my face to stop the tears. 'I will get back as soon as I can.'

Young bodies crowded round me, raggedly dressed, mostly barefoot. The Groot Vis might not have raged through the township as it raged through Bree Street, but the rain swept away the simplest possessions not moved to higher ground. And it delivered hacking coughs to these youngsters forced to take classes outside on damp ground.

'Miss! Miss, when is our lesson, Miss?'

'She was proud of you, Ada,' he called over their heads. Dina, overhearing us – for Dina always contrived to be close to the latest news – put her arm round me.

'Now you must come back to the township,' she shouted in my ear. 'We need you here. But I know she was good to you,' she admitted. 'I didn't think such white kindness existed.'

The bell rang again, this time for longer.

The youngsters reluctantly packed up their games and their scheming, and made for the classrooms or the bare earth outside that served as a substitute. Snatches of ANC talk, the new black consciousness, pan-Africanism, the latest protest vocabulary swirled about me like the flood waters so recently departed. The eyes of the policemen in their vans followed me as I walked out of the school gates. There was a larger yellow vehicle, called a Casspir, parked a little further down the road. Casspirs usually carry soldiers, not police. Soldiers in khaki uniforms with helmets and long guns. Phil would have recognised them. He would have been astonished to see them here, for Phil was only used to soldiers fighting wars far from home. Soldiers don't usually make war on their own people.

I walked to Lindiwe's brick house in Lingelihle. The new houses had filled up since I was last here. A new 'Township Bach' was growing from the cries and hammerings and snatches of song. Even a few thin dogs had attached themselves to the place.

I found Lindiwe mixing cement in her tiny yard.

'There are holes in the walls,' she muttered. 'How can they build houses with holes in the walls? Ada – what's happened?' She wiped her hands on her frayed dress and hurried to greet me.

'It's Mrs Cath,' I said, the tears falling.

'Oh, Ada.' Lindiwe wrapped me in her powerful arms.

She made tea in her new house for me. There was no running water yet, so it still meant a trip to the standpipe every day. And there was no electricity, although it had been promised. Even so, I think Lindiwe is pleased with her new place, although it is colder than her old hut.

The tea helped. We did not talk much. There wasn't a lot to say. Lindiwe will attend the funeral. She will stand at the back with Mrs Pumile.

'I don't believe in God,' she said gently. 'But if He is there, I will ask Him to bless Mrs Cath for what she did for you and Dawn.'

I tried to find Dawn, but the phone number that she'd given me after her arrival did not work. Instead, it played a long, hard middle C in my ear. So I went down to the post office and sent a telegram to the address she wrote on her last letter: *Mrs Cath died. Funeral Friday. Try come home. Love Mama.*

Wednesday and Thursday came and went but there was no message from Dawn. My arm was stiff, and its stiffness spread down my left leg. My head gave me no rest.

'Is it possible to wait until next week for Madam's funeral?' I asked Miss Rose, where she sat in Mrs Cath's bedroom, sorting through her mother's jewellery. Phil's military brooch, the pearls she wore with the soft cream day dresses before the war . . .

It was not just me who wanted it delayed. Many of Mrs Cath's farming friends were unable to be in town at such short notice. The Colletts were shearing sheep, the Van Der Walts were in Port Elizabeth at a farm equipment auction.

'We can't do this for your convenience,' retorted Miss Rose, rifling through an embroidered pouch with impatient fingers. 'I've told you already, it's so I can get Helen back to school in Jo'burg. The arrangements must suit the family first.'

I waited for a moment until Miss Rose looked up at me.

'Dawn is family too, Miss Rose.'

'How dare you?' she hissed, springing up and coming towards me. 'My father would have lived longer if you hadn't—' She broke off, her face inches from mine, her eyes marbled with venom.

'Mrs Cath loved Dawn like her own.'

'I don't care,' she spat. 'I'm not having this funeral becoming a spectacle.' She turned and flung herself down at the dressing table.

After this outburst, I left it for a day before asking Miss Rose how she wished to arrange the seating in church.

'Where do you want me to sit, Miss Rose?' I asked, as I stood in the kitchen, mixing ingredients for a lemon loaf cake. We were constantly besieged with visitors. I had been up at first light, baking. Helen was out picking lemons for the topping.

It was not only Miss Rose who might want me in a less prominent position. Despite the applause from my recital at Mrs Cath's school, despite the knowledge that Mrs Cath valued me, my spell in jail – and the reason for it – had annoyed some of Mrs Cath's friends, who felt I'd used her, and banked on her rescuing me, which of course she did. I'm not sure how much of this Miss Rose knew.

In any event I could give thanks for Mrs Cath's life and pray for her soul just as easily from the back of the church, where the cold eye of the congregation would not find me.

'You must sit behind us,' Miss Rose replied, not looking up from the list in her hand. 'And don't forget, I want the best tea set used for afterwards.'

For all her short temper, I could see that Miss Rose was well organised. And she'd always been good at giving orders. I wondered why she had not found work that would pay her to exercise such skills.

'Will you sit with us, Ada?' came Helen's soft voice. I turned to her. She was standing in the kitchen doorway, the lemons in her hands.

Miss Rose sighed and flicked a hostile glance towards me.

I reached for the eggs and cracked them one at a time into the mixing bowl. 'If your mother wishes it.'

Miss Rose shrugged. 'Very well.'

And so it was that I took my seat in the front pew of St Peter's Church, with the organ playing the music I'd selected – Ada will choose the music, Miss Rose ordered – and felt the breath of the white congregation on my neck, and prayed that Mrs Cath would forgive Dawn for not being there.

Lindiwe came to the funeral. She sat with Mrs Pumile in the

back row, for the minister at St Peter's was a man who did not believe in the laws on skin difference, and would not allow his congregation to practise them within the church walls. Lindiwe does not have smart clothes, so she looked quite ragged in her cement-stained dress, and attracted many glances. Mrs Pumile was already known to the congregation from the previous funerals. She carried her shiny black handbag and wore her Sunday hat and sang with gusto.

'Your Madam was a lovely Madam. Never mean,' she sniffed to me before I went in. 'Not like others I know.'

It was a service that was now familiar. Even so, I forced myself to listen to each word that was spoken, and identify each note that the organ played, and separate each flower in the arrangement that stood near the pulpit. Mrs Cath's favourite pink roses, wands of creamy jasmine, a fragile minor key, a gentle pianissimo . . . All these things were necessary to stop the tears.

'We have been through dark times,' intoned the minister, his robe smooth and well ironed. 'Our town was nearly destroyed. But out of destruction can come hope.'

I didn't want to cry as I'd cried for my dearest Phil. Back then, my tears had been for the waste of a life still to be lived, and a love still to be found – or so I thought. Mrs Cath, on the other hand, had led a long and worthy life. It should be a cause for celebration.

'Cathleen lived with faith. Throughout her life she stood fast through joy and tragedy, and finally through flood.'

I felt the congregation nod its approval. Mrs Cath had indeed been brave. She'd ventured out to help others when the waters had been at their highest. The minister was right to praise her, he was right to focus on courage shown in this way. It was safer to contemplate this than the conviction she'd brought to other, more unsettling, crises.

'Let us pray for Cathleen,' he bent his head, 'dedicated mother, dear friend and faithful servant.'

'Amen,' murmured the congregation.

'Grant peace to Rosemary and Helen, and bestow upon them Your everlasting Grace.'

'Amen.'

And for my child, I prayed, clasping my hands hard in my lap. For my wild, beautiful child . . .

'And upon Ada and Dawn,' my head snapped up, 'whom Cathleen wished to be mentioned here.'

The congregation froze. There it was, shockingly out in the open – what they'd shied from for so many years: Mrs Cath's willingness to forgive my sin, her embrace of Dawn and me as family, her resolve in the face of the law.

Two small voices at the back said, 'Amen.'

I felt the stiffening of Miss Rose's body within her tight black suit, even from where she sat on the other side of Helen. Miss Rose would be outraged. This time there would be no Mrs Cath to save me. This time, surely, Miss Rose would do whatever it took to be rid of me. The organ began a quiet *Panis Angelicus*. Tension slowly ebbed, pews creaked. Over the muted chords burst the honking cries of hadedas on their way to their afternoon roosts. I once feared they knew my sin, I once feared they would carry news of it across the Groot Vis, and drop it with a triumphant cry on to Cradock House, and my shame would be exposed . . .

Beside me, Helen twisted her hands in her lap.

I looked at my own fingers, not young any more, not as supple as they once were, and I thought of Mrs Cath's fingers, and the pleasure they brought to all who heard her play. Scales rushing down the garden and into the *kaia*, marches for my dear Phil, sly Debussy melodies that echoed in the head for days afterwards.

I will carry on with the Chopin nocturnes that have been my gift to her. I will play the last few into the silence of Cradock House. I hope there will be time to do so before Miss Rose forces me out.

Chapter 54

'The lawyers want to see you, too.' Miss Rose smoothed her red dress – no black for Miss Rose – and picked up her handbag. 'I can't think why. I'll be in the car.'

I rushed into my best skirt and blouse, and my shoes with heels, and sat in the back of the car as Miss Rose drove – at the sort of speed that must be acceptable in Jo'burg – to the lawyer's office on Adderley Street. My arm was stiff from an afternoon of tea-pouring and cake-slicing and much washing-up. Helen had helped, while Miss Rose held court in the lounge and waited to be served.

The lawyer's office was on the second floor of a building overlooking the Dutch Reformed Church on Market Square, which had escaped the floodwaters.

'Good morning, Miss Harrington. Please accept my deepest condolences. Miss Mabuse,' the lawyer shook my hand as well. 'Please sit down, both of you.'

He settled himself behind his desk. There was a picture of him on the wall behind, like the Superintendent had at the town hall. It seems strange to me that people who are already important still need to reinforce their importance by displaying photographs to prove it.

'As you know, we have handled the family's legal affairs since the time Mr Harrington arrived from Ireland many years ago. It falls to me to present Mrs Harrington's will, of which you are both beneficiaries.'

I heard the intake of breath beside me, and felt Miss Rose's renewed anger. Apart from catering instructions, she had said nothing to me since the funeral.

'What do you mean, sir?' I forced my head to concentrate. I had not come across the word beneficiary before.

'It means, Miss Mabuse,' he looked at me over his glasses, 'that you have inherited something from Mrs Harrington.'

Inheritance. The mixing of black and white skins that would always give rise to a brown child. The mixing of parental blood that carries only some traits from one generation to the next, but not all. Inheritance is a fickle thing. It made Dawn's colour inevitable, yet it refused to pass on Mrs Cath's capacity for warmth to her daughter.

'How much?' Miss Rose's words were abrupt. For her, this was about money.

'Let me give you the overall picture.' He glanced down at the papers on his desk.

'Miss Harrington, you inherit the bulk of your mother's liquid assets, apart from three thousand rand that goes to Miss Mabuse, and five thousand rand to her daughter Dawn.'

I stared at him in astonishment. Together, that was far more than what rested in my bank book! With such money Dawn could pay for private lessons to finish her studies! With such money she could buy a new brick house for herself!

'In terms of property, Miss Helen inherits Cradock House and its contents, to be held in a trust for her until she turns twenty-five.'

'But—' Miss Rose half left her seat.

'All rental income shall accrue to the trust as well.'

'But the house should be sold, Helen doesn't need it—'

The lawyer held up his hand. 'One moment, please. Mrs Harrington states that Miss Mabuse', he inclined his bald head towards me, 'may remain as occupant of the *kaia* at Cradock House and, if required, act as caretaker until that time, under the current financial arrangements.'

'We can't sell the house now?' Miss Rose hovered on the edge of her chair, gripping the arms with white knuckles.

'I'm afraid not.' The lawyer gave a tight smile. 'That will be Miss Helen's decision when she is twenty-five. She may dispose of the house if she so wishes at that time.'

There was a pause. Dimly – for my head was aching – I began to grasp how skilfully Mrs Cath had dealt with those she was leaving behind: her decision to name Dawn and me during the funeral service not just out of love but as an enduring challenge to those who would dismiss us; her deftness in removing Cradock House from Rosemary's grasp and saving it for Helen, so securing her heritage; and finally, the gift to me of the *kaia* beneath the bony thorn tree, for as long as Helen kept Cradock House as her own.

'I can stay,' I found myself murmuring. 'Is that true, sir?'

'Yes, it's true,' snapped Miss Rose. 'You've been angling for that from the very beginning.'

Her words pierced the air between us, like the bullets I'd heard in the township. A series of cracks, a pulse of wind if you were close enough. Phil knew such sounds . . .

The lawyer took off his glasses and began to polish them on his tie.

'Miss Harrington, it is unwise to begin a disposition such as this in an adversarial manner.'

Miss Rose yanked open her handbag, pulled out a compact

mirror and examined her face briefly before thrusting it away. She tilted her chin.

'Did my mother change her will recently?'

'No, this has been her intention for some years.'

'Then there's nothing more to be said.' She gathered her handbag and cast me a furious glance. 'You have all my banking details. And I presume you will make the necessary arrangements to rent out Cradock House.'

She stood up. I remained seated. The lawyer stood too, and offered his hand to Miss Rose. 'It will be handled with extreme care. And we will set up the trust in your daughter's name. I presume you will inform her?'

'Of course. Are you coming, Ada?'

'I will walk back, thank you, Miss Rose. I need to understand what Mrs Cath wants me to do.'

Miss Rose extended her hand to the lawyer and swept out of the room. The lawyer looked at me for a moment, then closed the door behind Miss Rose.

'I believe you have been with the family for many years, Miss Mabuse.'

'I was born in Cradock House, sir. I have lived there for all but a few years of my life.'

'Your English is very good. Now,' he laid his hands flat on the table, 'we shall not rush into this. As soon as Miss Harrington and her daughter have returned to Johannesburg, we will begin an inventory of the house.' Seeing my blank expression, he explained. 'We need to make a list of all the furniture and possessions because these will belong to Miss Helen from now on. Do you understand, Miss Mabuse?'

'Yes. They have never been mine, sir. I will care for them for Miss Helen.'

'Quite so. Only once that is complete will we seek tenants to

take the house furnished. You will remain in the *kaia*. I believe
you're a teacher in the township?'

'Yes, sir. I teach piano.'

'Ah,' he nodded. 'I've heard you're very talented.'

'Mrs Harrington taught me all I know.'

'Indeed. And you will need to give us your bank account
number and identity details – and that of your daughter – so we
can deposit the funds that Mrs Harrington has specified.'

'Thank you, sir. I will write them down for you.'

My head was clearing and I was becoming aware of outside
things. The palms on Market Square, untouched by the floods,
swaying in the window.

'There is one further matter in the will, which pertains to
yourself only.' He stopped and searched for easier words. 'It's
only for you to know about.'

I waited. I could not imagine what he meant. He reached
into an envelope and drew out the red diary. 'This is for you.
Mrs Harrington wished you to have it.'

I took the book from him with shaking hands. It was the first
diary. I lifted it to my cheek and felt the downy velvet. The satin
ribbon fell from its pages. This diary had long since been
replaced, and I hadn't seen it for many years. I'd lately read from
the brown leather one.

'There is a separate letter that accompanies it.'

He handed over a loose leaf of paper with Mrs Cath's familiar
script, the slender upstrokes, the heavy downstrokes, the
particular flourish of the capital letter that began each entry.

He stood up.

'If you need any further help, we are always here.' He
hesitated, then held out his hand once more. Few white men
shake the hand of a black woman. 'Your faithful service has been
justly rewarded, Miss Mabuse.'

Chapter 55

My dear Ada,

This is the first time that I am writing to you formally, although we have been communicating like this for many years through my diaries. I have tried to be honest but there are some things that I have never written down, or spoken of, and which should now be recorded, on paper, so that you may always know them.

I was blessed by your mother's friendship when I first arrived in Africa, but it has been *our* lifelong partnership – daughter, friend, confidante – that has been the most influential, and precious, of my life.

You were also the beloved of my dearest Phil – I'm sure you know this, now. I knew it, before you realised it yourself. You were so young, Ada! And so beautiful . . .

I have carried with me all my life the regret that I never acted in time to help you find a way to be together, although it would have meant leaving South Africa and all you had ever known.

I wonder if you realise that most countries in the world now believe apartheid to be morally wrong. It may take a while for it to pass from this country, but one day there will be equality. It did not happen in time for you and Phil, but it may happen in time for our glorious Dawn. Please hold on.

And finally, the music. There are not enough words to say what it has meant to watch you and listen to you. Please play for me every day. I will hear it.

Cathleen

It was the winter after Mrs Cath's funeral when Dawn came back to Cradock.

'Child!' I gasped at the beautiful young woman who stepped off the train from Johannesburg, her hair straight and far lighter than when she'd left, her feet encased in high heels that Miss Rose would have been proud of, her dress a swirl of animal spots. Men getting off the train stared at her. I stared at her because her hair was the colour of Phil's, light and flopping over his forehead as he looked up at me in the garden by the washing line where I was hanging wet clothes . . .

·'Mama!' Dawn bent down to hug me and I felt her tears against my cheek. 'You look so well, Mama!' She was being kind, of course. 'I'm sorry it's been so long. I tried to get back for Mrs Cath—'

'I know,' I said, slipping my arm through hers, trying to find my breath. 'She would have understood.'

The Groot Vis was low on the day Dawn arrived, just a narrow channel glinting between washing rocks. Nowhere in Johannesburg, she told me gaily as we walked across the bridge, was there a river that matched ours for laziness one day and tumult the next. Her good humour was infectious, she smiled at strangers, she slipped off her heels and carried them in one hand. People turned to look at her, or whistled at her from passing cars.

Dawn stayed with us for one luminous week, a week that was divided between my *kaia* and Lindiwe's house. A week of embracing old friends who'd survived so far, a week of hiding her exotic face from notice by the police. A week that said nothing about where she lived or if she had a proper job in Johannsburg. A week devoted to laughter and love and to dance, as I played for her once more. Gershwin, *Rhapsody in Blue*, her body twining and folding about the opening glissando like water curving around rock . . .

'What of the future? When the dancing is over?' This from me, finally, in the quiet of the *kaia* on the night before she left, with the thorn tree scraping on the roof and a candle throwing shadows against the wall. She was lying on the bed Mrs Cath had bought her, wearing the dressing gown that had hung on the back of the door waiting for her to return.

'Don't worry, Mama,' she whispered into the flickering gloom. 'I earn enough through dancing. And Mrs Cath's money is safe.'

'Do you dance for whites?'

She sat up, eyes gleaming with the defiance of old. 'They like me. They don't think of me as coloured!'

Ah, child, I wanted to say. I remember when you ran with your black friends here in Cradock, when you tried to be more black than you were in order to fit in with them. I said one day they will turn on you for being different. It is the same with whites, even if you are pale enough to match them. And, please God, don't try the thing I have read about in the newspapers concerning coloureds as pale as you. Don't try to cross over, don't attempt to live as a white. Don't 'try-for-white' – you'd have to leave behind your black family and never see us again. You'd have to cultivate whites and hope they will never betray you to the police. You'd have to pretend every moment of the day.

But I can't say the words. Why is it that those we love are the hardest to question? Is it because we are too afraid of the answers we might get?

'Don't worry, Mama.' She wriggled out of bed, defiance making way for tenderness, and came to lie alongside me, just as she used to as a child. 'I'll be fine. Jo'burg is different from here, but it's my home. Like Cradock House is yours.'

I don't remember how many winters ago it was that Dawn came. Just like I don't remember when it was that I lost my job. Or rather, the new headmaster told me there was no more money for a music teacher.

'But, sir,' I said, holding my stiff arm with my good hand, 'I don't need money from you. I will still teach if you wish to have me.'

He looked at me warily. He is a new headmaster, Mr Dumise is retired, and so are Veronica and Mildred and even Sipho who loved numbers. Only Dina remains, her turbans ever more colourful, her anger with whites unabated.

'There will be a reckoning,' she hisses, 'and when it comes, when it comes . . .'

Aside from Dina and myself, the school is now staffed by new teachers who will do as they are told. Bantu Education rules the curriculum, policemen patrol the grounds, soldiers sit in their Casspirs on the township edge, and only the students have no fear.

'Liberation!' they yell, to the watching skies. 'Liberation before education!'

I do not mind being unpaid, I have enough money sitting at the bank. In fact, because I am not an official member of staff, my classes are not official either. So I open them to anyone who wants to come. I have only one rule: I refuse to allow political chants or protest songs. Not because I have lost sympathy for the struggle, but because I've reached my limit.

'I've been arrested before,' I shout above the noise at the first lesson of a new term. 'If I'm arrested again, I know I won't survive. I have this arm,' I hold up my lame arm, 'and this hand,' I hold up my ever-swollen hand, 'from being in jail. If you want to keep me here, playing for you, then you have to protect me from the police who listen at the door.'

So they agree. And, once again, we find escape in all manner of music. 'Halleluja!' they sing joyously from the *Messiah*. 'Halleluja! Halleluja! Ha-lay-e-lu-ja!'

'Unforgettable,' they wail, like Nat King Cole, 'that's what you are . . .'

I hope Mrs Cath hears this music too.

And, as I limp home at the end of the day, the youngsters take turns to walk with me to make sure I am safe. I don't let them walk alongside me, because the police still watch me even though I'm old, so they walk behind me, or at the side of me.

It is not just the police that are the threat, it's other blacks, too. Something called a 'necklace' has arrived in Lingelihle, although it has been known in Johannesburg for some time. Dawn has told me of it. It is another example of a word that can be persuaded to take on a new mood. In this mood, the necklace is no longer a strand of jewellery to be treasured but a means of neck adornment that is lethal. To make it, a tyre is put over the head of a traitor and petrol is poured into its rubber cavity. Then a match is thrown, and both tyre and wearer are set alight. This is the new kind of necklace. I have seen this horror close to me. I have heard the screams. I have torn my gaze away from the burning, writhing victim and watched the oily smoke curl towards the *koppie* where the outdoor church used to be.

Where are you, God? I weep to the ironstone rocks that look down upon us without expression. Why do You allow such things to happen? I never understood why You took Phil so soon but this horror is surely not Your will? When will You decide who is right and who is wrong in this war and strike down the guilty party?

There have been several tenants in Cradock House since Mrs Cath died. Most have been kind, most have welcomed me inside to play the piano and to cook in the kitchen. Some have been less inviting, and I've had to buy my own paraffin stove for the *kaia*, and the Zimmerman in the alcove has lain silent and unplayed.

At the same time, the opposite of a boom has fallen upon the Karoo. Many farmers have sold their sheep and left the land, while the earth itself has dried up, as if to prove that the Great Flood was indeed a rare thing and that the Karoo is a growing desert that may one day become another Sahara. Dina says it is indeed God the Father's punishment for the ongoing sins of apartheid. After all, Steve Biko is dead, Mandela has been in jail for twenty years, and still the whites do not relent.

The opposite of a boom is a recession and recession has found its way to Cradock House. Lately there have been no tenants. I dust the house and play the piano every day for Mrs Cath. Cheerful pieces, polonaises, marches, waltzes, especially waltzes. The gentle Brahms in A flat, Chopin's *Grande Valse Brilliante*, Weber's *Invitation to the Dance* – they stream out of the piano to fill the empty corridors and build chord upon chord, phrase upon phrase, until the house is replete. I've known emptiness in Cradock House before, and I don't want it to return. While playing for Mrs Cath, I can keep the house alive for Miss Helen.

The lawyer sends someone to cut the lawn. People come and view the house, but they don't choose it. There are more modern houses for rent in the newer parts of the town, higher up beyond Market Square, further away from the threat of another Great Flood. The house next door is also empty, and the *kaia* beyond the plumbago hedge is silent. Mrs Pumile has finally gone to the Transkei. I hope the man she knew possessed patience and was still waiting for her when she arrived.

And then the lawyer dies, and the new person who manages Cradock House forgets about it. And forgets about me. One day the locks on the house are changed and my back door key no longer fits. I put on my best dress and my shoes with heels – although they are hard to walk in – and I limp along to the lawyer's office overlooking the Dutch Reformed Church.

'Good morning, Ma'am. I am a beneficiary of Mrs Harrington's estate,' I tell the lady at the front desk. 'I take care of Cradock House for her granddaughter Miss Helen Harrington. But someone has changed the locks and I can't get in.'

I wait on a couch, holding myself upright. They let me sit on the same couch as the white customers. This is unusual.

'Can I help you?' A young man with slicked-back hair stands in front of me.

I repeat my story. He sits down at my side.

'I'm very sorry,' he says, his young forehead creasing. 'Miss Helen Harrington appears to have left the country. We're unable to contact her. And her mother died last year. So, for safety's sake, we've decided to close up the house. There's no market for such old places these days anyway.'

'But, sir, I'm supposed to care for it until she tells you what to do. It was in Mrs Cath's will.'

'It doesn't need anything done to it,' the young man asserted.

'And without tenants, it's costing us money just to keep an eye on it. Better to lock it up until there's a resolution.'

I stared out of the window. The aloes in the Karoo Gardens still poked their orange heads to the sky. The benches still remained for whites only. 'It is my home,' I said.

Don't you know, young sir, that the apricot tree carries me in its sap? That the banisters know my polishing of them, and the piano gives me back more than I can ever put into it?

The young man spread his hands. 'I believe you inherited funds from Mrs Harrington. You could buy your own house in Lingelihle. It would be for the best.'

I left Cradock House once before, crossed the Groot Vis, and headed for a township future. And then returned to Cradock House, and to a life divided between the two places. I value this divided life. It is the Cradock House half that keeps me strong for the township half. But this time, surely, if I leave, there will be no return. I'll be sucked for good into the noise, the fear, the casual violence, the struggle. There will be no escape. It will own me, from when I go to fetch water in the Karoo dawn to when I try to sleep in the shouting, dog-barking, gunshot-torn night . . .

I left the lawyer's office and walked back from Market Square. Dundas Street slept in the waning afternoon sun. Poor Miss Rose, gone now as well. She didn't love Cradock House, she saw no need to preserve it. I went in through the back gate as I always do, and stopped in the doorway of my *kaia* and thought about what the young man had said. Across the garden, past the apricot tree, the house lay silent and dark. Yet when I'm inside, I hear Mrs Cath, or Phil, or Mama calling to me! They laugh with me, Phil teases me, I hear Mama's hands knocking down bread dough in the kitchen. Here, from where I stand, the only sound is the chafing of the kaffirboom leaves, one against the other, in the autumn wind. Soon some of the leaves will fall and crunch under my feet.

There are some things that I know, even if my brain is not as sharp as it used to be. I have gathered such knowledge by reading, and through a lifetime of hard experience, and built it into a pyramid of knowing – and unknowing – that has become my particular wisdom. For example, I know that wills cannot be broken. And I know that I'm correct about Mrs Cath's will. I have the right to stay in the *kaia* until Helen sells the house. If that happens, then I must leave. But until that time, no one can evict me. A suggestion by a young man with smooth hair does not have the force of the law behind it.

I've also learnt some practical things: I will be able to continue drawing water from my tap. If I only use a small amount, it will be below the level for which payment is required. So it will be possible to manage in the *kaia* without having access to the house.

I stepped into the garden and walked slowly past the washing line and the tumbling granadilla vine, then round to the front of the house. The grass had grown long and wispy, with the kind of nodding seedheads that I used to touch when I walked into the veld with Dawn. Grass will not behave like lawn unless it's cut regularly. It would rather bolt and rush to seed and try to outgrow its neighbour.

There is, of course, my duty.

Duty once tricked me and gave me a life beset with shame, but this time my duty is right and honourable. I have promised Mrs Cath to take care of Cradock House until Helen no longer wants it. Even if I can't get inside, I must stay on the property. If I leave, squatters could move in. I will not allow this to happen. I will guard Cradock House. I will guard it with my life.

I tell no one about my conversation with the new lawyer. And I begin to be careful about how I behave. Although I have an electric light in my *kaia*, I now revert to candles so that it may not become known to the lawyer that someone is using electricity on the property. Although I can do nothing about the grass, I can use my scissors to keep the shrubs from getting untidy, and I can sweep the *stoep* from time to time and perhaps even clean the outside of the windows. I want to keep Cradock House looking as if it is tended enough to deter squatters or robbers, but not enough to make the young lawyer curious if he happens to drive by.

Chapter 56

Dearest Mama

It is the winter here. It is colder than in Cradock and your funeral coat is not warm enough when I come home from dancing, so a friend has bought me a new coat made of wool! Remember we used to talk about the wool from Karoo sheep that we could never afford to buy? Well, now I know why white people like wool. It's warm, and it doesn't crease. Mama, you must take some money out of the bank (I know you have enough!) and go down to Anstey's Fashions and see if they have a wool coat in the window and then buy it, Mama. Buy it! If they see you've got the money they will sell it to you even if you're not white. In Johannesburg this happens all the time.

Everyone gets sick in the winter. There is so much smoke from cooking fires, and the air is very dry and gives bad coughs. There is also another illness here, something that must come from working in the mines, because it is mostly men that die from it.

Send my love to Lindiwe. Please take care, Mama. I will be back to visit you someday. It's been five years since

I was last in Cradock! You must go to the clinic if your head is still bad. All my love,
Dawn

Sometimes, in the evening, when the painted sunset has faded and the *koppies* are grey shadows against the horizon, I creep out of the *kaia* and go round to the front of the house and sit on the *stoep* with Mama's blue shawl about me. The shell chairs are no longer there, they have been locked away in the garage since the house became vacant, so I sit on the wooden floorboards with my back against the front door.

I listen for the owl that used to hoot in the kaffirboom when I was a child, and sometimes I hear it again. And I watch for bats – dark spirits of my ancestors – and I watch for possible intruders. Sometimes I think I hear something, but often it is only the creak of the red tin roof as it loses heat, or the rustle of a mouse in the overgrown grass. Mostly, though, I go there because the house calls me to do so. It needs company. I flex my fingers in my lap and pretend to be playing the piano. A *fantasie impromptu* in C sharp minor. Hands at full stretch, the bounding notes giving way to a sly melody that hangs in the air, waiting to be caught . . .

When I am not on the *stoep*, I'm doing something illegal.

The kitchen door has two parts to it. The lower part is wood, but the upper part is made of small squares of glass set in wood frames. I am using my scissors to score away at the gluey material that holds one of the glass squares into its frame. I have chosen the square that sits next to the door handle.

Every day, when I come home, I check to see no one is about and then, when it gets dark, I bring my scissors and scratch at the glue. It is easiest when there is a moon. Even so, I must be careful that the scissors don't slip and cut my fingers.

Each evening I do this.

Each evening the groove in the glue gets deeper.

Lindiwe says there is one hopeful sign in the township. A group of young men – nurtured by Rev. Calata – has sprung up. They say they want to improve the lives of township residents. One of the men is a gifted teacher called Matthew Goniwe, and I have met him. Another is Rev. Calata's grandson. Matthew Goniwe tries to recruit me; he holds my swollen hand and fixes me with his kind eyes and says it is still my war. He is right, but I know that my head and my body are no longer fit for such work. I can only watch from a distance and pray to God that they succeed in their means to make a revolution in a different way, like I once tried. Whenever I come across such peaceful efforts, I wish that Jake might suddenly arrive in their midst, turned from violence. But he, like Phil, is forever gone from me.

Like my students, who regularly disappear.

Their frantic parents rush to the jail and wait hours on the pavement outside in the hope of hearing something, any small piece of information. Maybe they try to speak to the people who own the black hands that deliver food to the cells and collect latrine buckets. Sometimes the parents' vigil is rewarded and the children return, but more often they're gone for good. We're getting used to disappearances. It is a terrible thing. Like necklacing is a terrible thing to get used to. I pray to God so often but He does not hear me any more. I think He has forgotten us.

Lindiwe transfers her worry about Jake to me. She says I should not be on my own so much, I should not be walking such long distances with my weak leg and arm. 'Come stay with me,' she urges as we drink tea after my unofficial lessons are over for the day. 'It will be easier for you, not such a long way to go to school. We can read together.'

'I can't,' I reply. 'I have to take care of Cradock House.'

'Not every day!'

'Yes,' I insist. 'It must be every day. There are houses that have been broken into when they're vacant.'

I love Lindiwe but I can't tell her that the real reason for not taking up her offer is that the house needs my company, and that I crave my quiet *kaia* after the violence of a township day and the steady loss of some of my most vivid students.

And I can't tell her that I intend to break into Cradock House myself.

I have spoken to Edward about Ada but he is not keen. Shades of being unwilling to consider proper schooling... I suspect he believes I am clutching at new occupations that will somehow heal the pain of losing – I can hardly bear to write the words – our beloved Phil. That may be true, but I have seen lesser talents than Ada's succeed and go on to great things. Ada deserves the chance to try. I have been negligent in other ways, but I will not be negligent about this.

One part of me wants to sweep her off to Cape Town right now, where she can be examined and put forward as a candidate, but the other half wants to keep her here a little longer, for we need her youth and beauty in the aftermath of death, and Cradock House needs to be filled with the glorious sound she makes. There is also the matter of Rosemary, whom I will be visiting shortly in Johannesburg, and attempting to steer towards a sensible future. That may take some time.

But Ada is twenty, and if she is to find a future as a pianist, or even a teacher, then it has to be now. As soon as I return from Jo'burg, I will take this further.

Not just for her music, but also for her own heart which I know is only now realising what it has lost.

Chapter 57

The only time I have needed a telephone was when I was trying to reach Dawn after Mrs Cath died. But now Cradock House is closed to me, and the telephone inside it has been cut off by the lawyer's office. This means that even if I have no need to make calls, no one else can call me.

So it was that I was pulled out of my class one day.

'Miss Mabuse! Miss Mabuse!' the headmaster shouted across the hall to me. 'You have a telephone call.'

'Sophie,' I gestured to one of my piano students, over the terror in my heart. No one but Dawn would need to phone me. No one but Dawn in an emergency. 'You play the accompaniment. Listen to Sophie,' I raised my voice to the rest of the class. 'She is better than me these days.'

'Ada,' the headmaster said with pursed lips, 'the telephone is not for private calls.'

'I understand, sir. It won't happen again.'

Dawn, my heart whispered. Dawn . . .

The headmaster pointed at the phone on his desk, then closed the door behind him. He has spoken to her, he knows something already that I don't . . .

'Hello?'

'Mama? Mama – is that you?'

'Yes, child. How are you?'

'I don't have much money left for the phone. Mama, I'm not well—' She broke into a fit of coughing at the other end.

'Dawn! Come home, child!' I cried into the phone. 'I'll make you better!'

'Mama,' her voice steadied, 'I'll write and tell you when – I wanted you to know—'

'Have faith, child. All will be well. Dawn? Dawn?'

But there was only the hard middle C in my ear.

The small pane of glass in the back door is loose. I have been scraping away at its fixing for many days, and now it is loose. This is where I must be careful.

I chose a windy night. It was winter and the Karoo was preparing to deliver frost. The kaffirboom creaked in the gale, the apricot tree rustled, I stood at the kitchen door and stared about me in the dark. No human sound. The *kaia* was in darkness. The scrape and fall of the glass would not be heard. Even so, I must try to protect it, I must try not to let it smash. I need the glass to remain intact. I need to be able to slide it out, without breaking.

Using my good arm, I pressed the points of the scissors into the grooves that had taken me so long to carve. The glass shifted. I lifted the scissors and pressed them against the grove on the left side. Then swapped over to the right side. The two sides of the glass were loose. The upper and lower part still held.

Now, I thought as I rubbed my swollen hand, if I can loosen one side completely . . .

I scraped further and felt the glass begin to give. I passed the scissors to my bad hand and pressed my fingers against the loose side. It swivelled slightly and I tried to lodge a fingernail around

its edge to pull it towards me and prevent it falling into the
kitchen. Then attacked the opposite side, scraping and scraping
until that side gave way and pushed out the part I was holding.
It crushed my fingernail but I held on. Then gradually worked
the rest of the fixing loose. Then lifted the glass out of its
frame. Then sank down on to the step with the square of glass
in my shaking hand. Even though it was cold, sweat ran off my
forehead into my eyes. No one reared out of the darkness. No
headlights like the eyes of night animals captured me in their
glare. Soon I'd be able to look after Cradock House as it deserved.
It needed dusting and polishing. It needed to be kept clean for
Miss Helen. This is why I have done what I have done. And
maybe – if I was quiet – I could even play some music into its
dark corridors.

And with Dawn coming back, I could put her to bed and care
for her in our old room. I know Mrs Cath, or Helen, wouldn't
mind. It will be warmer in the house than in the *kaia*. She will
get better sooner. But I haven't had a letter from her. Not for
some weeks since the telephone call . . .

I laid the glass down carefully and then reached into the
kitchen through the hole in the door and felt for the lock.
Twisted it open, and then turned the handle. The door needed
shaking because the wood in the door frame had swollen since it
had last been opened, but after a while, the door opened.
Cradock House lay before me, dark, musty, mine once more.

I only go in at night.

At first I was afraid of the darkness. It seemed to me that the
ghosts that used to torment Phil in his sleep were all about me.
I felt their passing in the breaths of air that suddenly touched my
neck, or lifted the curtains even though the windows were
closed. Mama and Mrs Cath and Phil himself did not come to
me as they used to during the day. They were silent, their

reassurance suspended. The night belonged to restless spirits, to evil thoughts, to the possibility of discovery, even to the men that had lain in wait in the shadows when I stumbled home from jail . . . Every looming cupboard, every creak of the roof made me jerk in panic.

It took me several visits before I began to understand that the house bore me no evil intent. It just required me to learn its new geography. Stairs hid their treads, surprising me at the top with an extra one, or making me stumble at the bottom on one that was missing. Furniture that I walked past in the day had to be relearned as a particular shape at night. The light that struck through the windows and lit the lounge one moment, then plunged it into shadow the next, came not from the stabbing beam I'd suffered in jail but from the natural passage of the moon between clouds.

Once I started to dust and to polish, the shapes I feared formed themselves back into those that I knew and had cared for all my life. They became chairs and tables and banisters again, and they rewarded my work with the familiar smell of linseed oil and soap.

And still Dawn did not come.

The telegram arrived at school. I tore open the orange envelope with shaking fingers. Dina stood at my side, ready to comfort me. But comfort was not necessary.

'Look!' I gasped, thrusting the flimsy paper at her.

'Meet Dawn Friday train,' Dina read, then flung her arms around me. 'She's well – she's coming back! Oh Ada!'

Lindiwe is joyful too. She knows how my heart has been desperate for news of my child. I have forced myself to school every day so that the piano can drive away my fears of Dawn alone, Dawn ill, Dawn unable to call me . . .

'She can stay with me,' Lindiwe said, 'if you can't manage.' Lindiwe knows my weakness; she knows my head and my body sometimes fail to work together properly. Yet somehow I can still play, somehow the piano gives strength to my arms, to my fingers.

'Thank you.' I took her hand and pressed it to my cheek. 'But first let me see how she is.'

Many years ago, Mrs Cath returned to Cradock on the same morning train. Master left the house early to meet her. I, too, leave the house early to meet Dawn. The station is not as busy as it used to be now that people prefer to fly to Port Elizabeth and then drive up to Cradock. Now it seems that the railways are for poor people only.

There is no one else waiting to meet the train from Johannesburg, via De Aar. I remember Dawn's last visit; her triumphal walk across the bridge with her shoes in her hands, and the eyes of all passers-by drawn to her. Perhaps she will be weak, I must prepare myself for that. Perhap she has picked up a disease that is only found where there is gold in the ground, and it will be cured once she is away from such unhealthiness.

I heard the whistle as the train rounded the *koppie*. Soon! Soon she would be here! And perhaps she might never leave again.

The man from the ticket office leant out of his door. Clouds of dust rose up around the approaching train and dissolved into the sheer Karoo light. The pigeons on the roof beams scattered, as if expecting steam and explosions, but these days the engines use electricity so there was just a sigh and a jerk as the carriages drew in and settled beneath the station roof. A man and a woman stepped off and hurried away. The guard at the far end jumped down, stretched, and then began to unload boxes from the goods carriage. The ticket man wandered over to the engine and stood talking to the train driver up in his seat. No other carriage doors opened.

Maybe she was on the next day's train?

Then the guard came down the platform. He was holding a piece of paper in his hand.

'You waiting for someone?'

'Yes,' I said, clearing my throat. 'My daughter, Dawn. She has been ill.'

He looked at me. 'Come this way.' He set off for the end of the platform.

No, I thought, my steps slowing. No, it can't be. Not like Mama . . .

I stopped.

He turned round. 'He's fine,' he said to me. 'Come along.'

He?

I stumbled after him. Amongst the boxes sat a small boy. He had a label round his neck, on a string. He was very pale. He wore tattered shorts and a shirt that was clean, but too big for him. His one hand was curled in his lap. The other hand clutched a cardboard suitcase. Mama's suitcase. My suitcase. Dawn's suitcase.

'Here,' said the guard, fishing into his pocket and handing over an envelope. 'They gave me this letter for you. Asked me to look after the *klonkie*. Said you'd take him, but he looks white to me.' He shrugged. 'I'll get the other things.' He turned away and climbed back into the goods carriage.

I stared at the boy.

Then went closer and knelt down in front of him. He drew back a little.

'What's your name, child?'

He looked at me with eyes blue as the morning sky, and fair hair that flopped over his forehead.

'Thebo,' he whispered.

'Where is your mama, Thebo?'

His eyes filled. He turned back to the carriage and pointed with the hand that was not holding his suitcase. 'There.'

The guard was levering a plain, brown coffin on to the platform. The boy stood up on spindly legs, abandoned his case, and ran to it and tried to put his arms round it.

'Sign here,' said the guard. 'It was paid for at the Jo'burg end.'

Chapter 58

We have buried Dawn across the river near the railway station, where there is a small coloured cemetery. Lindiwe came, and Dina, and Mr Dumise, and a scattering of friends who still remembered her. My students formed a choir and sang 'You'll never walk alone' into the trembling air, and the tune rose up and swept over the *koppies*. Out of Mrs Cath's inheritance I was able to pay for a stone above the grave with her name and her dates, and the words 'Our beloved Dawn' on the front.

I think she is happy there, for the cemetery is not fenced in but is open to the Karoo veld. Low bush and wild golden grasses surround her. The *koppies* look down on her, the Groot Vis murmurs to her. The trains heading for more exciting places go past where she lies.

Thebo and I go there often.

I show him the furry dassies that sunbathe on the nearby rocks. He follows shiny ants along tiny paths. I point out a bony thorn tree, like the one above our *kaia*. He giggles at the grasses that tickle his legs as he runs.

Thebo is a happy child now. And he has brought happiness to me. I don't ask him about his life in Jo'burg. I'm not sure I want to know. Maybe one day he will tell me, but perhaps it will fade from his mind and that will be better. Certainly, he is whiter than Dawn ever was. I am nervous about his whiteness, and about the possibility that he may have a white father even though Dawn has given him an African name. I remember Mrs Pumile: 'Don't parade the child about . . .'

There was no mention of his father in the letter the train guard gave me.

Dearest Mama

This is Thebo. He is my beloved boy, now three years old. I am dying and there is no cure for what I have. I will give this letter to a friend of mine. She will get it to you. Don't cry for me, Mama. Dancing was all I wanted to do, but Thebo is now the most important part of me. Please take him and love him for me.

Dawn

The writing is spiky and uncertain. I have had no word from any of Dawn's friends in Jo'burg.

I bought some strange material at N.C. Rogers General Dealers that I used to stick the glass lightly back into its space in the kitchen door. This means that if anyone looks around the house, they will not notice that the door has been tampered with. Then it is easy just to take the glass out whenever I want to.

We take a risk and go into Cradock House during the day now. We can do this because the garden has grown up and the shrubs reach over our heads and they screen the house from the road. Mrs Cath would be horrified, but this cover not only hides us, it also muffles the piano that I play each day.

'More!' shouts Thebo at the *marche militaire*. And, 'Teach me, Grandma!'

And so we begin.

From the book with the piano keys drawn and named on its pages, he learns one note at a time. Then he puts them together, notes making phrases, phrases turning into a melody that you want to sing over and over again.

'Magic, Grandma!' he cries, bouncing on the piano stool.

It's just like learning to read. Letters making words, words gathering into sentences. One day I'll show him how these collections of words and notes can take on moods far removed from their individual parts.

Soon he is playing simple tunes, *Dance of the Gnomes*, *Come to the Green Wood*. My black, swollen hands on either side of his light ones, his feet dangling from the piano stool, his tender forehead creased in concentration.

I teach one day a week at school now. And on that day, Lindiwe comes from her house in Lingelihle all the way to Dundas Street to take care of Thebo in the *kaia*.

'We'll explore the garden,' says Lindiwe. 'We will search for snails.'

I am careful with Thebo. I follow Mrs Pumile's instruction that I disregarded with Dawn. I don't parade him about. I keep him away from the township. I don't take him out if I hear sirens or chanting, or if I see smoke.

Lately there has been a lot of that because the young township men – now called the Cradock Four – who arose to start new civic organisations on behalf of their fellow blacks, have been murdered. More brutally, it appears, than would be necessary if robbery was the only motive. I gasp when I hear this and hold Thebo close, for Matthew Goniwe, their leader, was known to me.

Johannesburg has its Sharpeville martyrs, now we have ours. White Cradock turns away, not wanting to look, but black

Cradock is convinced the men were assassinated. Our wild youngsters goad the security forces that surround Lingelihle. It will only take one more provocation, one more stone to reach its target for the white soldiers to lower their sights. Bullets that once ripped over our heads will now find flesh.

'*Amandla!*' they scream, as the dust rises beneath their drumming feet. '*Amandla ngawetu!*'

They are ready to die too.

I creep home beneath the guns and the noise that is now more than mere 'Township Bach', all the while fingering my sharpened bicycle spoke – although my arm is too weak to use it as Lindiwe taught: thrusting in and up towards the heart. To avoid trouble, I learn that it's best to avoid the youngsters, even those that want to protect me, and walk among old people instead. Old people don't usually carry stones in their pockets. Old people are less of a target for the soldiers.

After several days, it is reported in the *Midland News* that the bodies of the Four were found on the sand dunes by the sea, outside Port Elizabeth, not far from the railway station where I waited all night for the train back to Cradock after burying Mama. Vast, swaying crowds attend the funeral of the Four. A white bishop speaks, and his face and words are captured by the cameras that arrive from overseas to record what is happening in our poor, dusty world. Green, black and yellow ANC flags snap in the brisk Karoo wind and ANC slogans are chanted to the skies, in defiance of their banning. The police sit on the edge of the township during this time, their tear gas and their guns and their truncheons stowed. They do not wish the cameras to be turned upon them. When the cameras leave, and the bishop and other dignitaries depart, the police and the soldiers move back. The attention of the world, like the beam of a powerful torch, shifts away from Cradock. Some people hoped that its blaze might bring some lasting benefit, but it has not happened. Cradock has returned to being a small town in the Karoo known mainly for its dust and its rocky *koppies* and its brown river, and – briefly – for its savage treatment of skin difference.

After the murders, I considered giving up my teaching altogether, but Dina and Lindiwe talked me out of it.

'If children come to school at all, then they come for the music,' Dina said intently. 'Not for my lessons, or anyone else's lessons, but for the music.'

'They need you,' added Lindiwe.

And they're right. There is little joy left for our youngsters. If they make the effort to attend, then they deserve their musical escape. But I don't take Thebo with me, as I once took Dawn with me to the school across the Groot Vis. It's too dangerous. I will not risk it. He is too white. Whiteness, even in a child, can be a spark.

I make a will. The money will go to Thebo to send him to a private school that will take blacks – or whatever colour it is decided that he will be.

Seasons pass. My head troubles me. The memories that I once could call up as fresh as when I first made them now reappear with reluctance, faded at the edges, like Market Square seen through the dust of horse carts, before tarred roads. While I struggle to hold on to the past, some people say there is now hope for the future. I have not felt it yet – that rising newness that I have known twice in my life – but others are convinced it is here. Fragile, as easily damaged as apricot blossoms in a late frost, but finally here.

Perhaps Mrs Cath was wrong. Perhaps apartheid will pass from the country in my lifetime?

When Thebo is asleep in his mother's bed, I read from the red diary, and I read from the brown diary that I saw in Mrs Cath's bedroom when she died. I found it again recently. It had been pushed into a dressing-table drawer, perhaps by Miss Rose.

Helen has grown so tall!

I am thrilled to see she has somehow contrived a mind of her own, despite the trenchant views of her mother. Once again, I'd hoped that Rosemary would have mellowed, but it's not to be.

I am so weary these days. Ada summoned Rosemary and Helen, of that I'm sure. How can I ever tell Ada what she means to me? I know she still carries deep shame over the affair with Edward, and I wish I knew some way to tell her that she was never to blame. But alas, I don't think she will believe it from my lips. So that is why I have decided on another way, a public way, provided the minister follows my wishes.

I must rest, as I said to them just now. First a little of my favourite perfume, then sleep and the thought of seeing my lovely granddaughter again tomorrow. If only Dawn were here too . . .

Chapter 59

A key turned in the front door. The hinges squeaked. The door has not been opened for some time. I grabbed Thebo and picked him up with my good arm. Then began to limp back to the kitchen. Even with the stiff door, I was too slow, I wouldn't be able to get out in time, they would discover me and throw us out—

'Who's there?' A female voice. Tentative steps.

I stopped. My heart pounded in my head, squeezing it, hurting my eyes.

'Anybody there?'

I set Thebo down and put my finger against my lips to keep him quiet. I shuffled back, peered through the crack in the door. A young woman stood with keys in her hand. She had golden hair. She was a little younger than Dawn would have been. I thought I'd seen her somewhere before, but the pounding in my head was starving it of memory. I stepped out from behind the door.

'Ada?' She started forward, a shy smile forming on her face. 'Ada?'

'Miss Helen!' I gasped. 'Oh, Miss Helen, you've come home!'

I felt the floor tilt and I reached for a chair and sat down heavily. It wouldn't do to fall over like I'd done before – when was that?

She looked about her, at the open piano with its propped sheet music, the gleaming furniture, the ordered interior compared to the wilderness outside. I felt a rush of feet.

'Hello,' I heard Thebo say. 'Can you play the piano too?'

'No,' Helen said, and squatted down to his level. 'Nothing like Ada.'

'You've got hair like me,' said the boy, reaching out and touching Helen's blond strands. 'Did you know my mama? She was Dawn, but she's in heaven, now.'

'Yes,' said Helen gently, with a quick glance at me. She stroked the child's arm. 'I knew her. She was a wonderful dancer. She danced for me when I was about your age.'

And so it began. The new hope that people talked about. God the Father's new plan. It could not bring back Jake, or Steve Biko, or the Cradock Four, but even so it rose up in the country and threw out the laws on skin difference and the people that policed them. It ripped the signs off the benches in the Karoo Gardens for good. It began to string wires for electricity and telephones in the townships. It gave Lindiwe her electric light. It allowed people of different colour – like Phil and me – to love each other and to marry. It flung open Mandela's prison cell and led him blinking into the sunlight. It changed my belief that skin difference would continue while men had eyes to see the difference between black and white. This new hope proved to be stronger even than that.

It ended the war.

It ended my war. It banished enemies-in-waiting, it healed inside wounds, it softened the shame I have carried with me all my life.

And it opened up Cradock House.

It brought Helen to stay, it tamed the wild garden, it fired up the stove and the laundry, it gave Thebo a room of his own, it welcomed me back to the old room I'd once shared with Mama. It welcomed me home.

Helen is going to stay. Once she has finished restoring Cradock House, she intends to work on some of the other old houses nearby. This is her talent. She has also decided to become Thebo's guardian so that when I'm gone he will have a family. She has enrolled him in the school which once would not hear of me, and where I later played a concert, and where Dawn danced with abandon behind the back row. The school where Mrs Cath used to teach. They have given him a place without any questions.

And as for me, my greatest joy is teaching my grandson to play the piano. Somehow, my head is still good enough for this, and my damaged fingers still know their way over the keys. We sit at the old Zimmerman, and the music rises in both our hands, and we play together. A little classical, the *Moonlight Sonata* with him on the melody line and myself working the difficult base, a little jazz, then perhaps some African jive like his mother's favourite *Qongqothwane* – the Click Song.

Dawn is here with us, now. I can see her, hair flying, slender legs flashing, hands twirling above her head. Helen is watching too, and clapping her hands. Or maybe it is Thebo clapping . . .

Then, in the evening, when the purple light falls through the window and the beetles fall silent in the plumbago hedge, I will play Debussy. Tunes that wander about in your head the next day. And the next, slowly revealing their meaning.

I can see Phil. He comes to stand by the piano, he touches

my shoulder, he smiles at me with eyes light as the earliest Karoo dawn.

Mrs Cath will come into the room too. Or maybe she has been here all along? I know what she will ask.

'A little Chopin? The *Raindrop*? Please, Ada.'

Glossary

amandla ngawetu!	power is ours!
bossie	small bush
dassie	rock rabbit (Rock Hyrax)
doek	scarf or cloth tied about the head
dompas	pass or reference book (used disparagingly)
dorp	small country town
hotnot	offensive mode of address towards a coloured or mixed-race person
kaia	detached servant's quarters
kleurling	coloured or mixed-race person
klonkie	young coloured or mixed-race boy
knobkierie	stick with a knobbed head
koppie	a hill, often flat topped
lappie	cloth used for cleaning
riempie	softened strip of hide woven to make seats or seat backs
shebeen	unlicensed tavern
skollie	street hoodlum
spaza	township shop
stoep	verandah
tokoloshe	evil spirit
tsotsi	street thug, member of a gang
verdomde	damned

Acknowledgements

Many people helped to create this book, but there are some who deserve particular mention. I am indebted to Michael Tetelman for granting me access to his superb research thesis on Black Politics in Cradock between the years 1948 and 1985. His material provided me with the essential background to Ada's story.

The staff at the Cory Library at Rhodes University in Grahamstown helped me track down Michael's thesis, along with a raft of other historical documents. My thanks to them for their time and generosity.

Sandra and Michael Antrobus provided advice, invaluable referrals, and hospitality on the ground in Cradock, for which I'm most grateful. Thank you also to Duncan Ferguson, Cradock's local archivist, who answered my questions, and allowed me to sift through his photographs and extensive collection of memorabilia.

I would particularly like to express my appreciation to my agent Judith Murdoch and my editor Imogen Taylor. They helped me refine the manuscript, and provided much encouragement and wisdom throughout the publication process.

Finally, my most sincere thanks must go to my family whose patience, love and support were unfailing.

1. Do you think the author captures Cathleen's loneliness and did you sympathize with her sense of isolation?

2. How would you sum up Cathleen and Ada's relationship? And what does each of them bring to it?

3. Ada's character develops throughout the book. What words would you use to describe her as a child, a young woman, and then as an adult?

4. Why do you think Ada felt her relationship with Edward was her duty?

5. How do you feel South Africa's political background colors the novel?

6. Why do you think Dawn is so much more entrenched in the life of the township than her mother is?

7. Did you believe that Ada's method of approaching the mayor and the newspaper director about housing was effective?

8. What do you think happened to Jake?

9. Why do you think Rose behaves in the way that she does?

10. What do you feel the theme of music contributes to the book?

11. Did you feel that the author offered a real sense of hope with the return of Helen?

12. Did you identify any metaphors that the author uses to enhance the story?

13. What incident affected you the most in the book? And what emotions were you left with?

14. If you were to meet Ada today, what single question would you ask her?

St. Martin's
Griffin